Saga Hillbom

A Generation of Poppies

A Generation of Poppies

ISBN: 978-91-519-3834-9

This is a partly rewritten, as well as heavily revised and edited, version of my debut novel *A Generation of Poppies* (2018). Thank you to everyone, especially Robin, who had the patience to work with me on this book a second time.

'We thought it was for the Future. It was against the Future. Our future is dead; for the youth is dead that carried it.'

Remarque, Erich Maria, *The Road Back* (1931)

'In Flanders fields the poppies blow
Between the crosses, row on row,
That mark our place; and in the sky
The larks, still bravely singing, fly
Scarce heard amid the guns below.'

Lieutenant-Colonel McCrae, John, *In Flanders Fields* (1915)

Prologue

Early October 1915, Rouen, France

Rosalie

MY FINGERS ARE slippery with pus and I must swallow twice in an attempt to calm my nerves, preventing myself from rushing out of the stale room. Mrs Johnson's mouth is pursed, her eyes stern and her fingers flick as she stitches the wound together. How many broken bodies has she tried to mend? How many men's blood has sullied her hands, and how often in vain?

The man has fainted—thank God—hence he does not feel the pain. He will wake up, though, like they all do, and discover the skin on his leg puckered by grotesque black thread. Of course, a stitched-up wound is preferable to a stump, and the soldiers know that as well as anyone.

I was not there myself, but I heard from my sister Isabel that even the collected Mrs Johnson went alabaster-white when the man was rolled into the room. A shell detonated in the midst of his platoon, I heard. Four dead and twelve injured, they said. I should not be taken aback; it happens all the time. Nonetheless, it is four vivid, brave lives, or so I think. I cannot quite tell what bravery is anymore, never had a clear grasp of the term, but I do not know what else to call those soldiers. Charles once told me that—

Mrs Johnson's voice slashes through, her Welsh accent lilting. 'We're done with the needles. Go and fetch me some clean bandages, and by the mercy of Christ hurry up!'

I manage a nod and steer my faltering steps towards the cupboards containing the supplies. With a stack of tightly rolled bandages in my arms I return to the table, my polished shoes sounding against the floor amongst so many other pairs. There must be at least fifty of us, including educated nurses, doctors, Voluntary Aid Detachments like myself, and kitchen personnel. I cannot be bothered to estimate the men. There are too many rooms and too many beds—all I know is that there are hundreds.

I hand over the bandages to Mrs Johnson and together we wrap the white strips tightly around the freshly stitched limb. The flesh is swelling up and has taken on a sickly shade, but if fortune is on our side for once, infection has been prevented. We coax a few pain-killing pills down the man's throat and proceed to treat the men from the frontline at Loos, who are suffering injuries from chlorine gas. The gas was meant for the Huns, naturally, but some of it wafted back into the British trenches. Perhaps it will be more successful next time; after all, this was only a first. I shudder.

Afterwards, I allow myself to drop down on the timeworn floor, pulling my legs to my chest and resting my forehead on my knees. I squeeze my eyes shut until bright spots and swirling flames dance before the dark of my eyelids.

Why did I come here? To help—to do a duty? I do not know anymore. Perhaps because it was the prudent thing to do when others went. Perhaps because I was anxious to see what lay beyond England, or because I have always been that most impractical thing: an idealist. I wanted to behold and care for the soldiers who we sent off with cheers and waves. I ought to have realised that there was more to their day-to-day existence than a few gunshots and daring deeds, that their reassuring letters home were naught but compilations of fragmented white lies.

I flinch as a slender hand seizes my arm. Isabel surveys me, eyes serene, as if she had been stitching embroidery and not skin. She has tucked her hair neatly underneath her white cap, but a cocoa-brown strand has escaped and dangles in her face.

She frowns. 'Come. Don't just sit there like a languid sponge! I need you in the great hall.' Her tone softens as she beholds my sorry state, because I have no doubt turned the colour of cream gone sour. 'I know you are tired, Rosalie. We cannot afford to be tired. Now come!'

I force a stiff smile in return, push myself to my feet, and let her lead me through a cramped hospital corridor. The room we arrive in can hardly be described as airy, but the windows are flung wide open, and slated beams of sunshine bathe the floor in crisp light.

I cast a glance outside and draw a deep breath, a faint sense of calm settling inside me once more. Autumn has crept upon us, the garden shifting in amber, stark yellow leaves dotting the trees.

I only have a second or two to admire the colours before my sister places a bowl of steaming hot broth and a spoon in my hands. 'Be certain that he swallows everything. I must start folding the bedclothes,' she says and nods towards a scrawny man in the bed on my right. I bob my head in understanding and sit down lightly on the edge of the mattress, the bed creaking at even the tiniest movement I make.

The man's jutted bones and the bruised shadows under his eyes are prominent, but he has merely a bandage tied around his upper arm, so he appears to be far better off than many of his current roommates. To my surprise, his chapped lips curve, and I spot the tiniest sparkle in his eyes. 'Thank you, Sister,' he mumbles after I have fed him the broth, his voice cracking.

That night, as I am sitting on my bed in the room I share with my friend Mary, I stare into the spotted hand mirror for what seems like an eternity. My skin is covered in a patchwork of shadows and light from the kerosene lamp on my wobbly nightstand. I run my fingers across my cheek and tilt my head, trying to burn a hole through the reflection with my gaze. Is my skin smooth enough, my hair silky enough? Do people think I am beautiful, like Mama when she was young? Is my sprinkle of freckles as alarmingly unattractive as I suspect?

I brush out my curls with thorough strokes. The silver brush belonged to my mother—one of the very few things I have left of her, memories included. When she died, my father tried to erase her from our past, if only to mute the pain. Everything was auctioned off save a couple of her personal belongings that Isabel and I pleaded with him to keep. The trinkets which were to Papa such a pain were always a great comfort to the rest of us.

I put the brush down on my bed and transfer my attention to the letter that arrived for me this morning. The paper is crinkled and carries marks from perpetual dampness. The envelope has been opened but I doubt Fred has written anything worth censoring.

Little Sister,

Are there more wounded than usual? I suppose there would be, with the battle over at Loos and all that. My instructor told me that the British aerial attack there was the first strategic bombing, the very first, and I must say it is extraordinary. I only have to wait another week before My turn to cross the channel comes—you wrote and said you would be there to wave me off, so I heartily look forward to it. There is no need for Isabel to come, though. Papa will, or at least I think so.

If I may ramble on a little longer to you, I have to tell you that I made a loop today, and it went somewhat amiss. It was my last solo flight, so I thought I would show the chaps my best, but of course my safety straps were chafed at and so I nearly fell out of my machine. You should have seen it! Anyhow, I stayed calm but got a bit of a scolding down on the ground. But really, it was not my fault.

I should be more serious. You know how Greatly I always care for you, and if there was anything I could do to reverse what happened, I would, anything. Now, I will keep from dragging it up again. I am sorry. If you hear anything interesting from the patients, please write to me about it. I put a newspaper article in the envelope, as you can see. It is about Boelcke and Hawker, those smashing German and British pilots. I do admire them both, although my instructor dislikes it when I speak of Boelcke, says it is not Patriotic enough.

I will see you next week (what a cheerful thought!)

Your-very-soon-to-be-Pilot

I stick my hand into the envelope and extract the article. I will have to read it tomorrow, though, because Mary reaches to put out the light.

Sleeping proves impossible. I trace my wedding ring with the tip of my nail. It is time I took it off, but the act feels like another betrayal. My thoughts skip then to Charles, and I am tempted to slap myself. Charles D'Aboville is *nothing* to me. Nothing at all. Is he at Marne? Or Artois? Perhaps I will never know. Perhaps I will never see him again.

Charles

The artillery barrage is still rumbling. Poor bastards…but then I would not have wanted to stay out there myself in their place, not if I had been offered the moon and stars both. The support trench is bad, but the front is worse. A great deal worse.

I lean back in my chair, tapping my feet against the caked mud floor of the shadowed dugout. I can barely recall which tune it is I am trying to tap, but it must be one I heard at the Sorbonne. There were so many songs there. I would kill to relive a single of those nights, a night sounding of laughter rather than distant canons, a night spent watching silly theatre performances or driving around in Michael's car. Well, if I were in Paris, I would not have to kill anyone, and that is the crux of it.

The empty box of mints is smooth under my fingers. Rosalie's face when she gave it to me is an image I will never manage to erase from my memory, nor do I want to. The blush on her cheeks and the way the breeze toyed with her hair… It is a fine memory to have—but I wish it was more than that.

Chapter one

June 1914, London, England

Rosalie

WE CLAP OUR hands frenetically, exclaiming as the boys pull the rope. Finally, one side gives in, and the other team tumbles to the ground for lack of resistance. They are all soon on their feet again, though, shaking hands, laughing in grass-stained waistcoats and with sun-chinked hair.

Harry's cornflower-blue eyes hold mine. He offers me his arm and I walk over to rest my hand in the crook of his elbow, the hem of my skirt fluttering around my ankles in the summer breeze. Together we stroll along the booths and carousels, all the attractions one might expect to find on a summer fair in Hampstead Heath.

'Would you like some ice cream?' he asks, glancing at me, then looking away as if afraid to get caught.

I nod, granting him a smile. 'Strawberry, please.'

Harry leaves me to fetch the requested sweet and returns shortly, presenting me with a paper cup filled with pink ice cream. I accept the cup and tuck a spoonful in my mouth. This, I decide, this must be what summer tastes like.

Harry's face twitches with hesitation and he waits until I have devoured another spoonful before he speaks. 'Would you…would you mind terribly much if I kissed you, Rosalie?'

I am taken back by this, perhaps because I never saw timid Harry as one who would ask for a kiss, or because it is a rather odd thing to say. I throw a quick glance over my shoulder to ensure that Mrs Ellens—our English teacher, who is heading our expedition to the fair—is nowhere nearby. Tracing his soft jawline with my hand, I tilt my head backwards slightly and wait for his lips to brush against mine. He is ever so careful, almost as if he has never kissed a girl before. The moment sends honeyed thrills edging down my spine.

A familiar choir of chattering voices intrudes on us. Three boys and two girls come rushing towards us, their steps brimming with giddy youth. A few feet ahead of the others is Mark Crewel, the chap who never fails to charm and rarely in anything else either. Behind him come James and Jones Jenkins, along with Mildred Smith—the girl with the crooked nose and fair hair— and the aspiring pianist Mary Warner. All of them are classmates of ours from King Alfred's School, except Mark, who recently left Eton

'Will you write to her then, Harry?' says Mildred, her voice high-pitched as always, tinged with teasing.

Harry withdraws from our embrace with a felicitous expression, then frowns. 'What do you mean? I'm not going anywhere soon, am I?'

Mark slaps his back. 'Why, the war of course! Have you forgotten so soon, Harry, and you, Rosalie? It will be here any day now, I warrant!' His eyes are alight with anticipation and confidence both.

'Die for England or return home a hero—it doesn't get much better than that, now, does it?' James chimes in.

At the mention of dying, Mary lets out a small, horrified gasp.

James clutches her arm. 'Don't fret, Mary! That was a foolish thing of me to say. We will all be home before Christmas. My father said so, and many others, too. All we need is for some bloke in a suit to say it has started, or else I might go mad!'

The rest of us nod with feigned graveness. Like James, everything we know of the European politics is based on what our charitable fathers and uncles have told us: tension has rarely been this high, and it is only a matter of time before one nation or another snaps. Germany simply refuses to curb its own ambitions, and no other country wants to be left behind for that matter. The Balkans are one pot of hotly brewing conflict with Austria-Hungary and Serbia encroaching on what the other considers their own territory. With the knotty net of alliances stretching across the continent, a single spark could cause explosions like dominoes.

Still, the prospect of honour, glory, and adventure is mouth-watering. We are the 'youth of steel', especially the boys, or so the older generations have begun to tell us. I hope that it is true.

'My sister Isabel is a trained nurse,' I say, basking in the others' sudden attention.

Mary shields her eyes from the sun with a glove-clad hand. 'I know, Rose. Will you also be one? *I* would like it very much.'

I shrug. 'Perhaps. They always look so pretty on the posters, don't they? With starched uniforms and—'

'But it's, well, it's *work*. Besides one has to be twenty-three to be sent abroad as a Voluntary Aid Detachment! The war will be long over when we reach that age,' Mildred remarks.

I lower my eyes. My sister has almost reached the required age of overseas service; maybe I could lie and go with her. If the boys can pass for older than they are, then surely so can I.

Jones Jenkins nods. 'Our soldiers' training would take months as well. Let's hope the war will not be over by Christmas after all. Otherwise we might get no real chance at it.'

Mr Atkins, our history teacher, sneaks up on us, his bushy eyebrows knitted. He is a short and sturdy man with no more than a few strands of hair covering his shiny scalp. The beige tweed suit is the same he has worn every day for as long as I can recall, and he has a thick cigar in the corner of his mouth. 'Now now, what's this? Talk of war? What would children like you have to say about such things as war? You're yet underage, mind you.'

Harry fires him a subtle smile. 'We're not children, Mr Atkins, really. Besides, the government doesn't care to know if one is seventeen or filled eighteen. We can report to duty any day once the war breaks out…and it *will*.'

'I can't blame you if you do. But hear this, hear this! War isn't what you think it is. Unless you were sound asleep during my lessons, you would know that, even you girls. I expected better of you.'

Mildred pats his arm. 'Don't you believe England's troops will outshine all others, Mr Atkins? They will do just wonderfully.'

'If I were you, I wouldn't be so hasty.'

I have grown tired of all this talk of fighting, hence I suggest we join the jolly people on the outdoor dance floor. My friends receive my proposition with all the enthusiasm I could have wished for, and soon we have left Mr Atkins to his cigar.

Harry places a fine hand on the red sash that marks my waist and I put mine on his shoulder. Despite the rather delicate air about him, he is a good bit taller than I am. The musicians play 'On the Old Fall River Line' and follow up with 'Peg O' My Heart,' both favourites of mine. Mark dances with Mildred, and the Jenkins brothers have each taken a plump girl from our class in their arms. Mary sits with her hands docilely clasped in her lap, smiling, likely dreading that someone might ask her to dance.

'This is the right way to end a school year, Harry, don't you agree?'

'Yes, yes, it is, and the future is even better than so! At first, I thought I'd study… But now, with the war, you, and everything… There are so many adventures that I never thought of.' His cheeks flush coral.

For a little while we are silent, skirts sweeping and shoes beating, the melody soaring high. When the dance floor starts to clear and the musicians enjoy a well-deserved break, we naturally gather in our little group once more and scuttle away to avoid being caught in conversation with Mrs Ellens.

People are amassing by a booth a few feet away. Once we manage to break through the crowd, we discover that the object of their interest is a man in a smart black suit, operating a camera.

'Can you take a picture of us, Sir?' Mark asks.

'Of course! Stand tight together, and for *heaven's sake do not move!*'

We squeeze together in front of the camera: Mark cosy between Mary and Mildred, next to them Harry and me; and kneeling in front of us Jones and James. We all plaster on broad, genuine smiles and freeze so that the man can take a good picture.

When we are done, the man tells us to come to his studio and collect the photo in a few days. I cup my palms so that everyone can gather their tinkling pennies before I hand the payment over to the photographer.

Having left the crowded spot, we head next to the carousel, a glossy fairy tale mechanism. Since I was little, I have nurtured a certain affection for carousels: the magical animals and creatures, the fine details, the way it spins one around first pleasantly and then at a faster pace until one feels queasy.

One by one we present the last of our pocket money to pay for a ride. I pick a large, silver-grey elephant with oriental patterns. Soon, the first clucking notes of the playful music sound and the carousel squeaks before beginning to move. I flash Harry a smile.

'I will buy you your own carousel one day, Rose,' he proclaims from his place on the horse to my left.

I laugh. I do not doubt for a second that he will indeed try.

As the summer erupts in full bloom, Harry, Mark, James, Jones, Mary, Mildred, and I embark on our annual excursion to the sea. With Mary's scrawny governess for chaperone, we set course towards Brighton with its khaki beach and sharply cropped cliffs. The gravel crackles under the tyres as we park the three cars: one popping red and two more traditional, black ones. I have little interest in cars, but even I know with certainty that these particular vehicles are highly fashionable, because we only brought two chauffeurs, while Mark insisted on driving himself.

I fill my lungs with as much salty air as I can without bursting, then allow Harry to help me down on the ground. Dashes of foam dance on the breaking waves, contrasting against the vivid blue of the sky.

A giggle escapes me as I watch Mark struggle to lift Mildred out of the red car whilst she keeps her hat fastened on her head, defying the tearing wind. Defeated, he settles on opening the lacquered door for her so that she might step out on her own, hat firmly held down.

'A topping day, isn't it?' James says and we all chime in while tripping our way down to the beach. The salt spatters our faces and we have to squint to not be blinded by the sunlight.

'Where should we lay the blankets?' I ask.

Mark sweeps his glance over the beach, which is dotted with like-minded people and their belongings. After close consideration he points to a patch of bare sand, and we direct our steps towards it. The boys, carrying parasols, folded blankets, and chairs, tread carefully to keep their balance. Mary and I each carry a large basket containing sandwiches and lemonade covered with chequered cloth. Having arrived at our destination, the boys put their baggage down in the sand, and I place my basket right next to it before assisting in arranging the blankets and chairs *just so*.

Mary's governess and the two chauffeurs, who have trotted behind us, settle close enough to keep an eye on us but far away enough to avoid complaints.

'Do you know something, Rose?' Mildred says, her fine-spun hair escaping strand by strand from its coiffure and gathering like a halo around her temples.

'What?'

'Papa says that he heard from his colleague, who heard it from his wife, who is a secretary at the War Office, that once the war breaks out there might very well be a shortage of stockings, too! Can you imagine that, that a war should affect *those* things?'

I laugh. Even to me, Mildred sounds rather ignorant. 'I don't think stockings will be the government's priority, you know.'

'No, I suppose not. If it were, though, I imagine them—the stockings and all sorts of things—could come in stripes and in an infinite supply. Fancy that!'

Jones interrupts our conversation. 'I say we stop jabbering about clothes and get a feel of the water. I bet it's unpleasant at first, then just about perfect.'

We put on our swimwear in the huts built for this very purpose, and the boys emerge from theirs spurred on by some invisible force urging them to dive headfirst into the sea. I try to walk calmly but cannot contain myself, and soon we are taking turns in the surprisingly cold water, giving me goose bumps. My knee-length, soaked swimwear is unbearably heavy, and my cheeks heat at how tightly it clings to my body. My wet, stiff coiffure has lost all its volume and become loose, falling like a sticky veil over my face when I at last stretch out to dry in the blazing sun.

Around teatime—according to the broken gold watch that Harry keeps in his breast pocket—we decide that it must in fact *be* teatime, and unpack the baskets, stomachs growling and crêpe paper rustling. I munch, perhaps a little too loudly to be decorous, on a soggy ham and tomatoes sandwich. The one with pickles and mustard that Mildred tries to prop in my hands I promptly refuse, though, the smell being enough to make me nauseated.

The people on the beach only start to disperse when the afternoon is bordering on evening. I lean back on my hands after emptying my second glass of cloyingly sweet lemonade that our cook Daya sent with me. Like so many times before, we speak of the future.

'I'm going to have piano concerts at Covent Garden someday, and you can all come and watch,' Mary says, eyes glazed with dreaming.

Mark scoffs, but appears to regret it when Mildred shoots him a deadly glare. 'I'm sorry, truly,' he says in defence. 'As for myself, I intend to get bravely killed and then I'm going to marry some fine girl and be very cheeky.'

Jones squints at him. 'Don't be daft. You can hardly die and *then* marry and all of that, you bugger!'

'Well, I can't very well live bravely, now, can I? That requires far more effort.'

I smile, finding to my surprise that his rambling makes a great deal of sense to me. 'No. People who live bravely are remembered for a little while, but it's not the same thing, is it? But I still think it's rather sad. No one should want to die.'

Harry clutches my hand and I know he agrees with me.

'I don't want to die.' Mark laughs as if to lighten the mood and leans over to claim the last sandwich in the basket. 'Only if it's absolutely, *terrifically* bravely.'

On that modest note we gather our belongings and drive back to Hampstead. The sun is on the verge of setting, painting the sky with broad brushstrokes of russet gold and soft lavender. We have already neglected curfew. The wind tugs at my blouse where I sit in the lather-clad backseat of the open American Chevrolet, as James informs me that the car is called, sand still between my toes. I do not mind in the least, though. A summer evening such as this is meant to be enjoyed and enjoyed thoroughly.

The house I was born and have grown up in is of fair size and white as milk. Three stories high, it stands crammed between two buildings of similar style, though darker. We do have a small back garden and a bench by the front door, but ours is by all means a townhouse, hence our money is invested in furniture and paintings rather than any large premises.

On the morning after my outing to the beach, my father throws his freshly bought copy of *The Daily Mail* on the table in the vestibule. "'Murder of the Austrian heir and his wife: shot by schoolboy!' The bloody fools!'

I halt mid-step in the stairwell, gazing at him, suppressing a yawn. We ought to have driven home from Brighton earlier, for I am still exhausted after a night's sleep. Murder…shot? It is one of Papa's blunt jests, of course. I muster a faltering laugh. 'How awful you are, Papa.'

'I mean it.' He shakes his head and reaches for the newspaper again, then waves it under my nose. 'Read for yourself!'

I take the paper, slowly. This is the spark. I cannot imagine otherwise.

Chapter two

Rosalie

THE MONTH THAT follows is one of mounting expectations and increasingly bold headlines. Austria-Hungary naturally seizes the opportunity to proclaim the assassination a *casus belli*, and on the 23th of July they present Serbia with ten high-strung, unacceptable demands. Five days later, a state of war exists between the two nations, and I can almost hear the sound of dominoes falling. Russia is bound to support Serbia; Britain, France, and Russia are all allies; Germany is keen to assist Austria-Hungary.

On the evening of the 4th of August, I go with one of my dearest friends, Laura Hamilton, to Buckingham Palace, where a suffocating crowd has already assembled under the darkened summer sky, their predictions and murmurs drowning the birds' chirping. Only a dimwit would stop to listen to the birds, though. No, we are here to behold the royal family on the balcony.

Laura is a fair-skinned girl who has always known what she wants from life: a splendid time, a hat with feathers, and the right to vote. She clutches my hand compulsively, and I am grateful, because otherwise I would only have to blink to lose her in this crushing mass of people. Papa does not know I am here, of course. It is frightfully late, a mere hour until midnight, and an unmarried girl ought never to be out on the streets at a time like this. But today is different. Today, I could not have resisted the temptation for all the riches in the world—for Britain is at war with Germany.

Hearsay is that the German army marched into Belgium, a neutral country, in order to reach France and take Paris before the Russians could rally their forces. When Belgium implored us, the British, to provide aid, we were plunged into the armed conflict that has rapidly ensnared so many nations. Now, we at long last have the chance to put Germany and their foul Austrian lackeys back where they belong: in the shadow, rather than usurping the place in the sun that rightfully belongs to us and perhaps to France.

Laura gives me a light shove. 'Can you imagine waging war on your cousins? Although I suppose that's the way it has always been for that circle.'

'Well, I doubt it was His Majesty's decision.'

'Look! There they are!' She points as if she had spotted a mouth-watering prey.

She is right. There they are: Their Majesties the King and Queen, as well as the Prince of Wales, striding forth on the balcony with grace that comes from a lifetime of practice.

The crowd erupts in a burst of cheers, and confusion follows as the men try to distinguish their own hat from thousands of others thrown up in the air without a second thought.

Queen Mary raises her hand in a stiff, perfectly calculated wave. Her white glove and the contour of her sloping porcelain shoulders are the essence of elegance, her pearls catching glints of light from the street lanterns.

I crane my neck and squint, at once regretting that we are not standing closer to the palace. 'Isn't she just terrific?'

Laura ignores me. She has eyes for Edward, the Prince of Wales, alone. I have never grasped why he is so utterly adored, although saying so to my fellow young women would be equal to pronouncing oneself a heretic four centuries ago. I prefer the Queen and two of her other children. They are nineteen-year-old Prince Albert, who reminds me faintly of Harry with his shy sense of duty, and seventeen-year-old Princess Mary, whom I secretly pity for having been cursed with five brothers and no sisters.

A stealthy conversation between two men clad in worn jackets captures my interest. They are standing with their backs to us, but their accent marks them as labourers, and I imagine their expressions to be grim judging by their words.

'What are they all cheering for? The pricks on that balcony are as good as German themselves! I'll be damned if they don't know it, too, Gareth.'

The man who I assume is Gareth shrugs. 'Beats me. You'd think they'd at least change that name of theirs—Saxe-Coburg and...and Gotha, is it?'

'Before we know it, they'll be having a Sunday roast with their German family.'

I do my best to shut my ears to their bitter voices. The labourers are right and I loathe them for it. I cannot for the life of me believe, though, that the royal family would consort with the Kaiser under the current circumstances, and we ought to credit them with some trust rather than turn to misgivings on a whim. The man and the woman on the balcony are still our sovereigns, and we will need the unity that brings more than ever if we are to be victorious.

The first sweet notes of 'Rule Britannia' rise from the crowd. Laura is quick to join in, and after a moment of hesitation—my singing voice is comparable to the sound of a cat being forcibly bathed—I follow her example.

Time wears on and still the lot of us sing, even after Their Majesties and His Royal Highness withdraw from our sight, back into their gilded domain. I should think it is midnight before Laura and I scramble into Laura's car.

Her chauffeur has been waiting with anxiety carved deep in his face. If any harm was to come to us this boisterous, quivering night, he would likely lose his employment. 'Really, Miss, I wish you had asked Mr Julian to come with us.'

I roll my eyes at Laura and she leans her head on my shoulder, smiling. Our brothers, Julian and Fred, would perhaps not have balked at playing the chaperone, but they have their own friends and their own affairs to tend to. We can surely afford a few hours of neglected good behaviour. Is not this a moment to be remembered for decades to come?

The queues to the recruitment offices trickle down the streets, growing longer by the minute. Men and boys blend together in grey clusters of suits, caps, and cigarette smoke. When one takes a closer look, they are evidently of all ages and from all classes, from public school boys and dandies in speckless Oxford shoes to urchins in rags and time-worn family fathers.

Laura and I are sitting at a café, sipping steaming hot coffee despite the rays of sun beating down upon us, watching the spectacle.

'Do you think our papas will be called to duty?' I ask.

'I don't know. They served well in the Boer Wars, true, but they aren't young anymore. Mine has even been ailing with gout this past spring!'

'With all these volunteers, maybe there won't be any need for conscription.' I draw a sharp breath. 'What if…what if they don't come back? What if we're not alive for them to come back to? What then?'

'Now, that's some malarkey!'

I frown, my friend's love for odd words chasing away my sudden trepidation. '"Malarkey"? What on earth does that mean?'

'Nonsense. I think it's American, see, and very modern.'

Shortly thereafter, a remarkably tall, slender man with hair as red as his sister's stalks across the street towards us, a polished walking stick in one hand and a straw hat in the other. Julian Hamilton is three years our senior but often pretends to be the worldliest person in all of England. He *has* travelled to both Italy and Greece, but I do not think a few months spent gazing at nude statues justifies his airs.

'Miss Wilkes. Laura,' Julian salutes us, bending down to give Laura quick peck on each cheek. 'All this fuss is just unbearable, isn't it?'

Laura cocks an eyebrow and her tone is tart when she speaks. 'I think it's rather exciting, Brother. I assume you're on your way to enlist?'

'Not if I can avoid it. There are, after all, far more important matters to occupy my thoughts, are there not? Moreover, if I am to fight anywhere with anyone, I would have it be in the cavalry and not in the infantry with…'

'With what?' I take a sip of coffee to appear unbothered.

'With working-class men, Miss Wilkes, if you must know. What glory is there to be had in trudging in the filth instead of looking fashionable on a horse? I'm not in the search for glory, anyhow.'

'Everyone should want to contribute!' I swallow, cursing myself for allowing my temper to flare up. 'I shall join the Voluntary Aid Detachment, so there. And you, Laura, won't you come, too?'

Laura smirks; there are few things she savours as much as irking her older brother. 'Of course, no matter how dull it sounds.'

'Our father will never consent,' Julian protests. 'Never. You womenfolk have the most incredulous illusions sometimes! Now, I must be off, or they might mark my absence at the Athenaeum Club.' He gives us a tiny and highly perfunctory gentleman's bow, then turns on his heel and resumes his walk down the street.

I put down my cup, pouting. 'I bet the cavalry wouldn't even take him.'

As I step inside the vestibule at home, the familiar aroma of Daya's beef casserole envelops me. In the days of my childhood, Mama sometimes supervised the cooking. However much I mourn my mother, there is no denying that Daya has prospered when left to her own devices with the pots and pans. I have often watched the steam form beads on her caramel-coloured skin, but never have I seen her troubled by it nor have I tasted a single mediocre dish.

I lay off my broad-brimmed hat and abandon my scarf before climbing the wide flight of stairs to my bedchamber. There is no maid to help me undress, but I have little need of one. Ever since Mama died, Papa has made do with three members of staff, and the housemaid Minnie is only for cleaning. Once I deem myself presentable enough in my plain evening gown, I descend into the dining room where Papa, Fred, and Isabel are already seated.

On the table stands a pot of casserole, a platter brimming with roast potatoes and beetroots, a carafe of wine, and bread. We fill our plates in silence, hunger urging us to choose dinner before conversation in spite of our deeply ingrained manners.

Fred, however, is eager to discuss the events unfolding outside our door. 'It appears to me that Oxford is not what I should have put my time into.' He props another piece of bread in his mouth. His freckles are three times as bad as my own, a cascade rather than a sprinkle, and he looks positively flaming in the light from the chandelier.

Papa raises his eyes from his plate and shakes his head, the loose skin on his chin and cheeks flapping. 'It may be that a military training would have come in handy at this time, but you'll never hear me agree that Oxford was for nothing! It will do you well in life. A war passes but a degree doesn't!' He shouts the last words, as is so often the case regardless of the topic.

Fred grins. 'I meant no offense, Papa. Still, I'd like to be taken up amongst the air force. You know I have long marvelled at aeroplanes, and what could be more exciting than to serve in the Royal Flying Corps?' He does indeed have a childish fascination with planes. Fear makes my stomach flutter at the very thought of being so far up in the air with no guarantee of ever standing on solid ground again.

Papa's temper strikes again. 'The RFC? Don't even think about it, boy. You either fight the bloody Germans man to man or you do nothing at all!'

The three of us—Fred, Isabel, and I—sit quiet, patient. We know from many years of experience that our father means no harm.

After the gilded grandfather clock at the other end of the room has ticked another minute, I approach the matter from a different viewpoint. 'If Fred joins the RFC, Papa, he'll have to undergo longer training than if he enlisted in the infantry, surely. By the time he's finished, the war will be long over, and while he'll be awfully sorry for it—' I sneak my brother a smile, '—you can take heart in that he won't see any fighting. I know you would worry otherwise, and there's no point in denying it.'

Papa shakes his head. 'Haven't you heard what Lord Kitchener says? The man thinks we shan't have peace again for three years or something such at least!'

'Lord Kitchener isn't a prophet, is he?'

'No, but he *has* been appointed our Secretary of State of War, Rose.'

'As for fighting the Germans man to man, flying will allow me to do just that,' Fred says.

We dine in silence until our cook appears in the doorway to collect the plates and serve dessert. These tasks should be carried out by a footman or possibly a butler, but we have none, and Daya is perfectly able. Minnie, who rarely speaks but often casts mistrustful glances through long, thick lashes, follows Daya to assist.

Isabel clasps her hands in her lap and smiles. 'This was marvellous. I'd say you could cook for His Majesty himself.'

Daya glows at the praise, which is unusually lavish coming from my pragmatic sister. 'Thank you, Miss Isabel, thank you very much indeed.'

Isabel excuses herself before dessert, blaming an agonizing headache. Of course, the rest of us are fully aware that she is seeking an evening spent in solitary prayer. She can be on her stocking-clad knees hours on end, whispering gracious words to our Lord and Saviour Jesus Christ. I cannot for my life imagine how she does it. Sometimes, she reminds me of a Protestant version of Queen Mary I. Were I her, I would be long dead from sheer boredom.

After we have retired to the sitting room, Papa sinks down in his favourite leather armchair, tapping his feet against the plush carpet out of habit. Soon he has poured himself a fresh glass of brandy glistening in amber and gold, lit a pipe, and opened today's morning issue of *The Daily Mail* with a rustle.

I can discern the headline from my place in the sofa: 'Great Britain Declares War on Germany'. Below that, the paper says 'Summary Rejection of British Ultimatum, Cheers in London', and 'All Eyes on the North Sea'. At the bottom of the page is an advertisement for ladies' hats.

My father has a soft spot for hats. One might not credit him being a fine tailor, yet he is well known for his taste in clothes and precise measuring, well enough to forgive his brusque temper. Naturally, he does not touch the scissor or needle himself, but rather manages the firm and provides the most prominent customers with advice on what might suit their figure and complexion. He puffs on the pipe, which belonged to my great grandfather in the early years of Queen Victoria's reign, and releases a curling plume of smoke. I am accustomed to the smell.

To search for a man who does not smoke is nearly as futile as searching for one who does not drink tea at teatime.

I return my glance to the notebook in my lap. Over the years I have created the habit of writing down ideas and stories as they come to me, wild tumbles of the imagination being captured with ink on paper. There is now a collection of scribbled books in my room. Perhaps I could sell those stories someday. Of course, my husband will provide for me, but I would like a profitable pastime. When I was younger, I yearned for a role in the moving pictures—or movies, as some call them—but I have stopped entertaining that far-fetched fancy since I lack the looks it would take.

'How did you like the novel I showed you?' Fred asks, interrupting my musings, crossing his legs and leaning back in the sofa.

I smile and put down the notebook. 'It was delightful. I loved the part where Anna pretended she did not recognise the marquise!'

'That was my favourite part as well. Will you let me borrow the one you bought last week? The one with the pistachio-coloured cover.'

'Of course, I'll fetch it right away.'

The soft summer sun still shines through the sashed window in my bedchamber. The furniture drowns in it; my favourite kind of light. I grab the glossy new book on my drawer and close the door behind me, then return to the sitting room and the company I would not want to live without.

Fred never mocks my love for romantic, thrilling novels, for it is an interest he shares. It would be a tad unfair to claim that any man has ever treated me poorly, at least not those I associate with, but Fred is something out of the ordinary. There is a certain difference between escaping maltreatment and feeling like an equal on an intellectual level. This is especially true since I know my brother to be cleverer than most young men in his year at Oxford. For as long as I can recall, he has ignored the fact that I am a girl and therefore subject to being viewed as a Venetian glass figurine. It inspires a freedom I will be most reluctant to resign if he goes away to train in the RFC.

Papa has put *The Daily Mail* down in his lap. He sips the liquor at a slow, constant pace.

'May I have the paper?' I snatch it from him since he does not reply, then read the lead article while holding my breath.

Fred is next to skim through and then carefully study the black printing. I wish I would have read the entire paper before surrendering it to him, but my eyelids keep falling down. Time goes by quickly; the clock on the mantlepiece shows quarter past ten. If I had a governess, she would have sent me to bed by nine o'clock sharp every night until I married and my husband could do the very same if he wished.

'I think I'll withdraw now, Papa,' I give both him and Fred the kiss on the cheek they expect.

Once in my bedchamber, I change into the thin nightshift with ruffled cuffs and brush my hair with long strokes before gathering it in a tight braid to prevent a bird's nest from forming during the night. I dab my face and neck in lukewarm water from a basin, and brush my teeth. Lying in my bed, I kick the thick covers to a bundle by the bedpost. The heat in the room is sweltering, conjuring up images in my head of the summer festival.

I roll over on my side and stretch out a finger to trace each of the miniature faces in the framed photograph on my nightstand. Seven bright young things—and I am certain we will remain just that, come what may.

Chapter three

Rosalie

HARRY'S FATHER, WHO knew my own Papa when they were at university, hosts a farewell gathering for his oldest son and the other boys. When we arrive, I am as always struck by the beauty of the old house at the far end of the street where the cobblestones are swathed in the great oaks' shadows. High, grey walls meet charming details in dark wood, the same material that lines the windows and tower up in pillars supporting the veranda.

I often played with Harry and his sister Elsa in the blooming garden when we were little. Elsa used to tug at my braids and point her bony finger at my freckles, sending me into fits of fury. Then Harry would cry because he did not want us to fight, and the adults had to tell us to 'behave and be *nice* like girls ought to'. I cherished those days.

Elsa has matured but hardly improved, and I cannot claim to have warmed towards her, either. She greets me with an icy stare the instant I follow Papa and Fred into the vestibule, her thin face, high cheekbones, and neatly pinned-up flaxen curls making me simmer with envy. Apart from Elsa's pasted-on smile, she and Harry are two peas from the same pod in terms of appearance. However, their spirits are so divided that I sometimes ask myself how they can have come from the same womb.

Elsa opens her mouth, without doubt to say something frightfully polite dripping with sarcasm. Her brother and father

18

arrive before she has the chance to utter a word other than the welcome expected from a hostess.

With Harry by my side like an eager puppy, I exchange a few words with the other guests, making an effort to align with their endless, mindless chatter. I do not have to endure it for long, since we are soon show to the dining hall. I count the guests seated along the table. There must be two dozen. Papa, Fred and I, the Bride family, the Jenkins brothers, Mark Crewel, Laura and Julian Hamilton, Mildred and her sister Elizabeth, various members of their families, and in addition to this a clutch of people whose acquaintance I have barely met before. Isabel, though, is sunk deep in her bed at home, allegedly suffering from some mysterious illness.

The footman, who brings a penguin to mind in his black and white uniform, balances a series of steaming dishes in his gloved hands, presenting us with the courses one by one: soup with golden croutons bobbing at the surface, roasted pigeon stuffed with fresh herbs, honey-glazed vegetables, slices of veal, and for dessert pear trifle.

Edward Bride—Harry's father—rises from his chair at the head of the table and taps his glass with the dull end of a knife, silencing the room. His evening jacket is stiff and his hairline has receded to the centre of his scalp. He clears his throat several times and, finally, every pair of eyes in the dining hall has turned in his direction.

'Friends, family, dear guests. Let me, before I begin, thank you all from the bottom of my heart for joining us this splendid evening. I believe you all know why this gathering was set up, and what is to come. Our courageous, honourable sons and brothers are to leave us, but not for good, no, far from it. I think we can all agree, that with our earnest prayers, they shall be home before the New Year.'

At this, my own father mutters something under his breath.

Mr Bride continues, 'These young men will fight for the future of England, for our nation's pride, and for our gracious sovereign King George. We will all, older men and women and girls alike, do what is in our power to assist them in this most glorious endeavour. Cheers!'

'Cheers!' we echo and raise our glasses. The boys look about to crack with pride. If there is also a sprinkle of dread in their hearts, they have done their utmost to conceal it.

Once we have tasted every dish and spoken every encouraging word, I steer my steps out on the back veranda facing the garden, which is unusually large for a London house. The light is soft and tinted with a peachy sundown; the dark will not creep on just yet. The trees are rich and evergreen, the branches swaying with ripening fruit.

I lean as far out as the wooden banister allows, filling my lungs with flower fragrance.

Harry's footsteps halt behind me. 'Your brother said you might be out here.'

I turn to face him and he blushes ever so slightly, as is his habit. 'I've barely had the chance to ask what they said at the recruitment office. Tell me, please, and spare me no details.'

'Oh, that. We had to undergo a physical examination—it was quite easy and they were very understanding—and then…then we swore an oath on the Holy Bible to serve our king and country.'

'And what will you all end up as? Mr Bride made no mention of ranks.'

'Well, Mark will be a second lieutenant and can expect promotion—if he behaves, that is, which might prove tricky. The same stands true for Jones, and I suppose you already know that James will be posted on the HMS Audacious!'

'And you?' I return his smile.

'I settled for being a private. To tell you the truth, Rosalie… I doubt I could lead men in battle when I do not even know what a battle is like.'

I must be a blithering idiot, because this thought has not struck me until now. Boys barely older than myself will tell hardened veterans how to fight, simply because their fathers had enough money to send them to a respected school. An officer is expected to behave like a gentleman and enjoy the pleasures of a gentleman, thus the selection is narrow.

Harry's Adam's apple bobs as he speaks. 'Will you wait for me, Rose? When I come back…when…when I come back, we could marry.' When he has the courage to meet my eyes, his own are brimming with hope and fear both. The blush has risen to his temples. Strange, that they so gladly go to a battlefield but tremble before a mere girl.

I stare at him: the boy I have only kissed once. The blood rushes in my ears and alarum is ringing in my head. Then, my conscience takes hold of me. I cannot send him to face the Huns with no hope—I simply cannot. I cannot ask him to fight without anything to cheer him up when things feel cold or dark or alien.

And I know Harry. I grew up with him. I know in my heart that he would never hurt me or raise his hand at me. Never. Moreover, he is kind and brave, at times even clever. The choice is at once obvious to me. I believe I have no other.

'Yes. I will wait for you, and then…then we can marry.'

The bottomless dread in his eyes vanishes. First now does the idea of kneeling come to his mind, and so he does with admirable haste. Laughing, he places a thin gold ring on my finger before standing up again, still clutching my hands in his. The ring is terribly *a-la-mode*: simple, crafted from what I believe is white gold and set with a blueberry-sized diamond.

'I will do anything to make you happy, Rose. Anything,' he whispers.

I believe him.

When we return inside, I slip the ring off my finger and drop it into the pocket between the folds of my skirt. 'Only for now. I wouldn't want everyone to know so soon.' I do not dare to utter the truth, which is that if I change my mind, it is best to have been a secret all along.

Harry's face flashes with disappointment for a heartbeat, but he quickly regains his composure and nods.

Chapter four

Paris, France

Charles

THE WHITE GOLD foam splashes up against the edge of my glass. I take a deep sip and the fizz sends a tinge of pleasure all the way to my toes. After what some of us consider a long day of arduous study, and others think of as a children's game, we have earned the champagne. We say that most nights of the week, of course, but I cannot for the life of me see any fault in that. After a hefty dinner from the café down the street, drinking rarely has any regrettable impact—except on our allowances.

It is a sumptuous room, with leather armchairs placed in a circle, gypsy panels covering the walls, and a massive fireplace most recently used at the turn of the century. The high windows offer a splendid view of the street below the Sorbonne. I cross the floor to the spot-free glass.

Two little girls are playing with a jumping rope on the pavement. Their hair is tied in garlands with ribbons to match their school dresses.

An old man rides his rickety bike down the cobblestones, his basket overfull with groceries from the market. I wager they will spill over any minute and send apples tumbling down the street.

An upper-class couple with the tackiest clothes imaginable stroll arm in arm, a poodle trotting by their feet.

'A cigar?' Louis says. He is sitting next to the stout chess table in the corner of the room, legs crossed. The chess pieces are neatly lined up in black and white, but in a few hours, they will be scattered all over the floor in some poor fellow's sudden rage over losing a game.

I turn my back to the window and saunter over to accept the thick roll Louis holds between two fingers. Once he has lit his own cigar and is breathing out smoke, I bend down to borrow the flickering flame of his lighter. To me, it is the most troubling mystique how anyone does not enjoy a qualitative cigar. Inhaling, I take a few steps across what I think is a Persian carpet, my steps muffled.

The second year of my law studies has taken a rather gallant start. There is little difference from the first year, except that I can now righteously call myself an established member of our group. That is despite the fact that the others' families rank on the ancient scale whilst my own is merely what they call new money, and lack a title. New money is not so bad, though. I know with certainty that if my grandfather had not made a fortune from California gold as a young man, I would not eventually have entered the gates of the Sorbonne. Now, my mother presides in the countryside château her father bought when he was eager to assert the family's status in a pool of age-old aristocracy. There she sits in her perfumed shawls and hideous dresses. I suspect I will never comprehend her way of living, but then we all have peculiar ways of spending money when overwhelmed with it.

The spirit of the evening escalates in the usual manner. One glass of champagne turns to three before we open the bottle of American bourbon.

When we have no sensible topics left to discuss, we quite naturally turn to the war. There is always something to be said about the war.

'What about you, Michael? Are you about to enlist?' Louis asks.

Michael speaks with a clamped jaw. 'You know very well I've no intention of fighting their cursed war! If they prop a rifle in my hands and ask me to shoot a man dead… I won't do it. I won't, that I swear on all that is sacred.'

'How noble of you, Michael,' I say. 'I do agree with you on one point, though. This isn't our war to fight and it never was. It belongs to the Kaiser, his cousins and their generals, Monsieur Asquith, and of course the Serbs and Austrians.'

'And Poincaré. He was none too friendly with Germany even long before the war broke out.'

'Yes, yes, I suppose so.'

My assessment of the current situation, flawed and simplified as I know it to be, is met with mumbled agreement. Unlike a wealth of other young men, we are not keen on going to the front, and for good reason. To bring our country glory sounds grand, but life is a fine thing, and I should hate to spoil it. We have come to the conclusion that, were we to go, we might never manage to reclaim this haven even if we survived. The books would not speak the same words; the whisky would not taste as full-bodied or be as tinged with smoke. The bond between us would be altered. We would be birds torn from their natural habitat at the Sorbonne and curtailed in an outlandish place.

The older men will have a more established existence to go back to in the shape of daily toiling and a wife, even children. The boys who report to duty after rehearsing that, no, they are not sixteen but eighteen, will be fed to the enemy like piglets and shall not have to come back to anything.

We, however, are those *meant* to go to war, those *meant* to carry the burden on our shoulders. Yet we do not wish to, because we are in the bloom of our lives, intoxicated with privilege. I have the creeping feeling that were we to leave it all behind it might slip away like wet soap, so that we would be unable to pick it up once more. In a way, we are frozen in our tracks, disbelief and fear mounting rapidly. The Huns' audacity in plunging through Belgium to take Paris within weeks has turned us to statues, baffled though we do not often admit it.

'I hear they are recruiting officers from the best schools. In England, they cull them out until there is hardly anyone left at Cambridge, Oxford, and the like. I can only assume the procedure will be similar here,' Marcel says. He is a short man with slick black hair, who competes with his cousin Henri in being the Ancient Greeks' most ardent devotee.

Henri settles by the chess table and rests his elbows on the board, frowning. 'What do those students know of being officers? What do *we* know?'

I laugh. 'I don't think it matters to those in charge. Anyone can learn to fire a gun.'

'Well, I think it's bloody idiocy, all of it. Had it been up to me to decide—'

Marcel interrupts, flapping his hands to shoo his cousin away from the best chair. '"Let him that would move the world first move himself."'

'*Un autre verre?*' suggests Louis, and this time, the lot of us raise our glasses so that he can pour the last of the champagne.

Amongst all the members in our so-called club, Marcel is my favourite. His thin, elegantly trimmed moustache gives him a snobbish expression, but he is far more reliable and practical than one would expect.

Michael, who has sat in silence ever since I called him noble, now begins to play with a tendril of copper hair and hums 'In My Merry Oldsmobile', a Billy Murray tune. We do not need much persuasion to sing along.

We will linger here all evening, and the better part of the night too, before we each return to our own rooms. There, we will instruct our butlers to shake out our coats thoroughly and see to the breakfast. Yes, and so things ought to remain—if only governments would have the common courtesy to end their own damned conflicts.

In the midst of a lazy game of croquet, the first bolts of doom strike down upon us.

We hit the ball with our mallets, giving off a solid *clunk* and sending it like a speck of white paint across the lawn. We have made the effort to change into fitting attire: thick waistcoats in bold colours, with breast pockets and matching socks. The last August heat simmers in the air, and although the sport is one of leisure, I am soon clammy and itching with sweat. It will be some time yet before the air cools and the leaves of the linden trees grow spotty with butterscotch.

The young men on my team clap their hands and cheer when I score another point. Their shouts quickly subside, though, and

I turn around, curious as to what might have made their words fall flat.

A bulky man clad in a dark-blue uniform jacket and scarlet trousers, with several garish ribbons and medals dangling from his chest, is marching towards us. His kepi casts a heavy shadow over the better part of his thick face, allowing the sun to illuminate his mouth and cleft chin alone. When he is right beside our game, he halts and politely removes his kepi, revealing well-groomed hair and eyes with red veins running like a pattern of poorly crafted lace.

The five of us squint, half-blind in the cascades of sunlight.

'Can we help you with anything, Monsieur?' I summon every effort to disguise my distress.

The man does not move a limb and his fleshy mouth does not betray any emotion. 'Yes, I do believe you can. If I may be so blunt as to inquire for your identity?'

'Charles D'Aboville. These are some of my fellow students.'

'Monsieur D'Aboville. Very well. My name is Colonel David Laframboise, 6th Army Corps, 2nd Army. I've come to give you fine young men—or anyone at this university who you know to be a gentleman—the offer of an officer's commission. I assume you've noticed that there is a war going on.'

'Yes, Colonel, we have indeed noticed that.' I swing my mallet to hit the ball again. The breeze playing in the trees has ceased. The faint rustle of fabric when we shift our weight is deafening.

Louis clears his throat. 'When does this…this service commence?'

Colonel Laframboise looks as if awoken from a blunder. 'Why, at once of course! Don't you all wish to do your duty, to win honour for France?'

Before I so much as part my lips to tell him that we will if explicitly ordered to do so, Louis has stepped forward, glowing in his new bowtie. 'Naturally, Monsieur. We'd be *delighted*, wouldn't we?'

The remaining four of us look at each other, then at Louis, and at last at the uniform-clad figure. Marcel and Henri mumble something resembling agreement, their voices blurred. None of us dares reject the colonel's cause out loud. A cause that we do not understand and therefore despise, something decided by a government too ubiquitous for our disdainful young hearts.

'We need every good man in this country to fight,' the colonel says.

'I understand that but… This war will surely sort itself out, or the men who began it will.' It is a feeble excuse, and I squirm at it.

'Is ignorance a common trait at the Sorbonne?'

I shake my head, cheeks flaring hot. I cannot recall feeling this utterly stupid since I was a child caught pouring salt instead of sugar in my sisters' tea.

'We lost well over twenty thousand men three days ago, on the 22nd of August, and the casualties are still heavy. General Joffre is doing his utmost to win this struggle.' He makes a deliberate pause, evidently waiting for some exclamation or other. 'So, do you still think the war will *sort itself out?*'

I swallow once, twice. Well over twenty thousand dead. In a single day. I have never heard of anything like it before, but in this moment, I would rather chop off my little finger than admit as much to the grim-faced colonel.

Henri comes to my rescue. 'I presume they were wearing the usual flashy uniforms? That must have turned them into gratifying target practice for the enemy.'

'The uniforms deserve your respect, young man!' Laframboise places a protective hand on his own scarlet trousers, the veins in his face pulsating. 'There was a heavy fog and relentless rain! The artillery did not support—'

'Thank you, Colonel. I think we understand.'

A glance passes between Marcel and me. What the hot-livered old man has just told us only serves to dampen our spirits, but he does not seem to realise it, since he continues.

'Gentlemen like yourself will know all about France's suffering at the hands of Prussia in the previous century, I presume. You desire vengeance. That's a certainty.'

If we do not succeed in distancing the colonel from the lawn, he might start spewing out more so-called certainties, perhaps even complete prophecies, God forbid.

'You are right,' I say in a soothing tone, placing a steady hand on his shoulder to guide him back from whence he came.

The colonel does not return my placid smile yet allows himself to be led away with less resistance than I expected. 'How old are you, Monsieur D'Aboville?'

Ah. The one question bound to trump my every vindication. 'Twenty. I celebrated my twentieth birthday two weeks ago.'

'And your friends are no younger?'

'No, no, they're not.'

'How foolish of me not to ask at once! Then you're liable to serve three years in the army, just like every man your age, as decreed by the Three Years Law of 1913. Perhaps you will reconsider my offer of a commission. It's that or the uniform of a *soldat*, Monsieur D'Aboville, and I'd loathe to see you sink to such standards.'

I nod, muted, seething with fury as I watch him depart. In peacetime, my friends and I would likely have been able to escape conscription by pulling the right strings. In wartime…

We do not take up our cheerful chatter again—it is pointless. We stand in thick silence, my stomach twisting as I try to register the others' faces.

Marcel is the one who at last breaks the tension, but his small hands are twitching. 'I believe it's time for luncheon, don't you think?'

We all glance at our pocket watches, only to find that it is eleven o'clock, an hour and a half since we had apple turnovers for breakfast. Still, we are unanimous in saying that, yes, surely luncheon would be fitting. Michael in particular claims to be ravenous. Perhaps the colonel's talk has taken a greater toll on him who is the only one of us possessing genuine moral scruples regarding warfare.

We almost flutter away, leaving the croquet match unresolved, mallets and balls scattered on the combed meadow.

Chapter five

Rosalie

AT THE BEGINNING of my final school year, just as summer is about to shift into autumn, a sense of emptiness hangs heavy in the classroom. The overwhelming drain of young students who have left to join a training camp, teachers who have signed up.

Most of the boys who volunteered had already left school—the Jenkins brothers for instance—but there are still vacancies by the desks. There is a small pile of abandoned trigonometry books with glossy pages and doodles in the margins. Harry's own notebook will not be written in for several months. Although his and the other younger lads' absence is temporary, it nonetheless serves as a reminder to those of us left behind. We are useless, the lot of us. We do what we always have done: practise our spelling and repeat the names of prominent men of the past till we know them by heart but cannot explain why they were great. The Union Jack is pinned to the wall, flapping whenever we crack a window open. That flag is whispering our names now, whispering eagerly.

King Alfred's school is not the finest institution in London, but it is close to home, and its name carries enough weight to be accepted by the fathers and mothers from the well-to-do households of Hampstead. A smear of bitter controversy still sticks to allowing boys and girls our age to be mixed like confetti, but I am glad of it. Mildred, Mary, and Laura may be perfectly darling, but I doubt we should ever have as many conversations or exploits without our male counterparts.

By the time the first week of school draws to a close, I can stand it no longer. I might have spoken lightly before about becoming a nurse, but when every young man I know is scrambling to aid the nation, I will go stark mad unless I realise these plans. It will be an adventure. Besides, school is of course not mandatory at my age.

Mildred and Mary accompany me to the War Office, where we report to a woman in a very drab dress that we wish to join the Voluntary Aid Detachment.

The woman's expression is set in stone, and her voice reminds me of a creaking wooden door. 'Well then—how refreshing. If you'd like to follow me, please, and I will see what arrangements can be made.'

Just as my friends predicted at the summer festival—a day that feels impossibly long ago, a day when the war in itself was also a mere prediction—we are too young to be sent to France. But to France we shall, and that is that, because I am convinced that only a fool would willingly waste her adventure here when she could have a trip to the continent. Hence, the three of us agree that our own white lies can be no worse than those the boys must have told when they enlisted.

'Twenty-three,' I say when the woman with the creaking voice asks my age. I clench my fists between the folds of my marine-blue skirt, awaiting her judgement.

The woman pauses and surveys us. In the end, she nods and allows us to proceed. Never before have I aged five years so quickly.

'You will spend a few months training in a London hospital. If you pass your examinations, you may be put on the list of eligible volunteers for the stationary hospitals in France to pick from when they require personnel. No clearing stations, mind you, not until you're more experienced.'

The training hospital is a bustling place, young women being crammed into the building. We must pay for our own training, and there will be no salary once we are finished. We must do our best to cooperate with the prim-faced instructors and doctors sweeping about in their white coats and carefully trimmed moustaches. We must be taught how to make a bed flawlessly with a mere minute on our hands. We must learn how to best dress and undress wounded men, and there is a scattered giggle as the nurse instructing us describes the process of washing and scrubbing a soldier.

Most of the time, we are restricted to performing these mundane, elemental tasks for the patients, but we slowly advance to sterilising and bandaging gaping wounds as well as changing the containers for body fluids. Once we have gone through our examinations—which are scheduled to November—we might be allowed to encroach on the real nurses' duties if there is an emergency.

Only a fraction of the patients has come from the front; the rest are here for minor conditions like broken arms or fevers. I find them horribly dull, though I dare not say so. Instead, I latch onto every opportunity to care for the frontline soldiers, hoping they will give me a glimpse of what life is like out there. Their wounds are none too bad and they often beam at me, eager to chat about all sorts of nonsense. However, they say very little of the army. Either they wish to spare me something, or it is simply not as interesting as I presumed.

There is no room for hesitation or weak stomachs, no time to question what the seasoned nurses order us to do. This harsh fact is an unwelcome intruder in my own and, I daresay, many of the other girls' world. We scurry about with pinched cheeks and brand-new uniforms, dainty as daisies, and we are beginning to realise we do not belong in a hospital. Perhaps we will, someday, but as for now we are still too fresh.

In the evenings we are given simple but nourishing meals consisting of lumpy soups, bread, milk, and occasionally beef with potatoes coated in thick gravy. There is nothing in the way of luxury. Mary rapidly takes the simplicity to heart, though Mildred and I snigger at the food more often than I would like to admit. I ought to be more grateful, of course, but it is difficult when I am paying for my stay with pocket money accumulated over the years. Papa balked at me leaving him and refused to grant me more than a third of the fee.

I envy Mary how quickly and effortlessly she makes the nursing vocation her own. She appears wonderfully serene when she puts on her apron or dresses a wound, as if this is what she was born to do, a dancer at long last finding her ideal song.

Mildred, on the other hand, is all of a sudden squeamish and therefore poorly suited to nursing. She frets about breaking nails and is haunted by a phobia of blood that I knew nothing of until now.

It is a small comfort that I myself am free from such issues. Day by day, despite constantly forgetting which drawer is which, as well as being the last girl to finish making the beds assigned to me, I slowly adapt to my new chores. It is a wonder that anything useful at all has been crafted of me.

On the weekends, we may at times do as we please for a few hours. Mary, Mildred, and I make a habit out of writing to the boys at the training camp—they have been moved from Bisley, Surrey, to Crowborough, East Sussex. We ask whether they, too, have a little while to spare for a joint outing, but with without success. They are frightfully busy, even more so than we, though one cannot expect otherwise. After all, they need to learn a soldier's skills in a few months' time.

Mark and Jones, who are to be second lieutenants, naturally enjoy greater liberty than Harry. They could without doubt be granted leave more often if they requested it, but it appears they are so besotted with their new surroundings that they have forgotten about the rest of us. Well, not entirely; they still write a few times every week.

Harry writes daily. He recounts his monotonous routine in detail to me, apologizing at the end of each letter for being too dull. I reply with similarly minute descriptions of my own life. At least it keeps my handwriting pretty.

The days in the training camp of the London Rifle Brigade are strenuous. The men are relentlessly drilled in marching, parading, turning, falling into formation… They learn how to take cover and how to interpret various commands. Eventually, they are introduced to rifles and grenades and weapons bearing names too odd for me to memorise.

Harry writes that there is a grave shortage of uniforms, boots, guns and the like. The surge of new recruits has been so vast that the army lacks equipment and resources for everyone. For now, the newcomers are given blue Kitchener uniforms, so-called because our Secretary of State of War has been one of the loudest voices bellowing for fresh recruits. Some must even make do with wooden rifles.

Mildred and I find this revelation terribly amusing.

'Anyhow, they will surely have good and proper equipment before they go across the channel!' my friend says and tucks the sheet under the mattress as we proceed with our chores.

'Yes, I wager you're right. Speaking of across the channel, my brother tells me they might attack the enemy from the air soon. He knows quite a bit about aeroplanes, and says they'll fly to the continent easily and come back again before you even notice they're gone.'

'Fancy that!' She throws up a pillow in the air and catches it again, plumping it up. 'I wouldn't step into an aeroplane if they paid me—maybe a balloon, just maybe.'

'Me neither. It frightens me to think Fred could be a pilot, but I'd never say as much, not when Papa is already making a fuss. He doesn't care for aeroplanes at all. As long as they quarrel, Fred won't enlist anywhere.'

A third voice startles us. 'Don't let me catch you throwing the pillows about again, sweet ones, or I'll be honour-bound to tell Miss Gibson.'

Mrs Bryant is a kind woman and one whom I could easily see as my own dear auntie. When we err, she corrects us with a mild voice and benign frown, hair thoroughly streaked with grey falling into her face. On her arm she wears a broad, black ribbon. We do not inquire as to whom she has lost, but she shares the tale with us regardless. Her husband, Harold Bryant, died thirty-four years ago in tuberculosis. To think that a woman can be tied to a fading memory for such a long time not only inspires admiration but chills me.

However, Harry will live. To expect anything contrary would be pure silliness on my behalf. I refuse to turn into a grey Mrs Bryant, forever in mourning. I simply could not stand it. I shall be a true wife, not a widow, and I shall have a clutch of babies to spoil, too. The images in my head are as lovely as can be, tinted with silver and seen through a haze of sorts, like holding a looking-glass at a distance. Do I want those babies? It is beyond me to tell, but I believe Harry does, and I dare not try to alter the ready-made mould of a domestic life. While I have yearned for a different future when immersed in my improper novels, there is a clear contrast between fiction and reality. Once I am married, I will have become a reincarnation of my own mother. Allowing myself to be dissatisfied would be the height of foolishness.

Mrs Bryant is in truth an exception amongst the trained nurses I encounter at the hospital. Many of them are harsh, although I cannot blame them. They have occupied this profession for years and know their business—then hundreds of chirping new birds come along and they have to teach us how to fly. Nonetheless, the burden will eventually lighten, and with some luck they will be more grateful towards us. We *are* doing our very best, even Mildred, whose face frequently shifts sage.

'Oh, dear! I'm so sorry!' she squeals, eyes wide as cups and mouth shaped to an enchanting little *o* after spilling a bottle of clear fluid on the floor.

Miss Gibbons, one of the nurses in charge who also happens to be the most handsome and arrogant woman I have ever met, arches an eyebrow. 'What are you waiting for? Fetch some towels at once, and clean it up properly!'

Mildred gushes with confusion. 'Where do I find the towels, Miss Gibbons?'

Miss Gibbons sighs. Her chin tipped skywards, she glides out of the room, demonstrating just how tiresome we are.

Mildred does not care to ask anyone else where the towels are stored, but Mary comes to our rescue and opens the bottom cupboard in the corridor

Once we have wiped up the liquid, the clock has already struck eight sharp and we are late for supper. There are plates waiting for us by the long table; my stomach turns when I spot the turnip and leek soup, large chunks swimming in broth. We take our seats and entrust Mary with the unenviable task of making excuses.

Mildred accepts a slice of toasted bread. 'How I miss the evenings at the Brides! Imagine how fine it would be to visit their gatherings again. Maybe the boys will be free next weekend— don't you think so, Rose?'

Before I have the chance to reply, Miss Gibbons silences me with a reprimanding glance.

We begin to eat, quietly. I abandon my soup in favour of the golden bread, scattering crumbs all over my apron. The electric toaster is one of the many novelties my father refuses to have in the house, and I must savour the opportunity. I even manage to ignore the woman seated on my left, Elizabeth Graham, whose meticulous manners cast my own in a poor light.

We remain silent until we have nearly finished supper.

'My uncle rang on the telephone this morning to tell me that the German plans to take Paris are squashed,' one of the women farther down the table announces as if to enlighten the rest of us. 'The Battle of Marne, they call it. I rather like the sound of that. He works at the War Office, my uncle, and he also told me that the French brought reserves from Paris by taxi! Can you imagine? Several hundred automobiles—'

This is indeed a revelation of sorts to me. Of course, I am as curious as anyone about the events taking place in France and Belgium, but I have neglected the newspapers these past few days, being preoccupied with my siblings' shared twenty-third birthday.

Elizabeth Graham freezes in the chair next to me. When she once more raises a spoonful of soup to her mouth, her bony face shows bitterness alone.

I cannot curb my curiosity. 'Miss Graham? Are you quite alright?'

At first I think she is not going to reply, but then she puts down her spoon and addresses the dining hall in a clear voice. 'I lost two cousins at Marne.'

The talkative woman with the uncle opens her mouth and closes it again like a goldfish. Perhaps it is her, as well as my own, first time speaking to someone who has lost a close relative in the war. Two relatives, even. That knowledge in itself is enough to rob me of my appetite. I am being ridiculous… What did I expect? No, I expected nothing else. I am not a stupid little girl who cannot comprehend the meaning of the word 'war'. Only…only death has crept very near all of a sudden.

Little more than a week passes after that before Mildred gives up. She has her heart set on returning home in the attempt to be useful in some other way, or, to tell the blunt truth, chose a fellow to marry so that she might busy herself with responsibilities better suited to her character.

'Take care, then,' I say as we embrace, standing outside the building in the lukewarm breeze mingling with the lavender oil Mildred uses to keep her hands soft. A chauffeur is waiting with the car nearby.

'And you take care of those poor souls, for both of us.'

I nod stiffly and then step back, letting Mary have the farewell due to her.

Then there are just two of us left, and with every dear friend and acquaintance I part from—as temporary as it might be—it is as if another piece of a puzzle has been removed. I can only hope I shall be able to fill in the gaps, eventually.

Chapter six

Charles

I QUICKLY COME to the conclusion that my superior officers, as well as those below me in rank, have a dash of insanity in them. Caught in a Napoleonic fantasy, they are only too happy to lag a century behind the world I believe to be real. Every morning, we put on our stylish uniforms, fit for parade rather than what I assume is a bleak battlefield somewhere out there. Those who have medals to show do so as if they were wearing divine relics. Each ribbon stares back at me, mocking. I cannot help but detest them. They mean nothing to me yet everything to the old men forcing me to fight.

Once I dragged myself to the *Grand Quartier Général* in Chantilly, it took a mere fifteen minutes for Colonel Laframboise, who popped up almost as if he had been waiting for me in particular, to decide on a commission for me: *capitaine*. It proved a challenge not to laugh him in the face. There he stood, feet planted firmly on the floor of his office, telling me that I am to lead close to two hundred souls into battle. Me! What do they take me for? I will not deny that I enjoy the role of the leader and all that comes with it: a servant in the field, superior meals and so forth. But I have only fired a weapon when hunting on my grandfather's premises, and unlike animals, humans tend to fire back.

I have been given a sword also—another part of the Napoleonic fantasy. I might know close to nothing about

37

warfare, but I reckon that a bullet trumps a blade nine times out of ten.

Marcel shares my opinion. He, too, is going through the preposterous drill to become a junior officer. We parted with our three fellow students with a toast of bland cognac and humourless smiles, each assuring the other that we would not cast a backward glance as we walked out from the Sorbonne. Of course, we went with our heads turned like owls, stumbling over our own feet.

Louis gave his parents a slight shock by applying for the post of ambulance driver on the eastern front, choosing the most unexpected path possible. When I asked him about it, he shrugged. 'Well, I enjoy driving, I do, and who knows, it might be less dangerous. But to be frank, Charles, my mother is so scandalized that it doesn't really matter why. It'll be worth it, if only to see her face when I turn up on leave covered in oil and grime!'

Henri was honourably rejected and received a signed statement from the doctor. As it turns out, the lucky bastard suffers from both bad eyesight and an irregular heartbeat. To my disappointment, I myself was chirpily diagnosed as 'physically top-notch and ready for active duty'.

As for Michael, he has not reported himself to the army yet, but is determined to stick to his unpractical humanist principles come hellfire—or, I should say, shellfire. The state does not look kindly upon pacifists, far from it. Michael might have had a brighter immediate future if he was a lunatic just like others will probably think he is. As nasty as an asylum sounds, prison is not exactly an ivory paradise with a faint scent of roses, either. People will call him a coward, and for that reason he is the bravest among us, for he refuses to budge regardless. The rest of us, myself included, will rather run towards death than endure the full scope of humiliation. I am beginning to realise how infuriatingly intertwined courage and cowardice are.

I am also falling back into my bad habit of thinking too much and too long. I will have to stop with such nonsense.

The officers' training camp is adjacent to that of the *soldats*, giving us the chance to practice our commandeering on men rather than shouting orders to the thin air. The *soldats* usually answer to officers who completed their training long since, but I occasionally find myself with the blue blocks and lines of men. Seen from afar, they bring to mind something from a geometry school book. Up close, their faces are too animated for my taste. A few are younger than me, but a majority are between twenty and thirty, and they who survey me with a speck of criticism in their eyes are nearly twice my age. Their hands calloused and their shoulders broad from a lifetime of labour. They represent the quintessence of everything I am not and never will be.

'Garde à vous!

The men adopt the correct position with obvious nervousness, some adjusting their feet and hands when they think my gaze is elsewhere.

I drill them for a while longer before dismissing them to their rigorous exercise. I return to my tent, which is wedged between two other captains', where I discover Marcel slumped on my bed.

'Why, I haven't seen you all week!' I offer him my hand and he pulls himself to his feet.

'I have been making myself scarce. The *Général de Brigade* is looming over me as if I were Oedipus and he one of the Erinyes.'

'What did you do to deserve such a daunting pursuer?'

Marcel winks. 'I saw him receiving a girl in his quarters—by accident, of course.'

'I take it from the way you phrase it that she wasn't Madame *Général de Brigade?*'

My friend merely winks again and asks how my company is conducting itself thus far.

I shake my head. 'They're hardly *my* company, are they? It's not they whom I'll lead in battle when the time comes. For all I know, you and I will both be put on a train to the front and dropped in a section where one of the captains have just been plucked down by the Huns. And then the process repeats itself once all that remains of use, too, are gaps in the lines.'

There is something so queer and so gloomy about this prospect that Marcel and I give in to fits of laughing that racks our chests and plunges us down to sit on the bed.

'What a morass, Charles,' Marcel says after regaining his composure. 'I'm feeling positively buoyant just at the thought of it!'

One of the *soldats* sparks my curiosity: the nutcase Arthur Hudson, a half-American with a patchy baldness and the brightest teeth I ever saw. He is a man whom everyone knows but no one *truly* knows, because no one's patience lasts longer than a few minutes when talking to him.

One evening, as I make a detour to explore the *soldates'* mess hall, I discover him bent over a worn sketchpad. He is making sweeping strokes with the charcoal, his tongue flickering across his chapped lips. When he notices my glance, he locks eyes with me.

'What are you drawing?' I ask.

'People. You.' His voice is startlingly clear.

'Pourquoi?'

'Because your face is interesting. I draw everyone's faces: yours, and his, and his—' He points a finger at various men in the room. '—and I keep them so I won't forget how they look.'

'Why would you want to remember anything like that? For all I know, I'll try my best and forget most of these faces. They will be dead, anyhow.'

Hudson spreads his hands. 'Exactly. Isn't it fun?'

Part of me finds the idea of keeping a notebook full of strangers' faces repugnant. 'You're mad.'

'No. I know I am, but those who are never quite do, see.'

'I suppose there is something to that.'

'There's a lot to it—after all, what would be the point in telling you so if there wasn't?'

'Are you here of free will?'

Arthur Hudson spreads his hands again. 'I don't have much else to aspire to except dancing to their fiddle. I was too bored, and it's quite the career. Not even a real interview required.'

'Life is a fiddle to which we must all dance. And though I don't approve of the dance, I'd hate falling on my face instead.'

Hudson nods thoughtfully, then stands and leaves without a word and without having touched the crumbling, dry crackers he took such care to arrange on the table. When he is at a safe distance, I snatch one of them and take a bite, ruining the pattern. It is difficult to swallow.

In mid-October, Isabel says her farewells to me, Fred, and Papa. We are standing in the thicket of steam at Victoria Station, watching a young man in uniform hoist Isabel's coffer onto the train, his cheeks blotchy with pimples and his expression strained with politeness. People are crowding forward to step on board: men in long coats, women in muslin blouses, children tugging at their parent's hands grinning with excitement.

'Have a pleasant journey, Sister,' Fred says. His tone is distant, as if speaking to a young woman he had only ever met over a cup of coffee.

Isabel grants him a short nod. 'Goodbye, Brother.' She turns to Papa and kisses him on the cheek, then climbs the steps to the train.

'Isabel!' I skip forward. 'Remember what you promised me! You must ask the people in charge to let me come to Rouen once I've completed my training.'

'I promised I would *try*. I can't guarantee they have a place for you, much less for your friend. I'll keep you in my prayers, though.'

'But Mary is tiny—they'd not even notice her, only that their work became easier.'

A man blows his whistle, signalling that the train is about to depart, and Isabel disappears from the door. The locomotive huffs and puffs, dove-grey plumes rising from the chimney. Then my sister is gone.

I step back and Fred wraps an arm around my shoulders. At the same time, he tucks his handkerchief in his pocket after Papa borrowed it to discreetly dab his eyes and nose. Papa detests tears shed in public and would be insulted if I suggested he carry his own handkerchief in case the need arises again.

'It was good of you to come down from Oxford,' I tell my brother as we emerge from the station into the chilly London street.

'I won't be going back, I'm afraid. I go to train with the RFC on Thursday.'

'What?' Papa bursts.

'I think you heard, both of you. Half the young men I know are already in the army—the rest are talking behind one another's backs. There's no use in trying to dissuade me, Papa. I've decided. You know I've never been the excessively courageous type but… I want to fly and that's all there is to it.'

That is indeed all there is. While Papa sulks in his armchair, I do my best to humour my brother by letting him entertain me with harrowing stories. Fred tells me about how British aeroplanes bombed zeppelin bases in Cologne and Düsseldorf not long ago. When Thursday arrives, he leaves just as he said he would, and I return to the hospital after my three days of leave.

Papa converts entirely to the role of the businessman. He is a father, too, but his children belong to Britain and the war effort now.

On a sodden afternoon early in November, I am once more at a station, this time to see Harry and the other boys off as they embark on their journey to Le Havre. It seems to me that my loved ones are leaving in hordes but I continuously remind myself that this is as it ought to be, and I will soon travel myself.

There are so many familiar faces, not among the women and girls who are here on the station for the same purpose as I am, but among the smartly outfitted soldiers. They belong to a so-called Pals' Battalion, where friends and colleagues are given the chance to serve together rather than with strangers in haphazard units. I am convinced that the London Rifle Brigade is the finest section of the 1st London Division, and nothing could alter that conviction.

Harry has put on quite a bit of weight since I last saw him, the training and ample food broadening his chest. If I am not mistaken, he has added an inch to his height as well. His smile is the same, though, sweet and unassuming, at times flitting.

'Look,' I say and show him my finger where I have put the ring he gave me that evening on the veranda. 'If it makes you happy, I'll wear it for everyone to see.'

'It would make me more than happy, Rose.'

'Then that's settled.' I swallow. Announcing our engagement to the world somehow transforms it from a tickling idea to a fact. Still, I cannot deny Harry the comfort I know it would bring him, the bounce it would add to his step. If I regret it later… Engagements are not marriages; they can be broken off. My conscience pokes at me, sharp and reproaching. No, I will not do that, not to Harry, not to the fair-haired boy sticking his head out the train window to kiss me one last time. It would be too cruel.

'I'll send you a souvenir or two,' he promises. 'A Hun's button or maybe a medal, if I ever earn one…' His cheeks flush, all cherry blossoms and careful hopes.

'Do you know yet where you'll be stationed?'

'No, not yet, but I should think Ypres.'

I shudder. 'I heard the men there have dug themselves down! Isn't that odd?'

'It protects them—us—from artillery fire…I think.'

'Goodbye Harry. I'll see you before you know it.'

The train jolts and accelerates.

Laura, who is standing beside me in her best Sunday coat and hat, grins at me. 'Soon you'll leave me all alone here in London, isn't that so?'

I laugh, banishing the melancholy my fiancé's departure has made wash over me. 'It will be an adventure to go overseas. I've only ever been once before, when Mama took me to Cannes, and I was too young then to remember much.'

'Don't steam it up, you dingbat. In all seriousness, though, I'm glad my father didn't consent to me becoming a nurse. I have the vote to think of.'

'I envy you, Laura. If it bothered me less what people thought, I'd stand with you.'

My friend links her arm with mine and we stroll down the dusty platform. Daya, who accompanied me to the station, follows us, a basket of vegetables fresh from the market in her hands.

'You'll shake off propriety some grand day, trust me. This war could well change everything, and if it does, I refuse to see you chose last century's decorum over future possibilities.'

Mary and I are both successful in our exams—she more so, but I will not let that fact consume me. I am by no means hopeless, not anymore, and if Miss Gibbons is pleased enough, I shall be content. When I was little, the teachers in school sometimes passed around my spelling to show the other children what they should strive to achieve. Nowadays, it seems I must settle for 'good enough' or even 'average'.

Barely a week after the examinations, providence—or rather a medical board somewhere—rewards me as well as Mary.

'I have received a telegram,' Miss Gibbons says, signalling with a wave of her sinewy hand for me and my friend to step into her office. 'You leave in two days' time for No. 2 Red Cross Hospital, Rouen.'

'Truly?' I exclaim before catching myself. She might as well have told me we had won the lottery.

Miss Gibbons leans back in her chair by the desk of lacquered oak. 'Am I in the habit of making jokes, Miss Wilkes? Yes, *truly*. Now, I have your identity discs, spare uniforms, embarkation permits, travel instructions and so forth prepared. You may collect them.'

Mary and I do as we are told and pile the necessities in our arms.

Miss Gibbons dismisses us but raises her voice one last time before the door closes behinds us. 'It will be a pity to lose a nearly faultless nurse such as yourself, Miss Warner.'

Victoria Station is silver-misted and damp. I check my watch, which is dangling from a gilded chain: nine o'clock. The train leaves in precisely thirty minutes, and I have already been here for ten. I am poor with punctuality in general, and this time in particular I would rather be early than late.

Mary arrives at the station twenty-five past nine on the dot, and together we board the train. Two hours pass, during which we only exchange a handful of words. Without Mildred's sprightly presence we find so much less to say. Mary was often Mildred's confidante while Laura was mine. I eventually occupy myself with flipping the pages of the so suitably French novel Fred lent me, a fairly recent one called *The Phantom of the Opera*. Mary, meanwhile, goes through everything in her coffer twice to ensure that she has not forgotten any item from the kit Miss Gibbons presented us with.

Folkestone is a charming coastal town with cliffs of sand and clay. With our light luggage, Mary and I scramble straight for the port, the thought of our schedule spurring us on.

I point. 'There! Surely, that is our boat.'

My spirit stoops low as soon as we approach the steamship, though. The white steel and black, bulbous chimneys look almost treacherous to me. I have suffered from weak sea legs ever since I was little and Papa took me on boat rides on the Thames. With each step closer that Mary and I get to our vessel, I grow more anxious.

Mary, however, who has been unusually quiet during the first part of our journey, brightens like a match lit in a dark room. 'It's perfect. If Miss Gibbons had posted me on a ship and told me to perform my duties there, I would have been delighted.'

'You can't mean that!'

'I do mean it.'

'I'm sorry. It just makes me feel terrible, genuinely terrible, to think about it.'

After the Port Embarkation Officer—a pasty-faced man who reminds me of my old governess—has approved of our permits, we cross the polished gangplank to the boat.

Mary does not mind staying with me outside in the whipping wind and the cold that gnaws to my marrow. She claims she takes pleasure in feeling the salty sprays of foam on her outstretched hands.

With the sticky rail in a compulsive grip, my knucklebones showing through the skin, I swallow bile more times than I care to count. I may not always behave the way a young woman of good background ought to, and I am painfully aware of it, but I would hate to empty my stomach in front of the other passengers and experienced crew.

The French coastline expands as we cross another and yet another wave until, at last, we arrive in the port of Boulogne. The very moment solid ground is once more under my feet, I could cry from relief.

The city is swathed in fog, and with my curiosity dimmed by the ghastly boat ride, I have no wish to explore Boulogne further before our final train leaves. Mary agrees. After all, Rouen is just as French and therefore as foreign. To my battered and exhausted mind, the difference cannot be that noticeable.

Rouen sparks my affection within days. The architecture is exquisite. Tall half-timbered houses line the winding streets, practically leaning on one another, and the river Seine curves through the city. I soon discover that the most magnificent landmark is the cathedral, which reminds me of something from a fairy-tale with its sharp gothic spires poking the sky high enough to impress the most blasé of beholders. A few of the windows are still set with blue stained glass, likely medieval. The Old Market Square offers patches of grass amidst the cobblestones; here, Jean D'Arc was burned at the stake five hundred years ago. Although the front is at a safe distance, there hangs a tremble in the air, as if the entire city is crouching, preparing to sprint from artillery fire. I have to remind myself that it will not come to that. The girl saint who died here will watch over us if no one else does.

The Red Cross hospital is located in the house known as *Le Grand Séminaire*—a large brickwork building with dark roof panes and rows of sashed windows—in the midst of the city. The clean-cut corridors offer passages to countless rooms; the floors are polished until they might serve as mirrors. Every bed in the building is occupied by either soldiers or staff members. It dawns on me why Isabel could not promise more than to *try* to find me a place. Only the matron, the commandant, the quartermaster, and the small knot of probing doctors have the privilege of a private room. Still, the furniture is of fine quality, and I quickly begin to feel at home in my cramped space.

From the back of the house, swooping stairs lead down to a garden with barren fruit trees, linden trees, and thick-trunked oaks. The frost coats everything in sight, like a lace of crystals, but the weather is mild and no gusts of snow fall upon us. Here, in the garden, we relish stolen moments of rest. At times, we are allowed to exchange our regular chores for a stroll across the lawn, pushing before us a soldier in wheelchair.

Some of the men will never walk unaided again. Others will never write a letter, either because they have lost their hands or been shot blind. Their injuries are more serious than those I encountered during my training in London, and I frequently shudder at the sight alone. Nonetheless, I was keen to come here, and thus I must push through. All the while I chant in my head that I am *not* the one deserving of pity, not as long as I have my own health.

Isabel and Mary give the impression of being sisters whenever we are at work, leaving me in the periphery of companionship. I know it is not intentional, but it annoys me nonetheless. Their fingers are equally flickering, their placid expression the same.

'Scissors, please,' Isabel says one day as the three of us are gathered around one of the newly arrived soldiers.

Mary swiftly hands her the requested tool, and a few minutes later they have taken care of the yellow-rimmed wound on his side.

'I think we're quite finished soon.' My arms are aching from holding the water basin that they dip linen rags in.

'I'm sure we should fold the sheets, and the man in the upper right corner might swallow some more soup now,' says Mary, eyes glistening with joy from having a purpose.

Isabel nods. 'What if Harry was one of the wounded?'

My sister has hit a vulnerable spot. I announced the engagement a few days before I stepped onto the train at Victoria station. At the time, my loved ones' approving reception invoked a strangely frustrating feeling in me, as if all my actions were already foreseen. Now, though, I soften at the mention of my fiancé's name.

Without a word, I help Mary smooth out the sheets and bedclothes—fresh and stiff from the laundry and mangling, giving away a stench of clinic soap, glowing with whiteness—and we begin folding them into perfect squares.

Chapter seven

Charles

THE TRAIN SMELLS rancid. I already miss the officers' training camp like one might miss a childhood home, though I resented it before, and I would pay good money to be allowed back. Perhaps I could claim a stomach ache… They would not believe me, of course, but I *do* have one.

When I asked the *Général de Brigade* where I was being stationed, he had three words for me: 'the Ypres salient'. What I have heard about the fighting around the Belgian city of Ypres is likely censored, but even so, I know that thousands of troops have lost their lives there for a stalemate of sorts.

A handful of new recruits are on the train with Marcel and me. I insisted on sitting with them in a feeble attempt to forge a bond of trust between us. It appears such a bond will only come once I have led them into battle and returned with a large enough proportion of survivors. As it is, they peer out from the windows, chins propped in palms. The white-veiled landscape and the soft contours of French soil hold their genuine attention. The trees are naked and raw, their branches stretching out with fumbling greed. Occasionally, as we get closer and closer to the frontline, we roll past crude wounds of powdered, frozen earth and cascades of gravel. Shell craters.

'It looks awful, don't you think?' Marcel has sneaked up by my window and hangs with half his torso in the crisp air, the breeze tearing at his uniform. Said uniform makes the sky above look pale in comparison.

The wind is biting my own hands and face, but some spell rests upon me, persuading me to remain in the cold and not retreat back to my seat. 'Of course it does. I bet it is, too. What did you expect?'

Marcel is silent for a while. Then he says, 'Do you think a chap can smoke a cigar properly out there, Charles? I brought some very fine ones. 1880 International, they are.'

For the first time since he returned from his visit to the bathroom, I look properly at his face. Something is drastically, horribly, *comically* wrong. 'What—what did you *do* with it?'

'What?' He is evidently enjoying this.

'Stop playing *l'idiot*, won't you? That…hideous moustache of yours.'

'I figured it would be difficult to keep neatly trimmed and delicate out there, and no one likes those damn walrus moustaches with hair sprouting in every possible direction, so a shave was the only alternative.'

'True.' I twist my face in a grimace.

We remain thus by the window, tracing the surroundings with our eyes for a long while. Then, the train pulls violently forward only to stagger back again, and stops.

We have arrived at our rallying point. Here, Marcel and I part ways, since our companies have not been assigned to the same section of trenches.

'So. Do you have any final words of wisdom for me?'

'"Never let the future disturb you. You will meet it, if you have to, with the same weapons of reason which today arm you against the present."'

I force a smile. 'Why, I thought you didn't appreciate Marcus Aurelius.'

'Oh? Perhaps that's so.' His jaw is visibly clenched. 'I'm beginning to credit Michael with greater wits the farther we get. I never envied him his stout principles before but—'

'I will see you in Paris, Marcel. The others, too.'

He nods and turns on his heel, taking his men with him, leaving behind a subtle scent of shaving water.

There is a telegram with instructions waiting for me, sent by a general whose name I do not care to read. I am to lead my half of the new recruits from the train to the reserve trenches and then proceed through communication trenches. Eventually, I am to arrive at my section of the front, the Main Firing Line. I shake my head. I had hoped to be stationed in the reserves for a while first, but no.

The rest of the company are already there waiting for us. The new recruits and I will fill in the gaps left by those killed in a particularly disastrous night raid.

'Let's not put it off any longer. Come!' I crumple the telegram in my fist and start marching in the direction most probably correct. To my relief, a man with a sketchy map soon assists me in finding our way. The company—close to two hundred soldiers— follow single file like a wispy tail. Their eyes are shimmering with eagerness and with a fear of being afraid. They shall die, a great deal of them; perhaps I will join them in a matter of days. Their eyes will grow glazed and dead and the flies, like so many black speckles, will feast on them. I do not know a great deal of warfare, but I have read about the flies. They come when the bodies are not retrieved and properly buried. It is in their nature.

When the trenches first appear in view, a fine, lethal spider's web is what springs to mind. The zig-zagging network stretches out in the distance, scrawny lines carved deep in the ground. The following months—if not years, I think with an icy thrill—will be spent trapped in these lines. The bloody fools who think it will all be over by Christmas have obviously not checked their calendars, because Christmas is three weeks away, and the word 'peace' is still censored in Paris newspapers.

By the time we enter the communication trenches, which cut across from one line to the other, my heart is no longer thudding as if to break my ribs. Yes, the filth is everywhere and the cold makes my toes hurt, yet despite the eerie sound of shells exploding in the distance we are completely unscathed.

'Are we within the range of enemy artillery?' I ask the man with the map.

'I believe so, *Mon Capitaine*. But I don't think they're firing at us in particular, and it will be dark soon.'

'Yes.'

We arrive at our destination. The bombardment is now closer, but not as intense as I feared. Perhaps the Germans are tired. The smell is like a slap in my face. I cannot quite discern where it originates, but it likely involves rotten flesh and provisory latrines.

I soak up the gut-wrenching view: men dressed in blue squatting in the dirt or leaning against the sandbags in the side of the trench, smoking, poring over letters, playing cards… Playing cards! That is at last something I can do as well as or better than any man. Here and there I get a glimpse of tea kettles and metal tins, even a seemingly abandoned frying pan.

Something black scurries over my boots and I let out a whoop of surprise. It provokes bursts of laughter from some of the men before they remember that I am their superior, and salute as they ought to. A rat. I *hate* rats.

'Excuse me? *Mon Capitaine?*'

I look up to see a fellow in his late thirties with a pair of spectacles on his nose and a shock of hair sticking out from underneath his kepi. 'My name is Renard Bacque. I'm your servant.'

'I see.'

'Lieutenant Delevingne was wounded and sent home. We're going over the top at dawn the day after tomorrow.'

It takes me a few seconds to realise the implication of his words. 'I see. I suppose that means I must lead you.'

'Unless you'd rather have one of the Non-commissioned officers—'

'No. I can do it. With privilege comes responsibility…isn't that what they say?'

Renard removes his steel-rimmed glasses and starts to polish them with a spotty handkerchief. 'Very good, *Mon Capitaine*. And you needn't worry. You will be briefed from headquarters, of course, and afterwards we'll withdraw to the support trenches. You should order us to fix our bayonets soon, like we always do at dusk.' He squints at my boots. 'Might I polish those for you first?'

Had it not been for the rat, I would have turned him down, but now I nod.

Ten. The man to my left has puked on himself and stares down at his feet, embarrassed.

Nine. I eye my pistol—a Modèle 1892 Revolver—one final time, the metal gleaming. The handle is clammy with my sweat. I would have preferred a few more days to settle in before going through this trial.

Eight. I count out loud but the numbers are somehow more prominent in my head.

Seven. The ladder is slippery under my soles.

Six. My ears are ringing with the echo of drumfire. Whistling, booming…both theirs and ours. Noises that intrude on my every thought.

Five. Renard is on my left; he holds his rifle the way my grandfather used to hold his fishing rod, only more angled.

Four. I wish Marcel were here, no, I wish we were both somewhere else.

Three. Damn.

Two. Snow is falling, mingling with clouds of dust from the shells, flakes melting the moment they touch us.

One. I blow my whistle.

The barbed wire creates a defensive nest of thorns outside our trench. A wiring party has gone before us and cleared a path through it so that we can pass, but our defence has turned into a perilous foe regardless, tearing uniforms and slashing skin to shreds. The German wire awaits on the other side. I would rather not think about it until I must.

A shell detonates. I have been running with my lips parted, and dirt spurting up from the crater fills my mouth. I spit and cough, squeezing my eyes shut and opening them when I stumble on the stones jutting up from the earth.

There is thunder in my ears. The machine guns rattle through that thunder, mowing down the man next to me and in front of me and still others. My lungs hurt. My throat is parched, my legs are stiff, yet I must continue forward. I leap over a small shell hole filled with water and sink down to my knees in the hole that comes after it.

Where is Renard? His is the only name I can recall in this jumble. I do not see him.

I halt in my tracks by the German lines of barbed wire. My men have run ahead of me—maintaining order during an attack is even more difficult than I anticipated—and several are hanging on the wire like tragicomic rag puppets. One of them is moaning, shrieking. His entrails are strewn on the ground below him. Not until this moment did I realise what a lethal weapon a few metal strings and barbs are when a man is plunged against them.

The goal… What was the goal? Ah, yes, to cross No Man's Land, take the enemy trench, and turn it into one of our own. That goal feels as distant as the North Pole now. I will die here, I repeat to myself as I jump over a torn-off limb. I will die here.

I will die here.

<h1 style="text-align:center">Chapter eight</h1>

Charles

A LIEUTENANT-COLONEL assures me via telephone that I was not by any means an utter failure as we went over the top. While we were unable to take the German trench, our casualties were easy. That is what he says, though I flinch at this condescending description. In addition, we did not lose our own trench to a counterattack. When I am so bold as to ask him why there had to be an attack to begin with, considering that the Battle of Ypres is supposedly over, I receive no conclusive answer. Apparently, we must keep trying.

Just as my servant said when I first arrived, though, we are allowed to withdraw to the support trenches, another group of unfortunate men replacing us in the frontline. When I passed through the third and second lines a few days ago, there was no time to stop and notice how they differ from the front. The support trenches feel slightly less miserable. This is because the duckboards—a wooden walkway separating our feet from the worst of the mud—are placed at closer intervals, and the dugouts are far more spacious. At the front, the latter were little more than shallow alcoves in the dirt, too small for more than a single man to cram into. Here, some of the dugouts resemble small huts, even bunkers, with wooden beams and sandbags to keep them from caving in if shelled. I take care not to ask how effective those skimpy safety measures are.

Unlike in the frontline, here one can get steaming hot meals as well as medical attention. It is a far cry from restaurants and proper hospitals, but to my surprise, I am grateful for what small comforts we do enjoy. Even a slimy stew is better eaten fresh than after it has been transported through communication trenches.

What is more, the danger is not as imminent here. The artillery is still deafening, and there are parados to shield against machinegun fire, but the Huns will not come here themselves. Not unless they take the first line.

After five days, my company and I rotate to the reserve trenches, where our headquarters present me with a sight I can scarcely believe. In the nearest dugout reserved for commissioned officers, of which I am one, stands two beautifully chiselled chairs and a table with a chequered tablecloth. A pot of withered daisies stands on top, and a large poster promoting perfumed soap is pinned to the fortified wall. The scene is so oddly domestic—it does not belong.

Every day, I carry out inspections of my men's clothes, weapons, and feet. The feet are crucial. If left damp and filthy for extended periods of time, they eventually decay, turn gangrenous.

Every day, letters and parcels from home brighten our spirits ever so slightly, keeping life and hope burning. Every day, relentless boredom plagues us—that is when I resort to my abridged copy of *Decamerone*, which I always keep in my biggest pocket.

God must be favouring me and my men, because we remain in the reserve trench for a good nine days before we receive the dreaded command to return to the front. I take farewell of my flowerpot dugout.

The evening after we arrive, just as I am about to task my company with various nightly duties—patrolling, repairing the barbed wire, sentry duty—one of them taps my shoulder and offers me a slice of...*Buche de Noël*. The icing is dripping but the cake is otherwise intact, and I marvel at it.

'*Merci*. But how on earth...? And what is it for?'

The young man, Benjamin, smiles and tucks a strand of hair behind his ear. 'Surely, *Mon Capitaine*, you had not forgotten? Today is Christmas Eve!'

I am tempted to laugh but check myself just in time. Only to think, that in this savage mess there should be such a thing as Christmas! I do not get a chance to either answer Benjamin or dole out the night's work, because I am interrupted by what can only be a ghost.

It is the strangest sound. A strangled, lone voice is raised on the other side of No Man's Land, like cracks in the silent air. The words are guttural, German—I understand only a few of them— but the melody is cheerful and soft like that of a Christmas carol sung by of rosy-cheeked children. A second voice and now a third joins the first. Soon, the sound reaching our ears is no longer harrowing.

I frown at Renard, who is repairing his spectacles after having sat on them. 'Is this some kind of strange…trap?'

'I think they're just singing, *Mon Capitaine.*'

'I think it's some strange trap. On the other hand, maybe they *are* just singing.' I groan inwardly at the meaninglessness of our conversation. 'Does anyone volunteer to see what they're on about?'

No one stirs. I should order a man to do it, of course, but I pity them every bit as much as I pity myself, if not more. They pride themselves on their bravery and patriotism, yet their expressions tell me clearly that they prefer to keep their heads down.

'Well then. Hold my kepi.'

Benjamin's glance flits from me to the colourful headgear I land in his outstretched hands. If he dared, he might protest, but military discipline is ingrained in the troops. In this instance, I almost wish that was not the case.

I swallow, clutching my pistol in one hand and the ladder in the other. Slowly, slowly, I climb three steps, thereby placing myself far enough above the parapet to peer over the edge but not high enough to have my brains dashed out by an enemy sniper. At least, that is what I hope. I may be underestimating their precision.

The German trench is perhaps five hundred feet away. A cluster of warm lights, like a swarm of fireflies, sticks up from their parapet. At first glance I think it must be some new kind of lethal weapon and my chest cramps. Then I discern the contours of a small Christmas tree.

A figure climbs up beside the tree and thrusts his hand in the air, holding a piece of white cloth.

As for me, I hold my breath. With a frantic gesture, I order my men not to shoot.

The German takes one, two, three steps out into No Man's Land and raises his voice over the singing. *'Waffenstillstand! Nur für heute, für Weihnachten!* A…a truce!'

I jump down from the ladder, completely shielded once more, and turn to my countrymen.

One of the non-commissioned officers, who has apparently understood what is in the making, pushes his way forward, face frozen with indignation. 'Don't tell me you're considering it!'

'Mind your place,' I say, foremost to get him to lower his voice before he sparks trouble among the *soldats*.

'*Mon Capitaine*,' the NCO continues in a barely controlled manner. 'The swine on the other side of that strip of frozen mud have taken everything from us, everything! They've forced us to battle on our own soil, destroyed our villages, taken our land—'

'I'm not ignorant, *Sergent*, of what has occurred in this war. To tell you a truth you'd rather not hear, I don't care right now. If they had murdered my family, I'd still let there be a truce. Anything to escape this god-awful bombardment for a day. You want to see them die? I can guarantee you'll get the chance tomorrow.'

The men are all staring at me, having amassed as close as they can get in the narrow trench. I wish I could read their minds. There are assuredly both superiors and subordinates against me, but none of them raise another protest. I stand by my words: anything to not feel as if I am living my final hours.

I must have gone soft as a sponge, because I can find no other explanation for what happens after that. I open my mouth and, after a moment's hesitation, begin to sing along with the enemy carollers. It is the French version, for the German I know too badly and the English would not be as familiar to my own men.

Renard turns his head to look at me with wide eyes, as do several of the others, before they one by one chime in with quivering voices growing steadier. Perhaps they simply do it because I am their commander, or perhaps they are caught in the same heart-quickening daze as I. All across No Man's Land, the voices of a thousand madmen from both frontlines ring.

We soon climb over our own parapet, not with our former speed and violence but to take the enemy's hand and shake it like that of an old friend. One man even offers me a cigarette, and although cigars took precedence at the Sorbonne, I have quickly grown accustomed to the cheaper option. In return, I share the bonbons I received from my sisters yesterday.

Not only do we fraternise with the Germans, but we speak also to our allies the British, with whom we have not had a proper chance to meddle until now. We have been too busy shooting at the same target to be introduced to one another.

An improvised football made from shredded uniforms tied together with a tangle of telephone wire appears in our midst, seemingly from nowhere.

'Come on lads! Anyone up for a game?' bellows an Irishman.

Gradually, men from both sides accept the challenge by taking a step or two forward.

A boy with unruly hair and a playful grin pulls me by the arm and flashes me a smile. In clipped, clear English, he asks me to join them. A few words of butchered French enter his speech as well, and I cannot help but to return his smile. The spontaneous enthusiasm is contagious; I curse myself and oblige.

There are no organised football teams, but rather we kick the ball haphazardly from one to the other. Perhaps that is for the best, because I know for certain that animosity would rise again if we formed opposing groups even in this most trivial of settings. It is all great fun, but hardly a show of grace from my side, football being one of the many sports I have avoided before.

A German soldier kicks the ball with immense force, plunging the dark missile through the air, landing it in a birds' nest of barbed wire. No one is keen to retrieve it—we know all too well what an encounter with the wire might entail. Thus the playing comes to an end.

I catch sight once more of the boy who tugged at my sleeve. He cannot have been here much longer than I have, because his eyes still sparkle with mischievous youth and his steps are bouncy.

A blush flares on his cheeks like winter apples. A striped neckerchief hangs loosely about his shoulders.

'Do you play cards?' I ask in my best English, for the first time grateful that my father pestered me with learning to speak his native tongue.

The boy snaps around, immediately on the alert, smiling readily. 'I thought you were French. Sir...?' He adds the latter with a glance at the marks on my uniform. No doubt he has little idea of what exactly they mean but has learnt the wise lesson that it is better to be safe than sorry.

'Half French. Do you? Play cards, I mean.'

'I suppose I do, yes.'

We make ourselves as comfortable as possible at an improvised table that was originally a box. After digging deep in the pockets in my overcoat, I deliver a deck of cards, and there we remain more than an hour.

I clear my throat. 'We haven't been introduced.'

'No, no, I don't believe we have. The name is Mark. Mark Crewel.'

'Charles D'Aboville.' I stretch out a gloved hand and he takes it; his own is turning ghostly pale in the cold.

Our conversation is sparse yet surprisingly pleasant. I find myself developing a rare, genuine liking for my fellow card player. He plays well, too. Each time he slaps a winning card on the box, his face glows with smugness, though there is nothing even remotely arrogant about him.

'Where did you learn to play?'

'Home in London. We played with the girls, too, sometimes. Gin Rummy and Old Maid, mostly.'

I arch an eyebrow. 'Pretty?'

'A whole lot prettier than those German lasses in their pictures.' He nods towards a knot of German soldiers who are shifting their weight from one foot to the other to keep warm, the crust of ice crunching under their boots.

What would Mark make of the girls in Paris, with whom my friends and I spent endless hours exchanging brazen remarks? Their alabaster throats sparkling with jewellery, their eyes pools of amber, their lips releasing trickles of smoke... Their mothers chided us for not taking the cigarettes from them.

I liked those girls, as simple as that. They were a façade, as unreal as a reflection, but they were a convenient remedy for the loneliness that would come creeping late summer nights on the porch of Louis' father's house. They likely thought the same of us. The boy in front of me would be a great success in those circles, although he might be a rough diamond.

'Good luck,' Mark says as we shuffle the cards again.

We shake hands once more before parting.

I turn just as I am about to leave. 'Crewel? Don't let them land a shell on that face of yours. It would be most unfortunate for the girls.'

He laughs and raises a hand.

Dusk falls heavy and we retreat to our network of damp, self-dug graves. The sky is darker than charcoal, stars aimlessly poised as if a painter had whipped the air with bright paint.

The truce will be far-gone in a day or two, I know. Soon we will be massacring and being massacred by the very same fellows who passed us the ball over the frozen mud a few hours ago and showed us pictures of their coquettish sweethearts. Soon there will be naught but a rain of dirt and bullets and pieces of burnt flesh, banishing this pretence of peace.

I write to my mother, recounting my peculiar day. She will be glad to hear of it. Although she is as shallow as a puddle and impossibly priggish, she does share my belief that the men fighting have nothing to do with the actual, corrupted conflict. None of us signed the declaration of war.

I have to make do with the glossy backside of a postcard Mark Crewel gave me. Each one of the British troops received one of those cards from King George and Queen Mary, Mark told me. The picture is a portrait of the couple. The Queen is rather beautiful in a buttoned-up kind of way, and her husband is one big moustache and beard. I suppose they think themselves angels of mercy with their tinsel postcards.

Dearest Maman,

You might wonder what the British royals are doing in your hand as you read this, and the explanation is simple. I was given it by an English soldier and I had nothing else to write on. Please send more paper and ink.

I fold the stiff card in two and push it down the envelope with
the address already scribbled on the backside. Good God, what a
Christmas.

As I expected, the truce does not last.

The days fade and turn into weeks. Slow as torture, they drag
by and by, until at last it all resembles a film where the figures
around me are actors in greyscale. They are attached to me—they
belong to my company or to units operating in the same section
of trenches—yet they are terribly distant. Their names brush
against my mind like butterflies before floating away again. New
names are added while those of casualties are crossed from the
lists. Remembering which man is which is difficult.

As spring creeps upon us, the earth softens and absorbs the
showers of lukewarm rain, becoming marshy. I thought I knew
what mud was, but never before have I seen this kind of wet filth
that swallows bodies and belongings alike. Though we
continuously transfer to the support and reserve trenches, and
though I as an officer am entitled to greater cleanliness that the
troops, it is poor comfort. The ground is now the consistency of

porridge. We are increasingly afraid of venturing outside the trenches on night patrol. Despite having laid out boards to walk on, a single misstep in the dark can cause a man to sink down to his knees and make him an excellent target for German bullets. Our rifles are clogged; our feet are in danger of rotting away; our dugouts sag and cave in.

I have been fortunate in other ways, though, such as my personal health. A few sprained fingers, a shoulder popped from its socket—nothing that the medics cannot easily take care of.

In March, I receive orders from the chain of command to bring my company to Champagne, where a battle has been raging since before Christmas. Being stationed there must mean more frequent attacks and more time spent in the frontline compared to our stagnated existence in the Ypres salient. I have always liked the name, though: Champagne. It sounds much too fancy to be the sight of a battle.

Chapter nine

Rosalie

ISABEL'S SHOES CLICK as we walk through the corridor. 'How is our brother?'

I quicken my steps to keep up with her. 'Stupendous. The training is much to his liking. Aviation theory, Morse code, navigation, how the engines and instruments operate. I can't understand half the things he writes to me about!'

'But he writes to you?'

'Of course. I…I can show you next time, if you like.'

She nods slightly, and swerves to the left, leaving me for the patient she was sent to check on.

Did I somehow offend her? I fail to comprehend what bad blood there could possibly be between Isabel and Fred apart from where they differ in character. While they share a calculated cleverness and the ability to remain composed in situations where I might panic or falter, Fred has Mama's optimism and Isabel Papa's grim outlook on life. Where my brother loves gardening, music, and reading, my sister loves God.

Still, that cannot be all there is to it. And did I not catch a flicker of envy in Isabel's eyes when I spoke of the letters?

I hitch up the hem of my dress another inch and follow through the door on the left. 'Papa was upset, though.'

Isabel keeps her eyes on the man whom she is prompting to swallow two white pills. 'Our father has not cut me loose, Rosalie. I know very well that he is upset.'

'I don't blame him, really. First a zeppelin raid on British soil and then Daya sprains her wrist and can't cook for weeks! It's just too much.'

'He's wary about the Dardanelles business.'

I pour a glass of water from a nearby carafe and offer it to her so that she can in turn give it to the patient. 'That too. I think he's placing awfully little trust in our generals. They know what they're doing.'

The crease of concentration on Isabel's forehead is as dismissive as any words, so I venture outside to the garden, savouring the last bit of my free hour. Some days I am bolder and visit the streets of Rouen instead. There are a multitude of shops for trinkets, books, and sweets to spend my meagre pocket money on. All nursing staff and VADs have strict instructions to avoid excessive jewellery and above all cheek and lip paint, though. The former would be impractical and the latter is associated with another group of women serving soldiers.

The brothels are a more integrated part of the city than I could have imagined when we first arrived. The older women at the hospital think we newcomers do not know, but of course we do. The patients talk, and we have eyes. I have even come by the knowledge that the common soldiers are only allowed at the brothels with a red light outside. Officers, on the other hand, may visit those with blue lights and, I presume, higher prices. The thought makes me nauseous, because had I been less privileged, I could have been one of those poor girls.

The air in the garden works wonders, chasing away the shadows that often sneaks upon me these days. They never stay long, yet they always come. Whenever there is a surge of new patients with new gruesome injuries, and I have to wash away blood for hours on end… That is when I long to curl up in my bed at home in Hampstead and never again come near a sterilised pair of scissors or an apron. Was not the war supposed to be over by Christmas?

I lean against one of the knobbly trees, palms flat against the trunk, tilting my head back to watch the buds on the branches sway in the wind.

Soon. Soon, we will be done with it all. Soon, Harry will be more to me than a pile of heartfelt letters and a ring on my finger.

The others will come back, too, except…except for Mark. It still feels like thrusting a needle in my chest, especially when I recall how he did not lose his cheer even once, till his final hours. That is what Harry wrote. His letter is no longer legible, being splotched with both his own tears and mine.

I draw a deep breath and dismiss my dead friend from my thoughts. As long as I keep my purpose in mind and at heart, I can last through this. It would be selfish of me not to. I left my scribbled notebooks at home, not wanting to bring too much luggage, but there are plenty of other things to find solace in, plenty of pastimes to enjoy. I just have to get through this day, that is all—this day and tomorrow and the day after that.

Charles

I prefer the drink to the place. Champagne is frustratingly similar to Ypres, as I suspect the entire Western Front is, only the rats are bigger, like rabbits rather than kittens. They get fat gorging on our rations and our lost comrades, and grow ever bolder by the hour.

In the château where I grew up, or in the Parisian cafés where I spent perhaps too much time these past few years, the sight of a single mouse would have caused great commotion and disgust. I may be squeamish like a little girl—that is what Marcel would say—but the beasts are gnawing their way into my dreams, hairy tails whipping the duckboards. I should apply for furlough soon, if only to get a full night's decent sleep. The concept in itself feels foreign.

There are, however, more urgent matters requiring my attention: the battle. As is apparently custom in this damned war, there is so far naught but a stalemate, an inconclusive mockery. I am not surprised to find that I carry such scant credit with the Lord. I do think, though, that at least some of my men deserve better.

I stumble over a root sticking up from the mud. My breath tangles in my throat as I fall. A spray of dirt blurs my vison. I roll around twice before pushing myself up with a bruising chest. The sound of bullets drowns in the rumble of artillery as I repeatedly fire my weapon in blindness. I cannot know how many souls I strike down. I do not wish to know. There is no use in counting when it only leads to more troublesome guilt to shuffle away to the darkest corner of my mind.

Time is endless. Are we out here for years? No, it is minutes, an hour at most. The cheers have all faded at this point. We will need many new recruits after today to reinforce the company.

I continue forward, launching a grenade at a group of enemy soldiers. Yes, they must be the enemy, because they are wearing those stupid helmets. The force of the grenade exploding throws me to the right like a rag, down a pit. Two other men are next to me. I think they are alive.

Splinters pierce my arm and rip the skin open. The numbness gives way to a burning pain, the feeling of thousands of needles making me lightheaded. It will not stop. I clutch the wound, head spinning, trying to apply pressure like I have been taught. I put my mouth to the wound in an attempt to hold the edges together with my teeth. The metallic, warm liquid slips down my throat and, gagging, I must content myself with using my hand. The blood soaks me. It is darker than I expected, and oozes steadily rather than squirts.

Despite everything, I want to live. I want to live, even if it is in a cursed trench with dead companions, or in an overfull military hospital. The realisation of just how much I want it fills me with fury, because it makes me as human as anybody else here, while I thought I had a less bothersome view of life.

'Stretcher bearer! Stretcher bearer *now!* Here! We have a wounded CO!' The voice is the last thing I hear before something dull and hard collides with my forehead.

Rosalie

The ambulance staff vacate their vehicle as if their own lives depended on it. I spot three stretchers from where I am standing by the window. One of the men has already had his leg amputated while the other two have a bandaged head and chest respectively.

I turn on my heel and speed to the entrance of the hospital. There, I select one of the patients at random, starting to question the men carrying his stretcher. The trained nurses and doctors will want a full report on his condition.

'A concussion from a piece of shrapnel. Quite severe. A vein has been cut on his left lower arm, but the arteries are intact. Deep wound from wrist to elbow.'

Only now do I look at the blood-soaked cloth wrapped around the poor man's arm. 'How long since he sustained the injuries?'

The man knits his brows trying to recall. 'Twelve, no, eleven hours ago. His company was repelling an attack over at Champagne.'

'Champagne? But you should have driven him somewhere closer to the casualty clearing station!'

'I don't make the decisions, Sister. It was too full there to stop and think, that's my bet, and they wanted somewhere fit for officers.'

The ambulance staff help me transfer the wounded man from the stretcher to an empty bed, and it occurs to me that he is not British but French, which contradicts the hospital's guidelines about prioritising our own soldiers. His uniform is ripped to shreds, its colour just visible under all the dried mud and blood. His face is a pleasant one, in that rare sense of appearing both delicate and roguish, framed with hovering black locks. Bold eyebrows, skin as pale as the bedclothes beneath him. A strange desire to find out the colour of his eyes takes hold of me, but I dismiss the thought with a bitter taste in my mouth. Those are the musings of a schoolgirl, and I cannot afford to be that now.

Another young woman, a giraffe-like thing who only arrived a couple of days ago, goes to fetch clean bandages and returns. We keep the soaked cloth already around the man's arm as it is, because removing it would disturb the clotting of the blood. Instead, we wrap another layer on top, all the while maintaining pressure on the arm. The bleeding has petered out to a trickle, though, and so the giraffe woman and I decide between us to take the risk of cleaning and stitching up the wound. Maybe it is heedless of us to act without instructions from the trained nurses. After all, military discipline is supposed to rule the hospitals as well as the battlefields, but our superiors are busy enough.

The skin has been brutally torn apart and I can see the shining, thick veins as they catch a spatter of light filtering through the windows. By the time we have closed the wound, my hands are painted in various red nuances, from bright strawberries to the darkest burgundy.

One of the doctors at last makes a brief appearance. 'Miss Levin? Make sure that that this man is well cared for once he regains consciousness. *If* he does.'

The giraffe-girl nods, and the doctor struts off. Together, Miss Levin and I carefully scrub the soldier and change him into the customary hospital pyjamas. The uniform is not much to keep, but perhaps we can wash it and use it as future bandages if the fabric is not too stiff. I still have not gotten used to the undressing process and I feel my face flush.

The contents of the man's pockets—a few soggy playing cards, a lighter, a crumpled letter, a whistle, and a copy of *Decamerone*—go straight into the drawer by the bedside.

When Miss Levin leaves me, I remain with the Frenchman for what must be an hour, toying with his sleeve after I have wiped every speck of dirt from his face. Then, I turn to studying the three birthmarks on his jaw with blooming curiosity.

I shove my chair back with a screech and stand up. What is the matter with me? The other patients have as much if not more need of me. I should not expect time to freeze just because of some silly fancy.

Chapter ten

Charles

THE WHITE LIGHT burns my eyes and I close them again. Dull, throbbing pain rises and falls in my head like waves on the ocean, flooding my senses, blotting out the softness of the mattress and pillow underneath me. All of it is not lodged in my head… There must be something else hurting, too. Carefully, I squint. The curves and edges of a room dotted with occupied beds blur and my head only feels worse when I try to concentrate.

The cannons were firing, the corpses were scattered in chunks. I remember now, fragment by fragment. My arms, my legs… If they have taken them from me, if any doctor has dared to cut off so much as a finger, I will shoot him on the spot. But no, I can feel my limbs, every part of me, and my murderous alarum subdues. I cannot feel my pistol in my pocket, anyhow. I do not think I even have pockets…no, I do not, not in these ridiculous pyjamas.

My left arm is different than the right: stiff and sore. That must be where some of the pain is coming from. When I manage to raise my head from the pillow—the movement nearly makes me throw up what little food is still in my stomach—there is a broad patch of white on my arm. Bandage.

I glide back into a soft, warm lull on the verge of sleep. Without having seen my wound, I can guess that it will leave a scar but nothing more, and no one can claim that I am fit for the

69

front in my current state. Perhaps this is the luckiest I have ever been.

During the first few days, I lie like a dead fish in my hospital bed, being gradually fed sticky soup and regularly watched over. They ask me questions. What happened? How did I survive the attack? Do I wish to write a letter to anyone? At first, I lack the energy to answer any of them. When I have it, I pretend that I am asleep most of the time. It can be rather interesting: all the grand, whispered things one overhears while feigning sleep.

One of the men next to me is gravely impotent, one of the young VADs cheated her way through school, a pacifist is lying on the opposite side of the room, and one of the doctors had some improper business with a pretty cousin in Belgium. There is a confusing piece of talk one afternoon about a naval defeat in the Dardanelles involving a prominent British commander whose name never sticks—William Churchwell or something along those lines.

Before long, though, I am bored enough to be at risk of screaming like a lunatic. Once my body has regained a certain degree of strength, I check that no member of staff is present to stop me then rise from my creaking mattress and begin to stagger down the corridor.

One of the doors to the nurses' and VADs' bedrooms stands slightly ajar, casting beams of light on the floorboards in the corridor. On pure instinct, I slip into the warm room and survey my surroundings. Two beds stand pushed up against the wall on either side of the room. A chest of drawers with porcelain knobs is placed between the beds, and on the top is a silver hairbrush. At the foot of one of the beds sits a stack of hefty novels with bindings in red and blue, titles engraved in golden italics on the spines.

Lightheaded, I sink down on the bed with the books. One of the framed photographs next to the silver brush catches my eye. It is a far too idyllic picture, I decide at a second glance. Seven youths look back at me with what appears to be genuine smiles, entirely unlike the stiff expressions usually applied before a camera.

Two of the boys with unbuttoned waistcoats and identical trousers are kneeling in front of their companions. They have the same robust chins and slightly turned eyes. Perhaps they are brothers.

One of the young VADs—a Miss Wilkes, if I am not mistaken—stands behind them, dressed in a blouse and floral hat. This is the first time I get the chance to study her heart-shaped face properly. Her arm is resting lightly in the crook of a boy's elbow, an angelic boy with tendrils of bright hair.

The photograph makes me sick. The couple looks to me almost euphoric, so ideal, so polished, and I will never have all that. Does 'all that' even exist anymore?

I tear myself from the couple and turn to the two young ladies on the left. One is dark with swarthy features—I think I have seen her, too, scuttling around the hospital—while the other one is remarkably tall and slender.

Between them stands a formidable card player with a boyish grin and shiny shoes.

'You have no right to be here, Sir.'

I turn, my head aching as I do so, to a flustered Miss Wilkes. Her eyes are wide with surprise and fringed with a thick set of lashes, a stain of today's lunch on her apron.

'That's Mark Crewel,' I say, eager for this scrap of familiarity.

'Yes, how did you know?' Those in the very front are James and Jones Jenkins. And there is Harry and me.' Her voice softens. 'And then there is Mark, and Mary, and Mildred. It was a terrific day. Only Laura was away.'

All this information means nothing to me but I wish it did. 'You look splendid.'

'Pardon me—how did you recognise Mark?'

'He's a grand card player. I spent a little time with him this Christmas, see, when there was a truce and so on. You know about the truce?'

'It was in the papers, yes. Then…then you don't know?'

I get the feeling there is a nasty surprise waiting for me. 'Know what, Sister?'

'Mark died last month.' She sucks on her lower lip as if holding back tears.

'What…what was it? Machinegun?'

'Typhoid fever—isn't that awful? Harry, my fiancé, that is, wrote and told me.'

I start to ponder the ample amount of bad news fate must have in store for Miss Wilkes if she has an average number of acquaintances. A childhood friend blown in a thousand pieces, a neighbour missing in action, an old teacher being treated for so-called insanity, a brother or father wounded.

The bed squeaks as Miss Wilkes sits down next to me. We say nothing; there is nothing to say. My headache worsens when I try to remember her Christian name but it is well worth the effort. Rosalie.

After a minute or two, she asks if I am all right.

'I'm just dilly. Thank you, Sister.'

She shakes her head slowly. 'No, you're not. You are as far from dilly as I've seen anyone around here, and I've seen quite a lot of people.'

A hot flash of fury over being read like an open book surges through me. 'I don't… I would rather be alone, Miss Wilkes. Rosalie. Please, just…just go.'

The compassion and curiosity drain from her face in an instant, and she stands, clutching her elbows. 'This is *my* room— *you* should go now. I have other patients to look after.'

I trace my way back to the great hall and sink down on my own bed, which is still warm. Lassitude looms over my shoulder. I could sleep for a hundred years were it not for the nightmares. They always come. They come with cold hands and clattering noises and faces I know I must have seen in the field but can rarely recall when I wake.

The sky is spotted yellow and salmon-pink, testifying to the late hour, a thin veneer of clouds stretching across the horizon. A bird is chirping from a tree, seemingly inexhaustible.

The grass is lush and squelches with dew under the wheelchair, this loathed old thing that I am forced to use whenever I wish to get a breath of fresh air. I have received a pair of new shoes that are two sizes too big, but without any holes, at least. Arrangements for a custom-made uniform and boots will be made before I leave the hospital, of course. How would the proud army of the French Third Republic cope if one of their officers had to walk around like *this?* I can only hope I will not be issued a medal of some sort and obliged to wear it.

The nurse halts and stoops down to pluck a few snowdrops from the lawn. I stand up faster than I ought to and have to grab the wheelchair while a swift stroke of dizziness passes.

The nurse frowns. 'Sit down *immediately*, Sir! You must recover properly—no running about, that's what your journal says!'

'But, Sister, I only wanted to help you with the flowers. I can manage a short walk of my own. I'm feeling quite all right, *really*. Grand, even. You go and put those snowdrops in a vase so that they keep fresh and pretty, and then you can come back and pick me up.'

The nurse pauses to consider my suggestion. She returns her glance to the flowers, then to me, and nods. 'Only a short walk then, and for heaven's sake, don't go far.'

I offer her my most cordial smile and she trips back to the hospital building. It is immensely gratifying to be set free from the nurses' constant chatter and the doctors' precautions and the other men's whining, if only for a moment. With my arm in a sling, still swollen under the tight bandages, I slowly wander.

I could have sworn the nurse and I were the last people in the garden this evening, but I am mistaken. On one of the benches shaded by the great oaks sits a short figure. She has let her hair loose and it falls down her shoulders in puffy locks. In the fading daylight, I can only just discern the freckles sprinkled across her nose and cheeks.

'Good evening, Sister.'

Miss Wilkes keeps her eyes stubbornly fixed on her hands.

I drop down next to her on the white bench, although I probably should not. 'Care for a cigarette?'

'I don't smoke.'

'I hope you're not refusing because of my previous ungracefulness towards you.'

'No, Sir. It's just never been a habit of mine. You're not the first patient who has displayed rudeness. They—you—have seen horrid things, I know.'

I pat my pockets in search of a bonbon, then remember with a sinking feeling in my chest that I have no pockets and hence nothing that I would normally keep in them. 'I won't lie and say you're wrong, Miss Wilkes. It's worse out there than I imagine Hell to be, at least sometimes.'

For the first time during our encounter, the VAD meets my eyes. 'You're heroes, all of you. If the German soldiers had half your courage, they could count themselves terribly fortunate.'

I shake my head, frustrated. She must be living in some kind of dream…it makes no sense, no sense at all. 'You're mistaken, Miss Wilkes, Rosalie. Can I call you Rosalie? You are severely mistaken, because there's no difference between us and the Germans or the Russians for that matter, not when it comes down to it. You use the word courage too freely. We're sinking to new lows with every day that passes and—' My voice cracks.

'Don't talk like that, Sir. If you can't believe in this cause, then who will? Who will win?'

I sit silent, inspecting the damp grass under our feet. When I speak again, it is with a nagging feeling of defeat. 'Old men will, one or another. Old men with fancy hats and illusions from the past. They always believe in their goddamn cause, only they can't fight for it themselves.'

Rosalie says nothing of my reply and nothing of my language, but stares blankly at her nails, which she has bitten down to the skin.

After a moment of hesitation, I reach out to rest my hand on her cold and dry one. She tenses for a second but does not pull away until the nurse materialises, pushing the wheelchair.

'There you are! Come along now! It's getting late,' the approaching woman says in brisk, commanding tones. When she notices Rosalie, the crinkles on her forehead grow deeper. I can sense the reprimanding thoughts oozing out of her like the stench from a smelly cheese. 'What are you doing outside at this hour, and with your hair like that? I can't image what the matron would think.'

Rosalie jumps to her feet and squares her shoulders. 'I will be right back inside.' She turns and speeds down the path to the stair leading up to the hospital, shoes crunching against gravel, hair bouncing with every flighty step.

The nurse makes a vague gesture towards the wheelchair.

I sigh and comply, sitting down nicely again so that she can return me to the hub of wounded.

Chapter eleven

Rosalie

AS THE DAYS pass, I grow acquainted with the soldier who managed to get his arm slashed open and was unpleasant about all sorts of business. Charles, as he is called, and I exchange stealthy words whenever the opportunity arises. Genuine friendliness quickly buds between us. I cannot help but to throw him a sideways glance as I walk past his bed carrying a tray with clattering instruments or a stack of folded sheets. All too often, those steel-grey eyes meet mine, glittering when he smiles.

His arm is healing superbly, the doctors proclaim, and so I can see for myself. The swelling has ceased, and though the scar will be permanent, the wound is closing up, new tissue replacing the damaged. His concussion is entirely gone two weeks after his arrival, which is a particular relief to me since watching patients vomit always makes me feel sick myself.

In mid-April, Charles is deemed fit enough to move from the great hall, where we keep the patients who require intensive care. He moves to another room known as the Second Ward since this is where soldiers stay when in a state of semi-convalescence. The men there are a merry lot. They are no longer in grave pain but still in need of a nurse's attention, able to enjoy simple pleasures but not endure the hardships of the trenches.

The matron, and sometimes even Mary, chides me when I spend too long in the Second, but Charles being there only makes the temptation greater. He is a distraction and an unwelcome one at that, though I cannot put my finger on why. He infuriates me in a thought-provoking manner. He makes me laugh against my better judgement with his tart comments about the other patients and staff. Naturally, I only agree with a fraction of all he says—someone should knock some good-natured sense into him—but that is not necessarily a detriment.

Other men have fared worse than those in the Second. The poor fellow who arrived in the same ambulance as Charles with an amputated leg is sent away to another hospital with better capacity to rehabilitate him. The other patients in the great hall were practically on the verge of a murder conspiracy when the man refused to stop talking even at night. He was a footballer before the war, he repeated. His team back home will never forgive him for spoiling their chances of victory against the rivalling village.

Then, wounded officers start to arrive from Ypres, where a second battle rages. The stories they bring make me quake with anger. The Huns have resorted to using chlorine gas against our men. Charles claims that our own Entente troops will soon employ the same horrid weapons in retaliation, but I refuse to think gallantry is quite so dead as that. Regardless, the gas victims are not what causes the greatest commotion at the hospital in the spring of 1915.

'Will you look at this?' I smack the newspaper on the table, too bewildered to care about the harsh reprimand I am sure to get for exciting the patients. 'I nearly choked to death on my tea when I read.'

A lieutenant, Mr Harris, is the first to swing his legs over his mattress and trudge forward on crutches to read aloud from the paper. '"American liner Lusitania torpedoed by German submarine off the Irish coast. Hundreds of civilians presumed drowned."'

I sweep my glance around the room, content to see that every face looks as startled as I feel. 'I can scarcely believe they'd dare to do such a thing!'

'A damned mistake!' one of the men says.

Another shakes his head. 'They were sailing into enemy waters and knew it. My nephew is a marine and understands these matters. Submarine warfare is merciless nowadays.'

'Those poor souls,' says a third, whom I know to be a devout Catholic, and crosses himself.

Mary, who has entered the room with today's mail, peers over my shoulder, scanning the article. 'Do you reckon the United States will enter the war now?'

What follows is a heated debate in which Mary's voice drowns time and again. I pity her, because she has several American relatives and should know as much about the topic as any of us. In the end, we can at least agree on that the Americans' aid would be most welcome, especially considering that the troops who landed at Gallipoli are facing daunting resistance from the Turks.

'I'm not going there,' Charles states flatly. 'I would rather shoot myself in the foot than go tripping around the world just so I can die in simmering heat instead of rain.'

'You French!' Mr Harris says. 'I take it you prefer Ypres or Artois, then? You ought to be keener to show the Boche who is in charge.'

'What do you mean by Artois?'

'I mean the action is escalating there again, just like at Ypres. If you're discharged anytime soon, I think that is where you'll find yourself.'

I turn from their conversation and slip out of the room, pausing in the corridor. Of course Charles will be discharged someday, but I thought that day was further away. If he keeps recovering at this pace, he will be right back in the trenches by the end of May, a mere two weeks ahead.

Hard morning light is breaking through the milky sky. The darkness is fast-fading; soon it will be but a shadow.

The bulky military truck has a grey tarpaulin for roof, and has already started swallowing officers strong enough to go back to the base camp and from there to the tedious fighting. The engines are puffing and rumbling as the men climb on board with heavy feet and hollow faces. They are all Frenchmen whom we received from Champagne and Artois. In their uniforms they look like a group of mellow blue jays whose bread has been snatched from them.

I rest my back against the coarse, thick oak trunk. Charles is supporting himself against his own tree, and clicks his lighter a few times but without success. His new uniform, which is paler than the striking midnight shade that the French used at the outbreak of the war, inspires authority, as is so often the case with uniforms. His hair is dappled with sun, tousled dark locks swooping down across one brow. He would need to visit a barber to be fashionable as well as to meet military regulations, but I have become fond of his oddities.

I snatch the cigarette from his lips and place it gently between my own. I inhale deeply, just as I have seen him do, and have to use all of my willpower not to cough and gag.

'I thought you didn't smoke.'

'I don't.' I release the cigarette and let it tumble to the ground before trampling it under my heel.

'I was going to finish that, you know.'

'I'm sorry. I'm not very well versed in what they might be worth at the front—I can't say I want you to teach me, either. To tell the truth, I think chocolate should be more highly valued.' I pinch myself before I can continue my ramble.

Silence, awful silence, reigns while the truck gets fuller and fuller.

'I suppose I shan't have the pleasure of meeting you again, Miss Wilkes, Rosalie. Rose.'

With deft fingers, I dig in my apron pocket and extract a trinket: an empty little metal box that once held mints. The lid is painted in cheery shades of yellow and green, branded with *Altoids Curiously Strong Mints*. I hold it in my palm, offering him it. 'For good luck.'

Charles studies the box thoroughly before slipping it into his own pocket with an amused expression.

I cross my arms. Perhaps I have somehow embarrassed myself without realising it. 'What's so funny?'

Charles's smile is even broader now, but to my relief I spot no mockery in it. 'Nothing—just that it's so wonderfully ordinary. Thank you. I won't lose it. You have my word on that.'

All of a sudden, the situation feels devastatingly grave. The chirping birds and the buttercups and the scent of toasted bread wafting from an open window, all these things offend me, because they do not belong here. When I am searing with fear and already longing for my newfound friend to return, I would rather our surroundings matched my increasing gloom.

'Well…' I fumble for the right words. 'I hope we will, after all, make each other's acquaintance again. Then you can give it back to me.'

He chuckles and lowers his eyes for a second. 'Yes, I suppose so. Just to give it back. That's all.'

Without realising it, I have edged much too close to him and his breath is hot on my cheek. Surrendering to the impulses I know will be my doom one day, I let my mouth brush against his for a fluttering moment. The faint taste of smoke mixed with toothpaste is sharp, yet I do not mind one bit.

Guilt hits me like the waiting military truck. I take a quick, staggering step back. *Harry.* Harry is fighting for his life. Perhaps his spirits sometimes brighten at the thought of me, and what am *I* doing?

Charles must have noticed me turn as cold and still as an ice sculpture, for he opens his eyes again and now the glitter is gone. He digs his hands into his pockets, squinting at me, tilting his head the slightest. 'I ought to be going. Goodbye, Miss Wilkes. May you find the greatest of happiness in this odd world.' He speaks without even a hint of sarcasm, and I know he does not truly expect to see me ever again. Why should he?

My stomach twists, my chest cramping.

He turns his back to me and walks down to the truck. He is the last man to climb on board with the same crestfallen steps as those before him, kepi tightly clenched under his arm and eyes glazed with the kind of nonchalance that can only be achieved with great effort.

I cannot cry. I forbid myself to cry. I will not. Nevertheless, my eyes burn and my vision blurs. As furious with myself as I am over what happened, I wipe the tears away before they get a chance to fall.

The vehicle jolts and starts to move, purring like a giant cat.

With a surreptitious glance over my shoulder, I turn and sprint back into the hospital building. I would hate standing outside watching when nothing remains of the truck but a penny-sized spot on the horizon.

In the early summer of that year, Harry is allowed home for five days' leave. Travelling consumes a large chunk of the time, but we should nonetheless be able to have the wedding we speak of in every letter. The planning is swift, although my father has rarely arranged a successful social gathering since Mama died. Harry's family is more than competent, and his parents promise us as fine a ceremony and wedding reception as can be had in times like these.

The matron grants my own requested week of leave, which is a fourth of my annual ransom, with surprising accommodation. I stand slack-jawed, watching her write something in one of her binders, smiling. Perhaps she is one of those peculiar persons who find weddings to be the most splendid thing there is in life. This is convenient, because to marry and still be allowed to remain in overseas service is a matter of controversy. My relief was considerable when I obtained permission from the War Office to do so. However, both Isabel and Mary are obliged to remain at the hospital and carry out their duties.

My marriage is not the sole thing occupying my thoughts. I had a frightful scare a short time ago when news reached us about the zeppelin raid on London. Fearing the worst, I sent Papa an urgent telegram asking if he or any of our acquaintances had been hurt, but they are all unscathed. Still, the knowledge that my loved ones are no longer safe in their own homes sends chills down my spine and makes me ache to hold them close to me. I shall have to go back to Rouen within the week, but to see Papa's face will cheer me a great deal.

Chapter twelve

Rosalie

LONDON SLOWLY BAKES in the summer sun like a soufflé in the oven. On the platform of Hampton Heath Station stands a lonesome figure in the midst of the crowd. Steam from the train forms thick clouds above our heads. Harry has seen this station many times before, but he looks terribly lost, as if in a foreign country. A heavy trunk with leather buckles stands at his feet.

My heart almost skips a beat. 'Harry? *Harry?* Are you all right? You're not hurt?' I fling my arms around his neck and bury my face in his shoulder.

My fiancé returns the embrace, his hair tickling my ear. He does not reply, but presses warm tears against my head. He reaches up and wipes them away discreetly, though in the corner of my eye I see his hand shaking. We stand thus for a long while, longer than what can be considered decent, before I pull away.

His skin is ashen, his hair lustreless, and his eyes contain a strange glimpse of something that I cannot identify no matter how much I try. A nasty scar stretches across the lower lip, and when I take a closer look at his hands, they are calloused, likely from holding a weapon in pouring rain days on end. Apart from these blemishes he is in one piece and as clean as I dared hope.

'Kiss me, will you?' I have imagined this kiss for a long while, long enough to have pictured it in my head a hundred times. With a single touch, everything will be perfect, just like in the novels.

The shadows will flee from his face and my own heart, and that one kiss will mend anything there might be to mend.

I do not think we achieve all this; it is a fond rather than impassioned kiss. A protective urge I cannot remember feeling before overwhelms me, a maternal wish to keep him safe from the world. I want to locate any trace the war has left on him that is deeper rooted than his scar and calluses, and wipe it out. Will someone think the same of me one day?

'It's so dreadfully nice to see your face again, Rose. I do love you so much…'

I force a smile and slip my hand into his. 'Come, let's take the car home. Your mother and Elsa are very anxious to see how you're faring.'

By the time we arrive at the Bride family's house, Harry is wide-eyed as if in a trance. After five long seconds—I count them, holding my breath—he raises his hand and knocks. We only have to wait a moment for the rattling of locks.

Bess, the housemaid, opens in her ruffled apron and cap. She begins flapping her hands like a little bird—a comical impression considering that she is unusually tall and plump. 'Mr Harry! How swell to see you! And Miss Wilkes!' She shuffles to the side so that we might step over the threshold.

Harry has his trunk in a tight grip and I have shifted to resting my hand on his arm. Many months have passed since either of us was here, but it is as if the clocks had been smashed and time ceased to exist. The bare birch floor, the roof beams, and the collection of antlers on the wall give the impression of a highland hunting lodge, yet the view from the large windows show clearly enough that we are in London.

'Miss Elsa, Miss Elaine! Mr Bride, Mrs Bride! Mr Harry is come home!' Bess bellows up the stairs.

The acoustic in the house is outstanding, and her words bring four pairs of footsteps hovering towards the vestibule. The Bride family swarm around us, all in gratifying tears. They do not pay much attention to me—which is as it should be—but shower their golden son with kisses and endearments. Even Elsa is commendable in her affections. The sight of her younger brother lures her to smile, a feat I believe only a handful of people will ever succeed in.

Harry is eager to return his parents' and Elsa's embraces, like a love-starved child. However, it is Elaine, a girl of eight proud years, whom he has confessed to me that he loves above the rest. She is a pretty picture with short braids and two gaps where her milk teeth used to be. When Harry sweeps her off her feet, she shrieks with delight.

Mrs Bride invites us for tea in the sitting room, and Bess brings us a tray, lemon and honey included. I prefer my tea plain, but now is not the time to fuss.

Sipping from the painted china porcelain, I keep my spine erect like a crucifix. The Brides are not forgiving of bad manners, and besides, I have to maintain focus on something other than the conversation to keep myself from interrupting. The exchange is painful to hear.

'Is it very bad out there? Is it very *dangerous?*' Mrs Bride asks, eyes twinkling with wonder, hands as brittle as pressed flowers.

I want to tell her to not ask something so obvious, but she means well. It is not her fault that she is living behind a shield of rumours and naïve beliefs. I stab with my spoon at the mound of honey clogging the bottom of my cup.

Harry flinches at the question, then shakes his head. 'No Mama, not so bad… I'm sure you hear things much worse than it really is.'

'Are you doing well, then? Are the spirits good?'

What now? Will he tell the ageing woman of all the wounded and dead? Will he tell her about all those sights that I know he must have encountered? But no, *of course* not.

'It is… The spirits are all right, Mama. Don-don't concern yourself for me.' His face is at once blank, his glance skittish.

Mrs Bride appears not to notice, but simply pats his knee and offers to refill our teacups. It is easier that way.

My wedding attire makes me thrill with pleasure: creamy silk adorned with pale peach lace, plainly cut, with fitted sleeves that cover part of my hands. The veil is pinned to my hat along with a clutch of freshly plucked blossoms to match my bouquet. Papa commissioned the dress from his own company and Mrs Bride is responsible for the flowers. Little did I know that they would make such a terrific team.

Although it makes me feel vain to admit it, I have no qualms about being wrapped in layer after layer of expensive cloth, mightily uncomfortable as it is. I bask in the attention, for this the one of the very few times in my life when I may do so without being frowned upon. A girl only marries once, or at least that is the truth I have been brought up on.

Laura is waiting for me at Hampstead Parish Church, as are the other guests. It is a small gathering; there are so many dear ones whom I would have liked to see in the church but who are elsewhere. Fred, Isabel, Mary, Mildred... The former three are bound by their duties, while Mildred sent a note saying she was visiting a gentleman and his family, no doubt planning her own wedding. And Mark is dead.

Elsa is standing on Laura's right, the usual smile glued to her face. Her posture is rigid and she has chosen a fancier dress than mine, no doubt in an attempt to outshine all others. I cannot stand people who turn everything into a beauty contest, and not just because I would rarely be victorious if it was. This woman is going to be my sister-in-law for the coming fifty years. I squirm at the prospect.

The first notes of the wedding march fill the church. The rich, deep melody is one of solemn promises and sun-lit dreams, of a shared past and a shared future.

Papa walks down the aisle like an ambling bear, me on his arm. 'Be nice to the chap, eh, Rosalie. I thought I'd be telling *him* that, not you, but mark my words—'

My groom is impeccably dressed, even smiling as if he had been frolicking a good while. His shoulders seem to shrink under the loud music—it takes me a little while to realise it—but he is sensible enough to not complain.

We exchange our vows, words with the impact to change lives forever, heavy with grandeur and clunky in my mouth. We share a brief kiss. Perhaps it is only in my imagination, but I swear he is the same boy in that moment as he was on the summer festival one year ago, unchanged for the duration of a heartbeat. One year! So much has happened in one year that it renders me speechless to think of where we might be another year from now.

I belong to him now... Oh, God, what have I done? But I must belong to *someone*, that is simply the way it is, and Harry would never, *never*, be unkind to me. This I know with the same certainty that I know my own name. To be fair, I shall probably be the one slamming doors and causing quarrels—that is, if there need be any quarrels.

Outside the church, we have our wedding picture taken. A scrawny photographer with a cleft chin dives under his swathe of black cloth and releases a blinding flash of light, immortalising us.

Because of the obviously unfortunate circumstances, we did not have a wedding breakfast such as Mildred and I used to imagine when we were little. Instead, there is a more modest wedding reception in the sitting room of the Brides' house.

The entire time, my husband's calloused, slender hand remains in mine, our fingers entwined. 'I love you, Rose…I love you with my heart and soul. I *swear*,' he mumbles as if trying to convince me. There is no need, no need at all.

We kiss our family members and friends on the cheek, shake their hands, and greet the witnesses with genuine smiles until my own cheeks are starting to ache. The gifts we receive are but another cog in the machinery required for a suitable wedding: a set of shiny copper pans and pots, fine embroidery, five engraved silk handkerchiefs, a beautifully sculptured cradle for eventual babies, a jar of Daya's homemade fig marmalade.

Once the formalities and pleasantries are at last done with, I sink down on the plush sofa, where a radiant Laura is already sitting. Indeed, she looks thriving, the impish gleam in her eyes more prominent.

'Quite darling, don't you think?' I say.

'*Dashing.* And look at you, aren't you gussied up?' She smiles. 'See, Rose, I always knew you'd find happiness before me! You must consider yourself very fortunate. Harry is a sweet boy.'

'Yes, very fortunate.'

'And by the time the war is over, I'm sure you can find yourselves a jolly nice house to invest in. Do you remember when we were younger, and Harry always had enough pocket money from his father to buy us all wine gums? Life will be a duck soup!'

The two of us surrender to a fit of laugher until my stomach hurts and I am gasping for breath. It is the most marvellous feeling, one I have not had since Charles left Rouen. Charles… No, our fluttering presence in one another's lives never happened. It was a dream, nothing more. Even if it *did* happen, which I suppose it did, Harry need not know, and what he does not know cannot cause any rift between us.

I shake off the thoughts like a dog shakes off water. 'How is Julian these days?' I remember my friend's bother's arrogance well enough, and honestly, the matter of his safety is but a distraction.

Laura cocks her head. 'He joined the 3rd Dragoons and went prancing about waving his sword, keen on the idea when he fully realised the world of cavalry fashion. Then his horse was shot and he broke two ribs in the fall. Now, he's sulking in a hospital.'

'You know I'd never wish anything truly bad on him, but…'

'But bruises like those might be just the thing.' She winks at me.

'Yes, I bet they might.' My merriment dies and shrivels, though, because I cannot keep my thoughts from wandering and settling on what still hurts. Mark's fate was so much worse than bruises. 'I trust you got my letter,' My voice is husky.

'No, no I didn't. It must have been lost in the mail. You know what it's like, with so many millions of letters and parcels being shipped every week. Was it important?'

I recount what I wrote, which is not a great deal, since most cases of typhoid fever perish in a similar manner, suffering weeks of high fever and sometimes internal haemorrhage.

Laura keeps smiling, tugging at a loose thread in her dress until the seam is ruined. I know she secretly held Mark dearer than she would admit—though it was obvious by the way her face flushed and her eyes lit up every time they spoke to each other. It was that all-too-common infatuation with his carefree mannerisms that I failed to grasp or was perhaps fortunate to escape.

I encircle Laura's soft, rounded shoulders with my arms and pull her into an embrace made uncomfortable by layers of lace and silk and sharp hairpins. At last, muffled sobs come, though her body is still and steady. Soon, the only tell-tale sign of our conversation will be the wet patch on my wedding dress where her tears are being absorbed.

Eventually, she rises and floats away to some distant corner. I do not follow. Silence will help her more than any words of consolation.

I proceed to conversing with my father and my husband. *Husband.* The word is foreign on my tongue.

'You look swell today, sweetheart… Have I told you that you look swell?'

'You have, Harry. But I'd never mind. Thank you—again.'

He himself is far more appealing to me in civilian clothes than in uniform. The khaki was exciting at first, but now that I have seen the terrible things men do and suffer when dressed in it, I prefer what the soldiers call civvies.

Papa lights his beloved pipe and draws a deep breath. 'Your brother should have been here, Rose.'

'Nothing could have made me happier, but Papa, you know his request for leave was denied.'

'And what fine general did that, eh? Up in the air they send people, and not a speck of humanity!'

There is no more time for chatting, because the hour has arrived to bid our guests a good evening.

As we are standing together in the vestibule, Laura squeezes my hands and flashes me a faint but scandalizing smile. 'Good luck with the wedding night. You must tell me *everything* before you go back to that dreary hospital.'

I swallow a giggle. 'You may depend on it.'

Candles emblazon the old-fashioned bridal chamber, where Harry accompanies me after a light supper with the Bride family. There is no use in setting up a household of our own, since we are both due to return to France shortly, and the wedding circumstances were out of the ordinary. Hence, we are to spend the night in Harry's childhood home.

I crawl down between crisp, new sheets that exude a fragrance of lavender and mint. Blood rushes in my ears as I reach down under the covers to smooth any crinkles and folds of my lace-trimmed nightgown. Everything must be *perfect.*

Harry leans over and places a kiss on my cheek and then on my nose. His own lips are cold but I can feel his heart racing when I press my palm against his chest. 'Goodnight, sweetheart,' he mumbles. Then, he envelopes me in his arms like a child might hold a stuffed animal and rests his head on the pillow.

I lie still in his embrace, waiting, waiting. I am fairly certain that a proper wedding night should encompass more than what has passed between us this far.

When his breathing slows, I raise myself on my elbow. 'Harry? Are you sleeping?'

He turns to face me, his hands fidgeting with the sheets. 'I… No, I'm not sleeping. I just…I want to keep you the way you were before the war. I want us to be like that again, be children.'

'But we're not, Harry. We're married now.'

'I'm tired…I'm so infinitely tired.' At this he turns away again.

I do not need to see the expression on his face to know that it is one of apathy. Harry always had a delicate, shy nature, but the boy I knew was no abnormality. He enjoyed the same things as his mates, found the same things amusing, the same sins tempting. That boy is not the phantom lying next to me now, though it has taken me a while to understand it.

It shall not be forever, of course. As soon as the war ends and its yoke lifts from my husband's shoulders, the Harry I thought I had married will return. For now, a goodnight kiss is enough. I do not have the heart to push him where he does not wish to go.

Chapter thirteen

Rosalie

THERE IS NO time to enjoy a honeymoon.

Harry must report to duty again, and two days after our wedding, we stand in the midst of screaming whistles at the station, the air dense with goodbyes.

Harry is looking smart as ever in his uniform, although with every time I see him in it, he seems to have grown a bit smaller and the uniform a bit more overwhelming. I already miss his civilian wedding clothes and the air of normalcy that came with them.

He sweeps a hand across his forehead to brush away a few strands of hair. 'Promise to take care, Rosalie, *real good* care. Promise, will you…?'

I nod several times, grappling for words without finding any that might suffice. 'You will pull through just fine, I know. And then we'll be wonderfully happy.'

Harry bends his full height to give me a peck on the cheek before climbing the steps to the train. A moment passes before he sticks his head out the open window. 'I will be very…very brave, Rose. I promise.'

Before I can contain myself, I have leaped forward to kiss him on the mouth. The shrill whistle that follows thrusts a thousand icy needles into my limbs. Like so many other times, I am left with my hand frozen in a crestfallen wave.

I return home to Papa. We spend the afternoon reading, sitting five feet apart in idle silence. Daya surprises us with a divine rhubarb pie and we devote ourselves entirely to the caramelised crust and the tangy filling. Even Papa gives his grunting praise to the cook, who wipes her hands on her apron and rewards our good appetite with a fond smile.

'How was it? The goodbye?' Papa asks when Daya has returned to the kitchen, giving me a long glance. 'I don't often speak of…of your mother, but had she gone away so soon after our wedding, it would have put me out of joint.'

'It was fine. It really was.'

'Good lad, that. A little squeamish perhaps…'

'No, Papa. Harry needs time, that's all. He's tired. You would be, too.'

'I *am*. The years are getting to me, strange as it sounds. This morning, I had a god-awful back pain.'

If a back pain was all that was ailing Harry, life would be easy. I sink back in my armchair and turn a leaf of *A Room with a View*, which is my recently most fawned-over novel with all its brilliantly sculpted Gothic and Renaissance characters. I like to think I would be a renaissance character—I bet all the shiny poster girls are.

Three days later, I am sitting on a train to transport me back to my own duties. The landscape flashes past the thick windowpanes in a haze of monotonous green. An unpleasant boat ride across the channel follows, waves sloshing against steel, and after that yet another train, this time from Boulogne to Rouen. Upon arriving at my destination, I am warm with familiarity for the gorgeous architecture and the dirty water of the Seine.

Time at the hospital appears to have been standing still. The exact same pattern of activity as when I left is still the order of the day. I have only been absent for a week, yet so much has changed in my own life that I find it difficult to comprehend how little has happened here. Some of the patients are, naturally, new men, but they require the same care as all the others.

In the once frozen garden, the apple trees are blooming most refreshingly.

'We simply *cannot* afford to send every weakling back home with a pension and a legitimate reason, for there is none! This…*madness* hasn't been confirmed as a wound inflicted by the enemy, and that's all there is to be said. Beat some sense into the boy, for God's sake!' The officer's feathery moustache flutters when he speaks. A spray of spit lands on my cheek.

I clutch his medal-adorned, stiff uniform, my knuckles growing white as marble as I hiss under my breath, 'Don't send me back, don't force me out there, please—'

The other man, the slender one in white coat, sighs and adjusts his glasses. I believe he is a doctor of some sort. My vision blurs and I can only hear certain words of his polished talk. 'Shock…trauma. Not fit for battle…'

A bomb detonates right next to me. I snap, a burning bile of panic rising in my throat, no, it was only a book that someone dropped on the desk. Cramping, I at last release the officer, who brushes his lapels as if my fingers had left filthy marks.

I drop to my hands and knees and start to crawl with jittery movements. I cannot let them send me back out there. I *will not*.

The two men resume their seemingly pointless debate. Eventually, the doctor surrenders to the hot-headed, chubby moustache-man and makes his departure.

They send me back to the steel-rimmed bunk beds. My unit has rotated to the reserve trenches, thank the Lord. Still, it is only for a few capricious weeks. It never lasts long. Despite the drumfire being fainter here, it is just as loud in my head and the bullets are just as present. I cannot seem to force them out, because every time a sudden noise is too close to me, it reminds me, and all my efforts crumble to dust. I tell the noises go away. I scream into the void to drown out the voices nagging me, but they never do as I ask.

I curl up in my bed. We have no mattresses, only itchy blankets. I stare at the photograph in my cupped hand. It is from the wedding not long ago, and looks saturated with early summer sun.

I wish she was here now. Rosalie…Rosalie in that dress. She could soothe me beyond any doctor's capacity or officer's shouts, I know she could. I caress the glossy grey surface of the photograph. It is the only picture I can stand to look at. The one from the festival used to be very nice, too, but not anymore. Now, all I can see in it is my own grinning face, except I do not recognise it, and that terrifies me even more than going over the top. Mark Crewel is not so well either. Perhaps the pigs got hold of him. No, no, he was buried and I was there.

The trial—I think it is a trial—is swift since the officers are unanimous in their judgement. They have found me guilty of deserting my post, which I did, but…

'Ask Sir Haig to confirm todays' sentences,' one of them says.

I cannot remember if I know this Sir Haig they keep mentioning. Perhaps I do. Perhaps he is another doctor. I wish the doctor who was here before would explain. His voice was soft.

Dawn is cracking through the sky's canopy when the men tie my wrists together behind the wooden stake. I hate them for it—I hate being tethered to a stick, and the rope is carving into my skin.

One of the men pins a funny little piece of red cloth to my uniform, over my heart. Then, all four of them step away and vanish, though the moustache-man remains standing in the back, arms tensed by his sides. At his command, another twelve men with faces set in stone march forth and pick something up from the ground. They position themselves in an impeccably straight line, all holding rifles, preparing to shoot.

My heart is pounding against my ribs; I bite my lip until it bleeds. Are they Germans who have come to take me? Will they tear me apart? No, they are English soldiers, I can see that, can I not? Yes… And there is the moustache-man, too. He is English. I know that.

The eloquent words bubble up inside me but I cannot speak properly. I hear myself whimper. I do not care how pathetic I sound with my high-pitched, obscure pleadings.

The man who pinned the red cloth to my chest approaches again, this time with a strip of white dangling from his hand. 'Let me blindfold you, Private. That courtesy is granted to everyone put before a firing squad.'

To my astonishment, my thoughts brighten at his words. I no longer hear shells bursting and machine guns rattling in the distance. I no longer see the world through a haze of red. The magnitude of the situation is suddenly comprehensible to me. They want to shoot me for cowardice, for desertion, but they will be mistaken. I will make them see that.

'No, thank you. No blindfold'

The man raises an eyebrow, then jumps backwards when the order to aim sounds.

I stare at them: twelve men who could have been my neighbours or relatives, all of them terse and, I flatter myself to think, unwilling. Maybe they are wondering whose rifle is or is not loaded. I would very much like to know that myself.

'Fire!'

Rosalie

I swallow another mouthful of sticky porridge diluted with milk. The mail is passed around. Again, there is no word from my husband. Three mornings have passed since I last received one of his detailed letters. This might not be a noteworthy period of time for some, but Harry has not failed in writing to me a single day since he enlisted. Perhaps the London Rifle Brigade is at an inconvenient location at the moment.

There is one message with my name on it, though, a square piece of paper. I unfold it with and scan the laconic, typewritten lines, a tight knot forming in my throat. It is the telegram everyone fears like the death it signifies, the telegram that is not supposed to be for me. To think that so few words can cause a sour taste on my tongue and make my heart race as if competing against a locomotive. This must be some kind of sick joke, *surely*. But there is not the slightest indication of humour.

Those five fatal words dance before my eyes even after I have let the paper slip from my hand down on the table. *Shot for cowardice. Shot...dead...shot for cowardice.*

I rise, choking. I crinkle the damned piece of paper to a ball and hurl it to the ground with all the force I can bring forth. The gesture feels pathetic since the ball is as light as a feather. I speed out of the hall and continue through the corridor until the nurses' chatter is but a faraway murmur and all that remains is the sound of my own footsteps. I slide down the chilly stone wall and pull my knees to my chest, trying to squeeze myself together like a tightly wound ball of yarn.

He was no *coward.* I refuse to accept that. Harry was a young man who deserved better. I have not seen the horrors of the front with my own eyes, but I have heard enough from all the wounded coming here, enough to know that no sane person should want to fight in that hellish place. For almost a year now, I have kept my faith in the war, and I still believe it to be rightful, but can no longer blame those who are afraid of facing it. How bravely they marched to battle, all of them, and how do they return? Often not at all, having been buried in France or locked up in an asylum.

I wish I could cry for my husband and the façade that the telegram has shattered, a façade that should have been long gone already. I sit with my palms pressed against my burning cheeks, breathing in gasps, biting my nails to distract myself—but no tears come.

Footsteps once more echo in the corridor.

My sister's slender fingers rest on my shoulder. 'I read the letter, dearest. How awful for you. You must tell no one how your husband died—you know it wouldn't look decent. If it's God's will, the gates of Heaven may yet be open for him.'

I speak through gritted teeth. 'You…you read my telegram? Isabel, don't you see? *God's will?* Harry was not a coward…and even if he had been, I could never heed a God who cares so little for His world and people!'

Isabel covers her mouth with her hand, eyes shining with disbelief, even horror. 'You mustn't say such things, Rosalie! Never! Come now, come. You're tired and confused. You don't know what you speak of.'

I have no will to argue. I allow her to pull me to my feet and lead me to the room I share with Mary, where she promises to have the matron excuse me from my duties for the remainder of the day.

I lie absolutely still hour after hour. The clock ticks soothingly, predictably, safely. It will continue its ticking, which I take a strange pleasure in. I want no more nasty surprises, not ever.

Around dinner time, a middle-aged woman, Edith, pays me a brief visit to ask if I care to have a light sandwich. I do not.

The French captain, Charles… If Charles were here… It is horrid, I know all too well, to think of the lips which I only touched once, and not those of my husband—especially at this time—but I cannot help myself. Maybe he would put his arm around my shoulders…but I cannot think like that.

The following day, I eat, sleep, clean, and help tend to the wounded, but I am merely going through the motions. Everything has been drained of colours. Whenever someone asks who I am wearing a black ribbon for, I tell them part of the truth: that my husband was shot in France less than two weeks after our wedding. The person speaking with me then treats me with the same approving pity as if I was a regular war widow. That is the way I want it, though I will not receive any pension from the War Office. My sister was right when she said the whole truth would not look decent. No matter how insensitive I think her phrasing was, she is a pragmatist at heart, and understands society. I prefer not to risk being branded 'the coward's wife' simply because British guns found Harry before German ones did.

I wish I could have buried him. He deserved that at least, no matter what cause the high and mighty used to justify the murder. I do consider it a murder, though of course, I refrain from uttering the fateful word aloud.

The minutes and hours, not to speak of the days, pass by so dreadfully slowly that I fear time might have stopped entirely. Yet they *do* pass, and with them passes the immediate and vulnerable longing for what used to be. It fades like an old painting might do in rough weather, my pain flaking away little by little.

Isabel gives up her attempts to make me kneel at her bedside every night to pray. She claims that the light of the Lord is what I am missing, but I disagree.

What is missing me is companionship, and, perhaps, passion as well. With Harry I lacked passion but had companionship, although it was a love without much chance to bloom. I eventually admit to myself that it must have been a lovesick part of me that agreed to marry him, and that it was a selfish decision as well as one I made for his sake. I should like to think that I am less dependent on warmth than that, but I suppose we all are to a certain degree. It is simply human nature.

Chapter fourteen

Charles

THE RAIN IS pouring down, creeping along my neck and shoulders under my coat like so many vicious trickles of ice in the summer heat.

'Keep digging, just keep digging!' I have shouted this order so many times that my throat will hurt like hell tomorrow. That is, if there is a tomorrow, which is far from certain.

The men stomp on their shovels to push them down into the soil, summoning what little force is yet to be found in their strained muscles, slowly deepening the trench. Yesterday we went over the top, and those of us who survived are now improving the ditches we came from. To deepen a trench may be gruesome work, but it is our only protection against the enemy, since this particular section of the frontline was not well-established when we arrived a few days ago. The German lead whistles over our heads, inspiring a haunting urge to dig our own mass grave. If we do indeed live to see the morrow…if we live, I will write to my superiors and demand to know why my company was sent out to a place without duckboards or even sufficient sandbags.

Some men drop their shovels in the mud and crouch behind the now seven feet high wall to avoid having their heads blown off by artillery fire, and stay down longer than necessary. I should tell them to stand and keep digging, but I have neither the heart nor the stomach for it. I myself do not have to labour by their side, being an officer. However, my arm is still sore where the knotty scar is, and I prefer keeping my head just like they do. Hence, I sink down alongside them. French shells fly from behind us, destined to demolish everything that breathes on the other side of No Damned Man's Land.

There are always survivors, though, amongst the Huns and amongst us as well. A bomb or a hailstorm of bullets never end everything—no, it has to *keep going*, forever and forever, *on and on*. There is always another thousand men to fill in the gaps in the ranks, always another pack of ammunition to be found, always more screams to be heard while plugging one's ears with one's fingers to shut out the noise. I cannot do it any longer. I wish myself back to Rouen time and again, back to a freckled girl and polished floors that would not have yielded to a shovel.

My cheeks are wet with tears made invisible by the rain. I cry from pure exhaustion, from bitterness, and soon from fury, because I swore to myself that yesterday evening would be the last time I wept. It does not become a grown man, least of all one who is supposed to be a good example. Unfortunately, I have been prone to it since I was a child.

A bulky fellow lands on his back inches away from me. I resist the instinct to reach out and shake him alive. His one dismal eye stares up at me without seeing; the other is a red hole of glistening flesh. It is a small hole, the size of a uniform button, but that is often the trick with bullets. As I turn him over, moist brain substance sticks to the ground. The hole in his cranium, where the bullet exited, is ten times the size of the hole where it entered.

I let go of the soldier, then press my arm over my eyes until it hurts and I see bright dots scattered in the dark. It reminds me of the street lanterns in Paris at night and the river glittering with reflections.

Towards the end of June, the Second Battle of Artois is over. We add yet another stalemate to the tally. Although we *did* push the frontline towards Vimy Ridge, the casualties were heavy and General Joffre did not get the breakthrough he wanted. To be fair, if the British attack at Aubers Ridge back in May had not been such a debacle, the situation could have been another.

My company rotates behind the lines, which is even better than the reserve trenches and is the closest to leave that any of my men have come so far. I have not even had a word about my own potential furlough. We set up camp with what is left of our company's battalion in the open fields near a small village. The total of roughly one thousand men has been reduced to seven hundred, and we wait for reinforcements. We are entirely out of enemy artillery range, and there is no large-scale barrage either. Such silence frightens us at first, but soon becomes a blessing. I marvel again and again at the beauty of nature: simple, clean, whole. The grassy plain has been spared the destruction so prevalent on the front, and a rippling brook marks a border between us and the village.

Bit by bit, we develop a temporary society of our own, a haven which will surely be snatched away any day now. It is only a matter of time—how much is difficult to tell—before we are called back in line to an inevitable autumn offensive. Still, we refrain from mentioning that bitter fact, according to a silent agreement between us.

The families living on the other side of the brook are a scrawny lot with chafed nerves, but evidently accustomed to soldiers. It rapidly becomes common knowledge in the camp that there are already two brothels, one for officers and one for *soldats*, set up last year by some shrewd woman who knew how to earn a living in wartime. I always found the Parisian brothels distasteful, not least because Henri and Louis were disillusioned enough to think the women there loved them. Naturally, the women themselves fed this belief, no doubt fearing their madam's reaction if they endangered business. I can only imagine their miserable reality. However, to ask my comrades to abstain from visiting the mouldy whorehouses in the village would be as futile as asking them to stop drinking at the pubs now springing up on every street corner.

To my surprise, I have quite a few able footballers among my men, and they set up two provisory teams. A fellow from another company locates a part of the field that is stony but spacious and dry. I shrug to grant my approval, with the result that Wednesdays and Saturdays are hereafter to be known as 'game days.' It appears that the unity forged in this sport—a unity manifested during the Christmas truce, too—is as strong as the camaraderie of the trenches. Its popularity competes with that of parcels and rum rations, which is no small feat. The tackles are rough, but what else might one expect? I leave the supervising to the men and retire to my private sphere, a small hut conveniently adjacent to the officers' mess tent.

Said hut has become the informal headquarters of our new battalion magazine, *Le Pou*, which came about when we found a run-down printing press in the village. The newspapers we have access to are, as always, heavily censored, and although *Le Pou* is one of satire rather than news, it is more honest. I named myself editor in a surge of ambition, much like when I was a schoolboy and fancied myself a future croquet star player.

What strikes me as the most peculiar, though, is neither the football games nor the newspaper. No, the most peculiar pastime is acting. A *sergent* and a few friends of his discovered an abandoned Red Cross tent which they dismantled and brought back to our camp. The next day, they had their hearts set on erecting a theatre in it and did just that. One of the little girls from the village, whom we often spot perched in a tree, spying on us, shyly provided us with a few garments that once belonged to her dead grandmother. I admire the men who eagerly pull on the shapeless dresses and nightgowns from the turn of the century on the hastily constructed stage. Were I not a CO, and could afford to sacrifice the scant dignity I have left, I might join them, but of course etiquette forbids it. Therefore, I content with lending them my copy of Molière and watching them perform. The audience howls with laughter bottled up and kept at bay for too long.

My old servant, Renard, transferred to another unit while I was in Rouen. His replacement fell at Artois, and now there is yet another one standing before me to fill the position. He is a full head shorter than me, and my throat closes up when I look at his spotty face and awkward stance.

'How old are you, Gérard?'

He straightens up as if I was holding a measuring stick. 'Nineteen, *Mon Capitaine*.'

'And if you have my word that I shan't report you for fraudulent enlistment?'

A moment's reluctance. 'Sixteen. And four months.'

'I see.' I place a hand on his shoulder and turn him around to behold the camp. 'Don't make the mistake of thinking this is the war, Gérard. This is temporary. Soon, we will be back in the trenches, and it won't be nearly as grand—keep that in mind.'

'I will. Can I clean your coat for you, *Mon Capitaine*?'

I sigh. 'It's clean enough, but you may fetch Lieutenant-Colonel Trembley.'

'But…but I can't simply *fetch* a man of his rank.'

'Tell him that it concerns *Le Pou* and he will come. Ask for Escargot, too.'

Gérard returns with Trembley and Escargot, ushering them into the hut with, I suspect, feigned confidence, and I let him have my coat at last.

'Thank you, gentlemen, for coming so swiftly. Brandy?'

Escargot nods and strides forward, being so bold as to pour himself liquor in the mug he keeps dangling from his belt. The other man, though, politely declines, as he does every time I offer. They are an odd pair. Escargot, the lazy carrot-head *caporal*, grabs for more than his share and pacifies others by luring them to laugh. Trembley, the aging battalion commander, cherishes ordinances but rarely asserts his own authority. I doubt they would exchange a single word with one another if *Le Pou* did not exist.

The three of us gather around the small table that I bought from an old man in the village. That along with the wobbly chairs and a couple of other necessities cost me two months' pay and a bar of chocolate from Paris, but I considered it a bargain.

'I wanted to discuss this issue's commentary on Italy joining the war,' I say once we are seated.

Trembley nods gravely. 'We may thank God that they chose the right side.'

'That's one way to put it, I suppose.'

Escargot slams his fist on the table. 'I have the most *merveilleux* idea! Why don't I draw a picture underneath the article, with a bowl of tricolour pasta—'

That very evening, after my guests have left, I am preparing to leave my hut when I discover Gérard peering at me. 'Where are you going, *Mon Capitaine?*' He catches himself too late. 'Pardon. It's none of my business.'

An instinct to protect this youth or at least confide in him seizes me. 'To the village. I promised the officers who were here earlier to meet with them outside *Le Chat Bleu.*'

'The…the fancy brothel?'

'I don't know if anything here can be called fancy exactly, but yes.' I halt in my step. 'Why are you looking at me like that?'

The walk to *Le Chat Bleu* is a short but tricky one. Once Gérard and I have leaped across the brook, I lead the way through the village's spider web of winding alleys, taking several wrong turns. By the time we arrive in front of the three-story house, which brings to mind a block of cheese with its yellow paint and with windows like black holes, the hour is growing late. The sheen from the blue kerosene lamp dangling from a nail blends with the warm lavender dusk, painting our skin.

Outside the cheese block a small cluster of chairs fills up the narrow street. There, two familiar figures are waiting for me.

'Go on, go inside—unless you changed your mind. That would be alright too.'

Gérard shakes his head furiously. Then, he smiles and walks past Lieutenant-Colonel Trembley and Escargot, avoiding their stares, and disappears through the doorway.

'You cannot possibly bring the servant boy, D'Aboville.' Trembley protests. 'It's against the regulations.'

'Forget them for once, will you? He said he didn't want to die a virgin—you should have seen how pitiful he looked. I don't like it any more than you do.'

Trembley heaves a sigh and stands with the expression of one carrying all the trouble of the world on his stocky shoulders. 'Well, then, gentlemen. I shall leave you to it. I have reports to write.' So much for having a chat.

I drop down on his chair, watching him distance himself from what he considers to be a breach of a strictly regulated unholiness. I have sat here often, although so far, I have not ventured inside.

Escargot jumps to his feet and cups his hands around his mouth, shouting after Gérard. 'Hey! If the madam offers you Beatrice, turn her down! She's all mine!'

I lean back in the creaking chair. 'Did you hit your head or are you just determined to deprive the girl of all her customers?'

'Oh, no, but she's special.' There is nothing in his voice to remind me of Henri's and Louis' disillusions, but a note of secrecy.

'Meaning?'

'Meaning I'm paying her for something little extra.' He winks.

'I can manage without hearing the rest.'

'But you don't grasp it, do you? Syphilis!'

I laugh; I should have expected this from Escargot. It is a sorry day for the French army when a *caporal* would rather get himself infected with venereal diseases than fight. 'How very clever of you. Do tell me, though, if you'd rather your mother received a telegram saying how you died in a hospital bed after pestering some brothel girl, or if you prefer "killed in action"?'

'Malarkey! Syphilis is curable and you know it just as well as I do. Gunshots aren't always. Think about it, Charles. A couple of months or so in a clean, real bed…'

'You win, but you can keep that plan to yourself. As for me, I'll do without any disease.'

'If you change your mind—and this stands true for the rest of you, too—I can be charitable. For a small provision, naturally.' He is speaking to an empty set of chairs, of course, and perhaps that is for the best.

'You're nothing if not a businessman, Escargot.'

'Oh, yes, I am, aren't I? And what's more, I'm helping Beatrice. Every dime is worth something, yes?'

I stand up and tuck my kepi under my arm, eyeing my fellow soldier with amusement turned to disgust. 'If you're so keen on helping her, why not give her the money and ask nothing in return?'

The question is apparently the most incredulous he has ever heard. 'Why? Because I'm a businessman. You said so yourself.'

I leave Escargot outside the blue lamp brothel, entirely forgetting Gérard in my eagerness to return to the camp and my dreary paperwork—mostly letters in need of censoring. Poor Beatrice.

Chapter fifteen

Rosalie

I HAVE TOLD both my brother and my father that I would rather not speak about Harry. For now, I simply cannot. Just as I vowed to myself when I received the dreaded telegram, I have not told anyone except Isabel how my husband died. There is nothing particularly odd about this. Too many men die in the chaos on the battlefield for all of their last moments to be recorded; frequently, the location and day are the sole details their loved ones can find out.

Fred, knowing that I sometimes find it difficult to speak of my emotions, resorts to telling me about aviation instead. This becomes a welcome exchange for both of us.

Little Sister,

You will scarcely believe it when I tell you of the latest German innovation. They have launched a new type of plane, a so-called Fokker E.I., that can shoot from the centre of the propeller without hitting the blades. I have told you how our own Lewis guns are nearly impossible to synchronise, and the French Hotchkiss isn't much better. Just imagine, Little Sister, what an advantage the Enemy will have unless we see a similar development here. I know my luck, though. The men on the ground are frustrated because they are made to fight machines and so it doesn't matter how brave or skilled they might be, while up in the air there is room

Your Pilot-to-be

I smile to myself. Perhaps I can go home and see him off in
October, then.

Charles

Our respite lasts more than two months before the battalion is
ushered back to the lines at Artois so that we may take part in the
third battle so named. The autumn offensive begins in late
September. While my men and I are part of the Anglo-French
attack at Artois, a solely French force will strike again at
Champagne. I can predict the bleak outcome already. Of course,
there is no use in trying to mediate this premonition to the French
High Command—Generals Joffre, Foch, Pétain, and so forth.
Even if they do realise it, they and their British counterparts will
push ahead regardless.

Upon arriving in the trenches, we receive our first proper
helmets, finally catching up slightly with German equipment. I
turn my new *Casque Adrian* from side to side, studying the
polished metal. While it far from guarantees my survival, I would
choose it over my old kepi any time if a piece of shrapnel came
flying my way.

The days of theatre and footballing feels more distant than a
dream—how easy we had it! *Le Pou* is currently on a hiatus for
obvious reasons, but I still share a cup of coffee or liquor with
Lieutenant-Colonel Trembley and Escargot when the

opportunity presents itself. To his chagrin, Escargot showed a remarkable resistance to syphilis, and has now been promoted to *sergent*, which makes him second in command of one of my company's platoons.

My own impending promotion to *commandant* and thereby second-in-command of the battalion is based on one tricky prerequisite: that I am still alive by the end of the offensive.

A pungent odour of pineapple and pepper causes me to snap around. The thick cloud wafting towards us is a shade of greenish yellow. Chlorine gas. This is the dreaded weapon I have heard stomach-turning stories about, the weapon we are supposed to be outraged over although we French used teargas against the enemy back in 1914. I guess the difference lies in the lethality.

'Gas! Gas!' someone cries next to me. 'Put on your damn pads! And the goggles—don't forget the goggles!'

My mind is blank but I follow the lead of the shouting man, strapping on my bug-like goggles and a pad saturated with chemicals to neutralise the chlorine. Unlike some units, we have not been issued hoods for protection, but at least we are luckier than those who encountered gas earlier this year and had to urinate on their handkerchiefs or socks to cover their mouths.

Like a shot, I plunge down in a large bomb crater. It is already filled with soldiers seeking shelter. I lose track of time as we wait for release, wait for the goggles to crack and let the gas burn our eyes, wait in uncertainty as to whether we should move or if we are safe in our hole. As it turns out when the first whiffs of greenish yellow reach us, safety is the last term that should be applied. The chlorine fills our crater like water poured into a glass. If we try to escape, though, the risk of being mowed down by German guns increases significantly.

One of the men is too slow—far too slow. In the time it takes him to fiddle with his pad, the gas has made him start to cough, and this in turn prolongs his struggle. He drops his protective gear to press his hands against his throat, and is doomed. The rest of us can only watch as the coughs rack his chest and his breathing grows laboured. I have heard it said that if one listens closely to the lungs of a chlorine victim, one can hear them crackle like the sparking of ember. It is the chemicals causing fluid to build up in the lungs.

The unfortunate man falls limp on his side and remains there. It is impossible to tell whether he is dead or has just fainted. If the former is not already true, it will be soon.

Another man is hysteric, his screams muffled through his pad. He claws at his uniform and his very skin before attacking his goggles. Tearing them off, he scrambles to his feet and climbs out of the crater.

'Will he be alright, *Mon Capitaine?*' a third asks me, as if he did not know the answer himself.

As the minutes pass, it becomes evident that the gas is not about to dissipate in the crater where the wind cannot reach it. However, our narrow view of the battlefield above suggests that it is almost gone up there. We have two choices. Either we stay down until the battle ends and try to crawl back to our trench without being gunned down by a sniper, or we climb out without further delay. If we go now, we will be right back in the thicket of battle, but have escaped the gas. If we stay and wait, we have a harrowing night trip ahead of us and could possibly be court-martialled for avoiding the fight. Of course, our pads could fail us before that, or a shell could land on us since we would be sitting ducks.

I know what an officer is supposed to do—and I loathe it. *'Allons-y!'* I begin the climb.

Only two of the men following me are struck down as we emerge from our poisonous shelter, at least as far as I can see, and the relief of fresh air is immediate. I pause to remove my protection gear in order to see better, and inhale. The chlorine has indeed dispersed with the wind.

An enemy soldier rushes towards me. His grey uniform is much too large, flapping about his limbs as he goes. He is of slight build, but the expression on his face is one of ruthless determination. The razor-sharp point of his bayonet is raised and ready to be buried deep in my stomach—between the ribs if the man is a fresh recruit, in the stomach if he is experienced. Despite carrying a pistol rather than a rifle, I have learnt the valuable lesson that a bayonet thrust in the chest easily gets trapped behind a rib. If it does, the endeavour of unhooking it and pulling it out is both difficult and macabre, should skin and muscle tissue be torn away with it.

I raise my pistol, but before I can fire, the German soldier collapses on the ground with an agonised howl, pierced with led and shrapnel. Without understanding it myself, I fall to my scraped knees beside him. The man, no, the boy—for I see now that he cannot be much older than my servant Gérard—is on the brink between life and death. The left bottom half of his face, from chin to ear, is missing. A bloody dollop of skin dangles from a dark hole. Only a few teeth still remain in what was once a mouth; they have been cared for and are white like sugar. The boy's arm ends abruptly in a black lump. I recoil at the stench of burnt flesh.

His yelps are sharp enough to cut through glass, and they go on and on and on. I could not make sense of what he is trying to say even if I were a professor in his native language.

'Hush now. I will…get help.' I scour my vocabulary for any German I might have picked up over the years. '*Hilfe, verstehen?* It is a lie, naturally. Even if I, against all odds, could get this soldier to a hospital and the doctors agreed to help the enemy, there would be no hope for him. Perhaps he could survive, but if he did, he would for the rest of his life be a one-armed young man with a grotesque face and broken mind. My instincts tell me few men would choose such a fate before the serene nothingness of death.

He refuses to shut his mouth. If he would just *stop*…

'Quiet! Won't you shut up! *Camrade*…' I speak the last word in a fresh attempt of soothing. I press the muzzle of my pistol against the spot where his heart must be. White froth is erupting around the undamaged part of the boy's mouth, tricking down what remains of his chin. Hand trembling, I pull the trigger. At last, the mortifying cries end.

Rosalie

The autumn of 1915 is monotonous at the hospital. We receive wounded from the big Entente offensive, as expected, but our own lives trudge on like before.

I pay a short visit to England in October to wave Fred off. He is glowing in his uniform, reminding me of all the others who have glowed like that before him. I have to keep in mind what he has been telling me for some time, that at least there are no shells or diseases in the air.

'Are you about to tell me to be careful?' He squeezes my shoulders and lures me to smile.

'I'm not sure carefulness is possible in an aeroplane, but you usually act sensibly, more so than me. Keep doing that.'

'I will.'

'Did you tell Papa you're leaving today?'

Fred hesitates and straightens the cap on his head. 'I mentioned it some time ago. He wasn't too keen on coming.'

'Goodbye.' I lean in to whisper in his ear. 'Don't let them catch you.'

I return to Rouen the following day, anxious to keep myself occupied for the moment. I still wear my wedding ring. I am not ready to abandon all the memories, and though it weighs heavy on my finger, I am soon able to wrap my personal tragedy in layers of indifference, directing my attention to the patients. With all the buzz and running about, there is little time to ponder my own grievances and complaints with life.

In December, Isabel and I request another ten days of leave, which just about fits into our annual allowance, and go back to Hampstead for the holidays. I had high hopes of Fred coming home also, but to my disappointment, the Royal Flying Corps keeps their pilots on a tight leash.

We have bought ourselves a Christmas tree that is tall enough to reach the ceiling and wide enough to require Papa to remove two armchairs. We hang shimmering ornaments and angels made of straw and red yarn on the tilting branches, just like we have done every year. I like to run my fingers through the tree and watch its needles cascade down on the mound of gifts. The warm colours and the candles we light burn my eyes, but they are vital. All traditions, all security that can be found, calm me. Even the library is oddly comforting. Thick books bound in evergreen or vermillion leather line the shelves; a fire has been lit in the fireplace. The scent of nutmeg and cinnamon floods the house, which is a certain sign of Daya's Christmas cooking.

My sister perfects the Nativity Scene on the table in the sitting room, moving the Holy Virgin one inch to the left, polishing specks of dust off the lambs. I am on the verge of asking her whether it truly makes any difference. However, Papa shoots me a warning glance and I swallow my words. While he is about as religious as a bucket himself, he has always indulged Isabel in her faith. Perhaps that is wise, because the afterglow of her admirable piety reflects favourably on the rest of us.

There is no reason for me to feel lonely in this house—yet I am, and I cannot shake the feeling. I am lonely not because the Christmas fair is cancelled and not because I cannot make snow angels with my friends like when we were little. I am not even lonely because Fred is away, or because I miss my new acquaintances in Rouen. I am lonely because my husband has been shot for cowardice and all the while my heart aches with longing for a person whom I had hoped to forget. And how might Charles be spending his Christmas? In a freezing trench or on leave in Paris, seated in a fine salon with his family? I can only hope for the latter. And if it is the former, well… Maybe there is a truce at the front, like last year, in the winter of 1914. It was in the newspapers back then. It must have been an exception to the rule, though. Regardless of where Charles is, I refuse to nurture the thought that he could be dead.

I sit down by Papa's desk in the study, and search for an empty sheet of paper. Once I find a thin stack, I grab his treasured pen and put it to the blank surface. I want to write, but no words flow from my hand. I stare at the delicately woven fibres of the paper and trace the silver implants in the pen with my eyes. After a while, I begin.

Dearest Charles,

I only write to wish you the happiest of Christmases. I know it sounds silly, because there can be no such thing, but wishes are never granted unless you ask for them.
Do you have leave, or are you still at the front? I hope not—but I believe you would say there is nothing one can do about it.
It is snowing here.

Your Rosalie

I let the pen rest on the desk again. Why did I write any of it, when all that passed between us was a single kiss? I never gave him my London address—doing so would have been both strange and imprudent—and I cannot remember the name of his battalion or company, not even brigade. I scratch out 'Your' at the end and replace 'Dearest' with 'Dear' before crumpling the paper and banishing it to Papa's paper bin.

Downstairs, the others are putting a new kind of nutcracker to the test on a bowl of walnuts that did nothing to deserve such harsh treatment.

'My God, who invented this devilish mechanism?' Papa is nearly spitting with anger when another nut falls to the floor without so much as a scratch from the cracker.

The crinkle on my sister's forehead is deep enough to bury a penny. 'Don't blaspheme, Papa! Where did you purchase this thing, Daya?'

Our cook's melodic voice floats towards us from the kitchen, but no one is genuinely interested to know the origins of the nutcracker. We put it to rest and proceed into the dining room, where a sumptuous meal is waiting for us. On the crimson-clad table stands an array of Santa Clauses made out of crêpe paper, amongst other merry figures. The decoration is interspersed with food: glazed ham, a pheasant pie, roast goose, potatoes, a stew of carrot and peas, bread filled with raisins and figs, a pot of thick gravy, and the pepper pâte mandatory in our household. If the government introduces rationing, this might be the last Christmas dinner worthy of its name that we can enjoy for some time. It is a wonder that Daya has managed to scrape this feast together, considering the impact the war has had on trade and supplies.

'How is it that in Rouen they only know how to cook porridge, soup, and tea?' My melancholy has been chased away.

'There is nothing wrong with those things,' Isabel says.

'Did you hear about Sir Haig replacing French as commander of the expeditionary forces, Papa?'

My father tries to remove a smear of gravy on his white shirt. 'I heard all right. Too much is changing these days. First Asquith is forced to a coalition government, and now this!'

'You must be awfully pleased with Mr Churchill's…*reallocation*, though. Fred wrote of your feelings about Gallipoli.'

'And have I not been proven right, eh, Rosalie? A bloody fiasco! Mark my words, Churchill will never be absolved from this. That man's career is doomed.'

I stifle a giggle. 'I suppose switching from Lord High Admiral to fighting in the infantry is quite the fall.'

'Oh, he's lucky if one thinks of the fate others have suffered,' Isabel says and dabs the corners of her mouth with her napkin.

'The soldiers, you mean?'

'Of course the soldiers, although I was thinking of poor Edith Cavell. There was a poster with her on Victoria Station—I think you saw it, Rosalie.'

I nod and lower my gaze to the starched tablecloth. Nurse Edith Cavell has become a martyr in the months since she was executed on the 12th of October, a figure used to stir up the patriotism that has begun to slumber in Britain. What better way to provoke another surge to the recruitment offices than by plastering the story of an innocent victim on every empty wall? I believe she *was* innocent. She was working in occupied Belgium and aided Entente soldiers as well as Belgian civilians, which I cannot consider a crime. For this, though, the Germans sentenced her to death.

We remain at the table for another half-hour before pushing out our chairs and gathering in the library. Papa then opens the aged Bible on the page with Bethlehem and the birth of Jesus Christ, and reads aloud from the fragile book.

We have saved the presents for the evening, as is our own little tradition. They are charming, the gifts, and I tear open the wrapping and ribbons like an eager child. A gorgeous silver pendant, an embroidery, pickled cherries, a novel by Walter Scott, and a marigold-coloured skirt made from fabric both rare and expensive these days. All this my loved ones give me, and yet my thoughts once more stray to Charles. It is as if a bug had attached itself to the back of my brain, refusing to let go. I curse him with all the sincerity I can muster, which is paltry.

Once we have opened all the fancy packages underneath the tree, I manage to slip outside to our back garden. More snow is falling now. I inhale the flakes and stare at the stars scattered across the sky. The more I think about it, the more I believe Harry to have been my favourite star—but he was not my sun, for I have none. Not yet.

Chapter sixteen

Rosalie

AT THE END of March, Mary and I transfer to a convalescence centre south of Compiegne, which feels like bliss compared to a regular hospital. It is a very fancy place: an empty old château that has been converted to what the current circumstances require. Ivy climbs up the red brick, entwined with itself, and a lawn often drenched in dew surrounds the building. Farther away, there are clusters of trees and a small pond where the breeze creates delicate waves on the water, like ruffles on a blouse. The manor has four stories containing an old-fashioned array of rooms. The vast hallway is in marble, the ceiling high enough for our voices to echo, and I snatch every opportunity to walk through it just to admire the busts along the walls. Each time I think I have seen everything, I discover a new room or passage. At least that is what it feels like.

Compared to my stationing in Rouen, the convalescence centre is an oasis of calm. Here there are men in need of recovery and care, but their injuries are no longer fatal or fresh or repulsive. All of them are officers, some even as high as generals—it appears that the regular soldier is too common to recuperate in this luxury. I believe the man of lowest rank in the house, except for some of the staff, is a lance corporal. The other patients are not overly kind towards him.

Mary insists on solely speaking with the other women unless there is an emergency, which is received with mixed praise and annoyance. She only makes an exception for the doctor. As tempted as I am to follow her example of prudence, considering that my fellow nurses are generally more pleasant than the men, I find myself in the same spot as in Rouen. Once more, I become the intermediary between male patients and female staff, because one group has my loyalty while the other captivates me with their gruesome stories.

My relationship with the patients does differ from Rouen in one aspect. They do not sleep as much or take so many painkillers, meaning I am not limited to chatting in a single ward. Moreover, I am less naïve than I was, and I know full well that some of them have no genuine interest whatsoever in conversing with me, but are after something else. Hence, I watch my steps, careful not to tread too close to them where they sit. If anything indecent were to happen, the matron would land the blame squarely on me.

If Isabel had come with us, she would remind me of this fact often. However, she is still in Rouen due to bureaucratic reasons, and I bet she is glad for it. My sister could not stand how idle it is here, where one spends the days serving food and speaking soothing words. I tire of it myself—it sometimes makes me feel like a mother—but I am mostly relieved.

The best part of my new whereabouts is without doubt that I have been given a room of my own. I had grown accustomed to the cramped feeling at Rouen, and can only marvel at this enclosed little space that I now call mine. I can cross from one wall to the other in three steps and the furniture is sparse, but it *is* mine. When my shift ends, I sit cross-legged on the bed and open my correspondence with a paper knife that I snatched from Papa's desk this Christmas. The letters addressed from my brother are my favourites.

Little Sister,

How are things over there? I must say I envy you, because a convalescence home sounds like a fine place to be at when I write this. One of my Friends was shot down by the Huns when he was flying a reconnaissance mission. He's doing all right but it took a toll on his nerves. His name is Albert Ball, a topping fellow with a shock of dark hair, not much older than you, Little Sister. We get on marvellously, for he likes flowers and music even more than I do, and so we have built ourselves a little garden of sorts here. I think he wants to become a proper fighter pilot, though he's awfully shy and often flies without goggles and helmet.

Enough about that. Rumour here has it that the Irish are stirring up trouble again. I cannot understand why they do it. They should be thankful, or what say you? They are even getting their home rule once the war is over. If they try any funny business, the numbers will be against the. It is plain Logic.

Write to me about how you fare and so on, and tell me what you're reading.

Your Pilot

I put the letter in my drawer, where a pile of them is slowly building up. Now that I no longer have a husband who writes to me, Fred's and, on rare occasions, Papa's and Laura's messages are the only ones I receive. I treasure letters, I really do; they are almost better than ordinary memories, because they do not alter. If only I knew what had become of Mildred, I would write to her, too, though she rarely used to sit down long enough to reply.

I pay Mary a visit in the room next to mine. 'Mary? Isn't your grandmother Irish?'

'Yes, why?'

'Do you know anything about there being trouble brewing?'

She shakes her head but avoids my eyes. Just as I have turned towards the door, she speaks. 'Their traditions and history are not the same as ours, Rosalie. It's we who have made the trouble to begin with.'

On Easter Monday, an uprising does indeed break out in Dublin. It is difficult to access British newspapers here at the château, but I extract all the information I can from telegrams and hearsay. A man called Patrick Pearse and his band of volunteers have captured the General Post Office and declared an Irish republic—such madness! The rebels proceed to capture other buildings as well, but Dublin Castle is spared, and they fail to prevent the arrival of British troops. My countrymen establish themselves at Trinity College. In the days that follow, the stories

I hear about it chills me. Civilians are looting the shops and wreaking havoc on the streets while the soldiers build barricades and launch artillery fire. Like Fred wrote, the numbers are in the rebels' disfavour, as is the fact that the British have better weapons and better training. They quench the uprising on the 29th of April, after which they deal with the ringleaders. Some face the firing squad, while others are just imprisoned. I pity them, but they ought to have known better. I cannot grasp why anyone would want to live in an Irish republic when there is Britain to be had, and regardless, the rebels should have been fighting in France. I do not care if they consider it *our* war rather than theirs, not when people I hold dear are dying out there.

Charles

The days of the late spring of 1916 are filled with rattling guns. To an outsider, Verdun is the same as any other piece of land, but it holds a dear place in many Frenchmen's hearts. The Germans have taken Douaumont Fort and are bloodthirsty for Vaux Fort, yet all I hear is how we will soon have them retreating with their tail between their legs. It is one thing to say it, another to believe it when there are *flammenwerfer*—flamethrowers—and phosgene gas. The latter is far sneakier than chlorine, because it is colourless and the symptoms can take more than a day to appear. We have been issued proper gas masks, at least. Another bit of damned positivity, so to speak, is my promotion to *commandant*. If I ever see the Sorbonne again, I shall take great pleasure in boasting about it to Marcel and the rest of my friends, although the rank in itself feels more like a mockery to me.

Oftentimes, when not in the Main Firing Line, I let my fingers slip down my pocket and brush against the cool metal of the little box Rosalie gave me. I refuse to look at it, but tracing its contours is enough. The habit brings the kind of comfort a lonesome child might yearn for. I am finding it increasingly addictive.

One morning in a reserve trench, I lead the customary foot inspection, a medical officer walking a step behind me as we advance through the lines of barefoot soldiers sitting with their legs stretched out in front of them. It is the medic's task to

117

inspect, mine to give us both an aura of authority through the marks on my uniform. I am only glad to keep my eyes on the men's faces while the medic stoops to search for blisters and blackened toes destined for the surgeon's table.

'*Comment allez vous?*' I ask this man and that, repeating the simple words. I have discovered that it makes the greatest difference to those who feel as if they are becoming one with the mud and lice. It reminds us all that we are still human and it still matters whether we have dry socks or not.

The medic taps my shoulder and I swing around. He is pointing at a slim soldier, perhaps in his late thirties, who is still wearing his boots but has attempted to carve off patches of the leather. The flesh is swollen and pasty, protruding through the holes, and there is a slightly sweet odour in the air.

I frown. 'Good God, what did you do to your boots?'

'I couldn't take them off, *Mon Commandant*. I tried—I tried to cut them—' His words fall flat and one of his comrades gives him a sympathetic glance.

The medic shakes his head and his face is grim. 'Can you feel your toes?'

'Of course!' He hesitates, eyes glittering with fear. 'No, Doctor. No, I can't feel them much, not today.'

'Who is your foot partner?' I scowl at how the term amuses me even in this situation. 'You don't look as if you're wearing any socks at all, and even I can see that filth is as old as fossils.'

'My partner was killed when we last went over the top, *Mon Commandant.*'

'I see.'

He ought to have asked for a replacement, but the blame is as much mine as it is his, if not more, because I should have been more attentive to which men I had lost. The taste of guilt is tart.

The doctor scribbles something on his notepad and together we proceed down the line.

'What is in store for the poor bastard?'

'Oh, nothing out of the ordinary. We can't save those toes of his, of course, but he might be able to keep his feet. I'll petition the medical board to supply you with more whale oil to rub them with.'

I nod. Perhaps the soldier will be glad some grand day, glad to have escaped the war forever at the price of his toes. The remainder of the company only presents one more case of relatively mild trench foot. They have been diligent with their hygiene and oil.

One day—my intuition tells me it is a Wednesday, but I have misplaced my calendar—I am made to lead my men single file along a trail of duckboards laid out in the heavy terrain. The rain has not, as we had hoped, subdued, and the constant shelling has made the ground a slough of mud as deep as two men standing on each other's shoulders. We hold tightly onto the man in front of us to avoid losing our footing and with it the safety of the duckboards.

I am absentminded as I walk the front of the line, my sight fixed on the pale Paris skyline in my thoughts, the Eiffel Tower in particular. Before I know it, there is no steady wood under my left boot. My chest flutters. I blindly follow my first instinct: to grasp for the filthy army coat I imagine the man ahead of me would be wearing if indeed there was anyone ahead of me. I swoon for a heart-wrenching moment, arms flapping. I catch a glimpse of the line behind me and a hand stretching out to rescue me—too late. The mud rapidly swallows both my feet and calves, and I can only watch as my knees disappear inch by inch. I tramp and pull and trudge with all the strength I can summon, but I am only making matters worse. At last, I freeze on the spot to give myself more time.

The other men stand dumbfounded. They are probably well aware that if I sink much deeper it will be ten times harder to do anything to help me, but equally aware that there is little they *can* do. I am too far from the duckboard for them to pull me out of the quagmire without an extensive rescue team, and they have to arrive at our destination in time. After all, there is a purpose with our reallocation—not that I or the other officers have any coherent idea of what exactly that purpose is. What would earn them the harshest reprimand: to abandon a commanding officer or to disobey orders from headquarters? I bet they are weighing the consequences.

I stare at the soil now reaching my waist, fearing I might vomit. 'For God's sake! Get me out! *Now!*' My frustration is almost worse than the fright or remorse, and it only escalates. I try once more to struggle my way out of the hole. Everything below my belt is cold and clammy. 'Where is Escargot? The corporal, no, the *sergent*…you know who he is?'

Finally, the man who walked behind me steps forward. 'Yes, *Mon Commandant*. He's not here. He had a stomach bug yesterday, he said.'

'Did he now?' I clench my jaw, forcing calm into my voice. 'Then I guess it's up to you to solve this, *Soldat*. I would if I could, believe me, but I'm rather stuck.'

The man calls to his friends behind him and they make a mutual attempt to grip each of my sleeves and pull, the only result being that they themselves nearly slide over the edge of the duckboard.

My head is spinning. An overpowering sense of being slowly suffocated has begun to chafe worse against my nerves than any artillery barrage could. I fumble in the mud, trying to find something solid to hold onto—a branch, a piece of shrapnel, anything—and I do feel something. It is not quite solid, though, but…squishy. Slippery in a different way than the filth. There! There is a stick, no, a bone. And there another one and a third. I squeeze my eyes shut and slowly remove my hand from the open stomach and chest I imagine is lodged to my right. I prefer not to know how long it has been rotting there, how bloated it is.

'A few of us are running back to the trench, *Mon Commandant*, to fetch help and ropes. Just hang in there!' one of my men calls.

I nod. They better *bloody hurry up*.

My gag reflex sets in, though in vain since my stomach is an empty pit, when the mud reaches my face and somehow pushes into my firmly closed mouth. Then, there is pressure around my head and against my eyelids. My lungs hurt from the lack of oxygen and my thoughts are blurred, giving way solely for sharp needles of claustrophobia.

The last thing I hear through the thick layer of mud above me is muffled voices, but it is impossible to discern what they are shouting about.

Chapter seventeen

Rosalie

I DISCOVER HIM sitting on the edge of a plump armchair in the library—tense, as if afraid to sink too deep down between the cushions. A closed book with the title in thin, cursive blue rests on his knee, seemingly unread. His uniform is spotless and goes badly with his worn face.

I freeze in my track. At long last, I let the door close behind me and take a few hesitant steps on the thick carpet. 'Hello Charles.'

His head snaps up at the sound of my voice. 'Miss Wilkes.'

'It's Mrs Bride now.'

'I see.' He clears his throat. 'You married that boy in the photograph, then?'

'I did.' I manage a fleeting smile.

'And how is your husband?'

What can I say to him? What do I want to say? Before I can think about it properly, the simplest version of the truth emerges. 'Dead. My husband is dead.'

Charles stares at me, then nods slowly, as if he should have known already. 'I'm sorry to hear so, but you must be sick and tired of those words.'

'Can I tell you something?'

'You could always try.'

It takes me a moment to summon up the courage. 'I think…I think he was lost well before it happened. Sometimes, I mourn what he was before the war more than I mourn his death. But it wasn't fair.'

'How did he die?'

The dreaded question. Always dreaded and always impossible for me to answer truthfully. It appears that my silence suffices, though, because Charles puts aside his book, stands, and switches to another topic. 'Would you like your trinket back?'

I shake my head, flustered. I remember the empty box of mints all too well. 'No, no. It is all right, really. You might need it—it is good luck, you know.'

'Good luck, huh?' His laugh is strained from the effort. 'Seems I sunk in mud over my ears, literally. Grand luck indeed, wouldn't you say?'

'Well, it was not my trinket's fault. You should have watched your feet. What…what happened, exactly? Once you were in, I mean.'

'Once I was in, it only took a minute to free my head, which was splendid. At least then, I could see and breathe and drink. God only knows how, but my men assembled a rescue team and pulled me out little by little. It took hours. All the while, I was wet and freezing—there was a rotten body somewhere next to me, too.'

I swallow twice, shuddering. 'That must have been awful—'

'It was.'

'—but how were you injured, so to speak? With a hot meal and a day or two in the reserve trench, you could surely have recovered.'

'I guess so. But then I discovered my leave had accidentally been suspended a few months ago, and when I mentioned the error to a superior officer, he immediately arranged for me to go to Paris.'

'But you're not in Paris.'

'I am aware of that. We agreed that I might benefit from convalescing for some time first—learning to sleep and eat properly again, that sort of thing. Becoming more comfortable with tight spaces after the mud.'

I close the distance between us, and thrill when he reaches out to brush my arm with his fingertips, which are cold and as smooth as polished stone.

'It's a swell house, with swell people in it. You'll learn what you have to again. I promise.' I stretch out my hand, withdraw it, and then lift it again.

Pure intensity flickers in his eyes, something that I have rarely seen before, and then his lips are on mine. I have longed for this kiss, and it is worth the wait.

The days that follow are brimming with excitement, yet overshadowed by one unfortunate fact: our bliss will come to an end. Time is suddenly my worst enemy and reminds me of a swollen boil about to burst—just not quite yet.

My chores are entirely manageable; the pace is even tranquil, and I find plenty of time to engage in what I now refer to as The Affair. It is a silly name, but I by far prefer it to 'sinning' or what else Isabel might have called it.

Charles and I walk in the wide-stretched garden with its intricate gravel paths and uncut grass and knobbly oaks, under the pretext that he is at risk of fainting during his daily exercise and should therefore not be left alone. Perhaps the other nurses would question this if they cared to take a closer look at him, but they are preoccupied with other matters. Besides, it is true that Charles sometimes gets lightheaded.

The silence is the most enticing part, the silence that settles when so many words have been exchanged between two persons that the air feels saturated and one must catch one's breath. That is when I get the change to study every line and curve of his face, like I would if he was a classical sculpture. I try to memorise every detail. It was like that when he arrived unconscious in Rouen also, only now he is looking back at me.

Then, we launch into the conversation once more.

Harry and I never talked, not like this. Of course we *spoke*, at times, but he had little to say about politics or literature, and I refrained from saying what I did have to say. While Harry agreed with me on everything, Charles rarely does.

'Isn't it nice of us French to let your English kings and queens stay on our territory when their rivals force them into exile? It seems to happen all the time,' he says during one of our walks.

'Not since a good while now! And you've caused your fair share of trouble, too.'

'Like what?'

I run my tongue over my teeth, selecting from a myriad of answers. 'Like…like the Hundred Years' War, and Napoleon, and—'

'The former was your fault. The latter, I apologise for. In all honesty, some of our commanders in the army are relics from that time.'

'We have that as well, I think. 'Isn't it odd that we're allies to begin with? And Russia! Not that I'm comparing the two of you, of course.'

Charles laughs. 'If it wasn't for allies, neither you nor I nor most countries would have anything to do with this war.'

It is natural for us to mention the war, but there is so much more; there is Paris, for example, an illustrious city with street artists struggling to capture the coral sunset. As much as I have idealised it before, its appeal grows when Charles speaks of it. I am tempted to dream.

We are entwined like the ivy clinging to the château's bricks, impossibly close. Pinned against the wall, I cannot catch my breath, and my cheeks are aching from smiling.

I have just cupped Charles' face in my hands when I spot a flash of white and blue in the corner of my eye, causing my heart to leap.

Mary, otherwise quiet as a mouse, clears her throat with surprising force.

Charles is at once alert and withdraws from me as if my friend held a pistol to his head. He is quick to adapt a nonchalant tone, though. 'What now, Sister?'

'Mary—' I call after her as she turns and marches out. I am queasy with fear for what might happen, although I know Mary will not divulge my secret. She was never as gossipy as Mildred or as dutifully honest as Isabel. She loathes obstacles. I break loose from Charles. 'Stay here. You'd only make matters worse.'

He opens his mouth to protest, but I brush past him, hastily smoothing my clothes and hair. I sprint down the broad flight of stairs, which is empty but for my friend and myself, gripping the handrail as if it was my lifeline. 'Mary!'

She continues her descent.

'You can't tell anyone! Mary? Promise you won't…?'

She finally slows down and faces me with furrowed brow, her usually so swarthy complexion rosy. 'Why would you do that? *Why?*'

I take a deep breath. 'Because I…I don't know. Because I wanted to. I met Charles before, at Rouen. It is not as if I go about with every patient; he's special and—' I stop myself. It is not my lack of virtue that bothers me but rather my lack of common sense. I should know better.

'But—but Harry was still alive when we were in Rouen. How could you do such a thing? You…you...*whore.*' She does not raise her voice one bit, yet her words cut straight through me as if she screamed. I have never heard her use that sort of language until this moment, and certainly not aimed at me.

Before I can control the impulse, I raise my hand and bring it forward in a resounding slap.

Mary stares at me, tears brimming in the corners of her eyes, threatening to spill over but never doing so. She presses her fingers to the flaring red mark on her cheek

Regret floods me. I have trampled and squashed the last chance of us remaining friends. Perhaps I have not only lost Mary, also but mine and Charles's secret happiness. How is it that my temper must get the better of me when it is most crucial that I behave?

Mary turns from me again and sprints down the rest of the stairs.

Charles

The girl who interrupted us—Mary, I think—does not utter a word about the scene played out before her eyes, at least not to anyone who cares to take action. With each day that passes, my chest feels lighter, and the cautious gleam in Rosalie's eyes fades.

A sweltering July turns to a russet gold August with ripening fruit and clear skies. I can sense autumn approaching early this year. Having been at the convalescence centre for a full month, my time is ticking away, loud in my head like a massive clock, and I begin to strategically avoid the only doctor residing here,

Holtermann, in the corridors. Moaning and whining a little extra, I should be able to steal another couple of weeks at least.

Nonetheless, I do not mind recovery in itself. My appetite has slowly returned. My nightmares come less frequently—though I wager that is going to change when I return to the front, where sleep is more often a luxury. I still prefer open spaces to closed ones, and I cannot tell whether I will ever want to wrap myself in a blanket again for fear of being reminded of the mud swallowing me alive, but I expect that kind of oddity will be the least of my troubles in the near future.

I cannot help but wonder what those moustached men in white coats presiding over the medical board would say if I asked them the obvious questions. Who in their right mind would want to die for another few feet of ravaged, raw soil? Who would want to fight and kill and be killed for something that is not worth to live for either? Of course, I already know what they would tell me. Men of quality, men with courage and patriotism enough to point their rifles at the enemy and feel the hatred they are supposed to feel. Sometimes I catch myself chuckling aloud when I think of myself being a *commandant* simply because I happened to be playing croquet at the right school at the right time.

It is growing on me, though, slowly. Not necessarily my hatred for the enemy, but my love for the motherland, because that is the only way I can diminish the feeling of pointlessness. While I still know deep down what I knew before—that this war is without any good purpose—I have become more attached to France. This makes it a little easier to believe in the fighting, and I need every sliver of belief I can summon.

Rosalie tells me that I have to write to her. I wish I felt the same certainty. So far, I have only written letters to *Maman*, my sisters, and a couple of distant relatives who demands a first-hand account of the war. I censor my own letters the same way I have been forced to censor my men's, carefully selecting the words as I scribble. I tell them of *their* war, as they should like to perceive it, and they appear satisfied.

I do not want to do that to Rosalie. I cannot shield her from the horrors, for she has already seen them and heard of them, even known them herself in a way through the patients she has nursed. And yet…I am ignorant as to how one even writes an honest letter at all.

Did her husband use to write her honest letters? She never speaks of him, not so much as the staggering first syllable of his name, yet I can tell by the glazed look in her eyes sometimes that the memories still trouble her. I detest the pathetic jealousy one feels towards a man who is dead and buried, and I detest myself for succumbing to it late in the evenings. It is not mere jealousy, though, rather…rather jealousy and guilt both. I have taken his place without him ever knowing it.

Once, when on a quest to fetch Rosalie a hairpin, my eyes fell upon their wedding photograph in the drawer, next to the little casket of pins, covered in the thinnest layer of dust. The two figures in the picture were like two dolls from the same collection, possessing the same air that can only spring from many years of companionship and similar upbringings. The husband ooked about to burst with pride, dressed in civilian clothes, exemplarily neat. However, he was not the same as the boy I saw in the picture taken at that summer fair Rosalie mentioned—his smile was somewhat twitched and the hollows of his eyes housed too much shadow. What was it she told me? That she had lost him before he died.

I hope one day she might recount to me what *exactly* happened to Harry Bride at eighteen, because if it is possible to feel haunted by a person one has not exchanged a single word with, then God knows I do.

Chapter eighteen

Rosalie

I LAUGH AND rest my hand on Charles' shoulder when he takes me in his arms and we attempt a waltz. There is a sprightly feeling inside me. Like a new kind of flower, it blooms rapidly, promising delight and destruction both.

Paul—a captain who was a pianist before the war—presses the black and white piano keys as if he has found a long-lost friend, raising his voice to accompany the instrument. He would have intrigued Laura with his skill and peculiar face, I am sure. Laura… I have not written to her in almost a fortnight. The last I heard from her made me giggle, because she asked her father to let her work in a munition factory, which nearly made him faint and the maid to call for smelling salts. My friend must have acted out of pure boredom, knowing full well that if a VAD was not suitable in her father's eyes, she was more likely to wake up with a tail than become a munitions worker.

Charles and I move across the cleared floor of the salon and back again, stepping on one another's feet, the rhythm of the music mingling with the pulsating of blood in my ears. The men have shoved the furniture aside to create a provisory dance floor. The setting sun filters through the drawn curtains, bathing the room in a red haze. The officers who have gathered for the entertainment clap their hands to the melody, or stamp in the event that they have lost one or both hands. It is indeed marvellous what seemingly insignificant pleasantries can do for people.

'I didn't take you for the dancing type,' I mock as Charles once more steps on my toes.

'Is that so? I'm deeply offended! Would you like to know a secret?'

'I'd love to—you *know* I'd love to.'

Charles leans in close and whispers in my ear. 'Speaking of love, I believe I'm falling in love with you. There. Now you know my secret. It's a disaster, isn't it?'

My steps falter and I come to a halt.

Paul lets his beautiful fingers rest on the piano keys and his voice dies down. The soldiers do not seem to mind the abrupt ending, though; they applaud and whistle as if they had watched the performance of a lifetime, the discipline they otherwise adhere to gone for an hour or two.

I pull Charles by the hand out of the salon and behind one of the towering cupboards in the corridor. The lights are bright and hard after the red softness of the salon, hurting my eyes and chasing the shadows from Charles' face.

'What do you mean?' I whisper, heart thudding, clammy sweat breaking out on my back.

His hand is scorching against my neck. 'I mean precisely what I said.'

'How unfortunate. I recognise the feeling.'

'Then at least we're two in the morass.'

'Maybe I should never have given you that box of mints or kissed you in the first place.'

'No, you shouldn't have.'

I am tiring of our little game. Turning us around, I place his back against the cupboard and lean against his chest. 'What will become of us—truly?'

Charles tips my chin up and places a kiss at the corner of my mouth. 'How would I know? But let's not take anything for granted. That, at least, I've learnt.'

We eventually return to the salon—dear God, do not let the others have noticed our absence—and resume our merriment until the grandfather clock signals the time has come to eat our separate suppers.

During that whole while, the matron remains in her private room, likely with her nose buried in paperwork, granting us rare liberty. The trained nurses are not always as dull as I assume them to be, and although one of them forbids me to dance anymore, it appears they have realised something. Perhaps they have realised that as important as propaganda might be, music and games are just as vital in order to keep up morale.

Even Mary is present, and plays us 'Peg O' My Hear' twice to loudmouthed praise that makes her squirm on her pallet. Afterwards, she retires to a corner where she can watch Charles and me with disapproval etched in her face. To my relief, though, she says nothing that might spark suspicion.

When we are about to part with the officers for supper and, sadly, return to the regulated formality supposed to exist between us, I manage to speak a few hushed words to Charles amidst the racket of furniture being put back in place.

He looks at me thoughtfully. 'You know what the consequences might be?'

I force a nod. I have a feeling I will come to regret this paramount indulgence sooner or later, while Charles has infinitely better chances of walking away unscathed from scandal amongst other things, but I do not care.

'And which room is yours?'

Charles

I tread through the corridor on light feet, meticulously avoiding the floorboards I know will creak if stepped on. I have memorised the path.

Rosalie's door is the third on the right…or is it? I do not want to picture the commotion if I entered some other, innocently sleeping VAD's room and was caught. Suffice to say it would not put me in a favourable light. Yes, it *is* the third door. I close it behind me, and in the next moment Rosalie has wrapped her arms around my neck.

'I'll admit that this is more thrilling than I expected,' I whisper.

She grins. 'I was worried you might not find the way. The house is terribly large, don't you think?'

'You forget I grew up in a house like this.'

'Yes, I do tend to forget that.'

I brush my lips against hers and wrap a garland of her hair around two fingers. It is like silk against my skin. If I could, I would freeze this moment and keep it somewhere safe from time. The way her eyes glitter in the dark when she tilts her head up is mesmerising. I can feel the warmth of her back and shoulders through the thin nightgown.

Rosalie gives me a kiss more demanding than the ones we have exchanged in daylight. Then, she pulls back and drops down on the bed, waiting while I unbutton my pyjamas shirt. It is chilly in the room, but her hands are burning like embers.

'I doubt this bed was made for two,' I hiss as the mattress squeaks under my weight.

'Of course it wasn't.'

'And does it always make that noise?'

Rosalie arches an eyebrow and pulls her legs up, shifting backwards to make more room. 'How would I know? It's not really my habit to bring men in here—or what did you think?'

'Who am I to make presumptions?'

For a second or two I worry she might take my remark as an insult rather than the jest I intended, but I need not have feared. By the time she laces her fingers with mine and allows my other hand to trail up her leg, I trust her affection more than anything. Her movements are a little fumbling at first—I imagine Harry Bride was not the most passionate of lovers—but it does not matter. That night, the nasty dreams leave me alone.

Chapter nineteen

Rosalie

BETWEEN SUPPER AND curfew, when there are few duties to perform, I occasionally sit with some of the patients in the old smoking room, talking about a variety of things—but rarely the war. It intrudes on every other hour of our life in the most unsettling ways, hence even the most invested officers are reluctant to say a word of it when the hour is late, although perhaps this is because I am a woman.

The smoking room is rather masculine in style, not only because of the dark leather chairs and rustic tables with crystal ashtrays, but because of the atmosphere, and because of the fact that my mere presence in a smoking room is frowned upon. However, I manage to appease the matron with little bribes and nudges. Only one of the trained nurses presents an obstacle, a woman who always seizes upon the sweet opportunity to make me fold sheets that have already been folded a hundred and one times since last they were used. Moreover, she drives me insane with her habit of gnawing on her cuticles. I do my best to shake her off.

At any given time, there are one or several soldiers sunk deep into the plush sofa cushions, dunking buttery biscuits in china cups of lukewarm tea. Brandy and whisky are too rare here to drink it every day, and what we did have was consumed during our dancing afternoon in the salon. Thus, French and British alike have adopted the habit of four or five cups of tea per day. I

132

suspect they will all grow sick and tired of it for the remainder of their lives.

One of those evenings—it is almost unseemly late, and I am supposed to be asleep in bed like the other VADs within thirty minutes—I enter the smoking room and discover Charles alone on the sofa. A sketchbook rests in his lap and he is moving a pen with swift, furious strokes. His hands are splotched with ink; he takes no notice of my presence.

Ever since I received him in my room for the first time, there has been an additional thrill of secrecy between us whenever we meet. However much I enjoy the intimacy, it also makes me uncertain. There is so much more to be revealed now if we were discovered, enough to get me permanently banned from the Red Cross and forced to idle at home with Papa instead. Is it worth the risk? What happens when Charles returns to the front? Will I be just another old fancy? Partly because of this, I consider making my departure from the smoking room again, but I never get the chance.

'Don't go. Please.' His hands grow still.

They are only three simple words, yet they hold more meaning in them than a thousand might. I carefully shut the heavy door and stride across the floor. Settling comfortably by Charles' arm, I pull up my legs under me. He is not wearing his uniform jacket, for once, but a linen undershirt and suspenders.

The muscles in my back are sore and I flex my shoulder blades back and forth to ease the tension. 'I didn't know you enjoyed drawing.'

'Well. I haven't done it for quite a while—not since the war began, and as you can see, I'm quite rubbish at it. But I thought I might sketch something for the comic section in *Le Pou* to pass the time.'

I laugh. 'You and your magazine! I doubt you can find a printing press in the trenches, really, Charles.'

'I also doubt it, but who knows? Someday that project will be resurrected, trust me.'

He has put down the paper and pen facing the table. I reach for the paper, but Charles immediately snatches it up again, smirking, then holds it high over our heads where I cannot reach it.

'What is it you have there that's so terrifically secret, anyhow? It must be very special.'

'It isn't.' A rare, peachy blush stains his jaw. 'Just the comics, like I said.'

Eventually, Charles hands me the sketchbook, although he does not let go of it completely while I flick through the pictures. First comes the doodled satire he claimed to have been working on, but behind that there is something entirely different. The ink is swept in determined dark lines and marks, completing a patchwork of landscapes and people. The former are raw and ghostlike. The latter appear hollow and drained of all life. Charles was honest when he called himself rubbish, but it matters little, because these scenes are not meant to be beautiful. Without asking, I know they are drawn from life, or, in truth, from death.

'They really are…something.' I give the block back to Charles, unsure whether I ought to add anything.

We sit in silence for a good while. He rests his head on my shoulder and I play with his hair, thinking he must have fallen asleep.

However, he withdraws the slightest, avoiding my eyes.

'What?

'Nothing.'

'Evidently something.'

He sighs. 'I only wish they'd keep their eyes to their newspapers and books—the men, I mean. I swear they look like they could gobble you up sometimes.'

'I'm not encouraging it, nor enjoying it. Perhaps you should speak to *them* instead.' I count to ten in my head, like my old governess would tell me when I was a child and prone to throwing tantrums.

'And make the whole lot of them wonder why I give a tinker's curse? I was rather thinking we'd find a way to keep them at bay.'

My chest is still fluttering with anger. 'What are you suggesting?'

Charles attempts to place a brief kiss on my palm, but I flinch. 'We could get engaged.'

I cannot tell if he is serious or not and it makes me despair. 'You're out of your mind. You don't want to get *engaged*, not really. You're just saying that to…to…'

'To *what*, Rose? I mean it. It's true I didn't expect to marry yet, but that was before the war. I could be dead soon, and—'

I shake my head and his words fall flat. This conversation reminds me too much of one I had at the porch of the Bride family's house one August evening two years ago, when everything was budding fresh and lovely. 'I can't marry like that again, marry because I don't want someone to die without calling me his. That's not what I want and I should have known it long since.' What I forbid myself to say is that I also could not stand being widowed again.

Something hard sets in Charles' face when no further explanation comes. 'I thought you loved your husband. Harry. Maybe you don't have any love for me either.'

'You're not being fair! I loved him dearly, and—'

He is not listening anymore, though. The petty issue that begun the argument is now long forgotten. 'It didn't seem like it when he was still alive, when you gave *me* your trinket, and smoked *my* cigarette and kissed *me*.'

I would have preferred it if he had struck out and punched me in my stomach. I slowly stand up. 'That was low. *Too* low. Why are you arguing for a man I know you to be jealous of?'

'Because...because I don't want to lose you! You're damn near everything I have.'

'That's not true and you know it! You're frightfully, filthy rich, you have your family at home, and you have your men.'

Charles spreads his hands and shakes his head. 'I thought...I thought to make things easier for you, that was all.'

'Why not worry a bit less about me and a bit more about yourself?'

'Perhaps you're right. After all, you can go home as soon as your contract ends, should you so wish. Isn't that grand? They don't force you to do anything, much less die.'

I inhale sharply. He is an expert at finding my most sensitive points. Not a single day has passed since the war broke out without me wondering whether I am doing enough, helping enough. It is the most central reason for me to stay on duty. 'You make it sound as if I'm not contributing at all.'

'Of course you are! But it's not the same, is it? It doesn't mean you understand.'

I wish I could slap him like I slapped Mary, but I have regretted that moment countless times and I refuse to infect this relationship as well through my unrestrained actions. I could rip out and crumple the pages from his stretching block—but no, that would also be the start of a destructive spiral between us, and childish. I decide on simply slamming the door loud enough to wake everyone on the floor.

The following day, Charles startles me in the hallway, where I am catching my breath on one of the benches after an unusually hectic episode of cleaning. Yesterday's fury lingers like a hot glow in me. I rise and prepare to retreat, to save myself the ordeal of facing him there with his black locks contrasting against the white marble.

However, he is too quick and grabs my arm. 'Won't you speak to me at all now?'

I hesitate; I do not wish to do his every bidding. I do want to clear the air between us, though, because if anything gives me a nasty feeling, it is an unfinished argument. As it happens, apologies are rarely my strong suit, but this time I am confident he owes me one as well. With a lump in my throat, I slowly sit down again at a safe distance, the cold stone pressing through my dress. I stare stubbornly straight ahead at the bust of Apollo.

'Maybe I should write you a dashing poem and you'll forgive me.'

'I don't care for poetry unless it is Shelley. I try to think of the right thing to say, an apology, but I'm afraid I'm failing.'

Charles sighs, tilting his head back. 'I see. I'm not very good at apologies either—but I *am* sorry, Rose, I truly am.'

I finally avert my eyes from Apollo's chiselled face and turn to look at the man of flesh and blood next to me. Still, I cannot simply let go of the matter. 'I *did* love my husband, and I *do* love you, albeit in a different way…a stronger way. I just wish you didn't think of me like so many probably do, like someone who has spent these past two years sleeping.'

'I never meant that. I know the opposite is true, and the fact that you have a choice makes me admire you all the more. If *I* had a choice, I *would* be sleeping, or at least be at home.

Sometimes, though, I envy you. And when I get flustered like that…'

'Yes. Me too.'

Charles quickly turns his head as if to reassure himself that no one else is present and pulls me across the slippery bench until we meet. I rest my cheek against his chest and inhale his familiar scent for a short, sweet while.

'If you do change your mind, someday, then keep this.' He digs deep into his pocket and extracts a small, crinkled piece of paper and a pencil. He scribbles something before handing the note to me with a smile.

I read carefully, and swallow laughter. 'A free proposal when it suits me?'

'Why, yes.'

'You cannot know you'll be willing to marry me whenever I pull out this thing.'

'But I *do* know that—out of all precarious things I know that.'

'Then I shall keep it always, and hold you to your word.' I fold the note before slipping it safely into my apron pocket.

When I have to return to my chores, I keep my hand in that pocket, cupping the note in my palm. As silly as it might be, I want to believe it is my ticket to a future beyond Hampstead and the life I expected to settle for like a younger replica of my mother.

Charles

With mud dripping, the shovel is emptied over my head. The substance pushes through my eyes and nose, creates a thick coating on my tongue.

General Laframboise peers down at me with blood-shot eyes. He is clutching a croquet mallet in one hand and the rusty shovel in the other. Then, he is gone, and the shovel now belongs to Marcel, who lands another heap of mud on my face. They will bury me alive. A long line of men passes by— amongst them Mark Crewel and the German boy who I shot all those months ago—each and every one of them contributing more mud.

I awake with a cool trickle of sweat tracing down my neck and shoulders. The dark in my room is as compact as it was underneath the dirt, causing the panic to rise in my throat once more. I fumble for a source of light, and yes, there is my lighter on the nightstand, so familiar in my hand, the quivering flame a relief.

However, I am not alone. One of the older majors is standing at my bedside, and when he tugs at the sleeve of my pyjamas, I nearly hit him in my bewildered state. I can only just discern his knitted brows and the deep creases on his forehead. It is one of the British men—his name is Randolph, if I am not sorely mistaken—but right now I could not hate him more if he was Kaiser Wilhelm himself. In fact, I might be more kindly disposed towards the Kaiser.

I cling to my bedpost and try to claw his fingers from my arm while he tightens his grip. Randolph at last succeeds in hurling me from my bedroom out to the corridor, where whispering is safe.

'What do you *want?*' I sputter, straightening my crumpled pyjamas.

'You have to help me. He's so *damn heavy.* I've got to get him to bed.'

'Who?'

'Doctor Holtermann. The medical board, they're examining me tomorrow. They *were* going to examine me tomorrow, that is. And then they'd send me back.'

The fear of what he could be implying chases away my initial anger. 'And so you prevented it? What on earth did you do, *kill him?*'

'God, no! I just jazzed his camomile tea with a few pills to gain a bit of time to come up with something. Only—' Randolph rubs his temples, '—only I misjudged the amounts, and now the bastard is passed out on the third floor, which is *fucking inconvenient.*'

We take the stairs two at a time, though quietly, and after turning a few corners we catch sight of the poor Doctor Holtermann stretched out on the worn but expensive carpet. His head is tilted backwards, but the folds of skin and fat diminish the contour between chin and throat. The blond hair—faded, Norwegian blond—looks suspiciously like a toupee, and the tawny moustache flutters with every breath. Though he is mild, many of the officers including myself dread him since he has the authority to pronounce a man healthy enough to return to the trenches.

'And why, *why* would I help you with this? Couldn't you ask one of the others?' I say, crossing my arms.

'The other French speak too little English. And the English are all morons.'

'Perhaps you should have thought about that before, then.'

Randolph leans in close, a gleeful smile on his face. 'You wouldn't want me to tell them all about that little wench, would you? Sweet girl—though she can't be very clever, waltzing around with patients. I'm willing to bet she lied about her age when signing up, too.'

I freeze. He must have seen something he was never meant to see. Without another word, I lift the doctor's legs at his ankles. Randolph nods and together we proceed through the corridor and up yet another flight of stairs, the limp body swaying between us, head lolling. I curse myself, because the doctor's weight takes me by surprise. It should not. I have carried and dragged more bodies than I can count on my fingers; still I will never get used to it.

Having returned Doctor Holtermann to his bed, Randolph and I shake hands as if we had concluded a business deal. I can only hope he is satisfied and will not use his potentially damaging knowledge to make me his puppet.

Doctor Holtermann is not indisposed for long. While he is, though, Major Randolph comes up with and executes a plan that involves deliberately breaking both a leg and a wrist. He must have failed to think it through properly. He is transferred to an ordinary hospital since these injuries are deemed too serious for him to stay at the convalescent centre.

Much to my dismay, it turns out that I am next on the list of examinations. And, yes, Doctor Holtmann informs me with giddy eyes, I will be sent away within the week. This piece of nasty news is far from a surprise—but for once in my life I have gladly nurtured delusions and denial. It is a great deal easier than facing the truth. I have already lingered here for two months, longer than I can claim to have needed, and it is high time I went on that leave to Paris as was the original plan. After that…active duty, I suppose.

When I tell Rosalie, there is only one remedy to keep us both from drowning in abhorrent self-pity. Later, lying curled up in her bed, our breaths are stale with melancholy, heavy with passing pleasure that shall soon be long gone.

Chapter twenty

Rosalie

THE DAY I have been dreading finally arrives when it is impossible for Charles to maintain the pretext of convalescing any longer. He must use the leave granted to him and then return to active duty, or he risks being suspected of cowardice in the face of the enemy or some such nonsense. *Cowardice.* I hate that word. Why do we not call it common sense instead? Mayhap because that would cause mass desertion.

I am brewing coffee when I detect the familiar sound of a car engine. I put the kettle down with a clatter and press my nose to the window, watching as the military vehicle pulls up in front of the château and a French orderly of some sort steps out. My whole body is at once erect with alarm. That man has come to steal my happiness, just like Charles warned me, and there is absolutely nothing I can do to stop him. Maybe I could help Charles have an accident and break a rib falling down the stairs… But no, it would be selfish of me to suggest it, and a risky endeavour.

Charles is already pacing outside when I emerge from the main entrance. When he catches sight of me, he gives a subtle nod towards the back of the house, and together we disappear behind the building, shielded from intruding eyes.

I lean against the raw surface of red bricks, the ivy sticking up between my fingers. It feels good, as if the wall is the only thing preventing me from crumbling. Shifting the weight from one foot to the other, I inhale deeply and raise my eyes to face Charles'.

The first drops of summer rain tremble on his face and soaks his eyelashes. 'Tell me to stay.'

'Would you?'

'I would, but I can't.' He is wringing his hands.

'But I'll write, and you will too, and everything will be good.' I am disgusted at my own words, for they are so much like the words I used to speak to Harry. 'Forget I said that. I know it won't be good or anything remotely similar, but…but you've survived so far.'

Charles nods and tucks a strand of hair behind my ear. 'I love you.'

Unlike last time we parted, the kiss that follows is not timid but confident, and I feel no guilt. Every time we begin to separate, we collide again somehow—until at last there is no other choice but to let go.

'Goodbye, Rosalie. Rose.' His voice is as shattered as a glass smashed against the wall, and I can sense he hopes to escape me now.

I want to reply, to wish him well, but the words are stuck like syrup in my throat. Before I can speak, he is gone to the front of the château, and soon simply gone.

After Charles has left, every waking moment at the château centres around the Somme. Of course, there was talk of it before as well, but I was far too preoccupied with more pleasant things to listen. A few of the wounded have recovered enough to come here, and the stories they tell are by every standard the most appalling ones I have heard during these past two years. It never ends, they say. The drumfire is as long as the day—and the night too, for that matter.

Charles

My mother takes a generous bite of the golden pastry, flakes raining down onto the napkin spread in her lap, and leans back in her armchair. 'Mademoiselle Allais is a perfectly nice girl, *mon chérie*, and a real beauty, too, not to speak of the family connections it would provide us with. You go and call on that girl and take her for a walk, and put on a smile.'

I sigh. My mother possesses a strong will. I am almost starting to regret that I did not return to my men at once after my stay at the château, or at least refrained from telling my family that I was coming home. When I wrote to say I would be staying in Paris, they were quicker than weasels to pack their perfumes and take the car to our apartment suite in the city centre.

I do pay a visit to Mademoiselle Allais—the daughter of an old family friend—and ask her to take a breath of fresh air with me, seeing as it is pointless to argue. The entire affair is just as dull as I imagined. There is nothing so bothersome as shallow acquaintances, unless they happen to be members of some exclusive club. Mademoiselle Allais is most certainly not that. Her governess chaperones us, and I cannot shake the feeling that this woman trailing behind us is surveying me, anxious that I might spirit her charge away to a secret dungeon.

The wind tries to pull Mademoiselle Allais' hazelnut hair from its coiffure, but it is no use; she has pushed down the heavily decorated hat with great force to hold everything in place. Her walk is slow, gliding, her figure the embodiment of grace under what she informs me is a ridiculously expensive lace blouse. She leans a matching parasol like a rifle against her right shoulder to offer protection against the lucid September sunshine. It was years since I last saw her at one of my mother's tea parties, but she has not changed one bit.

I let my gaze drift across the Parc des Buttes Chaumont. The breeze ruffles the lovely, deep green lawns. Elderly couples stroll arm in arm on the gravel paths, as do clusters of ladies and the odd gentleman.

I clear my throat. 'Let's sit down, shall we? On that bench there.'

Évelyne—for some reason, I find it easier to refer to her by her Christian name—accedes, and we pause together on the bench, at a proper distance. Despite everything separating my world from hers, I remember now that I must never place myself too close to one of society's darlings.

'Beautiful day, no? I think it would be splendid, were it only warmer,' she says.

'Well, yes, I suppose so.'

Silence.

'I believe you're fully aware of why we're here, Mademoiselle? If you'll forgive my frankness, I'd like us to sort this matter out as soon as possible. *Maman* will not leave me be until we do.'

'Honesty is very often regarded with suspicion and wrath, I have come to notice. Fortunately for you, I find honesty refreshing.'

I grant her an abrupt, choppy laugh.

Silence almost settles again, but Évelyne rescues us. 'Do you think I am ugly, in any way? No one has ever thought me ugly before, mind you.'

It is a confident statement, and one I appreciate. No, Mademoiselle Allais could never be called ugly. Her long face is thin and delicate with a high forehead, skin as smooth as cream, and hands as fine as those of a porcelain doll in a museum.

'I confess I haven't given it a great deal of thought, Mademoiselle, but no, I wouldn't want to be the first person to insult you so.'

'But you will not ask me to marry you? If you speak frankly, then so will I.'

I look down at my own hands before meeting her eyes again. 'No. My mother would be delighted, of course, but there are…obstacles.'

Évelyne bobs her head several times, a smile still flickering across her face. She caresses the lacquered handle of the parasol. 'I do like you, Monsieur D'Aboville, and I won't deny it. But I'd never beg on my knees for the affection of a man who does not wish to have me, nor could spark more than my own liking.'

'I'm glad. Nevertheless, I'm surprised that you should believe in love. You don't seem like the type.'

'Neither do you, but it appears we are both false to our looks.'

In front of us on the lawn, two girls and a small boy are fighting furiously over a toy horse. I watch as the biggest girl pulls the toy from the boy with rare determination. She is strong, though she cannot be older than seven or eight, and the expression on her chubby face is surprisingly cold. She would make a finer soldier than the other two, I figure, before hastily putting the thought away.

Évelyne pays no attention to the children but to a tiny, skittish lock of hair that has escaped her pins. 'May I ask who the lucky woman is?'

I draw a quick breath. She is sharp-minded. 'You may indeed, but you may not expect a satisfying answer. Nor may you tell *Maman*.'

'Very well, give me whatever answer there is, and I shan't speak a word of it.'

'The lucky woman, if that's what you want to call her, is English, and the most special one I ever set eyes on, as biased as it sounds. I doubt you'd take a liking to her.'

'*Mon Dieu!* You've become a romantic.'

'As I feared.' I rise from the bench and hold out my arm for her to place her hand on as we resume our walk. The governess, who has waited at a suitable distance, tows behind us.

'You did ask, and I did tell you,' I say.

'Yes, I reckon you did.'

The magic of Paris makes a more subtle impression on me than I imagine it would if I had come straight from the front. My months at the château have already allowed me to grow accustomed to a peaceful idyll, varied meals, a clean bed, and so forth. However, not even there could I do quite as I pleased. There were regulations just like in the trenches, and I could not very well venture beyond the premises of the house.

In Paris I am as close to free as I have been for the past two years. I can walk to the other end of the city or drive out to the countryside; I can have chocolate for breakfast. I do not have a curfew. I enjoy all these things to the fullest, counting the hours until I have to leave them behind again—yet these are lonely days.

Marcel is at the front, of course, and Michael still languishes in prison somewhere in another province. Henri, who was spared military training because of his frail health, works like a maniac maintaining the family estate, and Louis…Louis was killed a few months ago in East Africa where I am told he had transferred. I spend an evening sitting in a café and staring at the chequered floor, drinking to his memory. That is all, though. I have not seen him since the war engulfed us. He was a mere memory to me long before this.

My effervescent sisters, Constance and Marie-Louise, are as chatty as always, insisting on bickering with me like we did in the old days, dragging me with them to various entertainments. I love them for it, but often catch myself not hearing their rapid words, dreaming myself away to the convalescence centre. Is Rosalie still there, scurrying through the marble hallway, smiling at some other officer? No, I cannot allow myself to think like that. Wherever she is, she will keep her word to me, just like I intend to keep my own. And even if she does not, she was never truly mine to lose, as much as I hate admitting it.

There is only one person I do my best to avoid: *Maman*. I am being selfish, of course, but I cannot stand the way she criticises my every move and how there is nothing, nothing at all, that we seem to have in common. That was one of the many reasons I loved being at the Sorbonne: she was not there. Now, though, it is worse, because when we are close together in the apartment, my mother is becoming as aware of the distance between our minds as I am.

She twists her silk shawl between her fingers. 'Well, I wish you would simply listen to what I tell you, *mon chéri*, and you would see that you are behaving like a…like a…like a common churl who does not care one whit for good manners or consideration. You use foul language in front of your sisters, you show little interest in resuming your studies, you almost never speak with me at length like you used to—'

'You want us to speak at length? Then you must listen to me.' I halt in my pacing and sit down in the armchair opposite her, drawing a deep breath. 'I don't want to be rude, it's not that, but things have changed. I have changed. I don't know what to speak to you about when I can already sense you frowning at every story I have to tell.'

'Is that so? Well then, tell me a story.'

Her tart challenge makes me want to bundle her up and drive her out to the front. Instead, I pick a memory at random. 'There was an old man in my battalion—not truly old, I suppose, but some forty years. It was earlier this year and some of the aging and the teenagers had been recruited in order to keep up the numbers. That was the thing, see. The man's two sons were also in the same company. They weren't very bright, or maybe they

were just inexperienced, because they played catch with one of
our grenades.

'Someone had the brilliant idea to pull the security pin to raise
the stakes. I don't have to tell you they both died that day. I had
to tell the old man, though, and when we rotated behind the lines,
he hid in a brothel and refused to come out at all. In the end, they
shot him for desertion.'

My mother's cheeks are ablaze, her voice a hiss. 'A brothel?'

'But of course, *Maman!* How else do you think we keep the
troops from mutinying?'

We stare at one another in incredulous silence.

'Perhaps you were right. I do find that story of yours
tasteless.'

'And that's what concerns you? I say *they* shot the man, but I
was their officer. It was I who reported him, because I had no
other choice. Can't you see why that sort of thing bothers me?'

Her grey eyes meet mine, but that is where our similarities
end, and she appears content with twisting her shawl tighter.

'This,' I say and stand up, turning to face her once I reach the
door. 'This is why we do not chat the hours away.'

It is a miracle, for I am glad to return to the trenches. My new
posting dampens my mood—the Somme has a gruesome
reputation—but I figure it cannot be vastly different from Ypres,
Champagne, Verdun, and Artois. Lieutenant-Colonel Trembley
will likely be there, as will Escargot and Gérard, if they are still
alive.

'Don't get up to any mischief,' Marie-Louise says and winks
while I climb the steps to the train carriage.

'I can't promise anything.'

Chapter twenty-one

Rosalie

I HATE THE convalescent centre with a passion. The pristine rooms and high-strung atmosphere make me itch. I used to be relieved and grateful to have been stationed here, but now I feel as useless as a doll on a pedestal. I miss home, too. I need a break. I need to speak to my own family and friends, as scattered as that circle is these days.

The matron grants my request for leave seemingly without hesitation. Days later, I am once more sitting opposite Papa at the dinner table while Daya serves us. It is like jumping from one world to another, from uniforms and rules to a crackling hearth and childhood memories.

Papa swallows without chewing. 'How is your brother, eh?'

'Quite well. He wrote to me about the enemy aviators they are up against. There's a new fighter squadron, the Jagdstaffer 11, I think the Germans call it. One of the pilots is apparently particularly good, even more calculating than Fred. And how is Isabel?' I marvel at the shreds that were once a close-knit family. While the rift between Isabel and Fred already existed—and I still do not know what caused it—the war has made Papa drift away from his son and me from my sister.

'Good, good. Still in Rouen.'

'Do you always get such plentiful meals as this? Now that conscription is the order of the day, rationing will surely follow.'

'I'm not a picky eater, Rosalie. Mark my words, if they try to starve us, I'll be the last man standing.'

I want to laugh but instead press my napkin to my mouth, swallowing bile, and push my chair back. 'Forgive me,' I manage once I trust myself to put the napkin down. 'I don't feel well at all. I've not been able to stomach much lately.'

Papa frowns but remains seated, contrary to etiquette. 'Nonsense. Daya can make you something with chicken if you'd rather have that.'

The thought alone makes me nauseous. 'I mean it. I'm going upstairs for a nap.'

'A nap?' Papa calls after me while I climb the stairs. 'One can't nap at eight o'clock!'

I ignore him; I am tired and I want my nap more than anything right now. In fact, I might as well go to bed for the evening.

I am out there, out amidst the soaked filth and feverish tension that lies like a suffocating veil over the landscape. The sky is bare and naked—vulnerable, if the sky can be such a thing. Not a single skinny, dead tree stands. They have all been blown to pieces.

I cannot see them clearly, the soldiers. They move around me, a phantom mass without name and without aim. Their faces are blurry, yet their eyes are razor-sharp, cold glass pearls. Frightened eyes, like those of animals tied down to be slaughtered, with quick, twinkling movements and bizarrely small pupils.

The air is not filled with missiles and shells as it ought to be, no, it is devastatingly quiet and peaceful.

Harry stands in front of me with a peculiar, serene smile. 'Queer, don't you think?' His voice is like plush velvet.

I cannot answer him. I can never talk in dreams.

However, my late husband continues. 'Can I buy you some ice cream, Rosalie? I hope you don't mind if I do.'

Just when his voice dies down again and he turns away from me, someone shouts 'Coward!', and a bullet pierces Harry's head. His body never smacks to the ground. Rather, he walks towards the convenient ice cream shop that has magically appeared in No Man's Land, painted in sunny yellow and cotton-candy-pink.

The scene morphs into a wide-stretched ballroom with glistening lights and crêpe paper snowflakes dangling from the ceiling. Full skirts are sweeping and twirling across the polished floor. The girls are all glamorous, while the boys have their black shoes all right, but are other than that in uniform. One man alone is in civilian dress: Mr Atkins, who accompanies the dance band on the small stage at the very end of the room with a violin coming to life under the spell of his hands.

A pair of almond eyes and unruly hair, a pale face and a jawline marked with three birthmarks. I want to throw my arms around his neck in pure relief and delight, but of course, I cannot.

'How now, Rose? Do you by any chance know Mark Crewel?' His mouth is smeared with clotted blood, his voice saturated with same drowsy ripple as the music.

There is Laura on the dance floor, an open wound rapidly spreading across her chest, a demure bouquet of blossoms in her hands.

'Grand, isn't she? I hope it doesn't vex you.' Charles says. 'Oh, here they come.'

And indeed, the pretty snowflakes in the ceiling transform into deadly missiles falling with a whistle towards our tilted faces—

The sheets are cold and clammy with my sweat. I must have screamed, because footsteps echo in the corridor, and after a knock, Minnie pulls the door open. Her plain nightgown hangs loosely from her shoulders and she is clutching a dripping candle. 'Are you all right, Miss? I heard noises—you woke me.'

I pull the cover up from my feet, where I have kicked it in my sleep. 'Quite all right, thank you. You can go back to bed now.'

She snorts and nods, shutting the door after her as she leaves.

I sink back into the plump pillows.

I know very well what has been ailing me other than the nightmares. My marriage to Harry was certainly a brief one, but I have seen enough of the world to realise my condition. I have missed my monthly course twice now. My nausea is persisting; parts of my body swell slowly, slowly. A scandal was one of the risks I took when asking Charles to come to my room that night in Rouen—and the nights that followed—and this was the other, more distant, more daunting risk. Of course, we took what little precautions there were to be taken, but to no avail, it appears.

I refuse to dive head-first into the tempting alarm. This time, I must be like my brother and sister: calm and composed when facing threats of disaster. I cannot know that Charles will come back, or when. I cannot know whether he is still willing to marry me. If I do nothing but allow this babe to grow inside me, I will have signed my own social death warrant, and I will never glimpse anything remotely like freedom again.

I shudder at my own thoughts. Am I not supposed to be brimming with motherly instincts? I have been taught to put my children and husband above everything, yet I have already been disloyal to Harry more times than I can count, and what I am about to do is perhaps worse... But I dare not keep it. Whenever my willpower fails me, the fear succeeds in renewing my determination. I have seen what becomes of the mothers of bastards, and I have no intention of joining their lot.

Trembling, I flex my arms and bend the coat hanger until I am holding a crooked metal stick in my hand. Forcing myself to stop shaking, I hitch up my skirts with a soft rustle, the coat hanger in a hard grip. The ice-cold steel makes me flinch as I trace it up the naked skin along my thighs. I close my eyes. The discomfort soon escalates to a gut-wrenching pain, and I have to remind myself over and over again like a chant: *What is the alternative?* To raise a bastard child without a father in the midst of a raging war? No. I keep pushing. There is no turning back now. Finally, *finally* the first splash of warm blood wets my clenched fingers. I push the weapon another dreadful inch, choking back a shriek.

Minnie informs me with bewildered eyes that she found me on the bathroom floor. She says Papa used the handgun he usually keeps in his desk to break the lock. The family doctor, McWright, has been to see me.

My shame is dense, the sickness I feel overwhelming. Empty womb, empty heart... For surely it must be so, that no woman with kindness and love in her would do something as brutal as murder a child? Why else would the matter be so unspeakable?

If Charles does return, I will have to wait and see whether I can bear keeping my secret from him. If he must know, he must know, and if he does not love me, I will have one less obstacle in my life. After all, it was his love and my own that landed me here to begin with. I barely recognise myself. The girl I was two years ago could never have been this pragmatic. I am unsure whether I should be glad or not over the change in me.

I remain in bed for a few weeks, receiving Doctor McWright at regular intervals. He says nothing of my actions; I suspect Papa is paying him extra to keep quiet.

Papa and I are about as talkative as two wooden boxes ourselves. His face is uncharacteristically mild when he looks at me, though, and I am grateful that he does not ask a myriad of questions. They will come, naturally, and I will answer them as honestly as I am able, but first I intend to put distance between myself and what happened. I can only pray the air between us does not fester and grow stale in the meantime.

I was lucky, Doctor McWright tells me. I could have done more damage than I did, and recovery should be imminent. Each day, the pain subsides and my strength returns. I dare not ask if I have made myself barren for life.

There is nothing to do but to return. Not to the convalescent centre, not after I seek permission to be transferred elsewhere, but to one of the freshly erected field hospitals. They erupt like weeds in the French soil, for there is a constant need of another one and another still. Though the number of beds is rapidly growing, there are never enough of them to house all the injured.

There, I know I shall be able to mute the unwelcome voices in my head by focusing on a new set of professional miseries. The soldiers will all be badly damaged, indeed the entire place will be one cluster of struggles, and oddly enough this works marvels when trying to forget one's own problems. Moreover, I can escape Mary's scorching glances which have followed me ever since the moment I slapped her.

The hospital is simple, consisting of rows of barracks and tents that shine brightly amongst a thousand shades of brown and grey. Between them stretches a basic network of duckboards to walk on. Figures clad in white and blue are scattered along them, going about their daily tasks, reminding me of bustling insects. My fancy shoes that were ideal for the château's clean floors stick stubbornly in the thick mud when I am forced to venture outside the duckboards. With every reluctant step I take, another layer of dirt adds to the sole. I have to bend my neck to enter the spacious tents. Empty, rickety beds form tight rows under the white fabric, waiting to be filled with delirious soldiers. Neatly folded blankets rest upon the thin mattresses in perfect formation with the pillows. There is something harrowingly neat about it all—so far.

Two days later, a cascade of patients flood in.

One of them in particular attracts my attention. The man is lying very still and quiet with his hospital gown buttoned up to his chin. His hands are clumsy lumps of white bandage, and nothing can be seen of his face, because this, too, is wrapped up like a butterfly's cocoon. Only one nasty, gaping hole where the man's mouth ought to be allows for a space in the bandaging.

One of the nurses resolutely sticks a thermometer down the pitch dark of the hole, and the temperature proves satisfactory.

First, the cocooned soldier repulses me, but then curiosity takes the upper hand. Once the nurse has snapped up the thermometer again and walked away with swaggering hips, I sneak up to the bedside. There, I stand tense and unsure for a few seconds. I tug at the patient's sleeve. 'Excuse me? Is there…is there anything I could do for you?'

At first, there is no answer, and I curse my own stupidity. What did I expect him to say?

Then sounds a surprisingly clear and rippling voice, like a mountain brook. 'If Nurse could help me to write a letter, that would be…just great. My hands…' He falters and holds up the white lumps with a helplessness that makes something in my chest itch.

'Oh—of course. If you'll just let me fetch a pen and a piece of paper, we'll see what we can do.' I return shortly thereafter and sit down by his bed. 'To whom should I address the letter?'

'No one. I don't know. I haven't…haven't told my father about my face.'

'Do you want me to tell him for you?'

The cocooned soldier shrugs faintly. 'He'll know once I get home.'

I put down the pen and paper and swallow the pity stinging me. I have to stop taking personal interests in these men if I am to be an efficient nurse. I have to be professional for once, cold even. 'Then I can't spend my time here, Sir. I'm sorry.'

I rise and do not look back at his sorry figure slumped in the bed.

At night in the dormitory tent, I sit curled up under my thin blanket and rest my chin on my knees while brushing my hair. After the war I would perhaps like a haircut—a short one, like the fashionable, shiny bobs starting to appear in the magazines I occasionally get my hands on. I do not know if I would be able to carry it well, though. I can imagine it takes a handsome head to do that.

I let my mother's old hairbrush rest on my pillow, its backside shimmering in the warm reflection of the lamp. I then unfold the letter from Charles, which I received with the mail this morning after giving him my new address, and scan the smudged writing for the third time today.

Rose,

I'm not a writer. You know that. But I'll tell you everything there is to tell, though my life is monotonous at the moment. There is not so much to be done about that.
I'll start with the paper I read the other night. I can't for my life understand why we aren't living in Bologna together, like the people in one of the articles do. Don't you think that would be grand, with all the gondolas? Maybe that's Venice, but no matter. I'd write you a bloody sonnet and everything, if you like.

It continues for three compactly scribbled pages, and as I read, I am swept away for a few glorious moments. Charles is actually a fair writer, despite what he might think.

I share the dormitory with eleven other girls and women. There is neither space nor finances for the luxury of one or two roommates, let alone a space of my own like I had at the convalescent centre. Once we have put the dim lights out, our chatter dies down quickly and what remains is distant moaning from the soldiers' tents along with a cat's meowing and our own muffled breaths. I lie in the dark, unable to drift asleep because

154

of the thoughts buzzing in my head now that I have no chores to tend to.

Anything could have happened during the days that have passed since Charles wrote the letter. Maybe his corpse is being shipped home to his mother whom he told me about, the woman who notoriously lives off flaky pastries. Maybe he will be buried in the field instead, like so many others.

Charles must live. Oh God, he must live. Sudden panic, the feeling of being pulled under water with no escape, seizes me. He is *not* dead. He cannot be. I would have known. I would have sensed it. I repeat this to myself like a mantra.

Chapter twenty-two

Charles

THE OCTOBER WIND is ruthless. My impression of the Somme has not been favourable, so to speak, but I have seen horrors before. Here in the support trench, the rough weather is more present on my mind than the troops gushing across No Man's Land where I myself was days ago. It is easier to think of autumn, so I do, except when some soldier or other sneaks up on us officers to fish for advice we do not have.

'But what do you think it means?' a man in my battalion says, holding up a paper.

'Perhaps it does not mean anything,' Lieutenant-Colonel Trembley says with a frustrated sigh, leaning back against the sand sacks.

The other man, whose name I cannot recall, squints to examine the letter in detail, searching for signs of his wife's supposed infidelity.

'I think…' Lieutenant De Villiers says gleefully, approaching us with long steps, 'I think your pretty wife is—as we speak—offering herself up to a fat innkeeper just to have somewhere warm to sleep, considering that the house might have been mowed down.'

The man with the letter stares at him, disbelief and rage clearly battling behind his eyes. 'What?'

De Villiers puts on a sticky smile. 'Why, yes. The Huns are everywhere in that region. What makes you think they left your village as they found it?' He is a tall, slender man with hair slicked to his scalp, reeking of pomade. His lips twitch to one side when he speaks, out of habit from holding a cigarette between them. The high forehead and Roman nose create a distinguished look that irritates me every time I see him. Trembley and I have decided to keep De Villiers, though, solely because he has the extraordinary gift of being able to find food for several men anywhere and anytime.

'Thank you for that, Lieutenant. However, I don't think we need your point of view. I suggest you get back to your post,' I say.

De Villiers smiles again and wiggles his feet. Without doubt, he has dry, warm socks. 'There's no need to be rude, *Mon Commandant*. Who knows—you may regret it one day.' After a deliberate kick at Trembley's knapsack, he struts back to his designated section of trench.

I try to burn a hole in his back with my glare. Of course, most men would rather have their food ration eaten by rats than speak thus to a superior, but De Villiers is not most men. If I disciplined him, I would get some kind of unwelcome surprise as retaliation within days.

'Do you think so, too?' the man with the wife asks, crossing his arms. 'Do you think he's right?'

Trembley sighs again and I shrug, shuffling a deck of cards. The little story about the wife and the house might very well be true, but there is no use in stirring up further conversation of this sort.

'Leave us, *Soldat*. Go clean your rifle,' Trembley says at last.

I push my helmet down over my eyes and do my best to find a comfortable part of the dugout to sit in. No matter how furiously I shut my eyes, seeing dancing fairy lights and strips of fire, I cannot sleep. All is as it ought to be in our support trench— German and French artillery is raging; men are chatting—but the familiar choir of noise is annoying rather than comforting.

Still, I am tired. Before the war, in another life and another world, I did not think it was possible to be this tired. I feel old. I *am* old, in a peculiar way, as is everyone in my battalion, save only Gérard. We have seen much and are often close to dying, and few of our friends have their good health. Is that not what usually defines old age?

I abandon my vain pursuit of sleep and slip my hand into my pocket. My fingers graze the chipped paint on the box of mints. I wish there were real mints in it, because I have run out of toothpaste and my breath must be worse than ever at this point.

Rosalie… She gave me that box and I gave her a note. That silly, saucy proposal note. I have not regretted writing it a single moment. Perhaps Rosalie holds it in her palm sometimes, a faint caramel summer tan on her wrists… The thought of her plants a seed of, if not harmony, then calm, and sleep at once feels closer at hand.

We rotate back to a reserve trench that is not a proper trench at all, though in a pleasant way. Barely within reach of enemy artillery, the landscape behind us is soft and green. After a couple of days I even approve one of the men's requests to take a stroll in the meadow. It is a highly unusual sight: a lonesome figure walking with his hands in his pockets along the trench, boots squelching in the wet grass. He knows perfectly well that if he tries to run the snipers will pluck him without me having to give the order.

No such thing happens, nor do we appear to be the target of shelling. Even our own artillery is situated far from this odd backwater. I telephone headquarters to confirm our good fortune, without making any mention of the outing I am planning to boost the men's morale.

'A temporary placement,' the scratchy voice on the other end tells me. 'Don't worry, *Commandant*. You and your troops will be transferred before you know it.'

'Thank you. I will do my best not to despair.'

As it happens, my decision to bring a small group with me on a so-called expedition to take advantage of nature is a choice I will come to regret. Maybe the mint box actually brings bad luck. I am heading the line of men when a blast plunges me to the side. I roll like a barrel, my breath pressed out of me, my eyes stinging. I struggle to my feet and glimpse the crater. If we are under attack, it will be safer down there than trying to run back to the trench, and so I run towards it, rubbing the dust out of my eyes. The others must to have had the same idea, because several figures are already crouching in the crater when I slide down into it.

A moment passes. There is no more fire. It must have been an old shell buried in the earth that detonated because of our own damn clumsiness. Because of my recklessness.

'*Mon Commandant?*' We are missing men.'

I curse under my breath. Of course we are missing men. Eight pairs of eyes are looking at me with expectation, quietly pleading with me to do what they do not want to, to do my duty and find the two soldiers missing from our battered group. The only choice is to obey, and I push my helmet down, hoping that the shade will conceal my unwillingness. The silence is denser than a block of steel, leaving no room for my own spinning thoughts. For reasons I cannot explain, peering over the top of a shell hole is worse than going over the top of a parapet.

To my shame, I only remember the full name of one of the soldiers who are sprawled a few feet from the edge of the hole. Achille Plessis is an unlucky man. The other one is no doubt dead, eyes staring glassily into mine, unseeing, head bashed against the ground. Plessis, however, is trying to reach for something without success, his chest rising and falling as it ought to—and his legs torn off mid-thigh, flashing white bone.

I clench the stones I used to climb this far up, draw a deep breath, and turn to the men waiting below. 'Jérôme? Jérôme Plessis? Your brother has been injured.'

Jérôme is a man of perhaps twenty-seven or twenty-eight, who wears his wife's stockings wrapped around his wrist to remind him of her. Now he emerges from the small cluster of people and climbs the wall of the hole before I get the chance to warn him. There is naught to be done for Achille, the blood loss being too great, but we ask anyways.

'Is there anything you want? A picture? I have one here of *Maman*—' Jérôme says and digs in his pocket, but his brother does not care to look at the elderly woman in the photograph.

'Stretch…stretch my legs for me. They're itching.'

I exchange a glance with Jérôme. We are spared trying to answer Achille, because when we look back, he has already gone limp. Jérôme opens and closes his mouth before stashing the picture in his pocket again and wiping his brow on his wife's stocking.

'*C'est la vie. Désolé.*'

He says nothing.

The accident does not result in any consequences on my behalf, although I almost wish otherwise. I have the blood of countless men on my hands: the Germans I have killed, the Germans I have sent my men to kill, the men I have sent to kill those Germans. This feels different. The outing was my idea, not an order I had to carry out. However, I am too tired to weep or rage or even think more about it. People die. For all I know, those two soldiers could have been dead the very day we return to the frontline, regardless. Their faces will haunt me someday, some night, but not now.

De Villiers leans in until his shoulder touches that of the other man, meanwhile digging in his pocket and producing two cigarettes, one of which he offers to his friend. They hold their little treasures lightly between two fingers in a strikingly similar manner, smoke trickling from between their lips

The other man is of short stature with a boyish build, yet he cannot be younger than twenty-five judging by his face. His complexion is that of honey, his head broad, his movements soft.

I close *Decamerone* with a smack and place it on the improvised table filling up our deep dugout. Lieutenant-Colonel Trembley sits opposite me with his coat bundled up in his lap, stitching through the coarse material to mend a rip. His fingers are dotted with red where the needle has slipped and penetrated his skin.

'Shouldn't your servant be doing that for you?' I tease. 'Surely the regulations say something about it.'

'It's supposed to be good for the nerves.'

'De Villiers has not been *too* agonising lately, has he?'

'No, indeed not.' Trembley keeps his eyes on his fumbling craft. 'It's the new fellow, Chevotet. Emile Chevotet.'

'They seem fond of one another.'

'I've heard it said they were quite well acquainted before the war. He's just been transferred to this unit. Thick as thieves, I gather.'

I arch an eyebrow. 'And that's all there is to it, you think? *I* think there is something more to it, only nobody will actually say so.'

Trembley's mouth is one thin line before he at last speaks again. 'What are you implying, D'Aboville? Nothing unseemly, I warrant?'

I tilt my head back to stare at the mud ceiling, specks of dirt occasionally drifting down in my eyes. 'The *world* is unseemly, so why not be realists about it?' I trace the almost unnoticeable patterns in the densely packed earth before returning my gaze to my companion, who manages to hurt himself with the needle again.

'And you would not find it repelling? Outrageous?'

'I don't believe in the popular definition of outrageous. These days…these days it doesn't matter much. I'm not one to deprive people of the only solace they find out here, and neither are you.'

'We mustn't have this kind of crude discussion again. After all, we have no real reason to form suspicions.'

I cease listening to him at that point, and turn to watch De Villiers and Emile Chevotet instead. How I envy them if it is true! That society would taunt and condemn them seems trivial when considering the joys of having one's beloved next to oneself.

Mademoiselle Allais was right. I *have* become a romantic, at least to some extent, and what an unpleasant fate it is.

Chapter twenty-three

Rosalie

THE AIR IS cool and flushed with sunshine, which animates the grimacing man's face as he stumbles inside the tent. He is as worn a creature as I ever saw, with a torn German uniform and a rickety limp. His eyes flicker like those on an injured deer, and his hair is the kind of dirty that will take an hour of washing to remedy. There is no telling what shade it was before the trenches got to him. His hands, pressed against his belly, are the deepest red, and the red drips down on the wooden floor like so many glass beads.

Doctor Barnaby—one of men in charge of the field hospital—stares at the man for a moment before collecting himself. 'Are you German?'

The man with the red hands nods, unable to speak, it appears.

We VADs and nurses glance at each other with doubt. After all, he is a Hun. No one moves.

Then Doctor Barnaby has a change of heart. 'For the love of God, fetch some bandages!'

Relief flashes in the man's face and he brings his hands together in what could be interpreted as a prayer of thanksgiving. When he releases his grip on his gut, his entrails spill out and pile up on the floor. The man gapes like a fish. His knees buckle and he drops down. The rest of us, including the patients who are conscious and awake, can only watch in horrified silence. Our German supplicant is dead. His eyes stare blankly at the tent ceiling while the puddle of blood around him grows. He must have walked miles with only his hands keeping him whole and alive, and now it has all been for nothing—not that I truly believe any of the doctors could have stitched him together, anyhow.

'Someone find a stretcher. A stretcher, *now!*' Doctor Barnaby barks.

Before I have the time to recollect myself, a stretcher has been brought forward, and I manage to break free from my paralysis in order to help one of the nurses roll the man onto it so that he may be carried off. The other woman hands me a bucket and a spade, then leaves me. I look at the tools, my confusion and disbelief similar to that I spot in the dead soldier's face. The rest of the staff have already scuttled out of sight and escaped the ghastly scene. It appears to have fallen on my unfortunate lot to scrape up the intestines from the floor and scrub away the blood as best I can.

I thought I had chased away every hint of squeamishness, but my instincts are screaming at me to run. *Run, run, run and keep running.* So I do. I drop the bucket with a resounding clatter and turn on my heel. Out of the tent, zig-zagging along the paths of duckboards, down in the mud and onto the withered, frostbitten grass. I pull my dress up above my ankles to keep myself from tripping on the hem. I sprint like a maniac. My breath comes in gasps and my heart pounds as if to bruise my lungs. My chest and stomach burn and I taste metal on my tongue. My feet work themselves forward, my expensive shoes taking me surprisingly far.

Finally, the voices screaming in my head tone down to a harrowing, tingling whisper before petering out entirely. I have exorcised the panic. My steps falter and I stumble over my own feet, falling heavily on my hands and knees. The grass stains will be a challenge to clean off, just like blood. I rest on my back, catching my breath, waiting for the rhythm of my heart to return to normal. The freezing air bites my cheeks and hands, slips down my throat and chills my whole body.

What on earth am I doing here?

I am not a little girl anymore…I am not a sheltered lamb. I ought to be in the field hospital cleaning up like a proper volunteer. However, I cannot trust my legs anymore, so I remain there on my back among the trees, studying the skeletal branches against the stark white sky.

A quarter of an hour passes, I think, before footsteps approach. A young VAD with a pointed nose ducks under a low-hanging branch and comes towards me. 'There you are, then. I've been looking for you.'

'Yes, here…here I am.'

The woman sniffles. 'Well what are you lying there for? Come on, get up.'

'I'd rather not. It is nice here. Peaceful.'

'Nobody likes guts but that doesn't mean we haven't all got them. And it sure doesn't mean nobody has got to scrub them off the floor when they happen to fall out of some Hun. That's just not how it works.' She sniffles again and I start to wonder whether this is a habit or if she has the influenza. Her accent is distinctly Irish. I must be certain not to mention the 'trouble' there was this Easter.

'Perhaps. But nobody likes guts, do they?'

She snickers and scratches a rash on her jaw.

I pull myself to my feet and together we trace our way back to the hospital, the air heavy with snow.

'No, no they don't,' the other VAD continues. 'Anyhow, it is gone now, but don't think you won't get a fine and dandy scolding. Oh, it will be such fun to see!'

I shoot her a glare. 'I can imagine you should think so.'

The field hospital is now in clear view, bustling with monotonous activity. The knot in my throat tightens when we step onto the duckboards and my companion opens the door to one of the barracks to let us both inside.

'The name is Miss Butler, for all that it matters. Susan Butler—you may call me Susan.'

Before I get the chance to answer, one of the nurses in charge, Mrs Hader, has risen from her chair at the desk opposite the door. Despite being a mere inch taller than myself, she appears to tower above me.

Susan knows her own good and quickly retreats to the corner of the barrack with a poorly disguised smirk. I both detest and envy her for it, although her presence has cheered me a tad.

'So, you have decided to join us once more, Miss…?' Mrs Hader lingers at every word, balancing her tone between hostile and professional.

'Mrs Bride.' It feels strange to pronounce those words, for they are true but it seems to me it was a lifetime ago that I married Harry. I might be impulsive but I have learnt never to stare a dangerous animal in the eye, hence I keep my gaze on the floorboards. They are clean without a stain.

'Mrs Bride. I would have you know and *remember* that a dutiful VAD always does what she is told. It is not so much about specific tasks as it is about the principle of obedience, and I must say I'm thoroughly disappointed. Perhaps you believe I care about fancy upbringings, but when you're here, you cannot afford to be delicate. Delicate cracks and breaks.'

I nod with feigned humility and mumble an apology.

Mrs Hader's feathery brows come together in one line across her forehead. She promptly instructs Susan and me—although I cannot gather what Susan might have done to displease her—to be off immediately and take on the laborious task of washing bandages. Dulcet relief washes over me for an instant; after all, bandages are only linen. Linen stained with blood and pus and dirt, by all means, but nonetheless plain cloth. Harmless.

We make our way to the washing area behind the storage barn on the south side of the hospital premises. A heap of bandages the size of a bed is lying in a big trunk, exuding the rancid, sickening stench of old body fluids. I resolutely shake off the shiver running down my spine. This is nothing, nothing at all. I have dealt with far worse.

We take to soaking and scrubbing the bandages, then we stretch them out to dry. After a while, the washing water shifts in in red, and I have difficulty seeing my own hands as I rub the linen back and forth until it is as clean as one of my old dresses. Perhaps if I could only wear those dresses now, I would feel clean, too.

Susan is an effective worker but has an intrusive and talkative nature. She latches out and grabs my wrist, inspecting each of my fingers with arched eyebrows. 'You're not married then? Where's that shiny ring? You said your name was Mrs Bride.'

I withdraw my hand and let it fall down with a splash back in the lukewarm water to protect myself from her impertinence. 'Was. I *was* married—not any longer. I still carry the name.'

'Oh. We-ell, they die like flies, I daresay!'

I stare at her in furious search for anything I could possibly say to such a remark. She is right, though. They do die like flies. I shake my head to myself. 'And you? Do you mean to marry?'

'Why would I? No, no husband for me, thank you very much.'

We stay on our flattened knees, our fingers already blistering.

'Not that I am—you know,' she adds after a few moments, wobbling on her knees like a penguin as if to add some adversity to our dull chore. 'I'm going to become a lawyer.'

This time, I fail to suppress a giggle. 'You could never become a lawyer! You'd need an education, a real degree, and you'd have to magically transform into a man.'

'Go on, laugh! But you'll see. Everything will be different after the war.'

'I suppose things will have to be different after all this, yes, but not *that* different.'

While we proceed to folding the bandages that have dried, and the day creeps to its end, I begin to wonder just how much the world will have changed.

The following evening, after we have finally been released from our penalty of washing, I lie awake in the dormitory for a good while. I toss and turn on the flat pillow and experiment with wrapping the blankets around me in every imaginable way. I even try curling up to a tiny ball. It is no use. The others are constantly moving in their squeaking beds, some of them snoring, startling me every time I am close to drifting off.

Susan, though, is also awake, lying on her back with her hair spread like a halo around her head. Her sunburnt arms are flexed and stretched out, and she is holding a book, reading in the light of a single candle. Occasionally, she gives a loud sniffle, reminding me that she is still present.

My thoughts stray to Laura, whom I have not seen it what might as well be forever. It is strange, because there never were two individuals more different than Laura and Susan. One is the scrawny picture of Irish coarseness while the other is the essence of peaches and cream, voluptuous and laughing. What they do have in common is their fierce conviction of the rights of women—at least I think Susan shares it—and their controversial ambitions. I wish I was more like that, I truly do. Perhaps I am and simply have not fully realised it. I suppose…I suppose I have always been a product of the world as I knew it before, and I am attempting to transit into the unknown, while they are products of the new and exciting, rushing ahead too fast.

After perhaps twenty minutes, I am desperate to strike up conversation, for I cannot stand this silence interspersed with guttural snores and petite sniffles. I prop myself on my elbow. 'What are you reading?'

Susan holds up the navy-blue cover so that I can read the title: *Penalties and their Lawful Principles.* It reminds of something Charles might read, or something he would read had he not been prematurely snatched from his law studies. In an instant, longing spreads through my veins and stings me.

Susan must have caught a glimpse of my expression in the candlelight. 'What now? You look as if you've seen a ghost.' Her accent is more apparent than ever, and I have to quench the impulse to ask her to please speak clearly if she will.

'I—it is nothing.' I sit and sink back against the cold wall with the blanket pulled up over my knees, hands tugging at the fabric. Sleeping is now naught but a faraway wish.

Susan does not put the book aside, but keeps reading. 'You're not good at pretending.'

'If you must know, I'm missing, and worrying, and feeling frightfully alone. Everyone does, of course, but I must be unusually sensitive about such things.'

'What's the object of your missing and worrying, then?' Her voice bears a hint of genuine interest, much to my astonishment.

I should guard my tongue. Still, I am overcome with the urge to reveal the secrets locked up inside me, even if it is to Susan. Therefore, I tell her about my time at the convalescent centre and the months since I left it. I tell her all but the most private details, finishing with a trembling breath.

Susan at last sits and closes her book. 'It seems like destructive business to me. I've never been in love and I've no intention to be either. It must be a pain in the arse.'

I sip on the water I keep by the bed and her language nearly makes me choke. 'It is. It steps on your heart until there's nothing but a mashed lump in your chest, but you want it nonetheless. And then it hurts again, and it makes you wish you had been more cautious.'

'There never is any point olagonin'.'

'Any point in what?'

Susan throws herself on the mattress with an ear-splitting noise from the springs. She opens the book again and flicks through the crisp pages back to where she left off. 'Sometimes you're just too *British*. Or maybe it's your own self. I'm too racked to think about it. What are you doing after the war?'

'I don't know. I think that's why I keep coming back, keep nursing. Maybe I could publish something. I enjoy scribbling all sorts of…stories.' While this is true, I have not tried to write anything but letters since I left for Rouen the first time.

'Let me read them.'

I laugh as quietly as I can in order to avoid waking the others. 'I don't have them with me. And writing isn't as glamorous as some of the other things one might do. When I was little, I wanted to be in the movies, but I'm not pretty enough.'

'No, you're not. You *are* easy on the eyes, in a sweet way, but not in that overly dramatic way that they call beautiful nowadays.'

'No,' is all I can figure to say. I did not speak with the vain presumption that she would contradict me, yet she is even more straightforward than I expected.

We sit silent for a while, and oddly enough, I feel at peace. *It steps on your heart until there is nothing but a mashed lump in your chest.* These might be the truest words I ever spoke. What I did not say was how immensely glad I am that my heart is no longer untouched and shiny. Perhaps I once wished I had been left as I was before, but I have begun to cherish my experiences, even those that have hurt. If nothing else, at least now I have memories worth telling about.

Chapter twenty-four

Rosalie

I AM PRESSING a damp cloth to the temple of one of the wounded when he mumbles a few coarse words in delirium. *'Sie kommen…schnell…'* The man is pale, a gleaming circlet of sweat crowning his forehead, the peak of his prominent Cupid's-bow dripping.

I flinch, withdrawing my hand from his head, casting a hasty glance over my shoulder to assure myself that no one is within hearing distance. Two other VADs are sitting in a corner, chatting quietly while sterilizing scalpels for the surgeons. However, they are too preoccupied to notice me.

'You're German?' I whisper, dread and perplexity stirring inside me. Apart from the man who spilled his guts out, I have neither seen nor heard of enemy troops in an English hospital.

The soldier offers no reply, but I receive one clear enough when he utters another string of words I recognize as German. He must be hallucinating, or perhaps just dreaming. Nothing exposes a person's true self like sleep talk can do.

I drop the cloth to the basin of water at my feet, rise, and walk away, clenching my hands between the folds of my dress and apron. The fresh air outside the tent does nothing to help clear my thoughts like I hoped it would. *A German. A Hun.* They have killed so many… Tens of thousands of telegrams sent to unfortunate families, tens of thousands of wooden crosses still smelling of resin. For all I know, it might even be hundreds of thousands. And yet they are not personally to blame for the war. They could not prevent it any more than we could, or the French, or the common little citizens of any other nation. Every country in this conflict have killed, not just the Germans. Nevertheless, I cannot find it in my heart to forgive the wounded man for his allegiance. All logic, all reason escapes my grasp right now. The soldier must have arrived in his uniform. The chiefs of staff must be aware of him, so reporting the matter would make no difference. What then can I do? What *should* I do?

I give my shoes their hundredth layer of mud as I make my way to the nearby mess hall, my apron scooped up in a knot in my hand.

Susan is devouring a bowl of brown beans and a spongy slice of bread when I spot her, and I have to pull at her arm to attract her full attention. '*What?*'

I squat down to whisper my freshly obtained knowledge in her ear, and immediately regret doing so when the chewed beans splatter out, landing on the back of my hand. Susan's feelings on the matter must be even fiercer than my own, because her face reminds me of heated coal. Perhaps it was foolish of me to tell, but I had to get it out before it started to chafe against my nerves. Funny, how once upon a time I used to be good at keeping secrets.

'What does it mean? What was it he said?'

'I don't know. I think he was afraid of someone coming for him.'

'And so they should! I don't nurse Huns.' Susan emits a distressed sniffle.

'What then? I don't want him here, but if he has already been admitted, there's nothing to be done.'

'Nothing to be done? I can think of a few things.' She empties another spoonful of beans in her mouth, gripping the bowl until her knuckles whiten.

'We could always sleep on it.'

She shakes her head and carries her clean-scraped dishes to the washing station, me following in her footsteps to inquire for my own meal.

While we say nothing more on the matter that day, it is far from settled.

I make my final round long after dusk has fallen, as is common practice in wintertime. A silhouette is hunched over one of the beds. As I approach, I discern the contours of a young woman sitting with one knee on the chest of the man lying under her. She is holding down a pillow firmly over the patient's nose and mouth, suffocating him slowly, slowly. The flickering light from the lamp standing on one of the nearby tables highlights Susan's clenched jaw. The man—the German—flaps his limbs, flailing weakly, like a pathetic duckling trying to fly away from an eagle. The other men are either sound asleep or unconscious.

'Susan!' My voice is a hoarse, urgent whisper. 'Susan, *stop!*'

She pays me no heed. I doubt my words have reached her.

Hustling through the aisle between the beds, I wonder whether I am right to interfere, or if I should simply leave the ghostlike silhouette to finish its task. But no, I cannot let her. 'Susan!' Louder this time, roughly pulling her wrists in an attempt to wring the vomit-spattered pillow from her. She is stronger than she looks, far stronger. Only when we tumble down on the cold floor do I manage to make her release the pillow and lie still.

'Are you *insane?*'

'He's a *Hun*. He kills them. You know it as well as I do.'

'And the English and the French and all the others—they are killing people too.' I barely believe this myself, but Susan must hear it.

After a few creeping seconds, she stands and retreats towards the tent flap without turning around, pinning me down with her eyes. 'Don't tell anyone. If you do, you'll be sent home after the medical board hears of your affair with that Frenchman. You don't want that.'

I form a void reply in my head, yet it is too unwieldy in my mouth for me to utter.

Then, Susan is nothing but a flighty silhouette again, speeding out into the damp evening air, dress twirling, stockings flashing bright in the dark.

I remain paralyzed on the floor with the filthy pillow in my hands and the German slumbering once again. When—no, *if—*

he regains his health and sense, the incident will be but a fragment of a nasty dream, unless erased completely. Thank God.

She is right, that aggravating woman. I will not allow the medical board to hear a whisper about my secret rendezvous with Charles. However, the threat was unnecessary. I merely wish to tuck tonight into the deepest, most faraway pit of my memory and disentangle myself from the mess I created.

The German dies two days later from an acute infection. As it turns out, Susan needed not have bothered to usher him to his grave.

I learn that the cocooned soldier's name is Arthur Hudson, a private in the French army. His English is good, his accent American. Every day he asks me again to write for him, and every day he claims there is no one he wishes his letter addressed to. The routine is irritating yet oddly comforting, perhaps precisely because it is a routine.

Arthur Hudson remains in his chalk-white bandages with his sugar cube hands, and I begin to dread ever finding out what exactly his wounds look like. If I do, I might not be able to speak with him in the same manner again.

There are so many new wounded lying limp on stretchers or crying out when they are carried inside the tents in a rough rush. We have not had enough beds for weeks and the patients must make do with sheets on the floor, like books tightly crammed into a shelf. Soon, we run out of painkillers, too, and have to ration our other supplies. My eyes grow weary from examining gaping wounds and wretched faces.

Despair is truly starting to get the better of all of us, leaving little room for my longing. Longing for Charles. Longing for hungry kisses under the knobbly oaks, longing for the musty smoking room and the library stacked with literature. I push these things from my mind, or rather the situation pushes in my stead, except at night. I still receive Charles's letters three or four times per week, and I send mine to him just as frequently. However, all letters in the world are a poor substitute for a breathing human being.

Ever since the German fools sank the American steamer Lusitania, I have been eagerly awaiting the entry of another ally in the war, one that would tip the scales definitively in our favour. Of course, my hopes do not come close to being realised—until the early spring of 1917. Germany resumes its gambling submarine warfare in an attempt to starve Britain by sinking merchant vessels, British and American alike. When it is revealed that they have offered to aid Mexico in a hypothetical war against the United States, the tension mounts further.

For selfish reasons, I take a renewed interest in Arthur Hudson, who's supposed recovery has ground to a halt. Amidst all the questionable, bordering on crazy, things he says, I occasionally access an American perspective on the situation, him having been born across the Atlantic. He explains terms I do not comprehend, describes places I have never visited, and often asks me to read out loud from the newspapers his father sends. I scarcely have the time to do so, but I try to find it.

However, what strikes me when I open *The New York Times* one crisp March morning is not another headline about America or Germany. '"Revolution in Russia; Czar abdicates".' I read the words again, this time in my head, ignoring the rest of the text. With all the anticipation about our potential allies across the Atlantic, I have been neglecting the massive powder keg in the east. 'How can they do that? How can they just...'

'Just what, Nurse?' Hudson says, his expression hidden as always. 'They don't want an emperor so they kick him off the throne. What more is there to it?'

'They have a war to fight—surely that is more important. What if the new government abandons us?'

'Bloody monarchist.'

'Anarchist!' I force myself to count to ten. It would look awful if I launched into a defensive argument with a half-butchered patient. 'I don't believe in autocracy, not one bit, but to be entirely without royalty isn't so terrific either. The way we do it home in Britain, with both king and parliament, that's the way. We have both tradition *and* a voice.'

Hudson giggles. 'Except their tradition made them starve.'

'How do you know?'

'My teacup pig Petal told me last night.'

'Insane one,' I mutter under my breath as I leave both him and the newspaper.

To my relief, the British government offers the tsar and his poor family asylum, but I sense reluctance in the air. Our own King George may sympathise with his dear cousin Nicholas II, but if a revolution can break out in Russia… Better not upset internal politics with the Tsar's presence and thereby poke a sleeping bear in Britain. I think it is only a matter of time before the offer of asylum is withdrawn.

I dare not ask Susan what she thinks. After all, she is Irish, and I have a feeling she condemns monarchy in general. Moreover, we have barely spoken since that dreadful night. The suspicious tension between us is mutual, for we depend on the other's silence. I am curious to know which of our transgressions would result in the harshest punishment: her indecency or my own.

Nonetheless, the rest of the hospital is buzzing with talk of the Russian revolution. Most share my own view: that it is all very fine to get rid of autocratic oppression, yet our eastern allies have gone too far. Even the few socialists who cheer for the Russian labourers realise the unrest we can expect.

'It's deplorable!' Doctor Barnaby says, abandoning his professionalism. 'Now what do they have, hmm? Two rivalling powers vying for control, and at least one lunatic in Lenin!'

I have joined some of the other members of staff in a spontaneous gathering outside the mess hall. Rays of spring sunshine beat down like white gold, but no flowers can grow in the mud.

'Lenin?' one of the elderly nurses says.

'Yes. That man is sprung from Satan himself. Never read Marx, Miss Ainsworth. Remember that!'

'Do you reckon something similar could happen at home, Doctor?'

Barnaby presses a blue-veined hand to the base of his throat as if the thought alone could choke him. 'No, no. His Majesty is not like the Tsar. The people all love him.'

I highly doubt this last statement, yet I keep my peace for once. Only time can tell, but I do believe we have far greater stability in England than they do in backwards Russia.

On the 6ᵗʰ of April, it finally happens. The United States declares war on Germany. I could leap and dance with joy. This is a turning point; it must be. This will be what ends the damned stalemate we are struggling to break through, because with American money and American troops, we shall be unstoppable. If only they had not taken such a long time to come to their senses, thousands of lives could have been saved. But still, today is a day of celebration for us and dread for our adversaries.

My joy is muted when I hear from Fred shortly thereafter. He has transferred to No. 56 Squadron, although the name does not mean anything to me. The allies have begun another offensive on the western front, near Arras this time. Naturally, the air force is a vital part of reconnaissance and patrolling.

Little Sister,

How are you? It seems I ask you that too infrequently. I'm sorry that I have not been able to write more often, but we are having a Hellish month so far. There is simply no other way to put it. I won't bore you too much, but in summary, the Germans are on the defensive while we are on the offensive, and our tactics clash just like we do in the air. We have already lost more planes than I could imagine, and the number is rising.

Do you remember the particularly skilled Pilot I told you about last autumn? He and his circus of planes, as they call it, have become our greatest Adversaries and bother. You will have heard of him by now: Von Richthofen. If that doesn't sound fancy to you, I don't know what does. There are two of them, but the older brother is the worst. He has had his plane painted glaringly red so that we'll never miss it, and we never do, except with our bullets. The younger one is daring in a different way and easier to tackle. My pal Albert says we will get them both down any day now, though, and I know he is right. We must not let gloom overtake us at a time like this. You might have read about Albert in the paper. He's still our leading Ace, though he has been home on leave (and happened to get engaged!).

Enough about that. A bird whispered in my ear—the bird was Papa, as you can surely guess—that you were ill last time you visited home. I wish you had told me and I would have tried to come and see you. I wish, too, that I could embrace you this very moment. Has it been a year and a half since we last met? Time is escaping us. Promise that you will help me

175

I am alone in the dormitory. Folding the letter and stashing it under my pillow, I sink to my knees and clasp my hands, elbows resting on the mattress. It has been long since I last prayed like this, but I have to at least try, for my brother's sake. Dear God…

Perhaps the Almighty is mocking me. I cannot tell. Two days later, I hold a telegram in my hand, much like I did after Harry was shot. I peel back a strip of skin from my cuticle and stare at the tiny droplet of blood emerging, desperately trying to find a good reason not to read my telegram. It will only feel worse the longer I wait, though, and I at last summon enough courage to tear it open.

The telegram is from Papa. Fred was shot down and crashed behind the English lines. He is alive, being treated at a special facility before he can be shipped home across the channel. He has lost his eyesight.

I swallow a sob. Before the war, I could imagine few things more horrible than being blinded—to never read or write, never see the faces of loved ones, never watch another sunset—but in this moment, I am truly relieved. Fred is alive. He is neither dead nor a prisoner of war, as would have been the case had he crashed on the German side.

He will not be sent back again. He is safe at the cost of his sight.

Chapter twenty-five

Charles

HER HANDWRITING IS pale. Ink must be in scarce supply. The field hospital likely has far more pressing expenses to cover. One particular passage of the letter causes something inside me to clench and twist and hurt.

> *It breaks my heart that he shall never be able to see again—but at the same time, I am grateful, for he shall never have to fight again, either. Is that quite right?*

All those loathsome actions I have witnessed and performed are trifles compared to the fact that one young woman is grateful for such a thing. It makes perfect sense, of course, but it is so utterly wrong. As I reread the paragraph, I cannot help but marvel at how much this war has affected people's way of thinking.

One night here at Arras, a few of the men and I find ourselves seated around a wobbling table in a candlelit dugout. It is in one of the communication trenches, where we really ought not to be. There are five of us: De Villiers and Emile, Escargot, Gérard, and myself. We are an odd mix of ranks, which is precisely why Lieutenant-Colonel Trembley has chosen not to sit with us.

And why on earth did *I* decide to join in this gathering? I had in mind an evening spent staring at my mess tin, pondering melancholy memories, writing back to Rosalie. Unfortunately,

177

here I sit now, crammed in between men's bodies reeking of old sweat.

De Villiers reaches with slender fingers for the remaining chunk of the loaf we are sharing, and I have to rip it from his hands. Hunger is gnawing in all of us despite the parcels we receive from home, but I would rather let Gérard have that bread. My servant boy has not been his usual cheery self of late. Small wonder, when the lice are particularly fond of him.

De Villiers throws me a venomous look before returning his attention to the fluttering candle where the flame has swallowed the wick in a glow of amber. Every now and then, his eyes dart to Emile, as if they shared a secret joke.

Gérard scratches his neck.

'Is it still as bad?' I ask.

'Yes, *Mon Commandant*. Pardon.'

'It's hardly your fault, is it? We all get them again sooner or later, believe me.'

Escargot leans back with his hands clasped on his stomach and whistles a low tune. 'Hey, once the Americans get here, it will be *finito.*'

'It could be months,' Emile says. 'I don't doubt they're trying their best, though.'

'Months! Pah! They've been preparing long since.'

De Villiers shrugs. *'Qui vivra verra.'*

'It's my birthday,' Gérard blurts out. 'Pardon, *Mon Commandant.'*

'Stop apologising or I'll get you transferred. Eighteen, is it?'

'Yes. My mother sent me a cake but it got lost in the mail.'

De Villiers and Emile are the first to withdraw from our little soirée. I remain for another quarter of an hour, casting stealthy glances at my pocket watch, yearning for the chance to leave without giving the impression of imitating De Villiers.

Five past one. 'Gentlemen, I think I will get a wink of sleep.'

The night is a clinging veil of tar over the trenches. I walk with brisk steps. The eerie silence, which is not really silence but the closest we get out here, is interrupted by a faint moan. I make a sharp turn to search the dark behind me for whomever or whatever might be following me.

Through the blackness and with an effort of the eyes, I can glimpse the contours of two figures, tightly pinned against one of the houses. A sleek cap of hair. French uniforms, gripping hands. A compromising sight.

I begin to trail off as quickly as possible, but a loose stone scrapes under my foot, and the two men raise their heads, staring straight at me.

'You seem to have quite the moment there—don't let me interrupt.'

'You saw nothing, do you hear? *Nothing!* De Villiers fires the words towards me in the most agitated tone I have ever heard him use.

Meanwhile, Emile fastens his belt with fumbling fingers, and if it were not so bloody dark, I could swear I see him blushing like a schoolgirl. He wipes his mouth on his sleeve.

'I think I saw *something*. Grand, really, however one would like to interpret it.'

'You keep your goddamn mouth shut.' His voice is calm now and as cold as the ice cubes we used to put in our whisky glasses at the Sorbonne.

'I don't care who you sleep with, and I don't feel restless enough to go gossiping about every juicy thing I see. But don't you ever tell me what to do.' I have taken a step closer to De Villiers. I then curse myself, knowing that the next time he opens his mouth to speak, his spit will land on my face.

He slams his fist against my chin. My face is numb before the pain catches up. I launch a sluggish kick, and before I know it, we have both tumbled down in a knot of limbs on the cold ground.

I could count the number of fistfights I have been in on one hand, and the late hour has dimmed my reflexes as well. The ripples of pain come again and again—my ribs, my ankles, my stomach, my head. I swing my hands and feet without aim, hitting my opponent surprisingly often. Nonetheless, there can be no question as to who has the advantage.

Emile cups his hands around his mouth and hisses something about being friends.

De Villiers is holding me down now, his knees on my wrists locking me to the ground. He pounds with his fists on my face *one, two, three* times. Bright spots flicker before my eyes.

Then it appears he is satisfied, because he scrambles to his feet and stalks away, leaving both me and his more affectionate companion without another word

I crawl to the trench wall and slump against it, panting. I let my eyes wander over the sprinkle of needle-stitch stars. My entire body is hurting from the beating, my head especially. Still, I *did* make a few good strikes… Or maybe I am just flattering myself.

Emile's breaths are light as a butterfly's wings next to me, cautious somehow. 'You don't look very shocked.'

'It wasn't a massive enigma. You're practically his bloody *pet*.' I reach up to wipe the blood from my lip.

The rest of my battalion will wonder how in God's name their *commandant* has been amusing himself, when I face them in the morning all swollen and bruised. I no longer give a fig about how much food De Villiers can find in No Man's Land. He will be packing his few belongings as soon as I can arrange for it.

Emile is too mild to turn to fury. What I read into his expression must be something far worse: shame.

'However,' I add, filled with the need to console him. 'I know one can't control who one happens to fancy. Or even fall in love with. It's godawful.'

'Oh? Will…will it break your heart?'

'I don't believe in broken hearts, although it might have already.'

Emile frowns. 'That's like not believing in broken legs or ulcers. It won't protect you from attracting it.'

I groan. The hour is just perfectly late for poetic exchanges, yet there is no room left for such pompous things in my poor head. 'I see. Maybe we are too old for it, then.'

'You *do* know I'm not withering away with age?'

'And neither am I, but say the average lifespan of a soldier is—'

'—weeks or months when in the frontline. Less for junior officers.'

'Exactly.' I search myself for broken ribs but find none. 'Then we're *frightfully* old.'

Emile nods thoughtfully, then he stands and offers me his hand. Grateful, I take it and pull myself to my feet, and together we return to the support trench.

Three days later, we rotate to the Main Firing Line. Pity stings me as I look at the dusty faces with shabby three-day-old beards and glazed eyes where exhaustion has ousted fear. Seldom have I wished for something as passionately as I wish now to be able to send them all home to their clean beds and fawning families.

The first attack comes at dawn. It is the enemy, not we, who go over the top this time, but we still find ourselves in an apocalyptic mass slaughter.

'*Mon Commandant?* There's a small bunker here,' one of my men says.

'There are never bunkers in the frontline!'

'There is here, *Mon Commandant!* One, at least.'

I should confer with Trembley, my superior officer. I should telephone headquarters. I should stay out in the open and prepare our counterattack. I have no time for *should* anymore, though. I intend to survive this, come what may, and I will be damned if I let half the battalion be wiped out in one morning. A battalion would not fit in a bunker, nor would a company, but perhaps—

A piece of shrapnel hits the man who spoke to me, flinging him down on the duckboards. I stand dumbfounded, watching his brain stain the wood underneath. I step over the body and continue towards the bunker with men gathering in my footsteps. The door looks solid.

'Inside, all of you!' With shaky hands, I wave the men by until the space is crowded enough to burst, before managing to squeeze myself down the stairs and bar the door.

Once inside, I draw a deep breath. The artillery barrage makes the room tremble. Our faces, dusty and sweaty, gleam in the sketchy light from a kerosene lamp.

'We'll be stuck in here for some time. The ceiling might cave in, but you have my explicit orders to *not go outside.* Understood? It won't do you any good, believe me.' I swallow my own tinge of claustrophobia, the last reminder of my near-death experience in the mud last summer.

The men shift their weight.

One of them is already turning the shade of bile. 'Does…does anyone by cha-chance have a deck of cards?'

'I have one. What do you play?' The familiar weight of the deck in my pocket is a comfort in truth. We play one round of Bezique, then another.

After an eternity, when the gunfire has ceased—and indeed nobody has given in to hysterical fits—we dare to stick our heads outside the bunker and into the blinding sun. The trench is ripped open and tattered with holes. It is still, chillingly still. The duckboards are drenched in blood. I can imagine them spreading across the landscape: red veins in blackened earth. A lonely hand with dirt shoved deep up under its nails is perched on the parapet to my right.

I gesture to the men to stay while I make my way down the broken boards, placing my feet with caution to avoid getting my boot stuck in someone. Either the rest of the battalion has retreated to the support and reserve trenches, or we are the only ones who have not been captured or killed. I round a corner and halt in my step.

De Villiers is on his knees, his back bent, his hair ruffled for the first time I have seen. He looks very much alive, yet I cannot take it for granted. Another figure is stretched out in front of him. Emile's face is unblemished, his torso the opposite, peppered with bullet holes.

De Villiers raises his glance. 'Go!' His voice is hoarse and his face is ruddy.

Contrary to my better judgement, I drop down next to him. My hatred has magically disappeared for the moment. For some reason, I cannot stop staring at Emile's peaceful face.

De Villiers gives me a shove. 'You did this! You made us go back! Just *go!*'

'It was not my—' I clamp my jaw. There is no use in arguing with the man, and in this moment, it would be unfair to do so. If it had been Rosalie lying there on the red duckboards no longer breathing… 'He was a good man.'

'I know that. You think I don't know that better than anyone?'

I slowly stand and back away, leaving De Villiers to weep for his golden-haired companion who believed in broken hearts. My own tears spill over before I can stop them, hot and wet and inconvenient. Although I know very well that there was nothing that I could have done to prevent the army from sending us back in time for the attack, De Villiers' words strike a chord of guilt in me. If we had marched just a little slower, then perhaps…

'*Mon Commandant?*'

I turn around. 'Gérard! Were you in the bunker this whole time?'

'Yes.'

'Our…friends have not been so lucky. Don't disturb them. I did.' I nod towards the men farther down the trench, my throat closing up.

'*Dieu dort, Mon Commandant.*'

'Sleeping? No. God is dead for certain.'

Another voice calls my name. A surge of relief rushes through me. Trembley's uniform is covered in powdery grey dust, but he appears unscathed.

I embrace him, ignoring his stiff surprise. 'What now? Where is everyone?'

'We have surrendered.'

I blink. 'Surrendered?'

'You heard. The entire brigade has surrendered to the Germans; they have taken the trenches we occupied. These trenches.' He is struggling to pronounce the words. He is a man robbed of pride and duty, robbed of command.

'Will the enemy let us live?'

'That remains to be seen, Charles. If they are men of honour and follow the rules, they will.'

'Forgive me if that doesn't sound reassuring. Our own men will be distraught.'

Trembley brushes and pats the dirt from his shoulders. 'Naturally, but these are the orders of the *Général de Brigade*, hence there was nothing to be done. I can promise you we'll be more comfortable in the officer camp than we have been out here.'

I nod. I want to ask about the others—what about their comfort? The answer is written in my superior's face, though. The men will suffer the fate of the prisoner camps, where the food is sparse and the barracks unfit living quarters for dogs, not to speak about the labour and the harsh Prussian climate in wintertime. Of course, most have already endured similar conditions in the trenches. The most prominent new aspect to their life will be the humiliation of defeat.

As for the officers, at least us Cos, it will be different. Yes, I wager we shall indeed be comfortable. To us, the surrender could well be a blessing in disguise, assuming the Germans let us live, that is. If so, I can tolerate what they call shame.

'Do I have to shake hands with them?'

'No. No, that won't be necessary.'

I usher the small group in the bunker outside, and together with Trembley, we climb over the top into No Man's Land, which is now German territory, more calmly than ever before. Having laid down our weapons, we wait for our sentence. Death, or life.

It is life.

The rest of the brigade—three thousand souls blended to a blue cloud—are already being organised and shuffled across to the German side of the front. I fail to spot the *Général de Brigade*, but there are several of the officers commanding the other battalions and companies.

We are to march for a few hours, the Germans tell us, until we reach the railways and can be shipped off to our respective camps. The *soldats* are not given anything to drink or eat during said march. While the other officers and I receive biscuits, sausage, and plenty to drink, the *soldats* will soon suffer from dehydration and malnourishment. The Germans appear to be doing splendid in contrast, though I have heard it said their civilian population is on the brink of starvation. They sneer and laugh, and sometimes poke my men with the dull end of their rifles when they fail to walk fast enough. They are slim, all of them, but to me their faces are well-fed and grisly. *Poke, poke.* There is nothing intrinsically German about this behaviour, only human, yet it does affect my opinion of our enemy.

The troops I am soon to leave behind will likely haunt me worse than the ones I have seen die or killed myself. I shiver. To think that my fate is so much better than theirs simply because my grandfather happened to find gold in California all those decades ago.

Chapter twenty-six

Rosalie

A FIELD OF the dead.

This is the sight that welcomes me outside the tent one warm and clammy day. The rain has been drizzling during the nights, and during the days the clouds weave a thick lid over us, keeping the heat from escaping and the mud from drying. The field hospital has become one massive swamp, infested with dead and wounded and the maggots that start to feast on them when we are too slow with the burials. There are rows of stretchers and sheets laid out on the ground, all with flies abuzz above. They are too many to fit inside the tents and barracks. Each day, I ask myself whether the men who arrive at this point would not be just as well off where they came from. Rumour has it that typhoid fever is spreading, too.

I barely manage to swallow the bile rising in my throat. All the little things I wish to forget comes bubbling to the surface when I set eyes upon this field of the dead. I cannot run like I could when that German let his entrails gush out on the floor. I can only stand frozen in my track, inhaling the stench of corpses in varying stages of decay.

If there is such a thing as a breaking point, then this is mine.

That same evening, I hand in my resignation to Mrs Hader. I will not put my name on another six-month contract, because I could not endure it. This time, I am going home for good, no matter how long this cursed war rages on, no matter how useless I might feel.

I must return home to London, to Papa and Daya, and to Fred, who will soon be sent home, too. I must help my brother mend and perhaps mend myself in the process. I must feel London's streets under my feet and taste berries with rich cream. I must walk in clean shoes and watch everyday people go about their everyday business. Otherwise, the field of the dead will be imprinted in my mind's eye, never to go away.

The first military truck leaves the following morning. After the chauffeur stops at the nearest station, I catch the train to Boulogne, then the steam ship across the channel. I do not experience even a tinge of sea sickness this time. All I feel is relief to fill my lungs with salty air.

I have a newfound appreciation for London. I try to blend in with the other civilians, though it is strange to think how most of them have lived under a shield of sorts, unexposed to the horrors on the other side of the water. Naturally, they have lost loved ones and heard the tales. They have had sleepless nights fearing zeppelin raids and possible invasions; they have contributed in their own way, read all the papers… Still, it is not the same thing.

Papa refrains from mentioning my sickly complexion and my silence at the dinner table. Instead, he takes every small measure to make me comfortable: fresh flowers in my room, my favourite blackberry marmalade for breakfast. I prefer this method to lengthy conversations. I do not know what I would say, anyhow.

Isabel sends me a letter to tell me she is disappointed that I have allowed my own happiness to trump the soldiers' survival. She has risen in the ranks at Rouen, and now occupies a post of prestige and trust as one of the nurses in chief of the hospital. I never send her a reply. If she was here, or if I was in Rouen, I would gladly be her dearest sister—but those are not the circumstances.

In early May, a week after my own homecoming, my brother's train is due to arrive at Hampstead Heath Station.

'Will you come?' I ask Papa, putting on my hat in the vestibule.

'I'll see him eventually.'

'Soon, you mean. Papa, pretending as if it hasn't happened won't make it better.'

He grunts something indiscernible and retreats upstairs. He is afraid, I suppose, afraid for who his only son might have become. I, however, nurture no doubts. Fred is my brother, injured or not, and the fact that I have not seen him for a year and a half only makes me more anxious to be at the station waiting for him. What kind of welcome would it be otherwise? And how would he manage the short walk home?

A while later, I am pacing from one end of the platform to the other, bracing myself. Steam envelops me. The train is here. I stand on my toes and raise my chin, trying to spot my brother in the cascade of people emerging from the carriages.

There! Fred is in the midst of the tumult, evidently waiting to be found. The pilot's uniform with the broad leather belt and cap gives him an air of expertise and confidence, but the rest of him contradicts the impression. Indeed, Fred reminds me of a newly born kitten tripping over its own pawns. His walk is hesitant, cautious, without any true sense of direction. It is a small miracle that he could handle the train journey on his own.

I quicken my steps and halt at a few feet's distance, not wanting to frighten him. 'Fred?'

His head turns in my direction. 'Little sister? Is that you...?'

I cannot restrain myself any longer but wrap my arms around him and hold him close, close to me and his home. He locks me in his own arms, and for a moment nothing else exists.

I at last pull back to study his face. To my astonishment, he looks the exact same he has always done, except that his eyes are unfocused. Maybe I somehow misinterpreted the telegram I received at the field hospital.

Fred must have read my thoughts or at least read my silence. 'Yes, well, I don't look blind, do I? Everyone says so. People expect me to have milky white eyes or nothing but burnt holes.'

I have difficulty breathing, for that is precisely what I expected myself.

'I better tell you at once, then,' he continues, 'that a blow to the head like the one I suffered only causes internal damage.'

'Of course. I'm sorry. I should have guessed, after all the patients I've seen.'

'There's no need. Truly.'

'Do you want to go home now? I do, very much.'

He clings to my arm, a link to safety as we tread through the streets of London, turning his head back and forth to absorb as many guiding sounds as possible. His walking stick rattles against the pavement when he searches for hinders in our path.

'It's all right,' I say, placing my hand on his. 'I won't let you step out in front of a bus or collide with someone.'

'I know, I know. I've not been walking anywhere but inside the ward since it happened.'

'They should have kept you longer. They should have helped you rehabilitate, not just…not just healed the physical damage.'

He licks his lips and I sense an impending confession. 'I hated it there, Little sister. I told them time and again that I wanted to go home, and when I mentioned you, they relented.'

'Me?'

'My own nurse, as capable as any of them. But no worries. I don't expect you to care for me always. I can manage quite well.'

I thought I was done with nursing forever, yet here I am now with a new patient who will be entirely my responsibility. But I am being selfish. At times, it appears to me that all I do is care for men—Laura would say with a scoff that that is all women are deemed clever enough for—but this is my brother. I can hardly turn my heart to stone. I smile, though he has no way of knowing that. 'Don't be silly! Of course I will care for you.'

'I'll learn. I promise. I just have to learn it all again: walking, swimming, writing. I can do that.'

'I never doubted it.'

We are almost at the doorstep.

'What are you wearing?' he says after a moment's silence. 'Last time, at the station in the autumn of '15, you were wearing a new muslin dress and a dark coat; I remember.'

I describe my clothes to him, then proceed to talk of the surroundings he knows so well, until we arrive at our destination. We share a reluctance to go inside our childhood home and face our father. We have changed, and perhaps he blames us for that. The atmosphere is suddenly thick between us.

The first few hours are the worst. Fred bumps into the furniture constantly, and we all agree that it will take some time for him to construct perfect mental images of the rooms. To my secret relief, on the other hand, nearly everything he requires assistance with are regular everyday tasks rather than medical wellbeing. Apart from migraine and nausea—which reminds me of Charles' symptoms the first time we met—Fred is as healthy as I am. To help him put on the gramophone does not feel remotely like the nursing I want to escape.

I nail Papa down with a glare every now and then, silently reminding him to behave. It seems to help, though, that his son looks like he did last. Papa's face brightens when Fred mentions that he still notices sharp light and shadows, and I, too, welcome this sliver of normalcy.

On the morning of our third day in the house together, I join my brother on the rickety bench outside the front door, where we sit together in a pool of sunshine. The street is near empty at this early hour, the only sound being the birds' chirping and a thin scatter of footsteps.

Fred's face is turned upwards. 'I'm just soaking up the light,' he explains before I get the chance to ask.

'Oh. And the sky?' I tense. Will he dismiss my subtle inquiry, or speak with me properly?

'Maybe. It's not so much my sight as it is the flying that I mourn for. When you're up there…it was everything I dreamed of and more. It's like being a bird. I know I've told you that many times already but…I will never have the experience again. I will never—'

'But you will *live.*'

'Yes. If you had told me that three years ago, I'd have been as relieved as you are now. But I'm not. All the best ones die young.'

I bite my tongue, clutching his sunlit hands in mine. 'Don't say things like that, Fred. Surely, the best pilots are skilled enough to survive.'

My brother starts to say something but chokes on the words and has to start over. 'Albert did not. He went missing during a dog fight the evening before yesterday. I just received a telephone call from a friend in Surrey who had a telegram from the squadron. Of course, it's only missing until the Germans confirm his death.'

'I…I'm so sorry. Yet you owe it to him, then, to live for the both of you, to make certain people remember him.'

'They will. That's the thing. I won't be remembered, not like some other aces. I wasn't as good as them, it's true, but I did have nineteen victories, and every single one made me feel topping. I will miss trying to wave to the troops on the ground—they treat you like a hero, though they're fighting just as hard themselves.'

What can I say that would be good enough, consoling enough? There is nothing. In the end, I give him a light shove, for perhaps too much seriousness will only hurt rather than help. 'I hardly even recognise my carefree brother. Did the glamour go to that thick head of yours?'

'It might have. In fact, you could say it made me blind figuratively and literally.'

We look at each other—or, rather, I look at him—and he is the first to laugh. I have seen too much loss and he has experienced it; we need that laugh like we need air in our lungs. I cannot recall even smiling for weeks.

When we have indulged in our little merriment for a while, I come to think of something he wrote in his last letter to me in mid-April. 'You told me Albert was engaged. Will you let me write to his fiancée for you with your condolences?'

'Please. Flora Young is very…young.'

'Come. Let's go inside.'

In the early summer, a bombing raid on London leaves us with well over a hundred dead civilians. As sorry as I am for them, I refuse to let the incident lead me to presume we will suffer defeat. Shortly afterwards, the first American troops land in France, carrying with them a promise of turning tides.

Rumours are circulating about unrest in some French divisions. I hear nothing more, but I suspect 'unrest' is too mild a descriptor. The French government must be withholding details to prevent morale from plummeting in the rest of the army and keep the Germans from profiting. The war was supposed to be over at Christmas 1914. The French have bled on and for their own soil without gaining more than a scrap of land. I do not blame them for being disgruntled.

I write several times to Charles to ask him about this and furthermore to inform him of my address in London.

I receive no answer.

Charles

Had I known I were to be a prisoner of war in a country retreat hotel, I might have suggested the surrender myself, and far earlier, too. I bet that was why no one told me just how well commissioned officers are treated. We do not live in luxury, but although the *offizierlager* in Neustadt is not Paris, it is a far cry from the trenches as well. My expectations are lower than they once were. To sleep throughout the night without being woken by machine guns is a blessing in itself. I have lost my freedom, it is true, but when was I last genuinely free? Not in the trenches. Perhaps my short leave in Paris or my stay at the convalescent centre could be called freedom of a kind, but when there is a war raging, every man in the army is a prisoner.

There are roughly eighty officers here. Ours is a small camp—I have heard there are those housing a thousand men and more—which suits me. Since COs are not put to work, we spend our days the way we did behind the lines two years ago: playing games, reading, smoking. We even take brief walks out in the open after signing a document wherein we give our word as gentlemen to not try to escape. Of course, the knowledge that the guards could in theory blow out brains out with a bullet also quells the temptation.

A handful of regular prisoners of war referred to as orderlies carry out the work needed to maintain our relative comfort. I do miss Gérard. At the moment, it seems implausible to find him and have him sent for, considering that Lieutenant-Colonel Trembley and I are the only two men from our battalion now lodged at Neustadt.

While the Germans do not withhold mail from our families—if they did, their countrymen would risk the same treatment in allied camps—they refuse to let me contact Rosalie. I have no formal attachment to her, and in a way she is actively working for the British army. Hence, the Germans are suspicious of coded messages. I get physically sick every time I remember I cannot

write to her, or at least explain why none of the letters I assume
she sends reaches me.

Chapter twenty-seven

Rosalie

MY SKIRT IS a new, sweeping thing that I delight in displaying alongside the matching hat and beige T-strap shoes. I am not always fashionable, and it feels marvellous to wear something fresh and pretty after years in uniform. A basket rests lightly on my arm, ready to be filled with autumn apples for one of Daya's experiments. She would have gone herself, but I insisted. I have been outside much too rarely since I came home, and besides, I am in dire need of a new almanac for myself.

Something in the corner of my eye makes me halt just as I am about to enter a bookshop at Piccadilly Circus. A young woman is gluing a large poster in purple, green, and white to the shop window. A bucket of glue dangles on her forearm, and a bundle of tightly rolled up posters peek out from the satchel slung over her shoulder.

'Laura?' I take a few steps closer.

The woman turns, and indeed, it is my own Laura Hamilton. All at once I regret not paying her a call sooner.

Her face cracks up in a blinding smile. 'I haven't seen you in, well, ages! I thought you'd be in France!

I itch with guilt. I should have written and told her of my whereabouts. 'Yes—yes, I was at a field hospital…but it was so awful, all of it is, and I was so fed up with blood and vomit and…'

She clasps my hand, her eyes reassuring. 'You did a great deal of work, you know. Don't feel selfish for coming home.'

I nod and turn my attention to the poster on the shop window. *A fearless indomitable womanhood, a fearless indomitable race— Votes for women.*

'It's a fine thing, the movement.'

I have heard much about the suffragettes, and though I would love nothing more than to see their demands met, there has always been a certain controversy holding me back from raising my own voice on the matter. People throw stones and sometimes vile, rotten food on them. It might be cowardly of me, but I am not keen to face that. Moreover, I have been preoccupied these past few years, to say the least. 'Are you—are you truly one of them now?'

'Oh yes!' Laura bobs her head. 'Don't you see? We've been shielded, you and I, from all the horrid things some women have to endure. All our friends, and brothers and fathers have always been terribly dear, though they can be a bit rinky-dink.'

I frown. 'How can you know?'

'Why, has someone hurt you? If they have, you'll tell me this instant.'

'No, no. I just mean that if something did happen, it would never see the light of the day.'

'See! You're already thinking straight.'

'I do believe we should have our own vote.' I speak in a low voice for fear of being overheard and called one of those things. An ignorant, feeble woman. But no one does hear, and perhaps that is part of the issue.

'There you go then. Won't you help me with these?' She gestures towards the posters. 'They're so many, and they all have to be up within the hour. I have to attend a meeting at noon.'

After a second's hesitation, I grab the bucket of glue. With giddy smiles and arms linked, we stroll down the street just like we used to do before the war, albeit with a far more meaningful task than we ever had in those days.

Laura shares with me some of what has happened since we last exchanged letters. Since her father would not let her work in the munitions factory and use her porcelain hands for manual labour, of course she found an even more provocative way to defy him by officially joining the suffragettes.

'What did he do when he found out?'

She cocks her head. 'He said I could live on the street if it pleased me. That hasn't been necessary, though. One of my friends in the movement offered to lend me a room.'

I stare at her. 'And Julian? He didn't oppose your father in the matter?'

'You know he didn't. He was busy inspecting his old cavalry boots.'

'But you haven't been arrested?'

Her silence suffices for an answer.

I smooth out a crinkle in the poster we have just put up. 'What did they do to you in there?'

'In the hoosegow?'

'If that's American for prison, then yes. I don't know how you find all these odd words.'

'I went on hunger strike. They shoved a tube down my throat to feed me.' She has turned pale as milk and closes her eyes, likely trudging through unwelcome memories. 'The guards said I was a disgrace.'

I can tell from the way the men and women on the street are looking at us with our posters that the prison guards were not alone in their view. Every slight I have learnt to take for granted throughout my life comes back in that moment. I shrink little by little, yet Laura has already recovered her gay spirits, and I straighten my posture to equal hers.

Perhaps a change of topic would benefit us both. 'Do you know what has become of Mildred? And what of James and Jones? Mary is still in France, as is my sister.'

'Mildred had a baby a few months ago—the ugliest baby I ever saw—but then her husband insisted that they move to York. I can't imagine living as far north as that! James and Jones are all right, I think, though James nearly drowned once. It wasn't on the HMS Audacious where he was supposed to be posted—don't know what on earth happened to that boat.' She glances at her watch and smiles. 'I must be gone, Rose, but do send me a note, and we'll meet up for tea.'

'Count on it.' I give her a peck on each velvety cheek, then she is gone. Daya's apples resurface in my mind and I steer my step towards the Sunday market.

I do my best to sound nonchalant when sharing the day's events with Papa as we sit by the crackling fireplace. He is in the process of rinsing his smoking pipe, yet I can tell he is absorbing my every word.

'If you care to take my opinion for once, there's nothing as valuable as tradition. Women never had the right to vote.'

I clench my hands in my lap. 'Am I of an inferior kind, then? If you haven't noticed, I'm a woman by every definition.'

'I don't believe in inferior and superior kinds, Rosalie, I believe in individuals—and you're most certainly not an inferior one of those.' His words are more encouraging than I have heard from him for a long time. However, they are not enough for me.

'I thought you were a liberal.'

'Eh? Not even the bloody socialists in Russia would approve of the suffragettes.' He puts his pipe down on the table with a click. 'Fred might—ask him.'

I rise, but before I can stalk out of the room, Papa speaks again.

'If I can't persuade you to keep out of it, then by all means, you have my support. But don't you dare get yourself injured.'

I sigh and stoop down to kiss his temple where the hair is turning grey like the smouldering cinders in the fireplace.

Laura's note consists of two cluttered sentences that tickle my nerves until I do not know how to curb my excitement.

With the arrival of Thursday morning, as the first rays of light break through the curtains in my bedroom, I slither out of my nightgown and into a modest blouse and skirt, then retrieve my hat from the top of my drawer. On light feet, I trip down the flight of stairs, praying that Minnie and Daya are not already awake and tending to their chores. However, the house is still and quiet, a bright mausoleum, and I suspect the two of them sleep more than they are supposed to.

Papa did give my new engagement his support, Fred even his applause, but I treasure the secrecy. Besides, I doubt either of them would be pleased to see me go to the kind of demonstration I am heading to. Laura's note warned me of potential violence.

Having shut the door firmly behind me, I quicken my pace. The meeting place is not far off; I reach it while this part of London—where there are few workers rising early—is still slumbering.

Laura is waiting, as are a group of other women, all dressed in simple but finely tailored clothes. A large plaque with a similar message to that of the posters is leaning against the red brick wall of one of the houses.

Laura latches onto my arm. 'You came!'

'Of course I did.' I embrace her for an instant and offer the other women a polite nod. Some have gloved hands and clipped voices like myself, while others are wearing dreadfully grey wool and seem to have been aged by labour.

Several others arrive shortly, and we embark on our march with a tinge of uncertainty. The atmosphere grows stronger, though, until it contains a decisiveness I did not anticipate.

The hour is not so frightfully early anymore. People are spilling out on the streets, many lingering to behold us as we pass by. Amidst all the faces cut in stone, I spot curiosity and perhaps even admiration.

Our chant is simple: Votes for every woman, equality for every woman.

A middle-aged man balks at us. 'Now what, votes for dogs too?'

'You already have your vote, don't you?' a tall woman shouts back.

The man's eyes harden, but he merely thrusts his fists deep into the pockets of his patched jacket, allowing us to pass.

We continue through the streets. The march is going rather well, until one of the women at the front spots an anti-suffrage poster in the window of a tobacco shop. She picks up a stone the size of an orange and fires it, smashing the windowpane. Her precision is impressive, and the glass shatters in a thousand pieces like sugar. The poster itself is now naught but a rag.

'No stone-throwing today! We all agreed on it!' Laura scolds.

'And we all agreed to deeds, not words when we joined! That's the only way they will ever listen.'

Before Laura has the chance to reply, turmoil has broken out and the shop owner comes hurtling towards us. His round face is pink with fury, his fleshy lips curling. He draws back his arm and before I fully realise what is happening, someone throws our stone back at us and it collides with another woman's shoulder. Shouts erupt as people on the street rapidly join the man in his pursuit for retaliation. Our formation scatters through brutal shoves. The sharp notes of a police whistle slice the air. For the first time in my life, the policemen seem like a threat to me. They give the woman who threw the stone a thorough beating along with two others. Afterwards, the victims lie on the pavement, bruised and battered, surrounded with a splatter of their own blood.

The rest of us stand frozen, watching. A single glance at the policemen is enough to know we would regret it if we attempted to help our fellow demonstrators. Instinctive dread skitters down my spine. Nevertheless, when I search myself, I cannot detect a trace of deeper-rooted fear, only anger. Before, the inhumane treatment of the suffragettes has been a nasty rumour, somewhat distant. Now, I am in the thick of it.

The policemen finally succeed in chasing us from the place. Laura and I run as best we can, our lacquered shoes hitting the pavement hard. After turning four corners, we afford ourselves to stop and breathe.

'What will happen to those women?' I ask.

'If they're unfortunate, they will be locked up for a few days or weeks. It's difficult to say.

'Parliament can't refuse forever, can they? When the soldiers return home and some of them are not allowed to vote either because of the property requirements… *They* will hardly be punished for demanding justice.'

'For refusing to admit that men exist just a little more than we do'.

'Do you know something, Laura?'

'What?'

I smile and tuck my dishevelled hair back under my hat. 'I was afraid I'd feel useless back here at home. I'm not afraid of that anymore, not at all.'

Throughout the autumn and winter, I devote all my energy to the suffrage movement and my brother's rehabilitation. These projects are plentiful in keeping my thoughts occupied and thereby serve as a distraction from the war. In fact, although the political and military business are impossible to escape entirely, I create my own bubble to some extent. Have I not spent three years reading every news article, listening to every speculation? I can do without that for a while now.

Passchendaele, Cambrai… The names of battles I know little of and wish to hear even less about. I could torture myself with picturing what it is like based on Charles' descriptions of previous offensives but I refuse to do so.

The one set of headlines that capture my interest are those that flood us during some biting cold November days. The Petrograd Soviet in Russia has performed a coup d'etat on the provisional government and put Vladimir Lenin—the man Doctor Barnaby hated with a passion—in charge. Doctor Barnaby would find an ally in Papa, while Fred is tolerant of the Bolsheviks, though it would be unfair to call him enthusiastic. As for me, all I care to note is that a separate peace between Russia and Germany must be imminent.

Our victory—not Britain's but that of my new cause—comes in February the following year, when Parliament finally, *finally* passes the Representation of the People Act. It is a partial victory, though, because only women over the age of thirty who meet the property requirements may vote. Thus, I myself am excluded, as are millions of others. At the same time, a vast group of young men gain the right, since their own restrictions regarding ownership and wealth are abolished. In addition, serving soldiers only have to be nineteen to vote, unlike us women.

However, it is a start, and a milestone. Laura and I celebrate to our hearts' delight, well aware that we must continue the struggle tomorrow.

Chapter twenty-eight

Rosalie

FRED THROWS HIMSELF down on the sofa with far less caution than he displayed during his first months of blindness. 'He's dead, Little sister. Papa told me. It was in the paper.'

I swallow, my mouth parched. 'Who? Another one of your friends?'

'An enemy, Von Richthofen. The Red Devil of Arras, as we called him. I hardly need to tell you he was the finest aviator I ever saw. We respected him in the squadron, more than we respected ourselves.'

I nod. Though his death is news to me, I was well aware of Von Richthofen's notoriety, not only from Fred's occasional mentions but from the press, who loves a romantic hero.

'Who had the honour of shooting him down?'

'Captain Brown, or so it's been said. A Canadian. At least, the men on the ground conducted a proper funeral with full military honours.'

'I'm glad to hear it. You were right, I suppose, when you said all the best ones die young. I've never been more pleased to have an average brother,' I tease.

'Why, thank you, dear one.'

We exchange a smile. Humour has increasingly become our medicine against dreary emotions, and it often succeeds.

America is proving a better ally than Russia was. The latter has made peace with our enemies so that the new Bolshevik government can wage war on their countrymen who oppose the political changes. British and French troops land in Murmansk to intervene, though frankly, I think we should leave the Russians to their lunatic infighting. However, in July, word reaches us that the Tsar and his family have been massacred by the revolutionaries—all of them, including the children.

Events like these used to plunge me into a state of bewilderment. However, the world is changing too fast for me to fully comprehend, and I have resigned myself to watching from the periphery as it shocks people anew. Europe is aflame, yet it has been for a good while, and there comes a time when one ceases to be surprised at atrocities.

'It's ghastly,' Papa says with gritted teeth as we stroll down High Street one summer's day.

'It isn't swell. Those poor princesses…'

'I can't recall when we last heard something *swell*. Can you?'

I bite my tongue, considering. No, not anything swell, precisely, but there are certainly glimpses of light. The German spring offensive has failed, and with our blockade, they are suffering dire shortage of food and supplies, worse than we ever have in England. I have begun to hope, hope that the war might come to an end before the year is out. On the other hand, I hoped that in 1914 too.

Papa jerks me to the side just as a woman coughing violently into her handkerchief walks by. Both he and I watch her with caution.

'Several of my seamstresses at the firm are gravely ill,' Papa says. 'Bloody influenza.'

'I feel as healthy as ever myself, but of course, it's very quick.'

The disease is sweeping through London, through all of Europe, I believe, and has done so for months. At first, the papers said little of it—an influenza is not exactly as cheering as a romantic hero—and claimed it was the Spaniards' issue, but there is no way to deny what is happening anymore. People are dying every day, and not the way they have been dying from bullets and barrages, but from a sneakier foe that does not spare women and children. It spares no one, especially not the young and fit who usually prevail. That in particular frightens me. I would rather not cough and wheeze until my lungs collapse, or have fever hallucinations like the ones my patients sometimes suffered. The hospitals are all full as far as I know. Isabel writes that at least a third of her patients in Rouen are victims of the influenza, not the battlefield. It must be the worst luck to survive all the violence, perhaps even be near the end of it, only to succumb to a pandemic. I shudder. If I simply wait a little longer, there might still be good things to come.

The clanging bells of Westminster Abbey sound across the rooftops of London, announcing the hour we have been anticipating with poorly disguised felicity. Eleven o'clock. Eleven o'clock on the eleventh day of the eleventh month. Our salvation day.

I stand on the pavement, paralysed, waiting. First there is nothing. Then, the people spill out from their houses like hordes of ants. With them comes a deafening blend of cheers and chatter. Women and children lean out dangerously far from the windows, laughing and waving British flags. A few men climb on top of a glossy black car and set off towards Trafalgar square in some sort of parade. They have to go slowly through the crowd that is growing by the minute. I have never seen this many people at once, not even when the war broke out.

Can this really be it? Can this really be the day that we all have been yearning for? It must be.

An old man with deep smile lines sculpted around his eyes hands me a flag before melting into the masses again. I accept it, and soon I have joined in the merriment, watching men fling their hats in the air and without a care in the world pick up a stranger's headwear from the ground.

It is the most trivial thing to convince Laura and Fred both to come with me to Buckingham Palace. My brother shrugs off Papa's misgivings, saying Laura and I will not let him from our sight, and regardless, he has learnt to manage remarkably well with his condition.

The royal family make appearance after appearance, satisfying their subjects each time we ask to see them again. Of course, it is not the virtues of the Windsors, as they now call themselves after having discarded their Germanic Saxe-Gotha, that have brought victory. Nonetheless, they are the symbol of our nation. We ought to be cheering the common soldiers and commanders— perhaps even the mutinying German navy—but where would the glamour be in that? Besides, the square-shouldered figures on the palace balcony deserve some measure of gratitude for their devotion to the men at the front.

King George in his admiral's uniform removes his cap. The band plays "God Save the King" and "Rule Britannia." We raise our voices and sing along. There is a cold shower of rain, and I tilt my head to feel the dampness on my cheeks.

Fred squeezes my hand. 'It's all right now, Little sister, isn't it?'

'No, but it will be. And at this moment, it's good.'

'Good.'

His optimism must have returned in full strength, because if I were him, I would begrudge those who have emerged unharmed. Perhaps other veterans with lasting injuries do. I push them from my thoughts.

Later that day, the King and Queen drive through London, greeting yet more people, some of whom are waving American or French flags, even Indian and Canadian. I tend to forget our colonial troops, but of course, they have been a tremendous help.

If I know London as well as I like to think, the celebrations will last the week.

I reject an invitation from the Bride household to come and dine. They have sent me notes more often than I would have wished ever since I returned from the field hospital; I have only accepted their offer twice. I do not deserve their kindness, not after what I did to Harry. To look them in the eyes, knowing my fidelity towards their sweet brother and son faltered towards the end of his life… If they hoped to find a new family member in me, they must realise at this point that they were wrong.

Instead, I persuade Papa that we ought to host our own spontaneous victory dinner. The Hamiltons are all invited, as are an array of other acquaintances.

I accompany Daya to the market in an attempt to secure ingredients fit for an evening such as this before the stalls are all empty. We push our way across the square, through the fluttering masses. Dear God, let them be happy a while longer. Many are mourning rather than rejoicing, having already lost the people who made their lives worth the hardships. There will be time for such things later, though. I will mourn my entire life if I can just keep these few, happy days free from despair.

Mr Buttons—one of the foremost vendors in Hampstead—is a short man with round, silver-rimmed glasses and a twinkle of humour in his eyes. His wild-grown beard has begun to shift in streaks of grey and white. When he catches sight of us, he sticks up a hand the size of a gramophone record and gestures for us to come closer. 'There you are, Miss Wilkes, and Miss Monell, too!'

The use of Daya's surname confuses me for a second. 'Good day Mr Buttons. A genuinely good day, isn't it?'

He grins. 'Yes, yes, never was a day any better, Miss Wilkes. I haven't seen Miss Monell or yourself so very often lately.'

'I'm sorry. Nevertheless, I trust you have some substitute salmon stashed away for us.'

'As a matter of fact, I've not only that, but real salmon! Here, see, the finest fish you'll find in all England—you can take my word for it. Pure luck, really, that I should be able to offer it to you on this special day.' He offers up a fat salmon for us to inspect. The fish beams in the crisp daylight, silver scales glittering.

I look at Daya for her professional assessment, and she nods.

'That will be just splendid, Mr Buttons, although we might need more to feed our entire dinner party.' I hand him the money from my purse, and he wraps the fish and another one in crêpe paper before placing them in Daya's outstretched basket.

Though I know it will make my fingers blister and ache, I help our cook scrub the potatoes when we arrive home, not wanting to miss a single moment of 'this special day'. Then we lay the table with Papa's best china and silver while Minnie folds the creamy napkins into flowers. I am certain to place Laura's seating card on my right so that I will have someone to converse with.

Two hours later, the hired footman lowers the plate so that I can serve myself, his livery bulging. I have not dined like this since the war began, and all the formalities are beginning to feel silly. The result of Daya's and my own efforts is well worth it: honey-glazed salmon with potato gratin, sugar snaps, and a white wine sauce, to be followed by a dessert of glace au four.

The atmosphere is somewhat tense between the four Hamiltons, and small wonder, considering Laura's clash of opinions with her father and Julian, but it would have been rude not to extend the invitation to them. Julian has thus far spent the evening dissecting his food and making remarks about the German Kaiser being unfairly treated. Much to my amusement, Mrs Hamilton, whom I have seen very little of in the past, is fully prepared to oppose her son.

'Was it not bad enough that the navy mutinied against him? And now the socialist plague has spread from the east. We must put an end to this brushfire of revolution.'

Mrs Hamilton sighs. 'Social democrats, darling, not socialists. All I know is that unlike the Kaiser, they won't engage in a war on this scale.'

'Because they can't, Mother. Not because they're decent people.'

One of the other guests gives the pair a subtle reminder to refrain from discussing politics at the table, and they obey with stiff smiles.

Laura nods at her plate. 'When the boys come home, we must serve them this someday.'

'Harry won't come home. Perhaps Cha—' I fall silent. I have kept Charles' existence from the two people I share everything else with, namely Laura and Fred. Although I trust either of them with my life, Susan's betrayal is vivid in my memory.

'Who?'

'Only an acquaintance. But let's not fuss about it.'

The food and drink soon take on the flavour of paper on my tongue. Somehow, the joy has been sapped from me, only to be replaced with melancholy as the night comes creeping. If Harry was seated at my right, I would feel loved and ridiculously adored. If Charles was seated on my left, I would feel alive.

I have not yet heard anything from Charles. I sent an inquiry to the French government a few months ago, but they have not yet replied, likely being busy with matters more important to the war effort. I do not know his home address in Paris, and no further possibilities spring to mind. Either, he is dead, missing, a prisoner, or…or he has simply lost all interest in me. I do not know which would give me the most pain.

I want to slap myself, tell myself to stop pining for a man I have not seen in two years. Yes, yes, I will stop. There is peace in the world and I am to turn twenty-two in the spring. Henceforth, I refuse to waste a single moment on wishing for what might have been.

Chapter twenty-nine

Charles

ON A DAY of clear, bleached skies, word spreads like a wildfire through the camp. It must be a sick joke, but no, it is the incredible truth. Not one more soul will have to die after this day, or so it is claimed. The hundreds of thousands who have already gone like filthy shreds blown away with the wind must have satisfied our leaders and Mother Nature.

Some of my fellow officers sneer at our guards, knowing we have a whole other leverage now than when we arrived. I pity the Huns, though, for they have wasted their youth to an even further extent than we have, and crippling disappointment twists their faces. I ponder bidding them a cordial farewell, but the mood is not quite right. When it comes down to it, we are all more or less void. War has been the fundamental of our reality every day for four years, and now we are required to abandon that reality. Where do we go from here? Home, yes, but then? The freedom I desired for such a long time is overwhelming and unsettling.

Lieutenant-Colonel Trembley alone appears at ease. He has created a formulaic letter which one of the orderlies copies for him and dispatches to his friends and family. This way, he can inform them exactly when and where to expect him.

Our train departs from Neustadt in the morning six days after the armistice. The journey is by far the queerest experience I have had for years, if not my whole life. We are going home without anyone protesting or trying to smash us dead. As reluctant as I am to admit it to Trembley, who travels with me, I would rather have stayed in Neustadt a while longer. Paris holds my heart, but it has become foreign in a way, while the *offizierslager* had grown familiar, shielded from the rest of the world. There, all my fellow prisoners were more or less like myself both in background, rank, and experience. In Paris, I will be an oddity.

'I must say I do not understand you, sometimes, Charles,' Trembley says while we watch the landscape flash by.

'And why is that?'

'If you feel out of place once we arrive, you can just return to the army. There will be no war, of course, but there's always *something* to do.'

'Return to the army? By God, that's the last thing I'll ever do. I have had quite enough of them for a lifetime, thank you very much.'

'But what about the parades?' He boggles his eyes at me. 'Surely you want to take part in the parades?'

'I think not. If they're truly grand I might be tempted, but no.'

The train slows down at a grey, dusty station and stops with a jolt.

I peer out at the platform. 'I might have lost my wits, but to my knowledge this isn't Paris.'

'No, it isn't. We are stopping for food supplies, naturally.' Trembley gestures at the men outside who have begun to load boxes and sacks onto our train.

'Do you reckon we can stretch our legs in the meantime?'

We step down on the platform and I fill my lungs with November air cold enough to hurt. Farther down the station, there is a grey mass of uniforms and helmets. It is a German platoon, or what is left of it, likely waiting for their own train home.

I take a few steps towards them, finding it difficult to hide my curiosity. So, these are the skinny, muddied creatures who have crouched in the enemy trench for four years while we did the same on our side. They are not what I pictured. They bear little resemblance to the Germans I encountered during the Christmas truce or the unusually well-off ones we surrendered to. The war has taken its toll on all of us but the men standing shifting their feet in front of me look like street dogs begging for scraps. Some have an aura of hostility, clutching their rifles as if their life depended on it, but most seem exhausted, just like us. They were flattered or forced to the front, just like us. However, we have a victory to prance around with, no matter how empty, and they do not. As much as I hate it, I feel sorry for them. All they have to show for years of struggle and hundreds of thousands of dead is bitter defeat. We are the lucky ones, the rich and victorious, and they are everything we are not.

I dig in my pocket. *'Schokolade?'* This word I do know, and I happen to have a bar of Moser Roth which I won it from one of the guards in a game of cards.

The Germans exchange looks of mistrust, then one of them takes a step forward. I deduce from his uniform that he is an NCO, and the other men appear to regard him as their unrivalled leader.

I hold out the chocolate and wait, ignoring Trembley's mumbled protest behind me.

'Wir wollen deine schokolade nicht, französische schweine!'

I cannot interpret his words but the contempt in his voice is clear enough. I stuff the bar back in my pocket. Very well. Let them place their pride above their comfort if they like.

Trembley tugs at my sleeve. 'Come, Charles. Our train is leaving.'

I throw one last glance at the enemy soldiers, some of whom appear to regret their NCO's decision, and follow my friend up the steps to the train carriage.

'Aren't they a sorry lot?' I say more to myself than to Trembley as we sit down once more.

'The people of France are a sorry lot. As the Bible says: "Whatsoever a man soweth, that he shall also reap."'

I nod. I believe, though, that we have all sowed things we denied when the time came to reap.

I am in Paris. *Paris.* There are so many civilians swarming on the train platform, the lot of them pulling us into their world and swallowing us whole. Their noise is entirely different from drumfire.

I take farewell of Lieutenant Trembley; we have travelled far, but the time has come to go our separate paths. The feeble breeze whisks his hair. 'Good luck to you,' he says after a moment of mutual silence.

'Yes. Good luck. Be certain to try the Cristal Brut I told you of, will you?'

Trembley nods.

Without another word, we turn in a decidedly military fashion, and walk in opposite directions. I have a feeling that I will never meet him again. I will not miss him. Although as harmless as a kitten, he is the dullest man I met in the army, which is saying something, and I suspect the fondness between us sprang from the years we were made to spend together.

I steer my steps out from the station and into the streets. The city is as it was when I was last here. It feels like an insult towards all of them…the ones who vomited and choked to death, the ones who staggered forward with limbs hanging by their tendons. How can the theatre scene still be so devastatingly beautiful, when the spectacle played out was so ugly? The sky ought to have crackled and fallen down.

My mother and sisters know I was to be sent home, but I cannot bring myself to continue my journey to the countryside just yet. Let me grow acquainted with Paris again first, I want to tell them, and then I will do whatever they ask. Unless they are already in the apartment…

I dismiss the thought as I walk down Rue Saint-Jacques with the belongings that I brought from the trench at Arras stuffed in my pockets. My stomach is an empty pit; I tear my gaze from the pristine, undamaged houses and search for a café. A familiar sign catches my attention. I venture inside and drop down on a chair by an empty table. The air is dim with cigarette smoke and steaming food. Here, we often sat to take our luncheon—Michael, Louis, Henri, Marcel, and I. A block farther away stands the Sorbonne with its stout, chalky walls, walls that were supposed to be strong enough to hide behind.

'Would you like to order, Monsieur?' a hawk-nosed waiter asks.

'I'll have what the chef recommends, thank you. And a glass of champagne to that.'

The tarte aux fromage that the waiter brings me clashes badly with the champagne, but I delight like seldom before.

Champagne! It must be more than two years ago since I last had any. This is what I have longed for so ardently; this is the very first taste of the life to which I intend to return. I repeat this silently to myself. Whenever that void expands and threatens to drown me, I have to remember that life.

I finish my meal, listening to the chatter of the other guests. Some of it concerns the war, but most is light-hearted everyday nonsense, which captivates me. Having paid the waiter, I rise and continue my walk.

Two hours pass before I decide I have absorbed sufficient views for now, and abandon my detour in favour of the apartment. Only when I am standing below the arched windows do I realise that I do not have a key. Well, if this is not stumbling on the finishing line. I ring the doorbell twice. Just as I am about to leave, the chains and locks on the front door rattle and our Parisian butler, permanently in residence here, opens.

'Monsieur!'

Without as much as a greeting, I take three long steps towards the stick-like man and envelop him in my arms. He reminds me of Trembley for a second, and I release him after an awkward pat on the back.

'Should I telephone Madame D'Aboville and tell her that you're home?'

'No. No, Timmele, let's wait a little. It's good to be here.'

I keep Timmele faithfully silent for two whole days before he beseeches me to let him at least send a telegram to my mother. Shortly thereafter, I leave behind my temporary respite and rent a car out to the chateau. With every mile, I wish more intensely to go back. The quarrel I had with *Maman* has festered during my absence; I can sense it. As for Constance and Marie-Louise, I do long to see them. However, I fear my sisters have too high expectations, and I should hate to disappoint them. After all, I do not return in glory but as an officer who lost a trench and agreed to surrender.

My mother hosts a dinner to celebrate my homecoming. She has invited every distant relative and half-forgotten acquaintance I have ever so much as had coffee with. They sit there around the table, waistcoats and gloves as impeccably white as the thick tablecloth, their manners perfectly polite. Some of them I know well, like my cousin Adéle. Others I cannot even name, much less recall when I last saw them. Marie-Louise alone is excused, since she has been indisposed with the influenza for a few days already. I almost envy her, because though people are said to be dying in the thousands, in the *offizierslager* we were isolated both from the disease itself and from many of the reports on it. This makes the threat seem absurd to me.

Only two of our acquaintances spark my genuine interest: Victor and Gabriel Allaire, for they were both at the Somme just like me. In all fairness, Gabriel is not present at the table—he is being treated for a lung wound and will remain in hospital for another few months—but Victor and I find a scrap of common ground. He knows what it is to go over the top. He knows what it is to squash lice out of boredom and expect them to have spread again within a day.

'And what of your brother? Phosgene or mustard or something quite different?' I ask him across the table, stabbing a few peas with my fork.

Victor swallows apparently without chewing, like we did at the front. It is a habit I am trying to get rid of myself. 'Mustard. He was lucky.'

'I'll be damned. Perhaps he has a guardian angel.'

One of the women whose name I have forgotten winces. It takes me a minute or two before I realise that she disapproves of my language. I was never one to guard my tongue with my friends, but my words used to become effortlessly refined on occasions like these. It seems I have yet another bad habit to unlearn. Out there, every fourth word was a curse. If a man spoke cleanly, we were alarmed, and that stood true for officers and common infantry alike.

My mother frowns and flicks her wrist, signalling for the footmen to remove the plates from the main course. 'Charles, why don't you tell everyone of your law studies?' she says.

I blink at her, dumbfounded. My law studies? 'I've not yet decided if I want to resume them.'

'Nonsense! How silly you're being.'

'With all due respect, *Maman*, I can't see what I'd do with a degree.'

The chatter around the table has died down. I am treading on the verge of dangerous territory. Money and inheritance and differences in opinion are not suitable topics to discuss at social gatherings—or so I think. I cannot recall any longer.

I direct my attention towards the dessert, relishing the sweet and the smooth. Now and then, someone asks me a meaningless question and I grant an equally meaningless answer, barely hearing the words coming from my mouth. The faces around me are so…pure. Untouched. Yes, they have lost loved ones. Yes, they have fretted about a possible invasion. However, they belong to another world. In early 1914, theirs was my world, too, but now it is the exception to the rule, the place where I am on a brief visit before I will surely be called back home again, back to the warzone where I belong.

When the guests are leaving, I draw Victor aside.

'Fucking hilarious, aren't they?' he says. 'The way they'd never dream of using a soup spoon for ice cream!'

I shrug. 'Different things matter here, that's all there is to it. I just wish—'

'That it was not like that.'

'Precisely. Or that… Never mind. What will you do now?'

'Thought I might play more polo.'

'I see.'

The guests drive off, leaving Constance, *Maman*, and me standing in the grand hallway with only one another to speak to. It is unbearable.

'You'll be more sensible in the morning, *mon chéri*. Then you will see I'm right about your studies,' *Maman* states. 'Sleep well.'

I stare after her as she disappears up the flight of stairs.

Constance stretches out a hand and I clutch it.

'Did I spoil the evening?'

'Oh, never mind about that. But Charles?'

'What?'

'I'm still hungry. Come on, let's go downstairs.'

'*Splendide.*'

Sitting in the kitchen with my sister and a biscuit jar like when we were children, servants bustling around us, I get a glimpse of what true peace is supposed to feel like. It is the first time since the armistice.

Chapter thirty

Rosalie

ISABEL'S CLICKING SHOES are the very same that she purchased around the time of my seventeenth birthday. She is certainly a frugal shopper, and as she takes off her coat, I conclude that it must be even older than the shoes. The fur trimming is patchy, the colour of withering paper. Her face is as fresh and serene as ever, though. Despite the hollows of her cheeks I know she has enjoyed these four years of persistent work. The backbone of her mind is entirely different from my own. I have vivid memories of watching the gore run off her like water runs off a goose, marvelling at how she did it.

'Have you been managing without me?'

I nod. 'Would you like a cup of tea? Daya has baked, as usual.'

My sister would indeed like a cup of tea, and so easily, an orderliness I did not know we lacked is restored to our home.

However, over the days, I am also reminded of the frost between my brother and sister. There is a disenchanted edge that seems to have grown sharper by being apart and becomes apparent in the most subtle ways. Whenever Fred offers Isabel something at the table, she declines; whenever he hears her enter a room, he shies away an inch. Perhaps I was simply too caught up in my own merry life before the war to fully notice this behaviour of theirs.

One evening, I pull Fred aside in the gloomy corridor outside our rooms. 'Tell me what's the matter. I'm not stupid, Fred—I can see there's something.'

'You know what it is.'

'I truly do not, so I'd appreciate it if you told me, because it's driving me mad.'

'You really don't know?' He sighs. 'Then I'd rather spare you, Little Sister.'

I cross my arms and jut my chin out. 'Very well. I'll ask Isabel.'

'Wait! Do you remember her friend Catherine?'

'I think so. I was only ten when she and her family moved away.'

'Yes, we were sixteen. I was quite infatuated with Catherine, but it turned out Isabel was, too, in the same way as myself.' The bitterness in his voice is one I have not detected there before. Not even when speaking of the things he misses being able to see and do.

I draw a sharp breath. 'Do you mean…?'

'Don't make me say it out loud. I came upon them one day when we were out on a picnic. I'd gone to fetch something, and when I came back, there they were, all cosy. You've never been a sixteen-year-old boy, Rose, but it's not great fun to discover a girl prefers your sister over you.'

I cannot fathom the words coming from his mouth, nor can I decide what I find most disconcerting—that I was so clueless about Isabel, or that Fred would still hold a grudge. 'It's been more than a decade since! Catherine can't possibly have been that special.'

'You think I still care about Catherine? Of course not! It's Isabel—the way she…*is.*'

'I suppose it's a bit odd that she hasn't married yet.' This is true. My sister recently turned twenty-seven, an age when many women of our class would begin to wonder if they would end up as old maids.

'More than a little odd. Are you still glad I told you?'

'Yes, very much so.' I hesitate. 'What if it had been me? Would you have been as quick to forget your affection for me?'

'That's different. I never had the same affection for Isabel as I do for you to begin with. You know how prim she is, and you don't like it any more than I.' He turns his head to listen for footsteps in case someone should overhear our conversation.

'But that's just a difference in temperament! Speaking of temperament, she and you are more similar than you might like to think.'

'If Papa knew, he'd agree with me.'

My thoughts at once bounce back to when I myself was at risk of public shame, after I terminated my pregnancy. Then, Papa was surprisingly understanding. 'I actually don't think he would.'

We stand close, close together, taking one another's measure, waiting, challenging. If either of us fails to resist the temptation to rush downstairs and spill the secret to our father so that we can be proven right… I would no doubt be quicker, since I do not need the banister to keep my balance. But no. The tension slowly subsides.

'I thought you would feel the way I do,' my brother says at last, resigned.

'I don't know what I feel yet—it's all frightfully new. But I do know that I would get exhausted if I spent the rest of my life being unpleasant over something that isn't really my concern.'

'It's the family's concern.'

'It won't hurt us unless you decide to spread the rumour in Hampstead.'

He laces his fingers with mine and I let him, smothering the angry spark in my chest. He rubs my knuckles with his thumb. 'I shall do my best to treat her as if there was nothing bad between us, if you really want me to, though it's difficult to get rid of an old grudge. I suppose that was always part of it.'

'Good. I'll wager she's dismayed with herself as it is, praying so much.'

I watch him close his bedroom door, then I lean back against the wall, my hands flat against the tapestry. Fred, who shared my views when I told him of my involvement in the suffrage movement. Fred, who is less of a monarchist than any of us in the family… I expected him to be the most accepting, too, in that nonconservative fashion. And Isabel, who so frequently talks about the Bible, and who has not acted or spoken anything indecorous for as long as I can remember…

The confusion makes me sick. I hold Fred dearer than Isabel, yet I sympathise more with her, contrary to my common sense. Nothing has to change, though, not as long as he is friendlier and she returns the sentiment—then we can maintain our facade without crumbling under its weight. At least now I know there is a facade.

Fatigue pulls at my eyelids, luring me to sleep. I glance at the mantle clock. A quarter to ten. The dull pain around my temples has persisted for several hours.

'I have a headache. I'll go to bed early. Goodnight.' I rise from the sofa, tucking the small notebook under my arm. I have begun to write again, and I much prefer my own pencil to a typewriter.

'Goodnight. God bless you,' Isabel says. Her eyes remain on the delicate needlework resting in her lap.

I pause in the doorway. Does she know that I know?

Fred has already fallen asleep in one of the armchairs after having been unusually polite throughout the day.

I retreat upstairs to my room, my limbs heavy like solid granite. Perhaps I have not been eating properly, or perhaps I slept poorly last night without realising it.

When I wake the following morning, cool water is dripping into my eyes, dimming my vision. Through the haze, Minnie peers down at me.

She returns the soaked cloth to the porcelain basin on my nightstand and presses two fingers against my forehead. I want to tell her that she should not be drenching the cloth, only dampening it, and that she cannot feel my temperature after just having temporarily cooled me down. However, to my dismay, speaking is an effort in itself.

The harsh sunlight streaming through a slit in the curtains animates every speck of dust on her dress as well as the stains on her white apron. In that light, her lips remind me of dried prunes. Without a word, she stands and turns from me, skirts twirling, and leaves me alone with my pounding headache. My vision is still blurred, though the water must have dried.

A fit of coughing seizes me until it feels as if someone has torn my lungs and throat to shreds. The sheet is spattered with red. I reach up. Blood is leaking from my nose. Icy fright rushes through me. I have seen so much blood during these past years, but never has it been my own, at least not under circumstances such as these. This is new, this is sudden. I can come up with a number of diagnoses, and one of them…one of them is perfectly plausible, as reluctant as I am to admit it.

Doctor McWright enters my room shortly thereafter to perform his examination. It is a swift procedure, and soon I lie listening to the muffled voices coming from the corridor, along with my father's endless pacing back and forth. One word in particular strikes a chord of panic within me. *Influenza.* Before I can ponder this, raw coughs send ripples of pain through my chest again, shaking my body.

Papa enters and shuts the door behind him unusually carefully before sinking down on the foot of the bed. For a few moments he sits silent. He knows very well that I have heard what the doctor said. 'McWright will be back this afternoon. Try to get some sleep until then. And don't forget to eat, eh? Daya will bring some hot soup.' He leans forward as if to kiss my cheek, but catches himself just in time.

When the doctor returns, I have only managed half my bowl of soup. McWright claims that my health has neither improved nor worsened, which is a relief of sorts. His face is steeped in shadow as he tells us in a low voice that he has visited countless other victims throughout the day. Before departing, he discovers yet another one: our cook.

What follows is a period of delirium. I do not know when or if I speak, much less what I say. I cannot focus on anything. Sometimes, I find it difficult even to sleep.

Once my thoughts begin to clear and the nausea subsides, I can discern Papa shouting from the vestibule, after which the doctor replies with forced calm. The contents of their conversation remain a mystery to me.

The next time I wake from my drowsy sleep, there is only my own breaths, which are no longer as laboured. The familiar atmosphere of an extinguished life has dawned on the household, though. I have sensed it so many times. It is the feeling of a soul being sucked out from its bodily shell.

Left is only dense black.

Daya's funeral takes place on a Tuesday morning. The first trembling snowflakes this winter are falling, melting the moment they touch the wretched gravestones.

I have recovered enough now to stand on my own two feet, though my mourning garb and thick coat are weighing me down, as is the guilt. I was the first to be infected in our house. Daya could have caught the influenza anywhere, but I must at least consider the possibility that I passed it on to her.

The ceremony is brief, the attendants narrowed down to Papa, Fred, Isabel, Minnie, Laura, and myself. None of the deceased's own acquaintances are present, and she was never close to her family. When people are dying at this rate, most either have their calendar booked with funerals already, or they fear traveling and thereby exposing themselves to the disease.

Laura stands silent next to me. Her round apple cheeks are rosy from the cold, but her mouth is a thin line of anxiety. Her own father is ill, and the love that was never there between them has magically sprung up. She has moved back home, not to nurse him but to give her mother comfort.

I stare at the hastily crafted cross with the ornamental doves. Somehow…yes, somehow, I thought that now, with the war in the past, we would be out of reach from death's grasping claws. I should have known better.

Fred places a clumsy kiss between my temple and the corner of my eye, then accompanies Papa and the others across the graveyard and through the streets, back home. I remain standing, shivering. I was not even aware that I cared for our cook so ardently until now.

'Come. Let's go back and have a cup of hot tea,' Laura says.

I nod and allow her to walk me back into the warmth. We drink our strong tea—I suspect Minnie has laced it with a splash of gin for the sake of our nerves—and Laura leaves with a promise to meet with me a few days later.

That meeting is the last time I see her. Mr Hamilton does not survive his ordeal. I read his death notice in The Daily Mirror along with one I struggle to comprehend. It is Laura's.

What concerns me is that I feel little sadness, only a sensation similar to choking slowly, slowly. At times, I do not feel even that. I cannot grieve properly when I know it is not true. Laura is not dead, because that is not how these things work. Harry and Mark and so many others—*they* are dead, because they went to war and put themselves in danger, regardless of their reasons. Laura is at home, safe, untouched. She was walking arm in arm with me on the strand last week; she will be there again soon. A doctor must have pronounced her death sentence, but what does he know? He is a fool.

Having seen more people draw their dying breath than I can count or remember, I should not feel this distant from it all, as if the idea of Laura's passing was a bizarre joke someone insisted on repeating until I was tired of hearing it. I know I am just denying what I fear to be true, but… There are so many things she deserved to do first.

Day by day, my denial fades along with the lassitude remaining from my own illness. I am alone. My friends have disintegrated and vanished one by one, some of them through my own fault, others through forces and events beyond my control. My little family of four is so far intact, and for that I am grateful. Nevertheless, my circle has become almost too small for me to breathe.

Chapter thirty-one

Rosalie

WITH BUDDING SPRING comes the urge to emerge from my steadfast world at home. London is dreadfully dull to me now that nearly two years have passed since my coming home. My desire to experience something new—something fine and dashing, something exciting—grows more and more fierce. The question is not so much what I ought to do, but where I ought to go. In the right surroundings, I will surely find plenty of fresh opportunities. When I think of it that way, it is not really a question at all. England is too familiar; America is too far off. Berlin does not exactly occupy a place in my heart, and Italy is much too warm. Paris. It must be Paris.

One morning, as our little family is seated around the breakfast table, I summon the courage to ask for something I have never dreamt of asking before. 'Papa?' I clench the napkin in my lap.

My father is too distracted by his coffee to pay me any attention, though my siblings raise their heads.

I pour some buttermilk in my own cup and clear my throat, too loudly for him to ignore. 'I'm going away for a while. On a trip, if you will.'

'Going away? Why on earth?' He scoffs. 'Haven't you been away enough as it is these past few years?'

I take elaborate care in spreading marmalade on my bread in an attempt to postpone my answer as long as possible. 'Well, I have, Papa, but it has taught me that there's more to this world than…than this!'

His brows come together, spilling over his eyes, and the lines on his forehead deepen enough to hide a penny. 'Where to, then?'

'Paris. I intend to go to Paris, if you'll only give me a fair allowance.' My every trace of hesitation is gone. I want to see the spider-legged Eiffel Tower and high-pitched rooftops reflecting in the Seine with my own two eyes. I want to behold the paintings in the Louvre, and go to the theatres. I want to taste the grotesque snails and frog legs that I have heard so much about.

Papa's gaze is glued to his plate as if it could save him from having this conversation. Then, he shoves his chair back and stalks out into the corridor, leaving the testimony of a slamming door.

I rush after him, abandoning Fred, Isabel, and the now cold breakfast. 'I *will* go! It's not like it was before. So many women manage on their own now!' The statement is only partly true but there is no room for details.

Papa swings around. 'I lost all three of you for years! I had to come home from work every evening and stare at your empty places at the table—'

'There were important tasks to be dealt with.'

'And look where that landed your brother! Now he's…'

'Blind? Does that make him nothing, then? Do you want me to sit around at home all day, just waiting to get married again?'

'What would you do in Paris?' He flaps out a hand and is an inch away from knocking down a vase from the turn of the previous century.

'I would enjoy myself, have a jolly time, see things. Maybe write something or—' At last, I manage to lower my voice a notch and relax my tense shoulders. 'I had so little time to do that, to enjoy myself, during the war. You can't deny it, Papa.'

'How can you say that when all those chaps are gone, eh? That hapless husband of yours—Bride's boy—and all the others, too.' The blood that has gone to his face slowly drains until all that remains is grey ash.

'*You* didn't fight, did you? At least *I* helped to stitch them together again.'

Not even my own blunt Papa will easily forget such a remark, and indeed, that is the end of the argument. This time, I do not follow him.

Minnie tip-toes softly over the carpet, on her way to collect our plates. Her eyes are wide and she gives me an amused smirk. 'He certainly got hot under the collar.'

'Won't you mind your own business? Go on, keep going!'

Minnie trips ahead in a feigned hurry. Once she is gone, I allow myself to slump down on the sofa. I will *make* him see. He cannot keep me locked up behind bars. He would not.

With some help of persuading from Fred, I am proven right.

Papa refuses to speak of the matter after it has been settled, but he grants me a handsome monthly allowance when we are standing on the train station a few weeks later. 'I would not want you to spend this bloody, foolish trip worrying about money. You're many things, but you're not stupid,' he mutters and tucks the first check in my pocket.

I nod. I would rather accept the money and make the most of it than throw it away and join the working girls simply to salvage my independence. Although it bothers me to admit, easy living glistens brighter than labouring. I ought to know, for I have had my share of both.

I lock my arms around him and whisper in his ear, 'Promise you won't stay cross for long. I will send you some bonbons.'

His coarse hair scratches against my cheek and I withdraw.

Then Fred scoops me off my feet after a second of awkward fumbling in the air, hat barely sticking to my head. 'Come back soon, or I'll swim across the channel and track you down,' he says and laughs.

'We'll see. I can't know yet whether it will be a few months or more than that.' I brush my fingers against his cheek. 'Take care. You *have* to take care. Perhaps it will get better—'

He catches my hand in his. 'Don't get your hopes up, Little Sister.'

I bade Isabel farewell by the door at home, and I cannot think of anyone else I should have called on.

I climb up into the carriage, the hem of my skirt sweeping against the steps, steam encircling me. After some pushing and squeezing, I find myself seated opposite a man in hideous tweed and an old lady with her matching poodle. I smooth the folds in my skirt and rest my hands in my lap, tapping my knee with impatience. Oh, just to think of all the things I will do! I could even… But no, I must refrain from going on a likely futile hunt for Charles. I did promise myself to stop pining after a man who must be either dead or has forgotten about me. That is the only way to escape more pain, pain which I should like to leave behind now.

The boat ride across the channel is a trivial thing, since I have made it time and again. The nausea I felt when Mary and I travelled to Rouen for the first time is now a recollection I can smile at. The sun beams on my face in flaring waves of heat where I stand by the rail. The spring is a fine one this year.

In Paris, I rent a room at a modest but perfectly acceptable hotel on Rue Pasquier, so that I can live in comfort while I search for more long-term accommodation. It is wild to be here unchaperoned, by all means, but the fact that I am a widow proves a great aid, since it gives one a measure of respectability. Nevertheless, I have not been on my own in my entire life. The first few nights, I lie awake resonating back and forth with myself on whether I should return home at first light. I decide to stay.

I spend countless afternoons at a street café, perched on a wiry chair that digs into my thighs and leaves red marks. There, I watch the people pass by, or flick the pages of a novel whilst sipping on a beverage for as long as I possibly can.

The cobble stones are grey bubbles ready to burst any moment under shoes and tyres. Chinks of sunlight sparkle in the dirty water of the fountain in the square. Charming restaurants and boutiques are interspersed among opulent houses from the previous century. The Eiffel Tower's contours are stark against the chalky blue sky—the monument is thirty years old yet feels both ancient and futuristic at the same time. Paris is as beautiful as a certain officer once told me. Life is good, to put it plainly.

An impulse seizes me. My hair, long and prone to tangles, feels drearier every time I look at it. Now, a few strands are in my ice cream. This morning, I had to spend half an hour pinning it to my head before I could show myself outdoors. I used to be terribly fond of my hair once, but not anymore.

Without further ado, I push my ice cream to the side and leave the café, not halting until I reach the sign that I have passed so many times: *Coiffure*. Upon delivering my request to the hairdresser inside, he gives me a long glance, scratching the back of his head. 'Are you quite sure, Mademoiselle? All that lovely hair would be a shame to cut off.'

'I'm as sure as I ever will be, thank you.'

The man with the scissors shrugs and starts to comb through my locks to ensure that there are no undesirable knots. He then picks up the rest of his tools and there is a chippering, satisfying sound as he chops off my hair.

I close my eyes in anticipation. It is a bold move, but the bob is starting to receive more and more attention amongst women, far more now than when I first saw it in the magazines of 1917. I have high hopes of what the barber might accomplish. I am not necessarily trying to look boyish—that at least would calm Papa—but something one of the women Laura introduced me to said rings in my mind. That cutting your hair to your chin is a statement, a step towards freedom. True or not, it appealed to me.

At last, when my legs are numb from sitting still, the barber announces that he is finished and removes the fabric protecting my clothes. The floor around my chair is covered in brown clippings. I gaze at my reflection in the mirror. My hair is cropped neatly just above my chin, and the texture is transformed, too. The volume is retained, but instead of my old, lose curls, the surface is marcelled and shiny.

I slowly reach up to brush it with my fingers, allowing myself a moment of silent consideration. 'Thank you. It's just marvellous.'

'Well, I'm pleased you do not seem to regret the choice, Mademoiselle,' the barber says. 'You look like one of the girls at *Le Rongeur Dansant*.'

'Pardon?'

'A club where they play jazz. Horrid music, but you might take a liking to it,'

I nod and pay him, making a mental note to ask the woman managing the hotel where I live where I can find this intriguing club.

I reach for my hat, which I laid off when I arrived, but decide to carry it in my hand and leave my head bare. The street is alive and buzzing with people: fashionable young women, businessmen clutching briefcases, couples strolling arm in arm, and boys offering newspapers for sale. The air is vibrant with rapid French and the noise of car engines.

The club is unlike anything I have seen before. The people are dancing as if they will explode with adrenaline, and it only takes a glance to see that the women's skirts end well above their ankles. That is not all, though. The band, whose music the barber referred to as 'jazz', consists of coloured members only. Naturally, I am not a stranger to skin like theirs, but there were few coloured people in Hampstead, and certainly no coloured musicians. One of the sprightly young men I dance with informs me that the band is actually from the United States, though, and that its members served in France during the war, after which they chose to stay. Perhaps our years of struggle have brought something good, then. Perhaps they have brought more novelties than I knew was possible.

Charles

After Marie-Louise has recovered from the influenza, I return to Paris, having promised my mother to at least pay a visit to the Sorbonne and see whether I might not reconsider. The faces I encounter are to a large extent familiar, particularly among the elderly teachers, who likely stayed inside the premises of the building for the duration of the war. The nostalgia does beat down upon me. However, I feel no true longing.

One of the faces is special. If he had not allowed the pencil moustache to grow back like a streak of tar over his lip, I might not have recognised the man, who looks ten years older than I know him to be. Still, if I squint, I can picture him holding a croquet mallet in one hand and *Works and Days* in the other.

'What on earth are you doing here, Marcel?'

'Why, Charles, I'm catching up on the studies, of course. We missed quite a bit, being away and all.'

'I suppose we did. I don't know if I could go back, though. In fact, I won't.'

Marcel only shrugs his shoulders. They are brittle somehow, like the broken wings of a blackbird.

I stay with him for a while, exchanging stories in short, abrupt phrases. He tells me of the others. Michael has been released from prison at last and is toiling away at a bank since much of the family fortune was lost during the war. Henri is married to a certain Évelyne Allais and about to become a father. I recall her slender porcelain hands and rigid posture that day in the park, and wonder if the child will inherit those traits. My mother will be displeased when I tell her the news, for she has not yet given up the vain hope of making Évelyne her own daughter-in-law. What I hear succeeds my expectations: four out of the five of us came through alive, since Louis died in East Africa years ago. That is a clear majority.

As I make my departure, I am certain that Marcel and I are parting in truth. I barely even felt any joy seeing him. Too much has changed since I saw him last. We are not the same people; we have taken part in so many things that we are too ashamed of to share with one another. We are not the same people, and the world is not the same place.

The telephone startles me, and I pick it up.

'Charles? It's me.'

I frown. 'Michael?'

'Yes, Michael. I… Have you seen Marcel since you got back?'

'I encountered him back at Sorbonne. He looked awful.'

Michael pauses. When I am about to ask whether he is still there, he finally speaks. 'He was doing awful. He…he's dead. Killed himself. I was going over to ask him to the races when his landlady told me they had found him in the bath.'

I grip the telephone tighter, tighter. He cannot mean it. I waited to hear this fateful message for four years—but now? Now there is peace; now the dying is supposed to be done with.

'Dead?'

'Yes. Completely. I just thought I ought to tell you.'

'Thank you.' I draw a deep breath. 'Michael?'

'Yes?'

'You did the right thing. When you stayed at home, I mean. You knew from the start what kind of man you wanted to be, and it saved you a lot of pain, I think.'

The voice on the other end at once sounds guarded. 'Perhaps, although I can promise you prison wasn't the most darling experience I've had, nor was being spat at.'

'I'm not saying you had it easy, on the contrary, only that it must have been better than being dead.'

'Of course.'

I nod to myself. 'Take care, will you?'

'You too, Charles. *Au revoir.*'

I return the telephone to the wall. To spend every day for such a long time trying to survive, only to end it yourself as soon as you are granted your safety… It is the greatest irony.

Chapter thirty-two

Charles

I HAVE HAD enough of thinking about her. I chase her out of my head each time, but I swear she will be an everlasting ghost to me unless I see her in the flesh. Rosalie. Sometimes, she goes away for days or even weeks. Other times, she stays with me regardless of how many stupid Parisian frivolities I engage in and how many people I talk to. At last, in May, the solution strikes me. I turn to the telephone.

'Michael? I need your assistance.'

'What with?'

'Did I mention a girl to you last time we spoke? I don't think I did.' Too late, I remember that we have not spoken since he rang me to deliver the gruesome news of Marcel's suicide. *Of course* I did not mention any girl.

'No, I don't think so either.'

'Well, I have to find her somehow.'

An audible sigh. 'If you have plans of dragging me into a vain searching adventure—'

'Not quite. Just listen. You know a few British pilots, don't you?'

'I went to Downside School with Gerald Maxwell when I was a kid, before we moved to France, if that's what you're referring to. In fact, we went fishing together not long ago. He was in No. 56 Squadron.'

I could dance a jig in triumph. *Magnifique.* Now, how about you contact him as soon as I hang up, ask him if he happens to know the address of a man called Fred Wilkes, and ring me when you find out.'

Rosalie's family—I assume her father and sister are now involved, since they will have read her blind brother's letters for him—ignore my attempts for a full month. I tell them that I am an old friend of Rosalie, that we were close during the war, and that I simply wish to contact her. I have almost lost all hope when, one day, I receive an unusually cluttered letter that looks as if written by a child. It must be from Fred, and indeed, his signature is there at the bottom of the page, neater and more practiced than the rest. Only one line truly matters to me, though: Rosalie is in Paris. *Paris!* Fortune is kind at last. And in the same sentence, Fred has written the name and address of his sister's hotel. The very day after receiving the letter, I locate the building.

An old woman, likely a head of staff, informs me that Rosalie Wilkes is not in her room, and would I like to wait?

'No, thank you, Madame.' I want our meeting to be perfect—not in the presence of others, not on the bottom floor of an average hotel. 'Is there any other way I might cross her path?'

'You ought to catch her if you stay close to Place de la Concorde this evening. That girl always goes on a walk at night, though she really should not, and tells me the morning after how beautiful the Concorde is.'

'Are you certain?' I give the old woman a good and thorough stare, which she returns with equal determination.

She nods, her coiffure swaying like a grey cloud. 'I'm as certain as one can be, Monsieur. But you better have honest intentions with her, or I'll have to report this to the police, that's one thing for certain.'

'You have my word.' I highly doubt that the police would give a damn.

After emerging from the hotel, I push my hat down over my ears and tip it slightly to the side. Soon, I might have Rosalie in my arms again, if she will let me. I am afraid they will tremble too much to hold. The prospect of seeing her is at once daunting. What if all is not well between us? I could not blame her for having forgotten me, when I did not write for such a long time. What if…what if she has found another? The letter I at last received from her brother did not mention a new husband, but of course, she would not have to be married to have affections for someone. I know that better than anyone.

I *will* go, only not tonight. Soon. As soon as I muster the courage.

Marcel is walking with me through an underground tunnel. He is dripping a trail of blood after us, though I do not know where it is coming from. The tunnel is caving in bit by bit as we walk, the stones falling in our footsteps.

'We'll be late for the races,' my old friend says. 'That won't do. I've already bet on a horse.'

I try to walk faster but I cannot. My shoes stick to the ground with each step. The stones are rumbling behind us, the noise like an artillery barrage, coming closer, closer, closer—

I want to shake myself. I have to stop dreaming like this. I have to stop unconsciously feeling sorry for myself. The more I watch other soldiers walk the streets or stand on a train station waiting for their next transport, the more I realise my luck. The void is still draining me, true. I still feel robbed of my dreams and my friends and my youth, none of which I can get back. But I have the money to make a new life possible, and, hopefully, a woman to share it with. I even have all my limbs and at least some kind of common sense that stays with me through the nightmares. So many do not have any of those things. They have come home to some village that the war has wreaked havoc on, have lost not just friends but brothers, and will have no alternative but to find employment as a civil servant or a factory worker to earn their living. If they can find work at all, that is. They have not had the luxury I had of starting the repairing process in Neustadt, where I found the time and calm to slowly patch myself together.

I struggle to sleep while they struggle to walk with crutches. I have difficulties forgetting the time I buried my hand in someone's decaying stomach, but I can wash that hand under a silver tap and dry it on a creamy linen towel as often as I like.

I *will* go to see her. Tomorrow night.

The following evening, I set out from the apartment clad in my best suit and hat. The old woman's instructions were vague, but after passing the pillars of Palais Bourbon, I slow my steps to stand by the end of the massive stone bridge that is Pont de la Concorde. The warm June rain drizzles down in light cascades, forming beads on my face and soaking my khaki blazer. I lean back against a nearby lamppost, treasuring the saffron light while hoping it will not ruin my moment of surprise.

Rosalie should pass across the bridge; it is difficult not to if one takes a walk in this area. I am nearly slumbering on my post— reminding me of the poor fellows who fell asleep on sentry duty and had to face courts martial—when I spot her.

She is resting her elbows on the banister, clasping her hands above the dark Seine. I can only just discern her reflection in the water, for the moon is peeking out behind a cloud. It is her. I know it is, by the curve of her neck and the way she now brushes the rain off her arms.

Paris is never wholly quiet, but at this hour, the sounds are faded and few. My carefully measured footsteps, on the other hand, are painfully loud as I approach towards the middle of the bridge.

'Would you care for a cigarette, Madame?' I confess I have a soft spot for dramatic flair.

She keeps her eyes on the river, taking little notice of me. 'No. No thank you, I don't smoke.'

'Madame.' More clearly this time.

Finally, finally she turns to me. Perhaps ten feet still separate us, but recognition and shock are both written plain on her face. Neither one of us utters another word.

I dig in my breast pocket and extract a little box. The label on the lid reads 'Altoids Curiously Strong Mints'. I toss it to her and she lunges forward to catch it, but her hands are wet, and the trinket breaks the surface of the Seine with a splash.

'You should have aimed better,' she says.

'And you should have caught it.'

Rosalie crosses her arms, lips parted as she prepares to speak.

I cut her short, desperate to say what I came to say. 'I don't need it, anyhow. I found you.' I enclose the distance between us. 'Please tell me you'll have me. Just give me a moment to—'

'Right now, I…' She studies my face, shuddering. 'I want to punch you. Not slap—punch.'

'I wouldn't mind if you did.'

'I won't. But you better have a good explanation.'

I release a breath. 'To give you the brief version, I was sat in a prisoner of war camp since late April 1917. I wasn't permitted to write to you.' I give her the rest of the story, which is less brief than I would have wished.

When I finish, Rosalie is staring more intensively than when she first recognised me. 'That is quite some detective's work, Charles. If it's all true, you could become a private investigator.'

'It is all true. World you rather I'd forgotten you?'

'No. I'm glad you didn't. So very glad.'

At these blessed words, I dare to touch her cheek. The kiss we share is slow and hurried altogether, exuding bittersweet memories. I stroke the damp hair clinging to her scalp. It is not prettily pinned up like I remember, but ends at her chin. 'You got a haircut.'

'What do you think?'

'Grand. We should go inside.'

'I know a darling place.'

The café Rosalie leads me to is the smallest I have ever been in, with chequered floor tiles and cushioned chairs. A pudgy woman is sitting in one corner and a dainty-looking man is smoking in another, but other than that we are the only guests.

After ordering glasses of chardonnay, we embark on the quest of recounting the past two years of our lives to one another. Our drinks are still untouched after half an hour; we are too busy talking to drink.

Rosalie's face brightens bit by bit, though she appears reluctant at one point. Whilst telling me about the autumn and winter after we last met, she grows silent and takes to surveying her cuticles. Then, she carries on in her usual tone. I shuffle this moment to the back of my head, adding it to the collection of memories I do not want to revisit. Perhaps I was merely imagining—yes, that was surely it.

Eventually, the pudgy woman and the dainty man depart from the café. Not long thereafter, the waiter politely asks us to leave as well.

The rain has ceased and left is only the lukewarm air, heavy with the scent of linden trees and the sewer system. Our clothes are not yet dry, and my blazer has become a damp second skin.

'Where do you live?' Rosalie asks.

'My apartment is in the opposite direction of your hotel, I'm afraid. If you go missing for too long, that old lady might telephone the police, or so she threatened.'

'If you were a real gentleman, you'd accompany me to the door, but I know you don't like such silly formalities.'

I arch an eyebrow. 'And if you were a real lady, you wouldn't be out so late. There's hardly any taxi available at this hour.'

She slides her arms around my neck and inches closer until the tips of our noses touch. 'And do you mind the walk?'

'Not a bit.'

I stretch my limbs with a groan and sit on the creased bedcover, waiting for the drowsiness to pass. The embroidered pillows are neatly arranged behind me, and the only disarray in the hotel room is our shoes lying kicked off on the floor.

A grin spreads across my face as I run my eyes over Rosalie, who is curled up next to me, snoring lightly. Was last night nothing but a dream? No, I really did find her in the rain at Pont de la Concorde, and we really did lose the trinket box in the river. We kissed. We talked at the café, and upon arriving at the hotel, I managed to sneak upstairs with her. Then, we slept. Only that, nothing more, but it was the most soothing rest I could have wished for.

'Rosalie?' I place a hand on her shoulder. 'Good morning.'

She rubs her eyes and gazes up at me, then tugs at my shirt until I surrender and lie down with her again.

After some time, we rise and draw the curtains from the windows, filling the room with white morning light. The streets below are once more alive with people.

'Do you know something, Rose? I didn't dream anything last night.'

She removes a strand of hair from my jaw and traces my birthmarks with her finger. 'Is that a bad thing?'

'No. I always dream about horrible things—things I never want to see again, yet I have to see them every night—but not last night. I didn't see anything at all. I just slept like…like a baby.'

'Then it's a very good thing, but you ought to wake me up if you have those dreams again. You probably will.'

I nod and lean in for a kiss, but a sharp knock on the door interrupts us.

Rosalie breaks free from our embrace. 'That will be the maid announcing breakfast.' She opens the door just enough to look at the woman and keep me out of view at the same time. 'I'd like to eat in my room today, thank you. I don't feel quite fit to go downstairs.'

I escape to the adjoining bathroom as an extra measure of safety, though it turns out I do not have to stay there long.

Rosalie closes the door again before the maid can reply, and turns to me. 'I hope you know how improper it is that you spent the night.'

I emerge from the bathroom. 'Unless my memory fails me, we didn't do anything particularly daring yesterday evening.'

She laughs. 'Daring enough to stay in here until the coast is clear. Now, you can't have my croissant, but I care little for the roll and cheese—those are yours for the taking.'

'You're too kind.'

The maid brings up a tray with bread and pastry, a piece of cheese and cold cuts, a selection of fruit, milk, and a steaming hot coffee pot.

Rosalie changes into a fresh, dove-blue dress, while I have no choice but to keep yesterday's dishevelled clothes. Together we sit down on the wiggly balcony chairs with the breakfast tray on the veined stone table between us.

'Is it like you imagined it to be?' I ask, and pop a strawberry in my mouth.

'What?'

'Paris. Is it as good as I told you?'

'It's better.'

Chapter thirty-three

Rosalie

CHARLES AND I savour the weeks that follow, doing our utmost to compensate for the gaps in our time together. Gone is the intimidating threat of being parted without warning, gone is the agonising fear. Left are only pleasant visits to restaurants and gardens in daytime, entertainment in the evening, and caresses at night. I have not yet told Charles about the actions I forced myself to in order to get rid of the baby we might have had. However, I take every precaution to prevent another pregnancy. To my relief, he is as adamant as I am in the matter, and we have even greater care than we used to.

Together, we make frequent appearances at cocktail parties— a terrifically modern kind of gathering. The rules are simple: everything is gilded with tinselled glamour, one drops in and leaves at one's preferred times, and one does not have to be particularly familiar with the host to show up. It is an entirely different affair than the strictly organized dinners and luncheons and tea parties I occasionally attended before the war. Indeed, none of our new acquaintances pays any heed to archaic formalities, and no one hesitates to turn on the gramophone regardless of the hour.

I befriend a Miss Eleanor Belmore, who has come from Alabama, across the Atlantic. This fact—I have never made such a lengthy journey myself—as well as her being the author of two published works, makes a lasting impression on me. Her social incompetence is obvious. Somehow, though, it merely adds to her charm, her accent and way of dancing causing the young men and women at the cocktail parties to flock around her like curious birds.

Once, I discover her reaching into my handbag and pulling out my notebook, which contains my recent attempts at writing. I lunge forward to reclaim it, but Eleanor holds it out of my reach with a concentrated wrinkle between her eyebrows. After another minute or so, she willingly turns around and allows me to snatch it from her.

'What was that for?'

Eleanor grins, running a hand through her flaxen bob. 'Do you know something, Rose? You should use all that…all that scribble and notes. There's some interesting material, really.'

It is impossible to be angry with her for long, and I shrug, giving the idea genuine consideration. 'I suppose there is, but who is to say I can write? Would *you* care to read it?'

She snickers. 'I ain't going to read it, that's one thing for sure. I ain't going to read another aspiring writer's work. That's nothing short of self-destructive. But if you *do* come up with a good story, then you ought to try at the very least. You'll never know if you never try, mind you.'

I eye her with suspicion. 'I might.'

'Do you want another drink, then?'

'A mint julep.'

We steer our steps towards the cocktails, pushing through the mingling crowd and the heavy fog of cigarette smoke. I help myself to my drink from one of the hired waiters' exquisite silver trays, and Eleanor picks a glass of champagne punch. There is an array of decadent salmon canapés, devilled eggs, and salted nuts to go with the liquor, but I have not taken a fancy to the eatables.

I sip on my piquant cocktail. 'What will you do when summer is past?'

Eleanor tilts her head to one side and then to the other. 'What I usually do. Drink too much and spend too much time with Alfredo Amighetti—the Italian, if you recall. Write for that saucy magazine, if I ever get to it. And you?'

'Heavens, I don't know. Charles still mentions the Sorbonne every now and then, but I don't think he'll be going.'

'But you're certain you will do *something* together? You won't move on?'

The idea sounds absurd, and I laugh. I could hardly move on from Charles. That is a life I cannot imagine now that I know it does not have to be. 'Of course we will do something, Eleanor! We'll marry eventually.'

'Matrimony's so *dull*, you know, Rose. By God, you've been married once already. Wasn't that enough to put you off?' She pretends to cover a yawn.

'I wouldn't necessarily say so. My marriage was never an unhappy one—faulted, I suppose, but they were my own faults.'

Charles

After an evening in the blunt, amusing company of Rosalie's friend Eleanor, we retreat home to my apartment, too misty-eyed and too keen on one another to stay with other people.

I have told Timmele, the butler, that Rosalie is a dear friend of mine, and given him a hefty bribe not to mention the situation to my mother. Rosalie, in turn, has left the hotel and written to her family in London that she has found a room to rent from an old lady.

The nights we spend together are cherished hours of sweet indulgence. I take Rosalie in my arms; she is one mess of dangling pearls and warm skin, ruffled hair and an intoxicating scent of honeysuckle.

She pulls frantically at the layered necklace, and with a snap it comes off. She steps out of her dress, leaving a circle of olive-green around her feet. I send a thankful thought to the fashion designers who have made women's clothing infinitely much simpler in recent years. Rosalie reaches out to trace the contours of my face, laughing as I place a kiss on her nose and another one between her eyebrows. However, when I attempt to slide the corselette off her shoulders, she pushes away my hand takes an abrupt step back.

'Is anything the matter?'

'We cannot. Not this often.'

I frown. 'What are you talking about?'

'I don't want…I don't want any repercussions. I couldn't stand it.' She wraps her arms around herself as if the room was suddenly cold.

'We've taken measures. You know it as well as I do. And even if it *did* happen, I'd marry you in an instant. Not a tinge of scandal whatsoever!' I reach out and after a moment of unbearable tension between us, she takes my hand and comes closer again.

'I still don't want a child *inside* me before we're married, not agai—' she whispers.

'What did you say?' I withdraw ever so slightly, though my eyes remain fixed on hers. Something nasty spurs in my chest.

Her glance flickers for a second or two. Then she tells the ugly, frightening, guilty story with hardly any pause for breath, until the entire truth is laid bare at my feet. Once finished, Rosalie sits on the edge of the bed, her slender shoulders squared. Her eyes are the size of the moon perched on the sky outside, without a trace of tears, for which I am relieved.

'Why didn't you tell me in your letters?' I furiously wipe my own eyes dry, wishing she was not watching.

'You had enough worries as it was. And then you were in the camp.'

I clench my jaw, making my teeth ache. There are an infinite number of things that I would like to say to her, but they are like cloying fudge at the back of my throat. 'I'm sorry.'

'Promise me this won't spoil anything.'

'It could never. We must get some good sleep, and have breakfast in bed. Then we'll feel grand again. It's all those bloody drinks. I *told* you they weren't trustworthy.' I sink down on the bed, and with a tender kiss, it appears that my words have transferred from wishes to truth.

'You had six of them—I counted. I had four, at the very most.'

I force a strangled laugh, knowing it was the other way around. 'If you say so. They were sticky and sweet and filled with strange ingredients, that's all that matters.'

Half an hour later, sleep is indeed claiming us. We lie entwined on the mattress, covers and quilts bundled up at our feet, clothes in a disarray. Rosalie's heartbeats are a subtle thudding but my own deafen me.

239

It *will* be all right, though. I know it like I know that the sun will paint the city in burnished gold every sunset. What happened must be in the past, because how else are we supposed to manage?

'It will not always be like this. I promise. I don't want you to think you can never…never touch me or anything,' Rosalie mumbles just as I am confident that she is sound asleep. 'I'm only being paranoid.'

'You're always a little paranoid when you're tipsy.'

'That's what I was saying.'

I place a kiss at the nape of her neck. Then, before I can say anything else, her breaths are heavy and turn into faint snores.

Rosalie

On Bastille Day, a joyful parade begins at Champ Elysees. The uniformed men march in clean-cut squares, accompanied by prancing cavalry as well as several men of higher rank riding in cars. This is not just any other Bastille Day celebration, but also a victory parade to mark our triumph in the war.

The men participating are all survivors—by any logic, they must be—and it seems strange to me that such a great number escaped death. The nearly untreatable wounds and soggy mud and splinter of bones… Maybe I have a skewed image in my head of how all-consuming the destruction really was. It stands to reason that a large proportion of the soldiers who went into battle made it out alive.

I spot detachments from other armies, too, and I wave vigorously from my place in the crowd as the evidently proud British pass by. The detachments prop their fluttering flags high in the air: a symbol for everything that once was, of the former glory to which they hope to restore their nations. Hundreds of thousands of their fellow soldiers are buried deep in the battlefields, perhaps never to be found, but they appear determined that we shall recover. With the treaty that the high and mighty signed at Versailles little more than two weeks ago, the idea of prosperity is not so far-fetched after all, except for the Germans, naturally. I almost pity the country that was our sworn enemy less than a year ago. The way the French in particular crushed the Huns like a cockroach on Versailles' polished floor…but nothing less would have satisfied those calling for vengeance.

I raise myself on my toes for a better view through the heavy crowd.

Charles grabs my hand and together we make a leap up on the closest bench where we can gaze over the heads separating us from the parade, gripping a nearby lamppost in order to keep our balance as we lean out.

'Wouldn't you have liked to march in it? I'm sure you're more than qualified enough.' I have to raise my voice to be heard over the endless cheers and applause.

'Praise is appealing, but do I have as much right to it as they, when I sat in an *offizierslager* for a year and a half? Besides, I'll never put on a uniform again—that I can promise you. They call this a victory, but haven't everyone lost a hundred times more than we have won?'

'Well.' I turn my face to the breeze. 'I don't disagree with you, but at least we are not Germans.'

To my relief, he laughs. 'No, at least we are not Germans. I can imagine they wouldn't be in the mood for a parade at all.'

We remain there for a little while, leaning dangerously far out from the bench, always with one hand wrapped around the cold metal of the lamppost. Then, just as the soldiers have almost passed completely, Charles winces and deliberately tumbles down to the ground.

'What?' I land next to him.

He does not reply, his glance darting around.

I grip the lapel of his jacket. 'What?'

'I think I saw their silly hats. My sisters' hats.'

Before I can react, two girls have pushed their way through the wall of broad backs and draped skirts separating us. Both are of medium height, like their brother, though their hair is brighter and much straighter. The three siblings all have the same eyes; this must be the strongest family trait.

One of the girls has a bulging mole on her chin, while the other has childishly round cheeks. Despite these misfortunes, they are both pleasing to the eye, and breathe the kind of distinctive confidence that I have always wished for myself.

'Charlie!' the girl with the mole cries.

'Don't call me that.' His voice drips of disdain. 'Where is *Maman*?'

They are speaking rapid French now and I can barely follow the brief conversation.

'What's your name?' I manage, directing my question at the girl whom I guess is the younger of the two, since Charles has neglected introducing us properly.

The girl's expression hardens. 'Oh. You're the English one.' Her own English is stiff and faltering, like my French. It seems we have both made a mistake in trying to speak the other's native tongue.

It was naïve of me to expect the sisters in a household to have had as much practice with languages as their doubtlessly more experienced brother. Nevertheless, they must be equally half-English, and it puzzles me that they should feel so foreign.

Charles flashes me the look of a tormented man. 'This is Constance—' he nods towards the older girl '—and Marie-Louise. Constance, Marie-Louise, this is Madame Rosalie Bride.'

Constance asks Charles something in a hushed voice, speaking without pause for breath.

Unintentionally, my fingers creep up to my face at their own volition to cover my greatest insecurity. The freckles have finally begun to fade in the sun, though, and with some good fortune, they might be close to transparent soon.

'We ought to be going,' Charles says, this time in English.

Marie-Louise gives him a subtle pout, dapples of shadow dancing on the brim of her silky hat. 'I think *Maman* would like to see you more often. You should come out some day.'

'I'd agree with you, but then we'd both be wrong, and that sounds unnecessary.'

Constance kisses her brother on the cheek and exchanges an amused glance with Marie-Louise. Then, the girls turn their backs to us, and I watch them blend into the masses.

I bundle my shawl to a hard ball. 'Why don't we go somewhere?'

'Yes, let's go find something to drink. Impertinence makes one so thirsty.'

'Really, *Charlie*, they're just like you—annoying and somewhat impolite. I think you love them.'

Charles scoffs. 'Haven't you heard? "Love is a very serious form of mental illness". My friend Marcel told me once.' He pronounces the name slowly.

I search my memory until I realise Marcel was the fellow who killed himself. Maybe it is best to refrain from commenting upon it. 'Not always, I hope.'

'Yes, always. Only sometimes—'

'Sometimes it can be the most tremendous illness.'

A garland of his hair brushes against my cheek, tickling, before our lips meet. The breeze sweeps it away; we part again. Arms linked, we descend towards the nearest café.

'How did they know I exist? I couldn't quite keep up.'

'My mother thought to spend a few weeks in the apartment, and of course, we were out when they arrived this morning. Poor Timmele betrayed us. To his defence, it would have been tricky to pretend your clothes and books were my own.'

'Will they stay with us?' I cringe at the thought of spending even a day in such a strange constellation: the family and the mistress.

'God, no. *Maman* was properly scandalised and is making preparations for returning to the countryside. Constance and Marie-Louise convinced her to let them attend the parade before leaving.'

'Good. Not everyone likes me as much as you do.'

Chapter thirty-four

Rosalie

MADAME D'ABOVILLE CARRIES herself with rare grace. Her hairstyle belongs to another era and has begun to fade from bronze to matte silver. Her skin, however, is as smooth as a child's, making it impossible to determine her age. She stretches out a petal-veined hand and I take it, giving it a small shake rather than the kiss I suspect she would prefer. From that moment on, the atmosphere between us thickens until I could slice it up and serve it on a platter.

Charles, who seems to be on the verge between contempt and regret in his mother's presence, steals a quick kiss from me, and together we follow Madame D'Aboville into the parlour.

The idea alone of a parlour feels ancient—though perhaps I, too, am old-fashioned for using the term 'sitting room' instead of the more modern 'living room.' Gilded ornaments line the marble mantlepiece, and the room is heavy with shade. I have to round an empty oak desk, from which a photograph of the man I presume was Charles' father glares at me. I can only marvel at this fragment of the upper-class world that was designed for another reality. I hardly grew up in a stable myself, yet I nearly crumble under all the finery. We are here because Charles' mother insisted on meeting me and did not relent until we accepted her invitation to come out to the country for a short visit. Had there been a plausible alternative, I doubt either of us would have chosen this one.

Madame D'Aboville instructs a servant to bring us refreshments, and we gather around the oval table.

'Sugar?' Madame inquires.

I shake my head. 'Milk, please. Only a splash.'

The servant pours us each a cup of tea and I inhale a fruity scent.

'So. I understand you are English?''

'Yes, it appears I am.'

'Well then, tell me of your family. You were married before? How odd.'

I do my best to swallow the seething irritation. 'My husband died in the war.' I put down the cup on the table with a clink, having finished my tea in a hurry. 'We live—my family lives—in a house in Hampstead. In London, I mean. My father owns a tailoring firm. My brother was a flying ace in the Royal Flying Corps, and my sister a nurse like myself. My mother has been dead for some time.' I list this information like a schoolgirl demonstrating that she knows her homework.

'How *charming.*'

I sincerely hope that she is referring to Hampstead or my father's occupation, rather than to my mother's demise. I know now that what was considered a respected family with a decent amount of money where I grew up is nothing to this lady. Never in my life have I felt poor, and of course I am far from that, but her grandiose attire and manners, not to speak of the house, make me shrink to a church mouse.

Charles makes the tiniest grimace of agony.

'Charles, *mon chéri*, why don't you take the dogs on a walk around the premises? Madame Bride and I have womanly matters to discuss.'

I am tempted to tie Charles to his chair to prevent him from doing as she asks, but to my frustration, he nods and leaves us, likely rejoicing to have been excused.

The clock's ticking is slowly driving me insane. The fruity scent has somehow intensified and spread in the room.

Madame D'Aboville wipes her sinewy fingers on her napkin. 'I will be quite blunt with you, Madame Bride. I do not approve of your intimate relationship with my only son.'

I clench a fold of my skirt in my hand. 'May I ask why?'

'I hope you did not take me for a fool. I know my son. I know *men*, and I know frivolous girls, too. You're living in sin together, and perhaps you're under the illusion that your sinning will end when you marry.'

'Worse sins have been committed, especially of late.'

'With that being said, I don't consider you to be of that…certain calibre which is required to carry on the family name. You understand, I am sure.' By now, she is more than chafing against my nerves. She is stepping on them with razor-sharp heels. The way she twists her shawl and smiles joylessly at me only makes it worse.

'Well, Madam. You may think what you like of me, and of that precious name of yours, but *I* think your son can make up his own mind. As can I.' I am surprised by the coolness in my own voice.

'I cannot have my grandchildren be born protestant and English. Surely even *you* must see that.'

'Religion won't be an issue. I can compromise, and Charles isn't exactly pious. Besides, *Charles* is half English—or have you forgotten your own husband?'

Madame D'Aboville's glare is painfully intense. 'That is not your business, Madame Bride, and it never will be.' She picks up the brass bell from the table and rings for the servant to come and remove our empty cups. 'You may wait outside for my son to return with the dogs. *Adieu.*'

As we drive back in Charles' latest fancy—an American ReVere the colour of lemon zest—I manage to shake the lingering, unpleasant feeling.

'I apologise for my mother,' Charles says for the third time since leaving her company. 'She's not always so…'

'Daunting?'

'Precisely.'

'Why is she so horrified with me being English?' I ask after a few minutes of silence.

'My father was not a pleasant man, Rose. And my mother is narrow-minded; she has taken out twenty-nine years of grudge on the British nation as a whole.'

'Is that all there's to it?'

'Well—' He makes a sharp turn with the car. 'We don't have a particularly old or fine ancestry, despite what Mama might want you to think. New money and so on. I expect she wants her children to marry into truly *sophisticated* families to remedy that.'

'Do you like truly sophisticated families?'

'I like what they *have*. I guess everyone does, whether they care to admit it or not. I used to socialise with some of them, and they were decent people.'

I am in a mood for teasing. 'And their sisters? Were they awfully sweet?'

Charles appears to be considering his reply carefully, his eyes straying from the road to my face and back again. 'Some were, but they were not you.'

'If I had a penny for every time I couldn't tell whether you were being genuinely lovely or just ironic, I might be rich enough for your mother.'

'What would be the fun in that?'

'It's *not* a great deal of fun as it is.'

He sighs. 'I know. I'm sorry.'

I lean my head against his shoulder and coax his one hand from the steering wheel so that I can toy with his fingers. A few of them carry frostbite marks from the trenches, where no doubt he went gloveless occasionally.

Charles has to grip the steering wheel once more to keep us from slamming into an approaching truck. The ReVere's tyres screech, and after the initial fright, I cannot help but laugh.

The evening we spend at the Café Deux Magots is splendid.

Eleanor has caught an older gentleman in her net, and has abandoned all thought of the Italian Alfredo Amighetti. The new gentleman, whom I believe to be Japanese, is well-dressed with a sober tie around his neck and a matching hat pushed down over bold eyebrows. He and Eleanor exchange very few words, and I suspect that the relationship is based upon mutual physical attraction rather than any deeper emotion.

During our time at cocktail parties, Charles and I have accumulated a small circle of other friends as well. Liz Carter, whose fine hands are her great vanity, and the Massons, whose married life is anything but dull, are there, too.

Liz taps the table with two slim fingers to attract our attention. 'I thought I might inform you that I plan on taking my route to Spain for some time. I leave in August.'

'Is Spain so much better than Paris?' Charles says.

Liz raises a thinly tweezed eyebrow.

Eleanor claps her hands. 'I might go with you, then. It sounds so exciting!'

Liz smiles benignly at Charles and me but ignores Eleanor and her painfully southern accent. Their differences are numerous and pronounced as opposed to their few similarities. Where one is refined and sleek, the other is blunt and boisterous. Where one attracts artists alone, the other charms crowds. I think there is something more to it, though, because while Eleanor's grandfather owned a cotton plantation, Liz' family includes previous slaves.

'I doubt we'd have a pleasant time together.'

Eleanor's nostrils flare. 'I suppose not.'

Monsieur Masson—the amateur poet—sighs dramatically. 'Ah, the strife of disagreements; two souls at edge…'

'Don't start with all that bloody nonsense! Not again!'

'Honestly, Charles, he *is* trying!' I say, though unable to hide a smile.

We talk at length of Spain: the fields dotted with sunflowers, the pillars and arches, the salty Serrano ham. Afterwards, Charles and I part with the others to enjoy a stroll along the river in the mild summer air. It is only about ten o'clock, and a soft lavender dusk is cradling the city.

My hand rests in the familiar crook of Charles's elbow, and despite his refusal to get his own hair fashionably cut, he actually resembles the gentleman he was raised to be.

'We ought to do it, too, you know,' I say.

'Do what?'

'Take our route elsewhere.'

'I thought you loved Paris? I do—I really do.' Charles's voice is tinged with insult.

'I love it more than I could ever say. Only…'

'Only other places are glorious and lovable, too?'

'I wouldn't know, but they might be. I've never been to Italy, or Spain, or any of those hubs of culture, and although you might have seen more than I, I doubt that you've seen it all.'

We cross one of the numerous bridges over the Seine, slowly enclosing the distance between ourselves and the apartment. Charles braids my fingers with his and swings our hands back and forth. He tilts his head back to catch a glimpse of the sky before giving the door a resounding knock, waiting for Timmele to open and take care of our hats and scarves.

'No, I've not seen everything. I've seen too much of other places, but far from everything.'

'We've got all the time in the world to think about it. Isn't that wonderful? To have all the time in the world.'

Charles frowns. 'It's peculiar, if nothing else. I haven't thought myself to have all the time in the world for five years.'

The door opens and we step inside.

Charles

The clouds are waiting to burst. There is no pain, only suffocating fear as I dodge under a plume of shells and dirt and pieces of flesh. No, no. There must be no fear, because if there is then I am as doomed as the rest of them. Oh, but I am.

There goes a bullet—my bullet—burying itself in Emile's chest where he is already lying in the trench, gripping De Villiers' hand with bones shining through the skin.

'You did this! You killed him!' De Villiers screams.

And there…there is Gérard with a crystal glass tilted in his delicate hand and with a thick book tucked up under one arm: The Fundamentals of Law.

I have to bite myself in the arm—the place where the knobbly scar is—to keep from jumping out of bed and running.

Rosalie is turning slowly beside me, her bob dishevelled and draped across her eyes. I shake her shoulder. I need to know that this is real and that the dream was indeed nothing but a dream.

Squinting, she props herself on one elbow. 'What?'

'I was there again. And I killed him.'

'Who?'

Now we are both sitting up in the bed, sheets tangled around our feet as always when it is this warm.

I take two deep breaths to steady my voice, and tell her the story I have never told anyone before, about Emile and De Villiers and their misfortune.

Once I have finished, Rosalie eyes me up and down, the moonlight trickling through the window illuminating her face. 'You could not have avoided going back. How can it have been your fault?'

'I know, I know. I just—'

'Lie down, and I'll hold you.'

Despite the time we have spent together, I have not yet grown entirely accustomed to this kind of comfort, but I obey and once more rest my head on the small stack of pillows. I drift asleep again, and this time, I am left in peace. When I wake, her strong, sun-kissed arms are still wrapped around me.

I wish Rosalie would speak with me of her own ghosts; then, I could be of equal help to her. She does, occasionally, but Laura Hamilton is apparently not the tormenting type. If Harry Bride comes to visit, too, Rosalie never mentions it.

Chapter thirty-five

Rosalie

THE MASSONS' New Year's Eve gathering in the winter of 1919 is the most crowded place I have been in since the Bastille Day victory parade. The people range from high-born ladies to brothel girls, from snobs to rogues, from banking men to professional dancers. What they all have in common is that they are young and vivid and they all adore the extravagant shrimp cocktails.

Charles and I slip off our coats in the gloomy hallway. Through the controlled tumult, I spot Eleanor. She is chatting with a man I do not recognize, one hand placed on her rounded hip, wrist heavy with jangling bracelets.

A pair of young men in identical waistcoats latch onto Charles and sweep him away with them, leaving me to elbow my way to Eleanor.

She winks at me. 'You'll never guess where I'm going, Rose, darling.'

'Where?'

'Home to America. But I ain't just going home. I'm going to university. Can you believe that?'

I laugh, torn between joy for my friend and disappointment that I will be left behind in a way. 'No, not quite. Which one?'

'Brown University.'

'I didn't know they admitted women.'

She nods several times and grins at me. 'Oh, they sure do! Why don't you come with me and have a go?'

'Because—' I grapple for an explanation that she would understand, but in vain. 'Because America is much too far away. And Charles is here in Paris.'

'I'm sick and tired of you talking about him, honestly. You've potential. Don't waste it.' She taps my nose with the end of her cigarette stick.

'I'm not!'

'Really? Then why are you still here drinking and talking with me? What became of your plans to write?'

I stare at her. 'You are also here.'

'And I'm about to leave. Just think about it properly—what you want to do with your life.'

'Have you forgotten about the prohibition? You won't last a day over there.'

The word 'prohibition' alone seems painful to Eleanor. 'Must you remind me? Oh, here we are now!'

I join her and the other guests in counting down the seconds until midnight. It has been quite a year, and quite an autumn, too. We have celebrated the first armistice day. Home in England that entailed two minutes of silence, which made me want to laugh and cry both, because if we had accounted a single second for each fallen soldier, we would likely still be silent tonight. We have also seen the threat of the influenza diminish at least partly, and not a day too late. The sky-high estimates of death tolls chill me to the bone.

And now…now it is 1920. *1920*. How odd it is to think about! And how much more of a milestone of modernity it feels than 1910 did, when I was twelve years old and spent my time playing with my classmates at King Alfred's School.

Later that evening, or rather early morning, Charles and I are slumped in the backseat of a taxi car, driving back to the apartment. That is when my conversation with Eleanor resurfaces in my head.

'I'll order us two tickets to Florence,' Charles says, quenching a drunken yawn. 'We'll have a jolly time, don't you think? In a few months there will be nothing but sun and calm and…and other grand things.'

I hesitate for a moment. 'I'm not so sure I want calm and sun.'

'What do you me-ean?'

'Something Eleanor said about…' I search my hazy memory. 'About doing something with my life. I want to accomplish things. I want to know I'm capable on my own, too.'

'But you are! You were capable during the war. I know…know it as well as anyone!'

'I mean I want to *learn* things, Charles.' I push myself upright in the seat and force him to look at me. 'I want to be more than your accessory at parties.'

He cocks his head as if my words were a riddle. 'You're not! An accessory, I mean. Are you?'

'Maybe you are, too. But you remember how life was awful before? And now it's lovely. And then I want it to be real—with an education, a serious pastime.'

We ride in silence for a while, the driver making slow turns. Charles gnaws on his thumbnail.

I shift my weight, uneasy. This is the first time we have truly disagreed on what our future should be. The more I think about it, the more I yearn for England, and the more I wonder whether he will ever want to leave France. It will soon be a whole year since I saw Fred and Papa, and I long to talk to them. Isabel, also, but she does not spark the same feeling in me. How is it, that time has dwindled away so easily? One pleasure followed another, and while I have cherished them, this Parisian decadence is not made of stuff to last forever.

Charles at last leaves his thumbnail alone. 'You can't just say things like that and change everything, just because you're done with this life and done with me.'

'Did I put it that way?'

'Well, if by *education* you mean you want to go to university like Eleanor, then I won't be there! I can't go back when half of the seats are empty.' His voice is low, at once sobered.

'The Sorbonne isn't the only place and we both know it. There's Oxford and Cambridge, even America. There are places where the empty seats never belonged to anyone you knew.'

Charles sighs. It is as if he has already arrived at the finishing line and is content, which only serves to infuriate me more. Half the seats may be empty, but the rest do not have to be.

'You.' I poke him hard in the chest with my finger. 'You were going to become a lawyer, remember?'

'I don't want that anymore. Haven't I told you?'

'What *do* you want then?'

'For Christ's sake, Rose, I don't know!' he explodes, turning away from me. 'All I know is that I'm staying. I'm not letting Paris go again.'

'Why? It's not your girl or anything.'

Why? Because that was what we fought for! We kept the Huns from reaching Paris, from taking all of France. I might not be reeking with patriotism but—'

I throw my hands in the air and nearly smack him. 'I don't care, Charles! For once, I don't care!'

'I never thought of you as selfish before.'

'And I *always* thought of you as arrogant, but not stupid. Until now.'

We edge away from one another, sinking back into the seat, unsuccessfully trying to blend into the leather.

The poor driver starts humming a choppy tune.

I will go to England, and no matter what I will earn myself a place at a university. I am not dumb, and the world is not what it was at the turn of the century. It may be a rare sight, but I shall not be the only female student attending. I do not know what became of my old friend and enemy Susan, but if she were here, she would agree with me.

So would Laura. Dear, dear Laura with her suffragette banner. To my shame, I can barely recall her voice, but I do remember the prominent dimples in her cheeks when she smiled. She, Susan, and Eleanor—they would all tell me the same thing, just as they have done for years one way or another. Perhaps I have been listening with one ear up till this point, or perhaps their message has been seeping into me bit by bit, allowing me to leave home and cut my hair and enjoy myself.

In my drowsy state, I am convinced that I now stand at a crossroads. I can stay because Charles wishes it, or I can go because I wish it. The choice is far from simple, yet necessary, and there can only be one answer.

During the following days, our argument expands to include frequent snaps and resentful remarks from both of us. By the end of the week, Charles has retreated to his mother's estate in the countryside, while I am left in an awkward position with Timmele and the maids.

I refuse to give in, though. I have, after brief consideration, set my heart on Oxford. I was there a few times when my brother had just begun his first semester. The wind was ruffling the billowing lawns, and the stone buildings towered like the ancient symbols of knowledge and privilege they always were. I stood in awe before the Bodleian Library, craning my neck to behold this place of wonders, this place where I could find an answer to my every question. Young men in morning jackets and smart hats strode past Carfax Tower. Once, I even glimpsed a couple of young women with thin sweaters and leather-bound books. I want all those things—the grass and the sweaters, the buildings and the books. There was something about it that clung to my mind like a bug and has become more compelling in a short time.

Fred never quite appreciated Oxford the way he ought to have, despite being among the best students in his year, and so we did not speak of it a great deal. It feels like the irony of fate that it is now impossible for him to go back, while my own chances have likely improved with the war.

Papa has found a new cook since I left, a Mrs Carrie, and although she does not measure up to Daya, Papa appears happy enough. As he once told me, he is not a picky eater. My father and brother are both as I left them, except that Fred has started growing tomatoes.

My sister, however, is so light-hearted that I barely recognise her. After a few days, I ask her about it, unable to suppress my curiosity any longer.

She brushes me off, but smiles. 'It's nothing, dear. I'm simply pleased with my new lodgings.'

'Your new lodgings? You're moving, then?'

'Yes. I have a tremendous friend, Elizabeth, who is a widow since the influenza. She is very lonely in the house these days, and suggested I come and live with her. It's just next to the London Hospital so it is a matter of convenience, you see.'

I see well enough, although perhaps she does not understand just how well. 'I'm pleased for you. That you'll have such a short walk to work, I mean.'

'Thank you.'

Fred is in a far less cheerful mood, which becomes obvious when we are alone, taking a stroll through Hampstead Heath.

'I hope you realise that it's not about the location.'

'I'm not stupid, Fred.'

'No, of course you're not.' He sighs and touches my cheek. 'I've done my best to behave. I think you'd be content.'

'Good. I…I want to tell you something. I've let you think Isabel was the only hint of scandal in the family, but that is not so.' I bite my tongue; there is no turning back now.

'I'm all ears, Little Sister.'

Banishing further hesitation from my mind, I tell him the true story of my Parisian adventure. What I do not relate is the part about when and where I met Charles. It is overwhelming enough to reveal the least controversial part of my secret.

Fred kicks the gravel as we walk. 'I wish you had confided in me before. When that chap kept writing to us, Papa threw the letters in the fireplace, but I gave in once and wrote back. If I'd known how much you meant to each other, I'd have done so sooner.'

'You would? I thought you would have wanted to hide this as well, just like with Isabel, and perhaps scold me for being such a floozie.' There is a sharp note to my voice.

'I could never scold you! I'm not telling you to brandish it all around London, only that I don't blame you for heeding your emotions.'

'Yet you blame our sister. Is her virtue more sacred than mine, then?'

He shakes his head in clear frustration. 'It's not about virtue, Rose. That idea is outdated. It's about the fact that your emotions are natural and to be expected, while Isabel's are not.'

'Stop! Just stop! I withdraw my hand from his arm and stop mid-step.

'What? What did I say?'

'I thought we agreed you were going to be nice.'

'And I *am* nice when she's here, but that doesn't mean I've suddenly changed my every view. Surely you know most people share it?'

To my own annoyance, I make no attempt to resist when he reaches for my hand again and we resume our promenade. 'I do. Perhaps I even share it a little myself, but do you know something else? Isabel is far more fun to talk to than she used to be, and even if that's because she keeps this Elizabeth company, it's all the better for us.'

We make a sweeping turn through the park and set off home. When Isabel leaves the following day, having packed a trunk of essentials, I sense a great tension ebbing away.

Chapter thirty-six

Charles

WHEN I AM certain that Rosalie has left for England, I return to the apartment for the first time since New Year's Day. The scent is all too familiar: honeysuckle perfume and freshly baked brioches, wine and soap. The very quintessence of our time together. I cannot stand it.

Swiftly, the walls threatening to suffocate me if I remain too long, I collect my most vital belongings. One of Rosalie's dresses is dangling on a coat hanger, abandoned: the dove-blue one with shiny buttons down one side. I rub the fabric between my fingers, and as I do so, I encounter a hard, flat object. My curiosity sparked, I slip my hand into the deep pocket, and produce a small mirror in a case of burgundy leather. As I flip the case open, a brittle piece of paper sails to the floor. Bending down to pick it up, I at once recognize it.

'You cannot know you'll be willing to marry me whenever I pull out this thing!'

'But I do know that—out of all precarious things I know that.'

I still know it. I still would. Three and a half years ago, I wrote that note, and its content is as true now as it was then, even a thousand times truer. Without pausing to think, I stuff my things—along with the note and Rosalie's dress—in the trunk I brought with me and stalk out of the apartment. It is a spur of the moment decision, but I have a feeling that I shall not regret it.

Slamming the door to the yellow ReVere shut behind me, I shift back in the seat and stamp on the gas pedal. I have been a fool.

Two days later, I board a channel boat, having purchased the last-minute ticket from an elderly woman through bribes and pleading. Once comfortably seated in one of the chairs on the cold, sun-chinked deck, I cannot help but to hum a little tune to myself.

An older man is stretched out in the chair next to me. His full moustache is trimmed upwards and patched with grey; his coat is long enough to rest in folds by his feet. 'You sound like a cheerful lad.'

'It was not my intention.'

'Are we celebrating something?'

I raise an eyebrow. 'I wouldn't know. I might be if it all turns out for the best.'

The man grants me a thoughtful glance and takes his time before answering. 'Hmm. Is it business? A girl, perhaps?'

'I'm going to marry her. Maybe. I'm going to marry her if she will have me.'

'You sound superlatively excited about it all. Toffee?' He opens his small hand to reveal a few pieces of candy wrapped in white paper.

I shake my head.

'They're awfully good, you know.' He removes the wrapper from one of the toffees and pops it his baby-pink mouth

I sigh. 'Oh, give me one, then.'

So he does, and they *are* awfully good.

'What are you going over for?'

The man scratches his chin. 'Family. You know them—never satisfied to mind their own affairs.'

'Indeed I do know them.'

We sit in silence for a while, the waves beating against the boat, squealing seagulls circulating between ourselves and the cumulus clouds.

'I don't have a ring, to tell you the truth.'

The old man has just gulped down the last piece of candy, and it goes down the wrong way. Coughing and gasping for air, he repeatedly pounds his fist against his chest, but nothing seems to do the trick. The thick veins on his forehead bulge like wires.

Before I can do anything myself, two stewards arrive and start to violently slap the man's back, until the sticky lump of toffee shoots out of his mouth and lands on the sleeve of a nearby lady, who shuffles away from us under noises similar to the seagulls'.

The man's eyes are glazed with tears from choking. 'Don't–' he gasps between the last coughs and wipes away a tear with a crooked finger. 'Don't have a ring! How on earth are you going to do it, then? I've never heard of anything like it!'

I glare at him. 'Women don't care that much, do they? After all, it's only jewellery, and necklaces are prettier.'

'Oh, but they do, and so should you. That jewellery will nine times out of ten enhance your chances significantly. There's a whole science to it, believe me.'

'Are you married?'

'I was.' He chuckles. 'They were the worst years of my life.'

'How encouraging.'

The man smooths out the creased wrapper papers and folds them into tidy squares. 'Marriage is a race. You can't win it if you'd rather run against your teammate than with her. I never wanted to run with my Alice. It was all her father's idea.'

'Well, that's not the way it is with Rosalie. We make splendid teammates.'

'Good. Don't lose your pace.'

It is a fair-sized house, though meagre compared to my own childhood home. There are three stories, the stone walls coated in thick, white paint, the sashed windows and the roof panes dark. I know little of style, but the house must be quite fashionable, or at least it was a decade ago.

I climb the steps to the stout front door and knock. I am just about to raise my fist again when the door swings open and a small, fox-like face appears.

The girl is thin and practically tied up in her black dress and white apron, a mischievous sparkle in her drooping eyes. 'Yes?'

'Is there a Mrs Rosalie Bride living here?' I still wince at her last name.

The girl eyes me from head to toe. 'She's out. Would you mind waiting?'

'Not at all.'

The girl steps aside to allow me entry, though her expression tells me *she* minds my waiting. She leads me straight through the vestibule—I catch sight of a sitting room with dark furniture and a fireplace—and up a flight of stairs. Once we have reached the second floor, the fox-girl halts and knocks twice on one of the doors.

A voice floats through the keyhole. 'Yes?'

The maid cracks the door open and announces my presence. A low murmur of voices follows: one young and clear, one unmistakably older, the same that spoke first.

The maid slips past me and disappears through another door, and I enter the room. I had not anticipated having to face Rosalie's family, at least not immediately.

A man around my own age, perhaps slightly older, is standing by the window, hands clasped behind his back. His small, rounded chin reminds me of his sister, because although his eyes look healthy to me, this must be the brother who finally answered my letters.

Another man, who is indeed older, sits by the cluttered desk in the upper right corner of the room, face set in a frown. In his one hand rests a delicately sculptured pipe, and in the other he holds a pen. 'Yes?'

'I wish to see your daughter. I'm an old friend.' I stretch out a hand. 'Charles D'Aboville.'

Fred Wilkes navigates with surety around the furniture and shakes my hand since his father seems unlikely to, then introduces himself. 'Rosalie is not here at the moment, but she will be shortly. Would you care for a cup of coffee in the meantime?' His politeness sounds as natural as if he was speaking about the weather, yet there is a knowing undertone in his voice. He must understand at least to some extent who I am.

'A cup of coffee would be nice.'

We gather around the table in the middle of the room and the fox-faced girl brings us the refreshments.

'So, you're a Parisian friend of my daughter, eh?' Mr Wilkes the older asks. 'Your accent may be subtle but you can't fool me.'

'Yes.' For now, it is perhaps safest to label myself as the Parisian friend, not knowing how much the other two have been told.

'She's going to sit exams for Oxford in the autumn, my Rosalie. Terribly bright.'

I smile. 'Terribly bright, yes, I think that's the way to put it.'

The door bursts open, revealing a flustered young woman with her hat slipping off. 'Minnie said there was a young man waiting, one in dire need of a haircut.'

I rise and nearly drop my cup in the process.

'Well? What are you doing here?'

'Mr Wilkes? Might I speak to your daughter alone?'

Mr Wilkes the older starts to say something, but his son puts a hand on his shoulder.

Rosalie turns, gesturing for me to follow her. 'We will be downstairs, Papa.'

Once in the vestibule, I nearly stumble over my own words. 'Don't say anything,' I begin. 'Just know…know that I love you.'

'I know.' Her eyes soften. 'But I won't let you hold me back.'

'I would never want to do that. I only wish we could forget all the silly things we said. By God, I can come with you if you want me to.'

'Would you do that? Truly? What about not leaving Paris?'

Treading carefully, I reach out and tuck a wisp of hair behind her ear. 'Already have, haven't I? Forget about France. *You* are the greatest victory.'

Rosalie takes a step back. 'But that's just it, Charles. I'm not your *victory*—I'm not anyone's but my own, and if you can't see that, you shouldn't have come.'

'That's not what I meant! I swear that's not how I meant it.' I curse under my breath. 'You were infuriated with me for lacking ambition and direction, too, weren't you? Well, I do have those things. I want to go with you to Oxford, and then I'll start a newspaper or magazine. There.'

'A magazine?'

I nod, recalling the glory days of *Le Pou*.

'Will you marry me, then? I can even kneel down,' Rosalie says. It is impossible to tell whether she is serious or not.

'You can't say that!' I burst. 'You stole my—that was my line!'

'Don't make me take it back, you dimwit, just say you will.'

Perhaps the man on the boat was right and a ring has its perks. All I can offer now is a very crumpled piece of paper. 'I will. Now, don't lose this again.' I place the paper in her palm, closing her fingers around it.

'Is it…?' She studies the note for a moment, then at last kisses me.

I bury my face in the soft curve of her neck and let out a sigh of relief.

Rosalie

Dinner that evening really is something. My father, my brother, my fiancé, and I are all seated around the table, candlelight emblazoning our faces. Frequently, I catch myself smiling, making it difficult to chew properly. Charles, too, is neglecting the Franconia potatoes and chicken, fighting a battle with my foot under the table until I embarrass myself by laughing out loud.

Papa is suspicious of Charles, I can tell. Fred appears more friendly, and I am glad now that I spoke well of Charles to him. I might relate the truth in its entirety to them both someday, but for now, they have to be content with their limited knowledge.

As I sit here, I can hardly believe my luck. It is a wonderful thing to be alive, despite or perhaps because so many others are not. And this…this is only the beginning.

Ypres, 1963

Charles

THE POPPIES ARE swaying in the wind. They have sprung up from land so saturated with death that I marvel at anything at all growing here. Under my feet, my men lie buried in unmarked graves. I do not know how many, nor do I know whether this is the very spot—forty-nine years have passed since I first took them over the top—but it does not matter. I have never been sympathetic to superstition, but just as their bones are to be found in the earth along with bullets and buttons, their ghosts whisper in the air. It is the same each time I come.

Rosalie is walking towards me from the car, the scarf fluttering around her face. She takes my outstretched hand. 'Georgie wants her grandpa to come back and show her that daft card trick again. She's already eaten my sandwich.'

'Just a moment.'

'All right, Charles.'

I watch a bird sail across the sky, perhaps hunting for prey. 'I'm afraid…I'm afraid we won't visit these fields for a while— that very few will.'

'Why?'

'Because warfare always escalates. They could wipe this place from the face of the earth with their nuclear missiles. Anyhow, the latest war has already eclipsed our war. It is fresher in memory, and so that's what all the books and films end up being about. We're simply left in the past.'

'I don't think I've heard you call it our war before. It was always the war of the high and mighty.' She lets go of my hand and takes a few steps along the old shell hole. 'But I think you're forgetting something. The second time it was good for something; there were reasons other than patriotism to cheer for one side or the other. It was not pointless—and it was ours in a way, too.'

I squint, trying to spot the bird again, but it is futile. 'Not in the same way.'

'Perhaps. The poppies are beautiful this time of year.'

'We were a generation of poppies, Rose, ploughed down and ground to sticky red dust. But I'm being too sentimental. Come, let's drive back.'

'Yes.'

I drop down, knees aching as they so often do these days, and pluck one of the flowers. Rosalie accepts it, flicking a strand of slate-grey hair from her eyes. Together, we stride through the rain-soaked grass towards the car. Georgie has been patient enough.

Author's note

In *A Generation of Poppies*, I have done my best to merge the story with real events, although all main characters are fictional. I have taken care to not override dates and facts, as well as to create an authentic feeling by listening to interviews with veterans and reading newspapers from the period. However, I have also taken some small liberties, as is necessary in historical fiction. In addition, some details in the book can be described as atypical, though not in any way impossible, experiences. The largest inaccuracy in the book as far as I am aware is the fact that England did not send VADs overseas until 1915, while Rosalie, Mary, and Isabel are in France by the end of 1914.

The First World is easily perceived as a men's conflict on the surface, but it does not require much investigation to notice that the other half of the population were also frantically active in the war effort. Although it was mainly men who became casualties, men who commanded the armies, and men who attended the peace conference at Versailles in 1919, women were vital contributors.

It is difficult to find entirely reliable and inclusive statistics, but it is safe to say that the female employment rate drastically rose in several of the warring nations. Many working-class women spent their days in munitions factories, where exposure to chemicals such as trinitrotoluene sometimes made their skin turn yellow, resulting in the nickname 'canary girls'. Middle- and upper-class women became Red Cross voluntary nurses in masses, as Rosalie Wilkes does, and still others became ambulance drivers or fire fighters. After the February Revolution, Russian women could even join all-female fighting battalions, though it should be noted that the new Russian government did not necessarily allow this out of progressiveness. For many women, the armistice and the return of more male workers meant that they had to withdraw to the traditionally female sphere again, such as managing a household or working as seamstresses. Their bold move had been temporary to some degree. Nevertheless, their role during the war is frequently held to be the catalyst for women's right to vote in Britain and in other regions.

In this book, Charles D'Aboville and several of Rosalie Wilkes' friends become junior officers as a result of their socioeconomic backgrounds. This was a common practice that lingered into the 20th century. Although merit was becoming increasingly important, tradition still weighed heavily in the European armies. An officer was expected to speak like one, act like one, dress like one even when off duty, and enjoy expensive officer's pastimes. Furthermore, he needed the attitude of one accustomed to being above everyone else. If one had not attended a good public school, one stood an extremely small chance of becoming a commissioned officer. As part of the job, COs received various privileges: better food and accommodation, a personal servant, and as shown by Charles' experience in later chapters, entirely endurable POW camps.

Being a junior officer had its drawbacks, too, though, because it was one of the deadliest positions in the army. Around 20% of public schoolboys who fought in the war died, and the life expectancy of some junior officers at the front dropped as low as six weeks. Eventually, men with less polished backgrounds began filling the gaps, which contributed to a changing attitude towards social classes after the war.

Oftentimes, the initial impression one gets of the First World War is a war of stalemate and attrition, mud and killing without distinction. To a large extent, this was true. However, we should keep in mind that the war looked vastly different at sea and especially in the air. In *A Generation of Poppies*, I have attempted to emphasize the contrast between the trenches and the flying squadrons, mainly through the character of Fred Wilkes.

Many young men who went to the front in 1914 were hoping for an exciting adventure with glory as part of the bargain, but were sorely disappointed. There was no room for the individual to shine on the ground, at least not unless he was a high-ranking officer. The soldiers were likely to spend a majority of their time sitting around waiting, itching with lice and perhaps suffering from trench foot. In short, their everyday life was not headline material.

The opposite stood true for the fighting pilots. While their task was extremely dangerous—during 'Bloody April' in 1917, the RFC lost roughly a quarter of its strength in a single month, and pilots were not issued parachutes since that was thought to encourage desertion—it certainly was an adventure. Just to fly in an aeroplane was a brand-new possibility that people were astonished at, and unlike in the trenches, the individual's own skills were highly decisive. Instead of being mowed down by distant artillery, the flying aces experienced the thrill of the chase, and each victory was loudly acclaimed. The glamour that surrounded the pilots made them newspaper celebrities. Two of them were British ace Albert Ball (1896-1917), and German Manfred Von Richthofen (1892-1918), both of whom I mention in this book.

Because of their rarity, the fighting pilots grew to respect one another. Von Richthofen, who was the highest scoring flying ace of the war with 80 confirmed victories, wrote in his autobiography *Der Rote Kampfflieger* (1917) that: 'My father discriminates between a sportsman and a butcher,' and 'I honoured the fallen enemy by placing a stone on his beautiful grave.'

Parallel to these old-fashioned ideals of chivalry, the flying technology was rapidly modernising, constantly reaching new heights. For example, in 1915, the German Fokker Eindecker could fire a gun through the propeller arc of the aeroplane without striking the blades. By the end of 1918, aerial combat had gone from an experiment to a sophisticated and irreplaceable aspect of industrial warfare.

As Charles D'Aboville mentions in the epilogue, the Second World War presents a far more palatable story to remember and depict than the First World War. There were reasonably simple causes, a 'good' and a 'bad' side at least when looking at the overall picture, meaningful turning points of massive variety, and of course the fact that a third world war did not break out. It goes without saying that the defeat of Hitler's Third Reich was a greater ideological success than the defeat of the German Empire twenty-seven years before.

The First World War did not wipe out a whole generation. However, it did wipe out a significant proportion of certain classes and age groups in certain countries, and those targeted groups often felt near annihilated. There are very few wars that have seen as large a technological leap as the First World War did, and perhaps just as few wars that have marked such a stark line between an old and a new society. For all these reasons, I believe it deserves more attention.

Also by Saga Hillbom

Princess of Thorns

1483, Westminster. The bells toll for the dead king, Edward IV, while his rivalling nobles grasp for power. His daughter Cecily can only watch as England is plunged into chaos, torn between her loyalties to her headstrong mother, Elizabeth Woodville, and her favourite uncle, Richard of Gloucester. When Elizabeth schemes to secure her own son on the throne that Richard lays claim to, Cecily and her siblings become pawns in a perilous game.

The Yorkist dynasty that Cecily holds so dear soon faces another threat: the last Lancastrian claimant, Henry Tudor. Meanwhile, Cecily battles with envy towards her older sister, who is betrothed to Tudor.

The White Rose of York has turned its thorns inwards, and royal blood proves fatal...

Princess of Thorns is a sweeping tale of loyalty and treason, ambition and family bonds.

Also by Saga Hillbom

City of Bronze, City of Silver

431 BC. Greece is torn apart by war. The city states split into leagues: one headed by the militarized Sparta, the other by the sophisticated Athens.

Alethea, a young Spartan woman, leaves her home to accompany her brother on the military campaign. Taken prisoner by the enemy and enslaved in an Athenian household, Alethea's heart is set on revenge. However, her feelings are complicated as she is drawn to her abductor's amiable cousin, Eucleides.

Meanwhile, Efigenia, a child bride and Alethea's new mistress, struggles to navigate in a world dictated by men. The rigid norms she lives by are consuming her little by little. Can the arrival of the Spartan help her break loose from her chains?

City of Bronze, City of Silver is a tale of bloodshed and vengeance, oppression and love, set against the backdrop of an ancient civilization steeped in myth.